SIMON CLEARY IS the author of two novels, including *The Comfort of Figs* (2008), which was published after the manuscript was shortlisted for the Queensland Premier's Literary Awards. His second novel, *Closer to Stone* (2012), was inspired by his experiences in North Africa at the commencement of the Algerian civil war in the 1990s. It went on to win the Queensland Literary Awards People's Choice Award. He lives in Brisbane.

SIMON
CLEARY

THE
WAR
ARTIST

UQP

First published in 2019 by University of Queensland Press
PO Box 6042, St Lucia, Queensland 4067 Australia

uqp.com.au
uqp@uqp.uq.edu.au

Cover design by Christabella Designs
Cover artwork by Allison Kittredge // squidinkedstudio.com
Author photo by Patrick Hamilton
Typeset in 11.5/16 pt Garamond by Post Pre-press Group, Brisbane
Printed in Australia by McPherson's Printing Group, Melbourne

The University of Queensland Press is supported
by the Queensland Government through Arts
Queensland.

The University of Queensland Press is
assisted by the Australian Government
through the Australia Council, its arts
funding and advisory body.

A catalogue record for this book is available from the National Library of Australia.

ISBN 978 0 7022 6034 6 (pbk)
ISBN 978 0 7022 6192 3 (pdf)
ISBN 978 0 7022 6193 0 (epub)
ISBN 978 0 7022 6194 7 (kindle)

University of Queensland Press uses papers that are natural, renewable and recyclable
products made from wood grown in sustainable forests. The logging and manufacturing
processes conform to the environmental regulations of the country of origin.

For Dominic and for Liam

And of course, Alisa

Odysseus, clutching his flaring sea-blue cape
In both powerful hands, drew it over his head
And buried his handsome face,
Ashamed his hosts might see him shedding tears.
—*The Odyssey*

FLIGHT HOME

IT'S A LONG journey home, but he insisted he do it.

Brigadier Phelan sits alone with the casket in the hold, the roar of
the engines in his ears, the plane a giant stiff-winged creature, grey
across the slow blue sky, entire continents turning steadily beneath
him. He feels the weight of his duty: part sentry, part companion. He
is here because it is army protocol that a soldier accompanies the body.
He is here to bear witness to this journey. And he is here to atone,
though he doesn't yet understand his offence.

Phelan smooths out a crease that has gathered in the flag draped
over the silver casket. His temples throb with the plane and whatever
is beyond the sky's roar. He can't think for the noise, a blessing
really, louder than the ringing from the blast he still can't shake.
He is not ready to think, so he succumbs to it, and enters it like a
cocoon. His chin drops against his chest and he dozes, as sentinels in
outposts on the edges of civilisation have succumbed to sleep since
the beginning of the world.

When he wakes, it is to the sound of wailing. He starts, his blood
pounding. Yet it is only air rushing across a tiny gap that has opened
between plates in the fuselage, or catching, perhaps, under the head
of a screw. In the wind he hears again the bugle escorting Sapper
Beckett's body up the ramp. He hears its mournful cry as the casket
is strapped down, the ramp rises and is clamped shut, and all is dark.

Now he sits alone and listens until the bugler finishes his lament. How long he plays, Phelan can't say. The wailing stops. The plane drones on.

Again Phelan dozes. Again he wakes, gasping for breath. What this time? A whisper at his ear; a touch cool on his forehead, only half-imagined. Would he recognise another soldier's essence if it appeared before him? If Beckett's spirit rose, groaning from its body, seeking an answer?

Phelan shivers, then steels himself anew. Because here he is. Let no man say he lacks courage. Whatever happened when Beckett and he lay down together in their irrigation ditch, the last two men in all the world, Phelan is here still. Even if he has no answers, he will at least endure the questions. Yet, what then?

Phelan has no elaborate instructions to chant to Beckett's soul, no roadmap to the afterlife he can incant, no book of the dead to read aloud, air mile by air mile. He might murmur *rest in peace*. He might repeat what he remembers of the prayers and the *in memoriams* in Tarin Kot and at Al Minhad. He might seek to comfort the sapper with *The Ode* – that he fell with his face to his foe, that age shall not weary him and that he will be remembered – but there is too much he neither understands nor trusts.

In time, Sydney nears and Beckett has not yet spoken. Phelan listens, but beyond the whisper's echo there is silence. Perhaps his beloved Roman general Marcus Aurelius is right: that there is nothing beyond the sky's dome and the only task is to live honourably. In *that*, Phelan thinks to himself fiercely, I will not fail. I will tell the world what a fine young man Beckett was. I will tell them he was a brave warrior and that he fell in our service and they will know he did not die in vain.

The brigadier rises. He touches the casket one last time, then climbs up onto the flight deck as the plane begins to descend. He straps himself in. Ahead of him there are parents and politicians and ceremony, a long day, a sky of doubt difficult to dismiss.

PART ONE

WRITTEN ON THE BODY

Sydney, November 2010

KIRA LEANS OVER the body before her. The girl's eyes are closed tight and Kira studies the capillaries on her thin eyelids, looking for a pattern, some map of the frightened girl's eighteen years, some clues to where her life might yet lead.

She adjusts her lamp and the inside of the girl's right wrist is illuminated in a cone of light. A beautiful wrist, Kira thinks. There is a tenderness, a fragility despite its fleshiness. Already the transverse scar has begun to retreat behind the purple stencil she has laid over it, a scar that will merge with the tattoo when she is finished.

The tattoo machine starts. The girl looks into Kira's eyes as an anxious child might seek out its mother. Kira smiles at the girl – not much younger than her – pats her arm then bends to her work, losing herself.

The chain of bells tinkles as the studio door off the street downstairs opens. Kira lifts her head from the girl's wrist and her almost-finished skull and counts the seconds until the door clicks closed again and the bells stop. Just one person, she judges, and, from the weight of the footsteps on the timber stairs, a man. While Flores has taught her about tattooing and its gods, this practical knowledge she alone has won. She glances at the clock on the wall. It is nearly six. The heat has not yet broken; these November days with more summer in them than spring.

5

Kira watches the man emerge from the steep stairwell. He stops abruptly when he reaches the top. She guesses from his shoulders, his short hair, the way he scans the room, the way he weighs both her and the girl in the chair like they're objects in a landscape, that he's either police or military. Though it's unusual a man from the forces is alone – they usually come in pairs. Odd too that he's as old as he is.

'Be a minute,' she calls across to him, thinking he can wait, that it'll be good for him. Thinking too, how much she enjoys this part of her art – the unpredictability of the studio and who might walk in the door at any moment. What stories they might bring, what novelties, what fears, what needs. 'Take a seat.'

PHELAN CONTINUES TO stand. He's not entirely sure what he's doing here. Examine yourself, Marcus Aurelius, his philosopher guide urges, test your motives. Be unsparing. *That* alone is the way to doing what is right, what is great. Be untiring, be disciplined. Control your impulses, as true Stoics must. Know yourself.

Oh, Phelan thinks, he has controlled his impulses all right, how disciplined he has been. And how he has risen, how he has been rewarded. But now there is Beckett, now and always, no going back, that much he knows. Yet by what impulse does he find himself in a tattoo studio in a back street in Surry Hills after an exhausting day of ceremony and obligation, after delivering a young soldier's body to his parents? He has bowed his head before man and God today. He has expressed sorrow and gratitude and spoken words that lost their shape in the very act of their being uttered: 'honour' and 'sacrifice' and 'loyalty' and 'mateship'. Now he stands warily in the foyer of a tattoo studio, his uniform folded neatly in his overnight bag, this one final thing to attend to before taking the last flight to Brisbane. He is beyond the boundary of familiar duty, baulking at the edge of his world.

Phelan sees the tattooist and her client on his first scan of the room, the studio otherwise empty – the other two barbers' chairs vacant and no sign of anyone else through the open door to the backroom, a kitchenette or drawing space of some sort.

He examines the studio more carefully on his second pass. The six-inch polished floorboards and the high raftered ceiling and the whitewashed brick walls immaculately decorated with posters. There are framed mandalas and stylised roses and classic Japanese prints – *The Great Wave off Kanagawa*, and the *Fisherman's Wife* – on one wall. On another wall is floor-to-ceiling shelving, each shelf filled with books and folios, but too far away for him to read their spines. Near the wall of books is a chest-high pedestal. On it rests a human skull, illuminated by a ceiling down-light as if it's a trophy. His usually steady eye catches on the skull, and he blinks. Plaster, he guesses. But even so.

Then, suddenly, the throbbing pain behind his eyes returns, sweeping away the low-murmuring headache that's accompanied him constantly since Beckett. Phelan winces and presses his fingers against his temples. A weaker man would buckle. He'll count it out. Bloody annoying, though. He should have done a better job at hiding it – the headaches, the tinnitus, the nausea, the foggy head. But a TBI, a traumatic brain injury? For fuck's sake! Surely he should have been given the chance for it to pass before being ordered on leave, another week or two at least. He could be forgiven for thinking the Chief was looking for an excuse to send him home. *It's a demonstration of leadership,* the Chief had said. *You'll be showing how we need to take the injuries we can't see as seriously as those we can. You'll be back in no time. And Jim, you could do with the rest.* Well if he was going to have to return for treatment and a breather, then *he'd* bloody well be the one to accompany Beckett home.

When he opens his eyes, all is blur. He feels for the pills in his breast pocket, slides the packet out then waits until the room steadies. He pierces the foil with his thumbnail, four pills, but his mouth is too dry to swallow without water. There's a cooler in the corner of the waiting area, and he pours a plastic cupful, tips his head back.

It takes a while before he is able to refocus on the detail again. Detail matters. Always, and in everything. His nature, the army's habits. That the shaft of a childhood arrow be dead straight. That glue on a model plane not be visible. That radios are properly tuned and one's weapon is zeroed.

He continues his examination of the room, looking for cannabis pipes among the rings and slave bracelets and T-shirts and other paraphernalia in the glass cabinets at the front counter. He'd said to himself that if there were outlaw club patches among the flash tattoo designs on the reception wall he'd leave. But there are none, and no other traces of bikies, nothing discordant.

Clear, he thinks to himself, his reconnaissance done. Clear, he thinks, despite himself. Clear, but even so he cannot relax, cannot sit.

He leans forward to read the detail of a framed copy of a page from the *Hobart Town Gazette*. A reward note for a murderer, Kieren Patrick Dyson, posted 15 March 1837, his tattoos used to describe him:

> *KPD heart RR half-moon S stars fish inside right-arm, crucifix stars on breast, man cask of rum above elbow, man woman fish.*

'HI THERE,' SHE says when she's finished with the girl's wrists. 'What can I do for you?'

His skin is pocked, as if a hundred tiny landmines have detonated beneath his cheeks. His starched collar and his straight back and the neat part of his thin hair seem like efforts to subdue the ancient turbulence of his flesh. He looks old, but may be the sort of man who has never been young. His head, his shoulders, his entire body, not just his eyes, are steady as he examines her.

Kira doesn't flinch. She is twenty-three and this is her territory. She is in what has become her uniform: a black singlet, stonewashed jeans and silver-buckled black leather boots. Her right arm is bare, but on her left she wears an intricate sleeve of ink.

'Who is that?' the man asks, pointing towards the warrioress on her arm.

Kira straightens further, her hands on her hips. She looks straight back at him. 'Didn't your parents teach you anything?'

'I beg your pardon,' he says, surprised.

'It's rude to point.' She hears her father's voice as she says it. But she wants to fool with him. All these cocky men suddenly vulnerable in her studio. The fun you can have teasing them, playing with them. Upending their confidence.

'Well,' he says, 'I didn't mean—'

'Who do *you* think it is then?' she cuts across him, folding her arms now, her eyes sparkling with challenge.

He smiles. 'All right then,' he says. He leans towards her to examine the tattoo more closely.

She's young with raven-black, wind-whipped hair. She wears a crown of plaited ivy. Her skin is Kira's skin: her cheeks, her shoulders, her neck, her chest. Her left arm holds back a fold of her loosely flowing turquoise gown as she steps forward, the material gathering at her waist, her bare left thigh breaking from her dress. In her right hand is her sword, gripped tightly, the glinting blade pointing downwards, as yet unbrandished, her right arm itself tattooed with a knot-work of vines spiralling from shoulder to wrist. Her head is turned. Her shoulders are drawn back. Kohl-darkened eyes stare out at him.

'It's Celtic isn't it?' he asks.

She smiles. 'So you're not so ignorant after all.'

'But not Boudica,' he continues.

'And why not?'

She expects he'll say it's because her warrioress isn't red-haired, and everyone knows Boudica – or Boadicea, whatever her incarnation – was fiery red.

'The sword,' he says instead.

'What about it?' She is curious now.

'It's curved. Boudica would have had a broadsword.'

'Ten out of ten, Sherlock,' she says, nodding. 'So, what would you like?'

'I'm after a tattoo,' the man replies.

'Reeeeeeally?' she teases.

He laughs. He accepts the pen she offers and writes on her pad. He takes extreme care with each letter, as if each downstroke and each curve is a task he must get absolutely right.

Kira watches his hand labouring across the paper, pausing after each word as if resting from the effort. She watches the confidence leave him as he writes, but can't tell what is replacing it.

Samuel. Robert. Beckett.

The man checks and then re-checks the spelling. When he looks up at her, it's as if he's seeking affirmation. But then he seems to remember something and takes the pen again. Beneath the name he writes the date – seven days gone – before tearing the page from the pad and giving it to her.

She nods. Father, brother, or son? she wonders. Probably son, given his age. 'Where do you want it?'

He looks at her blankly for a moment, as if he hadn't yet considered where to put it. 'My shoulder,' he says, though tentatively, flustered.

'Are you sure you want to do this?'

'Of course,' he says, more firmly, affronted now, reasserting himself. 'I want it on my left shoulder.'

'Okay then.' She looks back to the piece of paper. 'You've got nice handwriting. Do you want me to tattoo it exactly as you've written it? In your own hand?'

'You can do that?'

'Sure.'

He looks at the name on the paper, but then shakes his head vehemently.

'Okay then,' she says, pulling an album from a drawer and placing it on the counter. She flips through its pages, leading the man and his uncertainties through different fonts and sizes. Eventually he chooses one, and she tells him she'll be ten minutes.

'Have a wander in the street if you want. Have a smoke.'

'I'll wait.'

'Suit yourself.'

ODALISQUES

KIRA SITS ON a stool at the bench table in the small room at the back where they keep the stencil machine, the laptop and the printer. Where in the early days she and Flores would draw and print and copy and cut. Where Flores first desired her. Or, she has begun to think, her drawings.

Of course, she'd always drawn: the angels she sketched while crouched under church pews, evading shoes and ankles all service long; surreptitious caricatures of teachers peeled off for her school friends from the backs of classrooms; butterflies in the margins of exam papers; sitting cross-legged on a gallery floor in front of a Whiteley. Her father once read one of Rodin's letters to her, his way of telling her she was okay, that her obsession wasn't abnormal, that she'd be fine. *Draw*, Rodin had urged a pupil, *draw and draw and draw and do not stop drawing*. So the day she arrived at Flores's studio, the day she abandoned her fine arts degree, she already had years of drawing in her. And an ache for purpose.

It's funny how something as banal as a widowed forty-three-year-old woman preparing a gin and tonic could lead you to choose one life over another. Kira can still hear the sound of her mother in the kitchen dropping ice cubes into a tumbler, the little cracks stirring her from a summer afternoon's ennui. She was nineteen, the end of her first year.

'I'm over it, Barbara-Ann,' Kira yawned as she lay on the divan, 'I'm not going back next year.'

'Oh no, Darling!' her mother exclaimed, responding to the bait, almost dropping her glass on the white marble benchtop. 'You mustn't even joke about such a thing.'

'Not a joke, Daaaaaarling.' Delivered with a perfect sneer. 'I'm going to quit.' Though the only decision she'd yet made was to rile her mother, expose her if she could. A disdain begun long before her father's death, a daughter's conviction that her mother was not good enough for him.

'You can't waste it, Sweet,' her mother was already imploring, pressing the palm of her hand to her heart as if that was the source of Kira's talent. 'You just can't. You're as good as any one of them …' She gestured out into the lounge room and beyond that, the sitting room – a practised sweep of the hand – to the walls crowded with paintings, to the coffee tables and their towers of art books, and to the library shelves tight with the years of catalogues she'd collected from every exhibition she'd ever gone to; from the blockbusters to the openings at Macquarie Galleries and Watters and then Legge when it spun off.

'There's a history of Australian art in those catalogues,' her mother used to say. 'Of names, and movements and fortunes. Of galleries and dealers and patrons.'

For months at a time Kira would take one to bed with her, turning pages compulsively till sleep overcame her. Or she'd sit at the kitchen bench, or on the deck in the afternoons after school, and it would be the exhibited artist's created scenes, rather than her own view of the ocean before her, that she'd try and set on paper.

'Come on darling, show Mrs Winsome how you can draw.' And her mother would pull out the sketch pad, and the collection of pencils, and set Kira up at a fold-out table, and have her copy Ingres' *Grande Odalisque* from a catalogue of a 1997 exhibition of Orientalist art at the gallery in the Domain. 'Isn't she amazing?' her mother would say, voice hushed, but not so low Kira couldn't hear.

In time, the pleasure Kira got from drawing for her mother's friends waned, and her mother's project of inserting *her* into the sweep of art history that those catalogues recorded became the burden it was destined to be. The words of admiration from the doctors' and judges' and churchmen's wives predictable and wearisome. Kira became bored.

And yet, it's difficult to ignore your abilities when there's little else you can rely on. The grades, the wins in school competitions or exhibitions sponsored by banks and charities, her watercolours hanging in the foyer of a town hall or the exhibition room of a regional agricultural show, her mother dutifully maintaining a scrapbook of her promising daughter's achievements. In her last year of school her major project was an interactive multi-media installation that was recognised by a showing in the Art Gallery of New South Wales with other finalists from schools around the state. Participants in her 'experience maker' (as she described it, pretentiously she'd later acknowledge) would answer a series of questions – date of birth, favourite colour, ethnicity, religion – resulting in a crude tribal personality profile. They'd then slide their bare arms into a sealed Perspex box where the bristles of small car-wash brushes, arranged along the length of the box and turned by a series of small motors, would paint stripes of colour onto their forearms. *War paint*, she called her installation, the country in the middle of a Middle Eastern war that, as far as she could tell, no reasoning person had wanted to join.

Surprisingly it was the motors of her installation that fascinated her most: the smooth silver casings and the shafts that rotated as if by magic when power ran through the little machines, the hum of them, the steadiness of it, their reliability. She knew enough to keep that to herself when she was interviewed by *The Herald*, a profile piece. She was learning how seldom people looked below the surface of things – that people could install her art or hang her paintings or write about her, without caring whether she was true or not. When her mother walked down to the local newsagent that Saturday morning to buy multiple copies of the paper, Kira left the house by the side door with her portfolio bag, the banksias in the street beginning to flower, and offered a series of charcoal self-portraits to a Bronte café owner, who blu-tacked them to his wall and handed her a joint. *Proceeds go to charity.*

'YOU CAN'T WASTE it, Sweet,' her mother said again. Though she must have known everything had soured, surely.

'I'm sick of it, Barbara-Ann. *You* made me sick of it. *You*! You know that, don't you?'

'Me? Me? Without me ...' she trailed off. 'You've got to understand the opportunity you've got. Look ...' Her mother disappeared into the living room and returned with a handful of recent catalogues from her favourite Paddington gallery, laying them out on the coffee table in front of the divan. 'Look at this.'

Kira sat up.

Her mother pointed to the price list in one catalogue, then the next, flicking through them, faster and faster, a frenzy. All the non-negotiable tens of thousands of dollars in their precise columns. As if what she was laying out was irrefutable evidence. But in support of what case?

'But you don't understand, Mother Dear. Read my lips: I ... just ... don't ... care.'

'No, you listen to me girl!' Her mother's voice began to tremble. '*You're* the one who doesn't understand! You're as good as any of them. Better! This is what you could earn. This is what you could make. More!'

Though what Kira heard was, 'This is what *we* could make.'

'After all I've sacrificed. After everything we invested in you …'

It was that last *we* that did it. Not just that her mother presumed to speak for her father. But that she'd so misrepresent him, could so misunderstand him.

'You shouldn't hide yourself,' Flores had said. 'The universe sees. It knows.'

Kira was on a park bench sketching out a swarm of bees, freehand, nothing before her. The words are similar to her mother's, but Flores gestures to some greater moral authority.

'Do you like it?'

'You've got something. Don't hide it. It's a talent. You gotta use it. You *owe* it to the universe.' Flores and his cosmos of interweaving debts, which she'd only later come to understand. 'Come and see,' he said, motioning for her to walk with him to his studio. 'We're hung in the streets, not hidden away in parlours.'

She remembers the first time Flores touched her neck, offering to tattoo her.

'We tattooists and surgeons and undertakers and whores,' he'd whispered. 'We body-workers, we lovers of flesh. The body calls and we respond. We are beloveds answering our lovers. A body cries and we answer it. We pull back the woven veils and begin our work. Our various blades, the points of our instruments, our hands pressing the flesh for a knot beneath the surface.'

So she joined him. She drew, and she cleaned, and then eventually, sooner than most apprentices, she learned to do needles. She started with one of his spare machines on grapefruit, then pigskin. Eventually old friends from art school, for free.

She changed shape in this studio. Her long hair went, and what was left she coloured: red, orange, yellow, moving through the spectrum like the colours were seasons. She added metal, experimenting, settling for a single ear hoop. She felt her arms strengthen, her shoulders, a new musculature building in her. She started wearing singlets, black Jackie Howes, showing herself off. Her name morphing as well, Keira to Kira, an early Japanese phase.

'You won't be missed?' Flores had asked, seeing the new creature emerge. 'Your mother?'

Kira shook her head. Her mother had ventured into the studio once and Kira almost laughed when she saw her enter, anxious, tightly holding a boyfriend's hand.

'You wanted to see for yourself what I'm wasting my life on?'

It had been unnecessary of course, as cruelty always is. Rebuffed, her mother would, she knew, go back to her glassed balcony overlooking the sea where she would shuffle her aspidistras and lament her fate.

How MUCH WAS it tattooing that seduced her, she wonders now, bent over her drawing desk, how much Flores? This question returning again and again on evenings like this one, Flores having disappeared from the studio mid-afternoon with barely a word.

Where do you go? she wonders. Who do you see? What are you doing there, you and your young brother?

If I told you I'd have to kill you, he'd said. But you can only tell a joke so many times before it stales. Before mystery turns rank and morphs into secret.

There is movement on the other side of the doorway and Kira looks up from her stencil. In the mirror she sees the reflection of a solitary man regarding her, his back to the flash on the wall, his head as still as the wall itself.

16

SKIN AND NEEDLE

'How does this look?' Kira asks, showing him the design.

The man examines it carefully. 'It looks good. Yes, that's fine. That will do.'

She leads him from behind the counter to her chair, and tells him to take off his collared shirt, which he folds neatly and places on the table beside him. He rolls up the left sleeve of his white undershirt so it gathers evenly around his shoulder, revealing a pale sweep of white skin above his elbow.

He's fit and he's hard, she thinks, inspecting him more closely now. There's power in his arms and shoulders, whatever his age. The skin on his pocked cheeks has gathered in jowly pucks from years of clenching his jaw. He has short thin hair parted on the right, and on the left side of his forehead is a cluster of splotches, each the size of a small coin, blossoms of imperfection.

She stands above him and touches his shoulder, sure of her business, her hands moving over him, searching for scars or bruises or pockets of fluid.

'You've got pretty good skin for an old bloke.'

'Not that good,' he laughs, 'and not that old.'

Kira shaves his shoulder, the cold blade and his light arm hair falling away. She wipes down his skin with a tissue, then takes a bottle of liquid from her cabinet, applying it to his freshly smoothed skin before holding the stencil against him. She feels his shoulder tense beneath her hand, sees his flickering eyelids, his shallow breathing. Some part of his body wants to run, some essence.

She peels the stencil away, leaving the purple outline of what will be his tattoo.

• • •

THE SLEEVE OF ink running the length of her left arm comes closer. From her wrist, up and over her shoulder, her tattoos interweave in a swirl of blue and green on the skin below her collarbones. There are so many tattoos – laced so neatly, beside and above, overlapping and interlacing, one forming part of the next, the Celtic warrioress the largest – that it's not easy for him to make out any one image.

'Good,' she says, inspecting the stencil, before retreating to the drawing room while it takes.

Phelan's eyes begin to dart. In the distance he sees her rummaging among papers. Outside the street is clamouring, a thousand sounds he can't tease apart; a storm of fire impossible to navigate a way through. When she returns he is sweating.

'Have you been back long?' she asks, wiping down his skin with ointment.

His head swivels to look at her. 'Back?'

'You're a soldier, aren't you?' Her voice is sure, and it's her turf.

'It's that obvious?'

'It's that obvious.' Though in fact, it's a guess.

'I got back today.'

A siren starts up outside, close, insistent while whatever vehicle it belongs to – police or ambulance, he can never tell the difference – struggles to get clear of traffic. The siren is followed, first by one car horn, then another, and then a third, as if a pack of wild dogs has cornered its quarry out there in the sweltering city. The siren's call changes to a short, jagged, staccato burst of electronica, before resuming its steady wail. The horns tire. The evening tires. The wailing siren moves away.

'So this is your first tattoo?' she asks him.

'Yes.'

'Usually I tell my virgins there's nothing to be frightened of, but … well … as a soldier there's no need to say that to you, is there?' She laughs, then falls silent.

Nothing to be frightened of. Phelan watches her clean hands, takes in the cheap rings and notes where the ink from her sleeve ends at her left wrist. He watches her pull a pair of thin black latex gloves on, hears them snap against the skin on the back of her hands.

KIRA GETS A new needle from its sealed plastic, popping the eye through the back of the packet and drawing the needle out, the point directed away from her. She then cracks open a new tube and rests it in the palm of her left hand before sliding the needle into the end of the tube, allowing the shaft to fall through till its point comes out the tube's tip.

She takes her favourite Micky Sharpz tattoo machine from its drawer, loosening the tube clamp enough so she can back the tube up through the hole in the machine's frame, eye and shaft and tube, till the eye is adjacent to the pin at the end of the armature bar. She flips the grommet off the pin, and settles the grommet into the eye of the needle itself, before working the eye and grommet over the armature bar pin till the tube and needle are in place and firm. She retightens the clamp. They're all so deft, these movements of her hand and wrist and fingers in perfect choreography. She stretches a thick red rubber band around the frame and the needle shaft. That give, that softness.

Kira savours the weight of the machine in her right hand; the custom-made metal frame, the two copper coils in their black plastic wrap, the plates and springs, the tube and grip and the needle she's just fitted. Damn Micky, she thinks, you're a goddamn thing of beauty.

'All right,' she says, gently pressing the floor pedal with her right foot. The surging electricity brings the instrument to life, and it becomes a new presence in the room, this buzzing object in her hand. The vibrations enter her, calling her body into her task. She lifts her foot, bends to adjust the voltage on the power pack, before letting the electricity flow again. That buzz, still a little ragged. She watches the vibrations of the armature bar, the current breaking and reconnecting, and tightens the screw, closing her eyes, working in feel and in sound until she's found its sweet spot and the machine is purring. When she opens her eyes she sees the wave in the armature bar, gentle and slow-moving, passing back and forth along the bar. The magic of it, how the first rapid violence of its movement metamorphoses into song.

'All right,' she says again, dipping the needle into a cap of black ink then pressing it against his skin.

THAT FIRST NIBBLE, a teasing at his shoulder. Phelan turns his head. Her hand pulls back an inch, the machine hovering above him. He watches the needle descend again and press against his skin once more, and is aware of a lag between what he sees and what he feels, a long second before the needle bites and he feels its sting. You see the lightning before you hear it. But by then it's become a different thing, a new word, a new name, thunder. If the thing one sees is different from the thing one feels, what is the thing itself? Does it even need a name?

He watches her lift the needle once more. A trinklet of blood remains on his skin. You could fall into the gap between seeing and feeling. You could disappear. But he doesn't, can't, not yet. He is not sure what he feels. He knows the needle is piercing his skin, entering him. He watches as she draws it away, wiping the blood off with the tissue she holds in her left hand. He feels the point of the needle on his skin. He closes his eyes and gives over to the buzz of the machine. How many machines his body has vibrated to: the Bushmasters and the ASLAVs, the M113s from the old days, sometimes a Hercules, even the simple burr of a camp generator shepherding him from exhaustion to sleep.

'Is it good to be home?' she asks, pulling him back.

Home. It's been a temptress all posting long, visiting him when he weakened. *Home*. And now she's whispering it. He sighs, then laughs, a hint of bitterness, but does not open his eyes. Home is too big a word for her, he thinks. She knows not what she is saying.

'What is your name?' he asks, finally.

She tells him.

'Like the *Wanted* poster on the wall?'

'One of my illustrious forebears.'

'So it's in your blood?'

'Literally.'

He waits for her to ask him his name in return, but she doesn't. Instead, the needle probes his shoulder, opening him, the light sting of it. He introduces himself anyway, as if it's the needle he's responding to, then returns to her question. 'It's good to be back, yes. It's good to be home. But ...' His voice catches.

Kira continues, needle, wipe, needle, wipe. 'But?' she prompts.

Phelan nods to himself, then turns his head away, lost.

'But ... Samuel Robert Beckett?' she finishes.

He looks up, startled.

'It doesn't take a genius,' she says.

A minute passes, maybe more.

'Do you want to tell me about him?'

He considers her question carefully, then looks away again. 'I don't think I can.' The old soldier grows suddenly ancient.

'Sure,' she says.

He closes his eyes again. The needle is at work on his shoulder, the soft pressure of her hand, the buzzing machine, the high song of his stinging skin. Outside the throb of traffic after the fallen day grows less threatening. There's a symphony here, he thinks, like the low hum of air through a chopper's blades, notes you can train yourself to detect above the engine. You really could lose yourself in this.

21

A FURIOUS BEAUTY

Chora Valley, Afghanistan, November 2010

PHELAN LEANS OVER and looks at the ground rushing past below. There are days he feels he could love this country. The furious beauty of it. These rose-coloured dawns, these unassuming villages, these rivers and streams that swell and narrow with the seasons, these kids who stop their play and look up at you with wonder in their faces. Phelan waves to them as the Chinook tips to the left and passes over a village. The chopper follows a bend in the river up-valley, its nose hard on some scent. The machine's roar is muted by the foam plugs in his ears, but its vibrations are pure and wonderful. Phelan gets out of his office whenever he can, looks for opportunities to take to the air, a certain magic in it for the infantryman he once was. He loves the throb, loves his chest vibrating with it, how you can shed the weight of a war's bureaucracy inside a chopper. That sweet shuddering, warm like a bath. It could lull an old warrior to sleep. Even one who's become a taskforce commander.

Ahead, the sheer walls of a mountain pass rush towards them, sharp with daybreak. As he peers at the southern rock face he sees the mouth of a cave, and thinks he detects a reflection of light on metal. He squints behind his dark glasses, looking for the stirrings of some many-headed Taliban Scylla inside the cave. But it is nothing, just the play of early morning light on prehistory, and soon they are speeding through the pass itself and the cave is behind them and a band of shadow falls and in a heartbeat they have emerged and are into the next valley, new villages beaded to a new river.

Grasso, his taskforce regimental sergeant major, touches him on the shoulder and holds up his open palm, fingers outstretched. Five minutes to go. Phelan nods.

• • •

NEVER ASK YOUR men to do something you wouldn't do yourself.

But it's a tough manifesto to live out from behind a desk. Tougher still for an officer who's risen to a rank as high as this without having seen active combat himself. Not that it's his fault. He'd stand in the face of enemy fire if he had to, he knows he would. He'd prepared himself for it, longed for it, greedily sought it when he was younger, but it never came – barely a shot fired in East Timor, and the postings in Iraq and Somalia only staff officer roles.

The history of his tribe is replete with armchair officers, he knows this too well and fears ending his career like that. To truly lead, to test himself, to stand with his men in battle, that is something to aspire to. If anything, he's found it harder to suppress his curiosity for action, to staunch his hunger for respect, to quell his envy when he sees soldiers return from enemy contact changed. But he makes do. He learns to plan an operation. Gets good at it. He's read Monash compare generalship to conducting an orchestra, and pictured himself with a baton in hand. He's sent warriors out on patrol. Again and again. Success after success. It gets almost too easy. That is, until they stop coming back.

It wasn't like this for Phelan's predecessor. Or for the commander before that. Their commands were spotless. But Phelan – there's no avoiding it – he's got dead soldiers on his watch.

The shock of the first, an earthquake of consequence, its tremors rippling still. Then a second, a third, a new reality entering the consciousness of the fighting force. Though his response – surely – couldn't be faulted. There is what his position demands, and there is everything else he's done. The visits and the letters and the reports. Standing beside their bodies in the camp morgue. Some days, his duties and his conscience stretching him closer to exhaustion than he's ever been, he doubts himself. His judgement. He's demanded review after review in an attempt to find a point – a decision perhaps – where he could have made a different choice. He's tried to uncover some resourcing failure he could blame. Or a training inadequacy. A hundred times he's replayed in his weary mind what he's heard, what he's seen. How can he possibly sleep knowing he has men who won't, ever again? How could he not begin to fear each coming day and whatever news it will bring?

Even the near misses offer no relief, make him queasy: a soldier who'd stepped on a pressure plate that didn't go off, or caught a leg in a trip wire, or had it explode only for the shrapnel to be buried too low to get fragged. Some nights he's been so sick with the consequences of the operations he's approved, he half-wishes it was someone other than him making the decisions.

Then the thought takes seed: go and see exactly what it is you're sending them out into. Stand with them, experience it. It'll be good for them to see you that far out in the field. And, Brigadier Phelan, it will also allow you to look yourself in the mirror, perhaps even to sleep. To know yourself as someone who would only ask his men to do something he is prepared to do himself.

He wonders now, flying over terrain he has only studied on a map, if he has created a reason where one didn't exist, concocted some vague logistical imperative to join a patrol out of the most isolated up-valley base. Not exactly defying the Chief, but close. For months he has pored over wall charts of the Uruzgan badlands. Each of their bases is a blot of friendly ink on a map that, in truth, is still being filled in. Our force is here to turn the badlands good, that's the strategic objective. Each blot is supposed to spread as the friendly territory expands, and eventually one will join with the other. *And then what will we have?* he overhears his RSM muttering to himself before answering his own question: *a fucking wildlife corridor.*

The operation is security for a meeting with local elders about building a ford over a river, one they can still use in summer when the snow melts and the water rises. The meeting is nothing grand – just a handful of locals, not big enough to qualify as a *shura*, and certainly

24

no need for a brigadier. But he's going to show solidarity with his soldiers on the front line, that's what he's been practising telling them.

THE CHINOOK ARRIVES as planned at exactly 0630 hours. What takes Phelan forty minutes by air was a three-day ordeal by Bushmaster convoy for the men who established the base here. As the helicopter's dust storm abates, Phelan follows his RSM and his warrant officer, Hartley, out of the chopper. Behind him comes a lieutenant from army media and another two soldiers, then finally the crew. His back is stiff as he bends beneath the blades, straightening fully only when he's beyond the reach of the rotors' gusts and he stops to grasp Lieutenant Anthony Gruen's hand on the perimeter, the two men yelling greetings to each other above the engine-roar.

Lieutenant Gruen is tall and lean, his dark hair clipped to a fresh stubble. He is barely older than most of his men. He gives Phelan a tour of the base, a simple wooden building, set in the centre of a small compound protected by HESCO-reinforced walls. As they match strides inside the perimeter wall, Lieutenant Gruen briefs him on the insurgency this far up-valley, only breaking his narrative to introduce the brigadier to his men – soldiers who take their earbuds out to greet him, or lay down their Bibles and weights to salute. Phelan looks them in the eye and repeats their names back to them. The base's Afghan interpreter salutes him too.

'Thank you,' Phelan hears himself saying to the terp.

'He's solid,' Gruen says as they move away, leading Phelan towards a break in the wall. 'Good and solid.'

Lieutenant Gruen points to the nearest village. Phelan looks over the HESCO down at the village and sees only desert and mudbrick and maize fields. There is no electricity, no steel, no cement. The water runs in open irrigation channels off the river, and the base is close enough to smell the smoke from their morning fires to know they burn their shit. There are fat-tailed sheep and barefoot shepherd boys, mules and water carriers.

'You'd do well to find a single thing out there that couldn't have been lifted straight from the Old Testament,' Phelan muses.

'Or the Koran,' Gruen replies crisply.

Phelan looks at the lieutenant. Was he correcting him? He turns back towards the village. 'Are they friendly?' he asks.

'Pot shots in the first week or two,' Gruen says, leading the brigadier away from the wall, 'quieter now.'

Gruen ducks his head as he passes through the doorway of the base's building, its flat roof laid not with harvested grain like the compounds in the village below, but sandbags. Phelan follows him inside, his entourage trailing short paces behind.

'Brew, Sir?'

'If you're having one, Tony,' Phelan replies.

Gruen hesitates just long enough to make Phelan doubt himself. 'We weren't going to, Sir.'

'I certainly don't *need* one,' Phelan responds quickly.

'We'll start the patrol briefing then, Sir.'

Route selection is everything, but in a narrow valley the options are limited: across the *dasht*, along the road that runs through the villages, through the fields, or some combination. Yesterday's patrol started out along the footpad beside the village wall, so today Gruen picks a route that begins in the harvested field this side of the village.

ONCE THEY'RE ALL kitted up a cocky young corporal, Starc, walks down the line of soldiers, checking their gear, making sure everyone's wearing dog tags – the brigadier and his warrant officer too.

It's obvious Lieutenant Gruen is proud of his boys and the way they've held up for the forty days they've been together inside this tiny base. Phelan imagines these soldiers putting themselves on the line, getting their arses shot at, having kids spit at them in the street, the hard work of winning hearts or minds up here. Forty days without shaving, without showering, sleeping on stretchers cheek by jowl. By now Gruen must know these men better than his own family. He'd know who've got wives, girlfriends, kids, who's taping glossy photos to rough posts beside their stretcher for everyone to share. Music, footy team, dick size. You train with blokes, you bed down with blokes, you fight with them, you get to know them. Who's running from what, who's hiding, how many of them are looking for their fathers.

Mothers don't like to hear it, wives even less, but there's no better way of getting to know someone than to fight with them. And here Lieutenant Gruen and his men are, exhausted beyond the point of sound decision-making, but still turning up patrol after patrol, perhaps for no other reason than their mates are there with them.

'Sir,' Starc says, pointing to Phelan's badges of rank, 'unless you need 'em, it's better to leave 'em. You don't want to bring anything that might give you away. And if anything goes wrong you don't want—' He catches himself.

Phelan guesses what it was the corporal thought better about saying – he wouldn't want to give the Taliban something they can use for propaganda. Because while Phelan's pack is lighter and he's got no antenna that might identify him as a commander, he's otherwise dressed as one of them: camos, body armour, webbing, helmet with its Australian flag sewn into the left-hand side, dark ballistic glasses, field dressings, hydration. Phelan strips the badges off his uniform, and hands them to his RSM, who's staying at base.

Beside him a sapper with a harelip is mucking around, flicking his unsuspecting comrades' testicles through their trousers with the back of his middle finger.

'Sapper?' Phelan addresses him, reading his name on the uniform, Beckett.

The soldier stands to attention, fearing an admonition, but Phelan gestures to his helmet cam which is already running.

'You need to tape down the lights better,' Phelan advises, pointing to the little green and red LED charge lights on the side of the camera. 'They could give you away in the dark,' he adds, pleased he has something constructive to contribute, even though he'd picked it up from a review of a special forces operation that had gone wrong rather than first-hand experience. 'Put more gaffer over the lights, Sapper, that will do it.'

'Yes, Sir,' snaps the soldier.

BEFORE THEY GO, Lieutenant Gruen breaks the patrol into two sections and has them practise formations inside the compound, the order he wants from them on the outside. Phelan feels the adrenalin rush. This is what it's all about, what it's always been about. He feels his surging strength, feels his fifty years as an accumulated vitality, sucks in the air. He has his place in the column, warriors before him, warriors behind.

Phelan watches the men who aren't on patrol take up positions on the perimeter wall, covering the line of soldiers about to leave the base. The gate swings open ahead of him. Phelan loads his rifle before following Starc towards the compound entrance. The soldiers in front of him pat the bony head of the base's pet goat before striking out through the gate, and Phelan does the same, something talismanic in the gesture.

They head down the scree in single file, the sappers out front, taking the path across the rocks to the edge of the green zone below. Beckett is lead scout, with Phelan positioned in the centre of the patrol, his warrant officer immediately behind him. Phelan's got cover front and rear. Gruen follows with the radio on his back, watching his boys gracefully scanning their arcs, and listening, for now, to the comforting sound of boot-crunch around him, while high above, out of view, the drone, Tiger Shark, is circling, feeding information down to him.

At the edge of the green zone, irrigation channels and low mud walls separate the crops. Phelan watches as two giant bales of golden maize stalks bob slowly across the fallow earth in front of him, the women carrying them obscured by their loads, the late-harvest grain swaying like lions' manes. The patrol breaks into two columns and crosses the stubble towards the village.

When they reach the first mudbrick wall of the first compound, Phelan's section makes its way down an alley that leads to the main road bisecting the village. He and his warrant officer, Hartley, work as a pair, covering each other as they move down the alley. You're never more alive, Phelan thinks, never more a part of the universe than at moments like this, never more at home.

The main street is swarming, even though it's not market day. The high mudbrick walls on either side of the street collect and funnel the men and the children. The walls are pasted thick with election posters. Phelan hasn't met President Karzai, not yet. A mule-man drives a dozen beasts down the road towards them, casually striking his beasts with his switch, puffs of dust coming off their flanks with each blow. Two men and a young boy squat in the doorway of a store, framed by brightly painted yellow wooden beams, grey shawls wrapped around each pair of shoulders. Their crooked toes protrude from their plastic sandals.

'Salaam alaikum,' Phelan greets them.

'Walaikum salam,' the men reluctantly reply.

From the shade of a tree near the marketplace ahead, a group of mat-haired children look up from their play. Phelan waves at them but they are impassive. He reaches into a pouch in his body armour for some sweets and drops to one knee. The kids come forward and take the wrapped lollies from his giant gloved hand. Not curiously like sparrows, but greedily like butcher birds. As they're finishing Phelan becomes aware of Gruen watching him. When he turns he catches an unguarded expression on the Lieutenant's face. Though fleeting, Phelan recognises it. Disdain.

Lieutenant Gruen orders the section to turn down another alley so they can link with the rest of the unit at the other end of the village. Phelan wipes sweat from his forehead, his hand momentarily passing across his eyes, when a bottle is thrown over a compound wall and lands just behind him, hissing. He dives before he's even seen it, like it's a grenade, and when it doesn't go off immediately, he goanna-scrambles forward as fast as he can while the thing's still spitting, not yet knowing it's only a chloroform bomb and in the scheme of explosive devices out here, harmless enough. When he turns a corner out of the alley, panicked and still coiled, there's a little girl running too, but towards him, straight into the barrel of his gun.

And somehow, someway, somewhy, Phelan doesn't shoot. He feels her forehead nudge the muzzle, actual skin against actual metal, and still he doesn't shoot. She screams. Phelan looks at her, this little creature dissolving into terror, and understands the pressure of his finger against the trigger. She's screaming and his finger's tight and he's looking at her, the little girl's scream filling up the entire world.

Lieutenant Gruen has nearly reached them when Phelan kneels and takes off his glasses, his helmet. Lays his rifle down beside him, smiles, or thinks he does. Phelan pats the girl's shoulder like an uncle might, three or four times, lightly, then produces what's left of his sweets. The girl is no longer screaming when her mother runs forward, and grasps her arm and pulls her away, knocking the lollies from Phelan's outstretched palm onto the dusty road.

Gruen picks up Phelan's weapon and silently hands it to him.

NO QUIET CORNER

KIRA REPOSITIONS THE pedestal fan. Its newly angled breeze touches Phelan as it moves mechanically back and forth, slowly passing across his body, cooling his skin in its steady sweep, ruffling the folds of his shirt. As he follows the blur of the fan's blades, he detects a barely audible clicking sound, and thinks that if the fan was set at a slower speed the sound would be louder, would be an irritant, thinks how often you have to go hard at something or else be exposed by it. He feels a sharp pain and winces. Kira pulls back.

'All right?'

'Yes, yes,' he says, settling back into his body.

Kira reaches for new tissues from the box on her work station, turning away from Phelan momentarily. He notices for the first time the patch of sweat forming on the back of her singlet. When she turns to resume her work, he looks beyond her to the wall mirror and its fresh image of this woman, Kira, bending over him. He is transfixed by her sweat-mark, and watches as it spreads across her dark back.

THE SOLDIERS PUSH on in the rising heat, village after harvesting village, their packs growing heavier with the sun overhead.

'That was close back there, Boss,' Hartley says to Phelan when they stop to slug water.

'We were lucky, son,' Phelan replies, a term he probably wouldn't use if he and his wife had children of their own, but truer than he'd like that the army is a family of sorts, that he'd be adrift without it. Phelan's manner appears perfectly matter-of-fact as he speaks – though his heart rate has still not come down – as if he's already reviewing the incident from a report on his desk. As if the heat and the pack-weight are nothing, and if others need to stop for a drink the weakness is theirs.

Phelan's not for wilting. He doesn't know a fifty year old fitter than him, and, as he now tells himself, he's more determined than any of the youngsters here. He's got a career to prove it, even one like his with his string of regimental and staff appointments, exchange postings where he could orchestrate them, his Chief Instructor roles, a term at the Royal College of Defence Studies in the UK, and then his 'strategy and preparedness' appointments on his return. What's his rank if not evidence of his determination to succeed? Some of these privates, he reflects, are just training for their first exam, cramming desperately. They might be ready – no army trains its soldiers better, equips them better, and, most controversial of all among the coalition forces over here, pays them better – but what's a year or two when set beside a lifetime of discipline and competition. The knowledge that might otherwise gnaw at him – that some of these young privates have seen the action that has eluded him – has been washed away by the adrenalin of the patrol.

He wills the aches in his body away, as Marcus has taught him, this power of self-control, and what it grants its adherents. People don't understand that discipline is more than just protection, more than effectiveness, more than moral strength. That if one knows where to look there's reverie in it too. When he stops for water, it's only after the soldier in front of him has stopped first.

Eventually, after a three-hour march, they reach their destination, and slowly approach the village square where they've arranged to meet the elders.

The sappers clear a stand of old cypress, and then the mudbrick wall of the adjacent compound. Nothing. The boys are positioned nicely, providing cover just in case, Starc's section near the entrance to the compound, Beckett's on the other side of the trees. His lips are pursed, an old Second World War tune, 'Whistle While You Work'. Where did a kid like him learn that? Phelan muses. It's midday by now and the heat is barely softened by the shade of the grove.

Phelan joins Gruen by a large cypress tree as the lieutenant listens intently to what's coming in on comms.

'Any chatter?' Phelan asks when he's got Gruen's attention.

'Nothing. Everything's quiet.'

'That must mean there were no spotters watching my helicopter arrive this morning.' When Gruen doesn't respond he forces a reply. 'You'd agree, wouldn't you Tony?'

'Let's hope so,' the lieutenant says, refusing to give him what he wants. 'How did you find the march, Sir?'

'Fine, Tony, just fine.' Phelan resists the temptation of saying he loved it. He has forgotten the encounter with the girl and all he can feel now as he squats near the base of the cypress are his stinging thighs, and it is a sweet thing.

Gruen takes off his helmet and glasses, and Phelan follows his lead. Though hot, at least the glare's not quite as brutal here. The elders will have been alerted to the patrol making its way up the valley, will know now there is a smaller group of four of them – he and his security, the terp and the lieutenant – waiting outside the compound for them.

Eventually three bearded *maliks* emerge, their flowing robes unable to conceal the stiffness of their joints. Even so, Phelan can see that Gruen is on alert, checking again that cover is in place.

'Salaam alaikum, sanga astai?' Gruen says to each of them.

'Walaikum salam, kha yam manana, taso sanga astai?'

'Shokor dae, zhuwande osae.'

Phelan waits as Lieutenant Gruen continues the long greeting ritual – family and health and prosperity – to gauge the men. Not just old, he thinks, but reluctant. Gruen spreads out the patterened sheets of material they've brought along, not the carpets the locals would normally use, but the best they can do, lighter for the march. The *maliks* join them sitting in the shade. Gruen introduces Phelan as his boss.

A big boss? One of the *maliks* asks. No, Gruen answers, just in case, *a little boss*, and they all laugh, the terp too, but the elders see the deference, see in Phelan not his age – though older than they are, he looks younger – but his careful dark eyes, his thin lips and bulging neck.

Phelan's Pashto is just good enough to take him beyond first salaams, enough for these ancient-eyed village elders to nod and murmur to each other.

We can build the bridge, Lieutenant Gruen says through the interpreter. By which he means his engineers can. It'll be so strong it won't wash away in a flood. You can get your crops to market faster. It'll help the entire village. If you agree to it, Gruen says, the whole community will be grateful, not to us, but to you.

The *maliks* nod. And yet. We'll consider, they say, directing themselves to Phelan, rising and shaking hands and touching chests lightly with the tips of their fingers. Phelan bows, lower than Gruen.

Kids have begun to gather around the sapper with the harelip on the other side of the grove. Through the trees they see him holding up a tennis ball he must have brought with him, and then miming cricket shots until one of the kids cottons on and runs off to get a stick they can use as a bat.

'Becks and his fucking cricket,' Lieutenant Gruen mutters in Phelan's direction, 'Becks and his fucking balls. If he's not juggling pebbles, or balancing a soccer ball on his head, he's tossing a cricket nut at you. "Sir," he'll call out, and if you're quick enough you'll catch it. Otherwise it'll hit you and the fucker will cack himself.' Though Gruen is shaking his head, Phelan understands it is with fondness.

The two men watch as more and more kids gravitate towards Sapper Beckett and his scratch cricket match. Eventually Gruen orders Starc's section to cover the game, while he squats beside a wall to radio in an update. Phelan stretches. Gruen strains to hear the comms operator above Beckett's enthusiastic hooting, the sounds of the sapper throwing down leg breaks, encouraging the kids. Maybe the sapper is right, Phelan thinks, and we've got as much chance winning the locals over with cricket as we do building bridges and schools.

When the ball is hit towards them, Phelan bends to collect it. Rather than lobbing it gently back to the boy who's come after it, Phelan jogs out with the ball onto the makeshift oval, leaving his warrant officer to shrug his shoulders and shake his head ruefully.

THEY RETURN BY a different route, leaving the green zone and crossing to the other side of the river, with Phelan closer to the back of the patrol. The river is thigh-high and cold, but slow. Some of the men take a piss as they wade across, pausing mid-stream. Not Phelan.

'That's an ideal place for a ford,' he says to Gruen when they're together on the other bank. 'They'd be crazy to knock it back.'

'They will though,' Gruen replies.

'Why do you think that, Tony?'

'Because they're not fuckwits,' Lieutenant Gruen says. 'They know the bridge is for us, not them. And because they think it's too dangerous to accept gifts from Americans. Or Australians. No difference in their eyes.'

It occurs to him how exhausted Lieutenant Gruen is. Forty days of being shot at in the middle of the night. Forty nights without a decent sleep. The man looks rooted. And now he's responsible for the safety of a brigadier who'd insisted on joining his patrol. A tourist. In the eyes of some of Gruen's men perhaps he's only here hunting for gongs. Phelan knows, of course, that Gruen's career is on the line if anything goes wrong and that the patrol commander is probably doing his best not to let any of it show. But before Phelan can think of what to say, Gruen apologises – 'Sorry, Sir,' – and quickly gives orders.

The soldiers move forward. The path rises above and away from the river, and the patrol passes a cemetery, the headstones barely discernible from the rocks of the dasht. After twenty minutes the path descends again to water level, where a high rock and timber footbridge crosses back over the river to the market village, the first they'd passed through earlier that day.

35

Lieutenant Gruen orders the patrol to halt while he takes stock. As Phelan squats by a knee-high boulder on the side of the rocky path, more exposed than he'd like, Sapper Beckett reports another bunch of kids crossing the footbridge. If there was anything coming in from Tiger Shark, any chatter being picked up, the lieutenant wouldn't risk crossing here. They watch as the kids move away on the other side of the bridge. Watch and wait till Gruen gives the order to move forward.

The sappers approach the bridge and peer under it, looking for exposed wires or fresh rockwork. Nothing. They move onto the bridge itself, swinging their metal detectors rhythmically from side to side, and then, when across, when the bridge is cleared, they secure it.

The first section of the patrol doesn't cross but continues seventy metres past the bridge, each man covering the other as they wade across further down-river, waist high, weapons above heads, the current jostling them.

The rest of the patrol uses the footbridge, man by man. Phelan's warrant officer crosses first, then Starc, followed by Phelan himself. When he is across he turns back towards Gruen on the other side and sees him stiffen, sees him press his earpiece harder against his ear, concentrating. The look on his face is short of panic, but Phelan can read it well enough, even from here: there's chatter coming in, enemy spotters somewhere in the area. Danger no longer latent.

Starc's section provides cover from behind a low wall as the rest of the platoon cross, one by one, bent low, moving quickly. Lieutenant Gruen squats by the wall, comms in his ears, scanning the country around them. A group of men watches them through the trees, but disappears when the terp calls out. Phelan senses the shifts in the atmospherics. Whatever Gruen is learning from Tiger Shark, whatever intelligence is beginning to pour in. Whether women and children are leaving the village to the north or youths of fighting age are gathering over a ridgeline, Phelan doesn't need to hear it to know something is off.

Lieutenant Gruen changes plan, orders the platoon to skirt the village rather than proceed through it, a new map home.

PHELAN READS KIRA'S arm as she resumes her work. The buzzing machine, the needle on his own skin. He sees again the dark-haired warrioress with her long, flowing dress on Kira's left arm. The three-blued dress, her skin, her arms, her neck, the curve of her breasts, the bared thigh and leg.

'Why the warrior?' he asks.

For beauty, she thinks, for kick-arse strength. Because that's what I am. Can't you see?

'Why not?' she returns. And then, after a slight pause: 'And why Samuel Robert Beckett?'

Though they may be reluctant at first, they usually end up talking. Pain does that, opens people up.

YOU MIGHT BE hoping for it, you might even be expecting it, but you're never ready. You're moving slowly, doing your arcs, eyes following the barrel as it swings. In front of you and behind you are highly trained warriors, bodies of nerve endings, twitching. Soldiers who've seen action say there's contact, and then there's everything else that happens in your life. They are right, thinks Phelan.

Breath, no breath. Hell, all hell.

Phelan sees Sapper Beckett squatting on the other side of the small almond grove. Even in that heat, even from his haunches, there's an agility about the sapper as he rises from the irrigation channel, a quickness in him as he steps over the low wall running beside the channel.

But it's then that the world explodes and you know there's no quiet corner left on earth, none that'll ever admit you anyway.

The sapper doesn't just drop, he's blown backwards over the wall on the other side of the ditch by the rocket-propelled grenade and there's machine gun fire and small arms fire, and the ground around them all is spitting with rounds.

'Man down, man down!' Starc yells.

Phelan takes cover at the base of a tree, fifteen metres south of where the sapper was hit, his ears ringing. Hartley is crouching beside him, popping rounds off, the enemy everywhere.

'Get low, Boss!' Hartley screams. 'Lower!'

Rounds are flying either side of them, others biting into the tree, a 270-degree engagement. Grenades are being launched from a compound on the western edge of the village, rounds from ahead and behind.

Gruen will be calling in the medevac, but there's no way a chopper's getting down in this without Apache cover.

Phelan calculates the distance to where the sapper has fallen. No one is closer than he is.

'Cover me!' he yells.

Hartley looks blankly at him for a moment, and then, when he realises what Phelan's going to do, grabs at the brigadier's leg.

'No, Sir! Don't Sir!'

But Phelan is already out from behind the tree, and Hartley props himself up and lays down what cover he can, no more than a guess at where the rounds are coming from, aiming at a lone building ahead of them, muzzle flashes from there at least.

Phelan rushes forward, staying low. He sloshes through the shallow channel this side of the mudbrick wall, then stumbles, his old legs, a lurching step before regathering and throwing himself over the wall where the sapper disappeared.

When he lands it's only a couple of metres from Beckett, and when he looks over, Beckett's head is turned towards him already, and his lips are moving.

Phelan crawls closer, and sees a vein in the sapper's neck twitch. Chunks of mud are bursting off the wall above their heads, showering them.

'Charlie …' the young sapper croaks.

'It's okay son, it's okay,' Phelan says. But as he nudges alongside he sees one of the soldier's legs is gone, and the other is shredded. Even if he had morphine, there's no thigh to inject into, and no bandage big enough. The sapper is a torso in a pool of dark coursing blood, and Phelan goes to reach for him, but it's nothing he's capable of imagining, and there's horror, there's nothing he can staunch, and this man is draining away.

TEAR DROPS

THE DOWNSTAIRS BELLS ring again and Phelan's body jerks at the unexpected sound, kicking out against it and the chair and Kira's hand. His own breathing.

'Whoa,' Kira says, quickly pulling the machine away from his violently twisting body. 'No sudden movements, soldier.'

She lifts her foot off the pedal and the machine falls silent. Together they listen to the footsteps on the stairs.

A thin, gaunt-faced man appears, his knuckly hand gripping the banister, his matted blond hair tucked into a Jack Daniel's cap, pulled low on his forehead, concealing his eyes. Kira can't quite make out what's on his black T-shirt, but guesses it's metal of some sort. The images on the shirt flow over onto his biceps, the spiderweb tattoos on his elbows, his crowded forearms. He's inked, but not by her, not by Flores, not by anyone she recognises.

'Give me a moment,' she says to Phelan, resting the tattoo machine on the tray and rolling back her chair, peeling off her latex gloves as she rises.

Lightning flashes beyond the window.

'Got any crowns?' the man calls out from across the room when he sees her, his voice high-pitched, strained.

'Sure,' Kira says slowly, tossing her gloves casually into the tidy bin. 'We've got crowns.'

'It's gotta be big. You know. From here …' he points from one side of his chest, '… to here,' pointing to the other. 'Like this. I want it like this. See? A big crown. Big. Big as fuck.'

Kira gestures to the coffee table where the large folios are displayed in a neat fan. 'Have a look in the folders over there, see what you can find.'

The man follows her pointing finger, twisting his head, but his gaze gets lost before it reaches the table and he swings back around, locking onto her again.

'Like this,' he says, his agitated hand drawing a jagged zigzag in the air. 'Pointy on the top, like. You know? A crown.' His bony index finger scratches at space.

'Sure,' Kira says, speaking as evenly as she can now, almost soothingly, offering her own voice as something he might follow, a way down from whatever he's on, whatever high is already collapsing around him. She slowly skirts the counter to where folios of flash are laid out on the table. She's managed situations like this before, is aware of the danger on this side of the counter, but not her limitations.

'Here,' she says calmly, choosing a design from the first folder and opening it out for him to see, pausing, then slowly turning the page, showing him another design, and then moving on to a third. 'Why don't you have a look through these? See what you can find.'

She holds the folder out to him but he just stands there, rocking on the balls of his feet, up and down, snorting, looking around with his tiny eyes, nodding his head, jacked right up still, teetering. On his left cheekbone are two crude teardrops, barely more than smudges of prison ink, the residue of burnt shoe rubber. Just out, she guesses, and already it's too much for him. He's going to burst, she thinks, he's going to blow.

'Is Prince here?' the man blurts. Her stomach tightens. Flores's brother.

'No,' she replies, carefully returning the folder to the table, then slowly stepping back. 'He doesn't come around here anymore.' She can't bring herself to speak his name. 'He hasn't been here for months,' she adds. Wishing it were true.

He stands there, looking at her, scratching at the side of his neck as if something is buried beneath his skin.

'What's the biggest crown you've ever done?'

'I can do big,' she says, taking another slow step back towards the counter.

'Well, bigger than that. Bigger than you've ever done. Bigger than anyone.'

A crazy exultation in him. 'And then ...' He begins to lift his T-shirt up, and she sees his stomach, thin and hard.

'It's cool,' she says. 'Keep your shirt on bro. It's cool.'

PHELAN MEASURES THE room, his chair to the counter, the counter to Kira, the gap between Kira and the man. Registers that the man's hands are empty, that the junkie hasn't even seen him yet. This set of scales Phelan was trained so long ago to employ, so finely calibrated before falling into disuse, now called on for the second time in a week. Phelan measures and waits for the moment of action.

The man pulls down his shirt obediently, but soon becomes agitated again, as if regretting his compliance. He looks around wildly. Only now does he see Phelan in the chair. His eyes dart back to Kira, as if to reassure himself she hasn't disappeared. He stands there, thin and rocking, his left hand gouging at his neck, his right hand slapping against his hip.

'So you want a crown?' Kira says.

41

'A crown ...' he repeats, then remembers. 'Yeah, then underneath, you know – *family*. You know ... the most important thing. In a banner or something, *family*. Because that's the most important thing, isn't it?'

When she doesn't answer he yells. 'Well it is, isn't it?!'

'Yes.'

'That's what I want – *family*.'

'Sure.'

'Family.' It's as if his voice and his body are operating from different realms, one splitting from the other.

'Sure.'

He looks at her. His fidgeting hands. He looks at Phelan again. Then he jerks round to the sheets of flash on the wall behind him, the designs themselves beginning to crowd in.

'Fucking bullshit!' he suddenly spits, and reaches for a knife at the small of his back, tucked into his belt, concealed by his shirt. Phelan recognises the replica Gerber – twelve centimetre, black-handled, double-edged – the type displayed in the windows of the army disposal stores in George Street.

Phelan is out of the chair, but the man has already lunged at Kira and grabbed her wrist with his left hand, swinging the knife wildly through the air with his right, snorting.

'Fuck yeah, fuck yeah, fuck. And you,' he screams at Phelan, 'don't move! Just fucking stay there!' He pushes Kira towards the register. 'Open it!'

Phelan remains where he is, watching their eyes. The terror in Kira's, a blazing emptiness in the man's.

'Do what he wants,' Phelan says to Kira, as calmly as he can, feeling the adrenalin coursing in him, too strong to rein in. Twice in a week. Use it, though not yet.

But Kira is cringing, pulling against the man's hold as if prepared to sacrifice her hand for her body. The man is thumping the pad of the cash register with the fist that holds the knife.

'Open you dog! Fucking open.'

But the machine resists.

'You need the key,' Phelan says evenly. 'The key!' he repeats, louder, reaching into his own pocket and pulling out a bundle of house keys, guessing the man won't know the difference.

'Here,' Phelan calls, holding them high, moving closer as he does. 'Here. You'll need these.'

The keys hang from a deep blue lapis lazuli pendant, jingling. The man's eyes come to him. Phelan offers the bunch of keys, holding them up between thumb and forefinger, high, away from his body, as if feeding an animal, drawing its gaze, distracting it while he steps steadily forward.

The man has the knife in one hand, Kira's wrist in the other. Phelan holds his keys out further, nearer the man's reach.

'Here,' Phelan says again, his voice soft now, almost song. 'Here, take these. You need them.'

The junkie releases Kira's wrist, reaches for Phelan's keys.

Freed, Kira pulls desperately away, stumbling backwards. Then, at the precise moment the man's bony fingers grasp for the keys in Phelan's outstretched hand, Phelan drops them. Their slow trajectory towards the ground. The junkie's eyes widen, following the keys as they fall, this development beyond his imagining. The keys clatter on the timber floorboards and the man is temporarily frozen, his dumb head and his open mouth, before slowly bending.

Phelan's boot strikes the stunned face before the grasping fingers even reach the floor, knocking him backwards. He kicks the man again as his body collapses to the ground, then slams his heel into the wrist of the knife-hand, the blade spinning on the floorboards, skittering out of reach, disappearing under the tattooist's chair. Phelan leaps onto him, flipping the man, wrenching his right arm behind his back, jacking it up, pinning him to the ground, the man's cheek on the floorboards, the manoeuvre surprisingly easy.

43

The man screams as Phelan ratchets his arm up his back, and Phelan knows the junkie is no match, that this is over. Feels his power. Pulls the man's arm back another notch, another screech of pain. Less power than control. Something lost beckoning to be reclaimed. The screaming gives way to a groan, as Phelan's weight presses oxygen out of the body beneath him.

'Shut the fuck up, now arsehole,' Phelan whispers, leaning closer, pulling the arm back even further, feeling it reach the end of its range – a little more pressure and it'll burst from its socket – readying himself over the petty thief's limp body.

'Hey.'

It is Kira beside him.

'Hey!' she yells. 'What are you doing?'

ANIMAL SPIRITS

THE MAN AND the knife have gone. The police too. He'd given them what they needed, no more, and when they return to take statements tomorrow he'll have left too. Phelan locks the studio door behind them, and returns upstairs. The air is bruised, heavy still with the stew of fear and violence. He can smell traces of himself. Kira slides to the floor and hugs herself, her back against the wall, arms across her chest, her hands gripping her shoulders.

'Are you okay?' Phelan asks, standing awkwardly in the centre of the room, looking over at her shaking. Her eyes blinking wildly. The warrioress' skin glistening with sweat, trembling.

'Yeah, I'm fine, but …' she says, shaking her head, '… fuck me.'

'You did well.' A stupid thing to say. Hoping, perhaps, that's what she might say of him.

She shakes her head again. She's still coming down.

44

The rain begins to fall. First Kira, then Phelan, turns to the window. Kira sniffs the air.

Phelan watches her nostrils flare, some animal spirit returning. He lowers himself to the floor beside her. He doesn't recognise the pattern of his own breathing. They sit wordlessly for a long time, the rain steady outside.

'How many drops?' she murmurs.

'How many?'

But she is musing, and hadn't meant to speak.

'Nothing,' she says.

A gust of wind blows a spray of rain through the casement window. Kira rises. Phelan watches the muscles beneath her shoulders ripple as she reaches up to lower the window, her black singlet framing her neck, her arms, the power in her back. She has to jiggle the window before it slides down. She leaves it ajar. The room needs to breathe, not just them.

'So,' she says in time, rubbing her hands together almost clownishly as if needing something exaggerated to get herself going again, 'where were we? Let's finish this thing, hey?'

Phelan smiles. His legs tremble as he levers himself off the floor and climbs back into the chair.

Kira stands beside him and prepares to resume her work, but when she raises her arm, tattoo machine in her hand, it is shaking uncontrollably. She looks at her juddering hand, surprised.

Phelan looks too, and then into her face. The doubt in her eyes as much as in her body, not sure she can do this. He reaches out and gently touches her bare forearm, her tattooing arm.

'It's okay,' he says softly. 'Just begin.'

She presses her foot on the pedal and the machine vibrates. Still she hesitates. She holds her right arm out, the machine in her hand. Phelan watches. She could be a priestess drawing some sacred energy to herself. She steadies. Hand, arm, shoulders. The machine's vibrations dissolving shock, erasing fear. She returns to the tattoo. To Phelan and to Beckett.

'Have a look in the mirror,' Kira says, pointing.

She watches as he stands and bends his head to his shoulder. He walks towards his image till he fills out the glass. Kira looks at this brave soldier again, a quizzical look on his face as he begins to make sense of the reversed text on his shoulder. His skin is sun-worn, nicked and blotched, his thick neck pitched slightly forward, as if from a lifetime of leaning into things headfirst. The hair on his head is thin, but perhaps it has always been like that, the hairline high. How many suns have burned that skin, she thinks. She looks at his arse and his still-firm buttocks. She tries to guess his age. Is he fifty? Is it possible? Is he that old?

In the mirror his brow is creased with doubt as he inspects his tattoo. He looks from mirror to arm to mirror and pulls his shoulder around, straining to see the tattoo in its fullness. To see what others will see. Kira is satisfied – the sense that comes from completing a difficult task, from doing what's asked of you, from knowing you've given everything and what you gave was good. 'It looks great,' she says.

'Are you sure?'

It's not the soldier who is asking, not the man of action from earlier in the night, but, she suspects, a man who a thousand times has privately dismissed the folly of tattoos, their cheapness, their crassness, and who is now suddenly anxious he has made a terrible mistake.

'Yes, it's great, and it's a great tribute to your mate, Samuel.'

Phelan swings back around to look at her, startled.

Well, she tried. Sometimes words aren't capable of reassurance.

'Can I interest you in a drink?' she aks, surprising herself as much as him. She should be exhausted, should be fading, but instead she's high on a second wave of adrenalin, more than the usual surge that comes with completing a tattoo and hearing the tattoo deities murmur their pleasure. How much of it is a reaction to Flores not being here – not being the one to tell her she's fine and to wrap a blanket round her shoulders – she can't possibly know. Realising, now, she didn't need him anyway. Whatever strange events have just touched her, whatever good strange things. She doesn't quite know what they are, but doesn't want them to end just yet.

When he doesn't immediately respond, she adds with a tone of self-mockery, of playful exaggeration, 'It's the least we can do. It's not every day a girl gets rescued by a soldier!'

EVERY HABIT AND every professional judgement he's ever exercised, every risk he's ever avoided, tell him to leave. Every obligation, every loyalty. Every Aurelian lesson. But this is where he finds himself. Beckett-led. This night. These random events. This woman. This now. This new him. This post-Beckett him. It is possible that everything is changed, *everything*, and who can ever say what can be controlled and what ought be left to fate and if a new world is calling him through a fissure in the old? What sort of man would he be to turn away?

NOT BLUE, AZURE

HE WATCHES HER with the bartender, a young bearded man in his twenties, his short hair neatly contoured, tight black T-shirt, dress-rings on the hand that pours the whiskey. A week ago, Phelan was approving operations to bring in men with beards like this, a week ago beards like this were trying to kill him. A week ago, he could not have imagined sliding his phone from his pocket in the bathroom of a pub and texting his wife.

Darling, I've been delayed again. So sorry. I'll be on the first flight home in the morning. Love you. James

She places the shots – straight, two each – on the table between them. She hadn't asked him what he drank. Raises the first of hers now, looking him directly in the eyes, smiling, waiting for him to raise his too.

'Thanks,' she says.

'My pleasure,' he replies, whatever ritual she's leading him into.

She knocks it back, then shakes her head, as if splashing the whiskey into every corner of her brain. Her mane of hair sways, mesmerising.

'So,' he asks, 'how long have you been tattooing?'

'No, no, no, no,' she wags her index finger, then points to his untouched glass.

Whenever he drinks there's a reason, never for mere pleasure, certainly never intoxication. Usually it's to make others feel comfortable. Sometimes just so it can't be said of him he's not to be trusted. You can train yourself to drink. Phelan lifts the glass and tips it back. 'Satisfied?' he asks.

She smiles to herself and settles a little deeper into the cushions on the bench.

'So,' he leans forward, 'you and tattooing?'

Kira sighs, shakes her head in resignation. 'No woman in history ever slept with a man who asked that question.'

Phelan turns away, an involuntary glance at the doorway, as if it's from the street dangers might come. When he looks back his heart is racing. When he looks back to her she's grinning.

'You're right. I don't need to know. But tell me this,' he says, touching her tattooed forearm with his right index finger, giddy as he moves further into the unknown. He presses his finger gently against Kira's warrioress, against her protector's flowing skirt, these women and their flesh. 'Why is she blue?'

The bass thumping from a speaker above their heads fades as one song dies and another begins. Kira reaches for Phelan's glass, sips from it, puts it down, leans into him, her mouth against his ear.

'Azure,' she whispers, her hand on his chest now. 'Not blue, soldier, azure.'

SHE WATCHES HIM at the bar ordering another round. Sometimes you can look too hard for reasons. Believe too much in the logic of the universe and in your own capacity to select one thing over another, good over bad. The soldier looks back over his shoulder, as if checking she's still here. This grand flux, everything aswirl. In walks a soldier, in walks a thief. Who can ever know how a dance ends?

HE FOLLOWS HER out into the night. The street is wet, but the storm has passed and the city sky is clearing. The buckles of her boots gleam in the streetlight. Her hips pivot over the kerb as she hails a taxi, her bare left arm raised high, still as a falconer's, waiting for the cab to come to her.

'Where you go?' The driver asks, turning to look at them as they climb inside, Phelan's thighs following Kira's as they shuffle across the back seat.

'Do you know Gordons Bay?' she asks.

'Gordons Bay,' he repeats. 'I know. What street?' His hand hovers over the GPS mounted on the dashboard.

'Just get us to Gordons Bay. I'll show you from there.'

The driver shrugs.

Kira pulls away from Phelan and leans out the open backseat window, resting her head on her arm like a wistful girl might. The soothing vibrations of the car, the night and all its movement big and loud beyond her, her black hair caught in its swirling, wisps of it near her temples playing in the currents. Strands of hair inviting him, Phelan thinks, to tuck them back behind her ears. But would his fingers even remember how?

Phelan detects a shift in the angle of the driver's head, and looks at him as he glances surreptitiously at Kira in the rear-view mirror. Phelan thinks he recognises something in him.

'Are you from Afghanistan?'

The driver's head jerks round, and Phelan knows he's guessed right, that he's Hazara. He repeats the question, this time in crude Dari.

'Dari Gup Mayzani!' the driver exclaims. 'You speak Dari!'

'Cumzara,' Phelan says, holding his thumb and finger together to show just how little, before asking the driver how long he's been here.

'Zeeyad wakht shouda ke da Australia astee? Australia – zeeyaad saal?'

'Aft saal,' the driver replies, seven years.

'Khush amadee,' Phelan says with a little nod of his head, a welcome.

'Kooja Dari yaad gereftee?'

But Phelan misses it.

'Mebakhshen. I'm sorry I don't speak Dari well. Ma dorost dari yaad nadaaram.'

Kira closes the window to listen. As she shifts, her left knee presses Phelan's right leg.

'You a soldier?' the driver asks.

Phelan sighs. 'Yes,' he says. Because truth is still important. Each press of skin, each of responsibility's demands.

'Thank you sir,' the driver says. 'Thank you.'

'Here,' Kira says, pointing out the window. 'This will do.'

The taxi stops and Kira steps into the throw of a streetlight, her tattooed sleeve glowing like a butterfly's wing.

'Come,' she says as he steps from the taxi, her hand outstretched. The night sky is now clear above them, the air a salty whisper. Come.

She is like a street urchin, leading him along narrow footpaths between red-brick houses, down rough porphyry steps, thick banksias on either side, the sound of the sea growing ever stronger. They find a staircase, the steps themselves hewn from the rock, the handrails rusting beneath the palms of their hands, big flakes of it.

The sky opens ahead, and they break out onto the ledge of a cliff. Before them is night sky and ocean, and a small horseshoe bay facing east, a bare sandstone escarpment cascading to a sandy cove below. The houses ringing the clifftop appear as just another layer of landscape, laid down in some more recent geological era, their lights glinting like quartzite.

Kira pulls off her boots, rolls the cuffs of her jeans, and, as if it is the convention in this place, hangs her legs over the cliff's edge. The moon is at her shoulder. She leans back and closes her eyes, propped on her arms. Her nostrils flare, like an animal's, her face to the stars, her skin drinking the ancient light.

'This is where I grew up,' she says after a while, turning to him.

Her eyes darken in the moonlight. Azure, he thinks, surprising himself. What might be a new universe is opening before him. If he were not with her, being led into the hidden pores of the landscape, he'd have cut the bay up already. His hours on patrol in the Chora Valley are burned into him, the practice of battle still raw, demanding he interpret landscapes as he was once trained to, the world alive with danger. Without her beside him he'd have tried to measure the bay, thought about sniper holes, where to find cover in the bushes and walls and larger rocks. He'd have marked the houses where the smoke rises into the night. He'd have mapped out what his next move would be and the one after that, and the options that would begin unfolding beyond even that. He'd have known how exposed he was. But here, tonight, she is overwhelming.

'Up there ...' Kira motions vaguely behind them, '... is my parents' house.'

He looks around, peering at the buildings clutching the rock. His heart quickens with a sudden desire to better know this place.

'Still?'

'My mother's, anyway,' and she laughs as if it is nothing. Mere words. A mistake.

She leads him further along the ledge until it narrows and they clamber, boulder by boulder, down to the beach. The houses disappear as they descend. Moonlight glances off the pulsing sea and the shell-flecked sand and her cheeks and the sides of tin fishing dinghies embroidering the beach above the high-waterline.

He goes to speak but he is made of earth.

'Ssh,' whispers Kira, whispers the sea. *Ssh.*

She lifts her arms and he looks up, thinking it's the stars her fingertips want to brush, but instead Kira is peeling off her singlet and dropping it to the sand, reaching back between her shoulders for a clasp.

Phelan turns his head away, as he does for his wife. But Kira's pull is greater than mere habit, sweeps away self-discipline. He wilts before her nakedness, and looks back at her, amazed.

This sea creature beside him, stepping towards the water. Some form of perfection he's never before encountered, moving like no woman he's ever known. Her dark hair, her long limbs, her hips and buttocks, the ancient markings on her skin. She glows, lit not by moonlight, but by something inside her answering the sea. The tattoos on her naked body silhouetted against her are glowing, their designs projected beyond her by that interior light, as if taking shape in the air itself. As if the warrior woman on her arm might come to rest in the palm of his hand should he open it.

A tiny wave breaks on the sand and sweeps towards Kira, lapping at her feet before withdrawing, leaving anklets of foam. She steps into the sea, and as she does he fears she might disappear forever.

'Wait!' he calls, frantically unbuttoning his shirt and throwing it to the damp sand, then starting on his singlet.

'No,' she commands, turning, raising her palm.

He freezes, the power of her. Each pebble, each grain of sand, every tiny piece of shell-grit is detonating around him.

When she continues, her voice is quieter. 'Soldier,' she says gently, patiently, 'remember your arm. You can't.' Kira points to his left shoulder and the plastic she has taped into place. Suddenly she is no longer siren but woman, no less beautiful, but more real, a professional who has not forgotten herself. 'You can't get your tattoo wet,' she continues, and then, when he opens his mouth to protest, cuts him off. 'You'd regret it if you did.'

Ah, Beckett. Though inked into him barely an hour before, Phelan has already forgotten him. It is Kira who hasn't, this woman who never knew him.

'Wait for me,' she says, laying a hand on him.

He nods in resignation, submitting to her authority. Armies cannot function without it.

Kira wades into the sea. Her thighs and then her hips and her waist. She brushes the water's surface with the palms of her hands as she wades forward. A moment of shimmering moonlight before she leaves. Then she dives, up and out and forward, the perfect arc of her body.

Phelan climbs back into his shirt, counting the buttons as he does them up, a little task to distract himself. He gathers her clothes and her shoes and folds them, never losing sight of her. He lays her things carefully on the sand above the high tide line, and watches her slow strokes, the rhythmic bobbing of her head as her breaststroke takes her from the shore.

Phelan walks along the curve of beach towards its southern tip, as close as he can get to her body out there in the glittering bay. Never has his wife swum naked before him. But is this for him anyway? This woman, this ocean, this night, these forces he doesn't understand. He squats at the end of the beach. These layers of darkness, and beyond them, imagination.

Gradually he becomes aware of voices, neither his nor Kira's, and swivels on his heels in the sand, staying low. The sound gathers, kids calling to each other, jostling, their shoes dancing on the bitumen as they descend the road. They pass under the last streetlight before the foreshore and Phelan sees three fearless teenage boys whooping and wrestling between swigs of beer, their bottles raised to the stars like bugles. When they reach the rocks ringing the bay they tip their heads, almost in unison, drain their stubbies and toss them against the boulders, shattering the night. They leap, rock to rock, as if they can fly.

Phelan turns on his haunches, back towards the water, but the surface of the bay is still and Kira is gone.

The boys climb onto the tinnies, balancing on the tips of their bows, arms spread like nautical figureheads, oblivious to Phelan's presence. They won't see him, he knows that, because they're blind to stillness. Instead, their laughter is filled with boisterous astonishment – that they are bigger than they could ever conceive, that there is nothing for them to find here on the beach that they cannot create themselves. Their talk of women, when it starts – their boasts about what they'd do and what they wouldn't – has no malice in it. Phelan can't help but smile.

He looks out at the bay again. He imagines Kira treading water and looking back at the commotion on the beach. Can she see him, too, squatting, all of it under control?

One of them spies Kira's clothes on the sand and hurries to investigate.

'Hey, check this out!' he calls.

'What?'

'Over here!'

'What?'

The kid lifts Kira's bra. 'What the—'

But Phelan has moved quickly and is almost upon them.

'Thanks lads.'

The three boys turn. Phelan's shoulders and head and bull neck, his outstretched hand.

'I'll take those.'

It's as if the boys have unwittingly conjured him out of their imaginings, and having created him, must heed him. The one with the bra hands it to Phelan.

'The rest.'

The boy bends and collects the remainder of Kira's gear, gives it to him.

'Thank you.'

Phelan says it slowly, deliberately, allowing no other option, and now it is sealed.

'Do you boys need help with anything else?'

The one closest mumbles something and shakes his head.

As they retreat, their courage returns. By the time they step off the beach and begin making their way up the road zigzagging its way to the clifftop, they slow and yell face-saving taunts back at him. But Phelan too has disappeared and the boys will have to imagine him anew.

HOME, INTO THE STARS

SHE SWIMS OUT so far that when she finally looks back to land she can see the buildings rimming the cliff. Treading water, she locates her mother's house. It is unlit, which means it is empty, because even after her mother goes to bed she leaves a light on, a signal – to whom Kira could never fathom – that the lady of the house was in residence. Kira guesses she's either away on one of her overseas vacations – usually Nice, sometimes Biarritz, never alone – or else she's temporarily moved into one of her boyfriends' apartments.

Kira puts her head down and swims back towards the beach. She closes her eyes as she strokes, opening them only to lift her head and check her bearings. The water is deep and dark and she swims hard. When she reaches the shore she is out of breath. She takes Phelan's hand when he offers it, allowing him to draw her body to his, feeling his shirt against her breast.

She laughs and pulls away. Phelan offers his shirt as a towel. Though she knows his torso already, she watches his singleted chest with different eyes as he unbuttons and peels off his shirt.

'Come on up to the house,' she says, nodding towards the clifftop.

THE HOUSE IS Federation red-brick, two gables and a tiled roof. An empty carport with carved timber bracing and matching tiles stands to the right of the block. There is a chest-high mock orange hedge on the footpath boundary, and an ornate wrought-iron gate that swings smoothly when she opens it.

'Won't we disturb your mother?' The 'we' with which he dooms fidelity.

'No,' she says. 'The house is all ours.'

Normally he'd want to understand how she knows but there's another impulse operating on him now. He follows her through the gate and closes it quietly behind them. A carriage lamp on the front porch switches automatically on. Phelan's heart quickens, but Kira ignores the light and leads him down a side path before kneeling beside a large terracotta pot and its tiny Port Jackson fig. The base of the pot crunches against the brick pavers as Kira tilts it in the dark and feels beneath it for a key.

'Hey, soldier,' Kira calls to him from her mother's bedroom, 'help me with this.'

Together they drag the mattress out onto the balcony, into the intoxicating stars. Of all the camps and all the bivouacs, of all the

56

swags rolled out in the trays of utes, and beside ASLAVs, and on the flat roofs of mudbrick hovels beneath star-bled skies, of them all this is the strangest. But he trusts this balcony, these stars, this night, this woman. He is beyond doubt, in the hands of fate. And, he suddenly thinks as he watches her move about the balcony, a passing benediction, that it is Beckett who has led him here, Beckett's spirit, and his own honouring of it.

But Beckett wants things of him too, makes demands he cannot refuse.

'Charlie, my cock, my nuts. Are they still there?'

Phelan's not sure he's heard right, though the words were clear and strong. All the thunder, all the light. All hell aswirl.

'It's all right, son,' Phelan yells into the boy's ear, 'you'll be okay.'

'I want you to check, Charlie.'

The sapper rolls his hips so Phelan can get at him. He still has his dark ballistic glasses on. The rounds are flying overhead, but Beckett reaches up with his right hand and pulls them off. Phelan lifts his too.

'Tell me, Charlie. Tell me,' Beckett says again with complete seriousness.

Phelan looks into his eyes. The sound of the firefight around them and the blood-mud ditch is somehow fading away, replaced by this urgency.

'Of course you're all there, son. You're right as rain.'

'Have a look Charlie. I need you to look.'

Phelan takes off his gloves and lays them aside. His heart is pounding. He unbuckles Beckett at his waist, and reaches into his trousers. He can feel something of Beckett through his jocks. It's probably enough. Probably. But Phelan owes him this, wants to know himself now, so he slides his hand beneath Beckett's jocks, and finds his penis there, his balls. He's moist, but it's not blood, not yet, and as

Phelan holds him in his hand he feels the warmth begin to leave the boy, and he shivers.

'You're all there, son,' Phelan says, their helmets touching, fire above, what might be a sacred moment. 'There's nothing to worry about, got it? Nothing to worry about. You just hang on, son. The medivac will be here any minute. Any minute.'

'Thanks Charlie,' Beckett says. Or Phelan thinks he says, thinks he remembers.

But now what? Should Phelan keep him awake or help him sleep?

PHELAN LOOKS AT Kira's tattooed body but doesn't know how to touch it. He fears it is beyond him. That it is too knowing. That it seeks more experienced men than he, truer men too. Whoever tattooed her, whatever intimacies, whatever the hands that have worked her flesh, whatever bodies have inspired her, whatever life she's taken into hers, he's inadequate. There is nothing her body does not want to know, nothing it does not yearn to record.

But who is he?

'You ...' he says, his voice trembling. 'I ...' But he falters. It is too much for him.

She just laughs, gently, as she might laugh at a silly child, and reaches for him, her teeth at his neck. This moment, this yes and this no, each folding into the other. Whatever his hesitation, it doesn't matter. She takes him.

MEMENTOS

SOMETHING IN HIS dreaming, some sudden movement, wakes her. Kira examines him in the glinting starlight and the late moon. Lying on his side, his right arm curves over his head as if protecting himself, even in sleep. His fist clenches involuntarily and he pulls his head down, balling, groaning. She reaches for him, takes his hand and gently strokes it, caressing the night and the scars and the gashes, wondering to herself, where has this hand been? Muses, as she returns to sleep, about what it might do to her own dreaming.

WHEN HE WAKES it is to a throw of morning light and a slip of breeze. He rolls to gaze at her. The tattoos on her arm are like foliage, a blanket of leaves laid tenderly over her shoulders as she lies on her side, the dawn rising easily around her.

He returns to her with a coffee he's made from the espresso machine he found in the kitchen, another new experience. He places it carefully on the tiles beside her head and watches her face respond to the coffee's aroma: the widening of her nostrils, her fluttering eyelids. The sky is not yet blue above her when she wakes.

'What happened?' she asks, pointing to a long scar on his left forearm. 'Here? And here?'

But he holds back. A gentleman never tells, or some such. He traces the warrioress on her arm, the hem of her blue dress, her hip, the sword's long curved blade.

'That azure,' he says. 'It's a fine colour.'

'Is it your favourite now?'

He continues to caress her skin. 'I don't have a favourite, but ... blue ... it's ... it's the most,' he struggles for words 'inspiring colour.'

'Inspiring?'

'It's the colour of the sky and the colour of the sea. You reach for the heights and explore your own depths. You don't accept what you think are your limits. You push yourself. Push the boundaries of what's possible. *That's* inspiring.'

'Do you give that little speech to all your men?' she replies, looking at her work, *Samuel Robert Beckett*, beneath its plastic wrap.

'Made me sound like a dickhead, did it?'

'Well,' she persists. '*Do* you give that speech to your men?'

'We all need people to inspire us.'

'Do we? Really?'

'In my experience, yes. Yes, we do.'

Kira looks away. He senses he's losing her. But he's not ready to give her up, to leave her. Not yet ready to return.

'Wait,' he says, rising. He goes to his shirt, neatly folded over the back of a recliner in the living room, and unbuttons a breast pocket. He returns with something held clumsily in his big hands and feels suddenly awkward. 'It's for you,' he whispers, his voice strangely hoarse.

The look on her face hovers between delight and disquiet.

Phelan lifts his top hand. The gift is covered in tissue paper. Kira reaches for it, unwrapping the trinket, fold by fold. A delicate blue crane, long-legged, its wings spread like a great feathered cape. He'd bought it for Penny in Kabul, but fate knows better.

The thought takes hold, fervently, as if a revelation, that this hand-carved bird had, in fact, always been destined for someone else. That when he'd read the line from *The Travels of Marco Polo* he was being led to this woman, *there are mountains there in which are found veins of the stone yielding the finest azure the world has ever known.* That when the Kabul merchant enticed Phelan into his shop, his figurines laid out on a table covered by a large velvet cloth – rows of elephants and lions and birds – and selected this crane from among the carvings, it was always destined for this blue woman.

'It is lapis lazuli.' He pronounces the words slowly, proud of this new language, sensing only now the beauty in the words. 'It's their national stone. Like our opal.'

• • •

BUT MERE WORDS have lost their weight and she has tired of using them. Already she is alighting, awaiting the first of the day's breezes. She is strong, and she is ready to fly.

'A memento,' he says, holding it out to her.

The places those hands have been, the things they've done, what they will resume doing now this is over. She looks into his face. He is sad, she thinks. And old and foolish. And while she was not mistaken, the sun is now burning the night away, and she fears its scars.

'Thank you,' she says, her mark on his shoulder.

PART TWO

HOMECOMING, DELAYED
Brisbane, November 2010

PENNY SITS ON the front verandah, looking out over the lawn that slopes down to the lilly pilly hedge bordering the street. Beyond the hedge, the red-tinned suburban roofs of Wilston cascade down the hillside. Further away, the city spreads eastwards to the bay and the sand islands on the horizon. Two sulphur-crested cockatoos screech at the rising sun, and Penny instinctively scans the sky until she finds them. Already the day is beginning to blur, and soon the islands will disappear in the early summer heat. Shortly after dawn on a clear day, with the aid of James's telescope, you can see the car ferries on the water between Dunwich village and the mainland terminal. Though it's not the traffic on the bay she's tracking this morning, but the planes in the sky as they slowly loop and descend to the runways in the north-east. One of them, soon, will be arriving with her husband. And soon enough she'll have to leave for the airport to meet it.

They've been texting each other for days, mundane messages filled with the dull detail of travel logistics, worth nothing to anyone if they were intercepted. That he'd touched down in Darwin and loves her. That they're leaving for Richmond in five – the army base in Sydney with its long runway. That Sapper Beckett's parents will be there when the plane lands to greet their son's body and he still doesn't know what he'll say to them. Later, that the ceremony was like nothing he'd ever experienced. That he had an afternoon of duties and a brief medical check ahead of him, but that he'd see her in the evening, will let her know which civilian flight he's on. Then the final text late – that he'd been unavoidably delayed overnight and would be home in the morning. How she'd sighed, conditioned as she was over the years to changes like that – *he's* reliable, it's the army that can't be trusted.

But it's a blessing he was delayed, she tells herself now. The first time she's ever felt like this. At the end of every other posting or return from leave her longing had been almost unbearable. Not that she's one to pine – not since their early years anyway. Nor has she learned to merely fill in time as some wives do, or resent each day's absence. If they'd had kids it might have been different, but they couldn't and she's dealt with that, as much as one ever can, the new commitment they made to each other. She got on with things, as the saying goes, has a career of her own that has offered consolations and, more recently, satisfactions. Still, there's nothing like a return date. No matter how full her life, a posting end-date – circled on the kitchen wall calendar – issues a solemn promise, daily: *I will return.*

Yet how different this return is, freighted by burden. For both of them. And then his arrival pushed back. Sure, it might have only put off the inevitable by a day, but hard as it's going to be to tell him, it would have been harder if he'd arrived home last night as he'd originally planned. He would have been exhausted after the long journey, after all the officiating, all the emotion of it. Even so, she couldn't possibly have hidden it from him. It wouldn't have been fair. She won't hide it from him now. She can't, even if she wished to.

This morning's text from Sydney was unremarkable. He'd been about to board, giving her the flight number and its scheduled arrival time. She'd replied immediately that she'd meet him at the airport – as she always did.

But now she's overcome by anxiety. She imagines him emerging from the gate searching for her, expecting she'll be in the middle layer of waiting people, as she usually is. She imagines his face seeking her in the crowd, the need in him palpable, overwhelming his usual equanimity. She fears that. But she also fears he'll detect something is different. Without realising that *everything* is different.

And then what will she say?

She's practised it a hundred times but still doesn't trust herself to tell him without tears. At least not in the airport, not in public. Suddenly she's sure of that much.

PHELAN STANDS AT the gate, his overnight bag beside him, waiting for his phone to come on, and what he expects will be a message from Penny that says – seeing she's not here – she'll be outside waiting. She is always on time, that fine quality of hers. You can build a relationship on that, he's often thought, because dependability is about respect, and what is respect but a face of love?

A message comes through. *Darling, welcome home … I'm sorry but can you get a taxi? P x*

A cold shudder. Does she know? How can she? Is she guessing? Does she sense something? Something he hasn't done? An ill-chosen word? Fuck, he thinks, fuck, fuck, fuck. He rereads his text from last night, but can't see anything in it, gathers himself, strides through the terminal and steps out into the humidity. He finds the taxi queue – he's on leave, beyond the privilege of a driver, not wanting one today anyway. His mind is churning with torrents of competing thoughts and plans, roiling. The buzzing in his ears seems to grow louder. He'll grab a taxi and hang on. She knows; she can't know. It is like an alternating current. Though if she knew, surely it wouldn't be *Darling.*

But what if she *has* guessed? he thinks suddenly. So damn what? What was it anyway? Though last night's thread hasn't yet snapped, the nearer to home he gets the more it stretches.

Even if she knows, she'll understand, he says to himself. In time she'll understand, in time she'll forgive. The war and its toll. She'll understand: a man under your command dies in your arms and everything is changed, everything, destiny setting you a new course.

The taxi passes the factory outlet clothing stores and takes the overpass. He sees the Airtrain curving its way on its raised track out to the airport. Another thought: why does he need to explain himself anyway? As if he's done something that needs justification. Hell, after the months of stiff emails he's received from her, the handful of awkward conversations, her reluctance to skype. After making half a dozen excuses to avoid a video-call – her responsibilities as nurse unit manager at the hospital, the unrostered extra shifts to fill in for junior staff suddenly taking sick, even describing her monthly book club as a 'commitment' – he assumed she simply didn't want to *see* him, preferred the controlled communication of email and those increasingly perfunctory phone calls.

She'd denied anything was wrong when he asked, said she wasn't upset with him, but he knows a cooling when he feels it, a withdrawal. So she can hardly be surprised, he says to himself. And now she is taking it a step further, now she can't even be bothered meeting him at the airport!

Suddenly he's angry, and it shits him he's in a taxi, returning alone from six months in Afghanistan with a soldier's death on his shoulders, that he's a brigadier without a driver to meet him, that his wife hasn't bothered to show, and that the Punjabi cabbie is taking the cross-city tunnel without asking him his preferred route and that it's him who'll be paying the $4.50 toll.

AGITATED, PENNY PACES from room to room. Where will she tell him? The kitchen? Their bedroom? The garden? She is passing through the living room and its great bookcase, when she stops abruptly.

Occupying an entire wall, metres long, is her floor-to-ceiling library, all the years of her reading life. Book after book organised chronologically by when she finished it, her library charting her reading history. Her childhood fictions at the top left, the start, leading to the handful of books she read between leaving school and meeting James, followed soon enough by the novels she completed on his first tour away, so soon after their marriage. Too soon. Those first novels followed in time by others. Thick bands of books gathered during each of his postings. Her library reminds her of a tree's growth rings – the bursts of intensive reading while James is away, her reading seasons more frugal when he is at home. All the events of her life are held in place up there on the shelves by what she was reading at the time – changes of house or city, milestone birthdays, extended visits, the deaths of friends and relatives, of princesses and movie stars. The entire decade of yearning for children – the hope, the treatment, the despair, the anguish, the arguments, the love, ultimately the love, all mapped out in shelf after shelf. The order of it gives her comfort. Finishing a book and then placing it – whether memoir or novel or non-fiction – in its proper place at the open end of the shelf. Irrespective of whether she enjoyed or was repulsed by it, whether she's ever likely to recommend it or read it again,

She halts before her recent reading, the thirty or so books she's consumed since James left for Afghanistan, almost no fiction among them, almost all the same topic, devoured with an urgency she's never known. Her heart races, a fresh anxiety at what these books will give away, too soon. Penny gathers them in her arms and carries them, half a dozen trips, to the laundry where she boxes and hides them away. Just for today, she thinks, just until I tell him.

In the kitchen, when she's done, she's panting from the effort. The face of the wall clock is suddenly enormous, its hands moving inexorably.

• • •

SHE IS WAITING for him on the front porch when the taxi pulls up. What seeing her triggers, what it sweeps away. She is standing there quietly, as if she's been waiting for days, and seeing her like that, his agitation subsides. She's wearing a dress as she always does, this one light blue and patterned with sunflowers, though not sleeveless, as she prefers. Her arms, usually gym-toned, are covered.

Phelan is overcome by the accumulated joy of all their previous reunions, the uncorralled excitement of those first moments of pure welcome. He wants to embrace her now. He calls out from the street, waves, and if she remains on the porch a moment longer than necessary, hugging herself tight before stepping carefully down onto the path, it signals nothing to him.

Penny's face is shaded by a wide-brimmed garden hat as she comes down the path. She removes her sunglasses when they are nearly upon each other, but he sees nothing unusual – the sun lighting her short brown hair, her high forehead, her face free of make-up, her strong jawline.

'Welcome home, Darling,' she says. 'Welcome home.'

Phelan hugs her, but she only gives him half her body. It's as if she's already twisting away in the moment of their first touch, extracting herself from his grasp, leaving him the instant he arrives.

Penny leads him up the front path, nervous words spilling from her now, evasive words about gardens and plants and seasons and rain. About how she's glad he's home. About how she's missed him.

But then, at the doorstep, just as he's about to ask if there's something he ought to know, she's crying, sobbing, telling him again and again how much she's missed him. It's uncharacteristic of her, not the strength of the emotion, but the tears. Yet when he reaches to embrace her she pulls away again, turns, and enters the house without him.

Phelan follows her into the kitchen, disconcerted, determined to find out what's wrong. But the aroma of freshly ground coffee beans stops him. The room suddenly becomes foreign, his head suddenly

70

dizzy. He is back in this morning's house at Gordons Bay, overlooking the tattooist's body and the sea, and once again he is kneeling beside Kira, a mug beside her face, stirring her awake.

'Where did you end up staying last night?' Penny says, wiping the tears from her cheeks, sniffling, smiling.

REVELATION

PHELAN FEELS A cold blade in his shoulders and freezes. He's vaguely aware of his wife continuing to move around the kitchen, making for the hot water jug, her back to him. He swallows. The rush of time, throatfuls of it, would choke him if he tried to speak.

Eventually she turns and repeats the question sweetly, as if perhaps he hadn't heard her. 'So, where did you stay last night?' She's looking at him innocently, her open face, the water jug suspended beneath the tap, waiting for him to respond before turning on the tap.

'With a mate,' he says in a voice he barely recognises, all authority drained out of it.

'Who?' she asks, still nonchalantly, filling the jug one-handed, not looking up, no need to. He has a network of soldier mates and she's entertained most of them over the years.

'No one you'd know,' he says, so quickly the words run together. His temples begin to throb, something trying to burst free.

She turns the tap off and looks up at him, meeting his eyes for the first time, a kitchen bench between them. She is confused. There's not a friend of his she can't fit into place. She waits for him, expectantly.

'Fuck me!' he suddenly spits. 'Christ!' His face is violent red. 'What sort of interrogation is this? Get home from a fucking war – take my own fucking taxi home – and here I am getting drilled. For Christ's sake,' Phelan snorts. He heaves his bag up from the floor, turns his back and strides angrily towards the bedroom.

'Sorry,' she calls out, following him into the bedroom just as he throws his bag on the bed. He's got his back to her and is aggressively stripping off his shirt and tossing it at the wicker clothes basket that has stood in the corner of the bedroom the life of their marriage. When she catches it.

'James,' she says softly when she sees his taped shoulder, thinking it's a wound dressing of some sort. 'Oh, James.' She moves around to get a better view, but he turns away, sheltering it still. 'Why didn't you tell me? What happened? You said you'd only had a slight concussion, that was all. You said you hadn't been hit. Show me. James, show me ...'

She goes to him confidently – all the certainty of wounds and their tending, all the old habits – and takes his wrist to still him while she bends her head near. He looks down at his shoulder too, as if remembering it afresh.

Penny pulls away, aghast.

'A tattoo,' she says her eyes wide in shock. 'You've got a tattoo!'

IT'S NOT AS if she hasn't been around them, she's an army wife for God's sake, and over the years she's admired as many as have horrified her. But not James. She can hear him at a barbecue twenty years ago, one of his mates pressing him, calmly knowing he was setting himself apart but not wanting to offend, seeking a tactful route: 'They're not for me.' And then, when that answer wasn't enough, when they kept pushing, he looked them in the eye, forcing them to wait on him, and told them he believed the body was sacred and who was he to mark it like that. He wasn't entirely serious, but knew that talk of sacredness frightened people off. No, it wasn't really about reverence for the body. It was about self-possession, and the projection of it. That he'd be beholden to no man.

'It's nothing, Pen,' he says. 'Don't let it ruin your—'

'Day ruined,' she fires at him. Then waits, staring. 'Well,' her challenge is fierce, 'what is it?'

But before he can answer she reaches across and finds the end of one of the strips of tape with her nails. Her husband submits. She rips the tape off, then pulls the plastic wrap away in one swift downwards unveiling.

For a moment she's not sure what she's looking at, and sees only a blur of black lines, raised on inflamed red ridges of skin. There's an anger in them, like fiercely wept tears. She tilts her head and reads the inked lettering – the name, and the date, and her husband's scarred flesh.

James hadn't mentioned Beckett's name in his first short email.

Dear Pen, There's been an incident. I'm fine but we lost a soldier. I'll call soon. Love, James.

She'd replied immediately, her fingers shaking, trying to get her first feelings down before they started to fragment.

Oh, no! That's terrible terrible terrible. I'm thinking of you always, James. Stay safe. Love you. Px

Then the second email, twelve hours later, odd, as if he'd entirely forgotten he'd sent one earlier.

Dear Pen, If you haven't yet heard, you will soon enough. We lost another soldier yesterday. Sapper Samuel Beckett. Everyone's gutted. He was such a good kid, and such a good soldier, and now he's gone. I can't help feeling responsible. Please say a prayer for him, and for his family. Love, James.

It was stiff, but she thought little of it: the army has its protocols about how much can be said. She knew that better than most army wives. And knew that James was often preoccupied with his responsibilities, these little gaps that would temporarily open between them. Though some of the holes that have grown between them on this posting, she knows, are because of her. But it *was* a surprise, asking her to say a prayer for the sapper. Not the notion of praying, but that her husband would *ask* her to. He who asked no one for anything, ever, let alone a god he'd never believed in.

Call me as soon as you can Darling.

The phone started ringing even before her computer had shut down, his voice quivering as he said her name.

'Are you okay? What happened, James?'

He told her, his voice flattening out as if he was reading from a report – giving her the same facts he'd given Canberra earlier that day, even referring to himself in the third person, Brigadier Phelan, before correcting himself, his voice only losing its way after he'd finished, after he'd paused and said, eventually, 'I'm fine.'

'What do you mean?' Penny exclaimed. 'You were *there*? With the patrol? You were actually there?'

'On the patrol, yes. The patrol was engaged. We came under fire. Sapper Beckett was hit and I … I … I was with him when he died, Pen. And …' He seemed to choke. There was the silence of a long marriage between them. '… And I couldn't do anything about it.'

She thought he might even weep. Penny had visited the hospital chapel that afternoon and lit a thin taper candle and pressed it into the bowl of sand beside the darkened altar, knelt and said her rosaries. The first for Sapper Samuel Beckett, the second for her husband, the third for herself.

'You must be grateful it wasn't James,' one of her colleagues said, stopping her in the hospital car park and squeezing her arm. Penny thanked her for her concern, responding to her nurse-mate's tone rather than the clumsy words. Even so, Penny found herself overwhelmed by irrational thoughts. Surely, she wished in desperate reply to her fears, James will be safe for the moment. Surely, while Sapper Samuel Beckett's death and life are in everyone's thoughts, nothing else will happen. Surely the universe will do the right thing.

She emailed again.

> *Don't think you're responsible, now, Darling. It's only natural – that's how leaders always feel. But you're not responsible. I saw you on the news this evening. Are you sure you're ok? Love, Penny.*

James's response: *He was just so young.*

IT WASN'T FROM her husband she came to know about Beckett, but from the profile pieces in the media, and from the other wives. That he was twenty, and the youngest soldier in the platoon. That he walked with a strut without being arrogant. That he loved a laugh. That he had a harelip no one regarded as an imperfection, not in a kid like this. That he was a natural athlete from the north coast of New South Wales who turned his back on a promising cricketing career to join the army on a whim. The story goes he'd nicked the first ball he faced at a national selection carnival, the very first ball of the innings, and before he'd even taken his pads off he was laughing, unable to take any of it too seriously. He applied the following Monday, left behind a prestigious cricketing scholarship, his hometown and a sprawling family.

Penny also read somewhere he was engaged. She'd heard that benign little phrase – 'childhood sweetheart' – often enough to know it was seldom true. But when she rang around she discovered there *was* a girl, Laura, and a wedding date. When Penny Facebooked her to offer support the girl was gracious, or scared, and told her how she and Beckett were planning to have kids and Penny wept because Laura was only nineteen – the same age she'd been when she and James were married.

SHE LOOKS AT his shoulder and the tattoo in memoriam of a young man she hadn't known existed until he was dead. She's staring, barely thinking, still adrift.

If someone had asked her, she would have said she was good with change, that she's learned to cope without being swallowed by circumstance, change the only constant and all that. These last months proof. The thousand adaptations she's made while he was away, all the work she's been forced to do on herself – that phrase the counsellor at the hospital employed every session.

But now … now the new wife she was going to unveil to him, the little ceremony she had in mind, has been derailed by Samuel Beckett.

'So, that's to remember him?'

She looks into her husband's eyes. His anger has given way, but she can't tell what's replaced it.

'Is that a question?' she hears him ask.

Is that the sound of contempt? she wonders.

'I've made a booking,' she replies, backing away. 'The usual place on the river. Do you want to go?'

James sighs as he, too, retreats from whatever edge they were at.

'You look tired,' he says.

She's not ready to respond to that.

'Do we still want to go or not?'

'Of course,' her husband says, something like tenderness ebbing back. He touches her cheek with his hand.

People trying to enjoy themselves

WHEN HE'S CHANGED she presses down the wings of his collar, and as she leans in he recognises her perfume. On any other return he'd whistle, comic-book style, both of them knowing. He'd reach for her, his right hand on the back of her neck, pulling her to him, finding her cheek then her lips, waiting for her to give. But today he is unbending, and she unwilling.

'Issey Miyake,' he says.

'Thank you,' she returns.

He blinks. She straightens his shirt.

When it's time to leave Phelan swallows two tablets to hold off the headache, slips downstairs to the garage and climbs into his orange BMW. He adjusts the driver's seat to his own height and sits quietly with his hands on the steering wheel, refamiliarising himself with the smell of the upholstery and the dashboard and the view from the side mirrors. He reads the mechanic's sticker in the top corner of the windscreen and sees that Penny has had it serviced. She's a good woman. He hears her shoes on the floorboards above as she moves from room to room looking for him.

'In the car,' he yells out when she calls his name.

'I was wondering where you'd gone,' she says, settling into the passenger seat.

He caresses the wheel's leather grip. 'You don't know how good this feels.'

She smiles.

Phelan turns the key in the ignition. The engine and the radio come to life simultaneously. Purr and chatter. Hear those revs, he thinks, beauty's voice. He pulls out of the garage just as the hourly news bulletin begins on the local ABC station Penny must have been listening to when she was last in the car. He glances at the digital clock on the dash and counts the seconds until it changes from 11:59 to noon. Eleven seconds. It's easily fixed, he thinks, but losing eleven seconds in six months …

'They covered you bringing Sapper Beckett home yesterday,' Penny says. 'It was on all the news.'

He turns off the radio. 'What did they say?'

She thinks for a moment before responding. 'That the nation was mourning. That despite their loss, his parents were thankful for the army's support. That every soldier matters and what better proof could there be than you escorting him home.' She pauses. 'Mateship and egalitarianism … that was a theme. The Sapper and the Brigadier. That our army is different from others. That we're different. That sort of thing.'

He's looking fixedly ahead as she speaks.

'They'll turn you into a hero if you're not careful,' she finishes, smiling, prodding him for a response. And when he remains silent, she reaches across and slaps him lightly on the thigh. 'More of a hero than you already are, James.'

When he still doesn't react she pokes him in the ribs and tries tickling something out of him, but he brushes her hand away with his elbow.

JAMES STOPS THE car at an intersection and taps the steering wheel while waiting for the lights to change. An irritable little rhythm, Penny thinks, not a tune she knows. Ah, well. She looks out the window as they wend through the Valley and the slumbering neon of its nightclubs and strip joints. She's never liked this double-faced part of town: the frenzy of its nights so different from its sullen days. On the footpath outside a newsagent's she spies the day's front page displayed in its metal frame, *Tragic Homecoming*. Under the headline there's a photo of Beckett's casket being carried from the plane onto the tarmac, honour guard and dignitaries, James leading the procession. She looks back at him behind the wheel, tense but inscrutable.

There's always a period of readjustment. As a general rule it's one for one, a girlfriend told her when she and James were freshly married and he was away on an exchange with the Americans.

'If they're away for a month, it'll take a month back home before the house returns to normal.'

'That can't be right,' Penny had replied, 'because that would mean for a six-month deployment ...'

'Exactly.'

'No!'

'Wait and see, young Penelope, wait and see.'

'But how does a marriage manage that?'

'Look around. Count how many don't.'

Too much of it was true. The weeks of finding their way again after each return, of wrestling a new equilibrium into place. Yet their marriage itself was unthreatened by challenges like these. You make a vow. You do it before God and Society. Though she has learned to ration herself. Anticipation for his return, yes, but only so much. Joy, but not unbounded. She sees frustrations and disappointments as irritants, nothing terminal. And anyway, her husband doesn't want to fight another battle when he returns. They love each other, need each other, rely on each other. That's what she will tell him.

They park on the circular driveway at New Farm Park. Penny is relieved to open the car door and let the breathing world in. As James gets out and walks around to her door, he reads a lost dog notice taped neatly to a lamppost.

'Spoodle!' he spits. 'Spoodle! What a stupid name for a dog.'

High clouds follow them as they cross the grass to the café. Penny takes his hand. He goes to shake her off, but she holds on. She points out the rosebushes as she leads him between the raised beds, naming the different species, looking for words to soothe, any words. They could be the names of racehorses or colours on a paint chart, her husband's face blank to the relationships between the name and the flower she's pointing to. At the end of one row is a bush with a single spent rose, a dead head missed by the gardener that morning. She watches as James snaps it off its stalk, a fall of shriveled brown petals, and lifts it to his nose.

WHEN HE AND Penny arrive it is she who steps forward and gives the young waitress at the door the name of their booking, adding that it's a special occasion.

'What are you celebrating?' the excitable waitress asks good-naturedly.

'My husband's home from the war,' she replies, gazing up at Phelan and smiling.

'What war is that?'

Penny's body stiffens and she turns slowly back to the waitress, but Phelan places his hand on his wife's arm. 'It's okay,' he says to her quietly. Then to the waitress, 'Which table is ours?'

The waitress looks dumbly from one to the other, blinking, before pointing towards a table with a river view.

Though it's damned-well not all right. Sure, we wouldn't want to be like the States where they stand up on buses and pay for your meals and clap as you walk past in uniform. Christ, all of Yankee Stadium rises when the on-ground camera picks out a marine in the bleachers. But we've got to be able to do better than limit our gratitude to ANZAC Day and all of its little rituals, that national bloody containment exercise.

As they take their seats the maître d', an older woman, hurries over and bows her head apologetically.

'Welcome home, Sir.'

Phelan nods and smiles. 'Thank you, Ma'am,' he says, reassured that sacrifice and recognition might still find their place here.

When they look out, the river sparkles. Despite everything, kids play on pieces of sculpture. A family of bikes rolls by, swerving around a ball-juggling clown spruiking for tips from the walkway. Shoppers wander past carrying jute bags filled with organic vegetables from the Saturday market on the other side of the refurbished old Powerhouse. The river breeze carries Penny's perfume to him once again, drawing him towards her until a plate crashes to the floor in the kitchen and Phelan starts violently, his head whipping back.

Penny is startled too, but by his reaction. Phelan is panting, desperate gasps, his chest heaving, his eyes wide.

She reaches across and places her hand gently on his arm. 'James?'

He looks up at her, almost frightened.

'James, what is it?'

He shakes his head. 'I don't know ... nothing.'

At the next table three cyclists in lycra discuss the Brisbane Lions' season, replaying games, reviewing the list, debating selections. One of the men is ruing injuries. Another is mapping out what the team needs to do to make the finals next year. At first, the banter is soothing, the sort of mess hall debate he's joined a thousand times, an army of soldiers filling weeks of downtime between operations.

'No, no, no, no, no,' one of them suddenly says.

'Hopeless,' another replies.

'You've got to admit, we're getting nowhere,' the third joins in, and the banter descends into a squabble over whether the coach should be sacked in the off-season. Two of them want his head, swearing it's the only option, that nothing will change until he's gone and it's suddenly too much for Phelan who gulps down his beer and holds up the empty glass to the waiter. Just days ago he was marching out of a forward operating base in the Chora Valley, holding off the forces of barbarism, a soldier about to die in his arms.

'Darling?' The second glass of alcohol in the middle of the day heightening her confusion.

Phelan compares his hands to those of the men at the table beside him. He likes his strong wrists, his hard skin, the way his muscles and veins rise off the back of his hands like mountain ridges.

'Hell-o-ooo', she croons softly, so only he can hear. 'Are you there, James?'

He turns his hands over as he counts the nicks, the scars, the white hieroglyphs marking his flesh and no one but him capable of deciphering them: the skin that came off a knuckle the day he was thrown around inside a Bushmaster that took a pothole too fast during a training exercise, the hairs on the back of two of his fingers singed off for good, the webbing somehow split between the middle and index fingers of his left hand during that Chora patrol, the infection that followed dirt and grit getting embedded in his palm.

'James? James?'

These men, he thinks, with their fat fingers and their sunspots and their warts and their never-ending jibber-jabber.

'You blokes done or what?' Phelan turns his body around as he speaks, opening his chest to the table of cyclists.

The closest one, his back to Phelan's table, swivels. 'Excuse me?'

'You've been banging on for half a fucking hour about absolute bullshit. There are other people trying to enjoy themselves here.'

LITTLE BLUE WREN

THEY STAY UNTIL the cyclists have gone.

When it's time to leave Phelan squeezes his wife's hand and they walk along the river in silence. The water has turned muddy under the high sun and no grass grows under the canopies of the great figs lining the path. In the bandstand beyond the figs, three small Chinese men perform tai chi, weaving out of harm's way, this left and right, this up and down, all in slow motion. The old men disappear behind the girth of the next fig as Phelan and Penny continue on their heavy-footed way. On the other side of the tree a foraging ibis appears, perched on a rubbish bin. It looks Phelan in the eye. For long seconds Phelan meets its wary stare, before the ibis drops its head and plunges its long beak into the bin. You're right bird, Phelan thinks, I won't hurt you.

Up ahead is a bank of the new yellow CityCycle hire bikes set up near the ferry terminal.

'Can't get away from bloody bikes,' Phelan scorns, but aware of himself, some part of it a joke.

'Come on then,' she says, trying to nudge him further out of his black mood, 'let's try them out.'

When he pauses she prods a little harder. 'I mean, it's not like you to let those cyclists back there get to you.'

Phelan grunts, a reluctant retreat. 'You win.'

Penny swipes her credit card at the ticket machine and points out which bikes to unlock. 'Don't forget the helmet,' she reminds him as he is about to head off. Then smiles to herself when she realises what she's just said.

They take the footpath on Oxlade Drive, past the art-deco block of flats on the corner, past the new riverfront homes, before cutting across to the water through the gap between the veterans hospice and the bowls club.

The movement's good, Phelan thinks, surprising himself. Feeling his body is good. They ride abreast for a while, the riverside path giving way to a floating boardwalk, water beneath them. Phelan sets the pace, travelling quickly enough to pull Penny along – faster than if she'd been cycling alone, but not so fast as to lose her. Because people need to be pushed, he thinks, they do, and in the end they're grateful.

How good to be working the stiffness out, the river sweeping by. And the solace of activity, of accomplishing things – the walkers and the prams they pass, the slower riders they overtake, the steel cantilever bridge that for a long time is ahead of them, but which they soon reach, pedal beneath, and then leave behind. The trick to any long journey is to break it down into smaller pieces, the buzz of achievement that gives. Penny falling in behind, the journey itself disappearing.

He reaches the city and its glass-faced cafés, its weekend shoppers, its skateboarders and its buskers. As the Botanic Gardens approaches, the tall buildings turn into a forest of mangroves, suddenly dark, and his bike's tyres are vibrating on the wooden boardwalk. It's like he's back in the cargo plane shepherding a young warrior home and all he wants to do is make the sound continue, to tunnel on and on, to lose himself in it.

When eventually Phelan emerges from the mangroves at Gardens Point, the light is stunning. It is too bright for either reverie or illusion. He turns his head to check on Penny, but she's no longer behind him. He stops and waits, but still she does not come. He doubles back and re-enters the mangroves, this time slowly, a feeling he's lost something in there. When he locates her, she is off her bike, exhausted in the shadows, leaning over the boardwalk's timber railings, staring at the dark mud.

'I got carried away,' he says, joining her at the railing. 'Are you all right?'

Her breathing is shallow. It sounds angry. She waves the question away.

Phelan waits with her while she catches her breath, looking down into the mangrove flats at the thousand tiny holes dotting the mudscape. There is a darting movement at the corner of his eye, but when he turns his head what he thought was a crab has disappeared into the wet earth. He settles in to wait it out, for it to poke its head up again, for the whole army of them to emerge from their mudholes. But crabs are patient too.

A group of walkers approach. Phelan raises his finger to his lips, hushing them. They look over the railing, but see nothing and continue on their way. A minute passes, perhaps less, no time at all, but already this little test he's set himself is growing hard. His mind will not be still. It is filled with engine noise, a low keening.

An upriver ferry passes on the other side of the mangrove forest. The sound of its engine, distorted by the canopy of leaf and branch, is somehow ghostly. Phelan watches the boat's wake work its way steadily through the taproots towards them, arc after arc, wondering if it will help flush the crabs from their holes. But nothing. Perhaps there were no crabs after all. A wren appears in the branches above, flitting azure, the colour reminding him of Kira, and he follows it, this flash of her, branch to branch, till she disappears. Everything is so difficult. Everything disappearing.

He has forgotten Penny entirely, and when she speaks her voice is a surprise to him, a thin woodnote, as if the wren is returning in admonishment.

'James,' he thinks he hears his wife say, 'I've got cancer.'

BIG BLACK CROW

PENNY STARES AHEAD. Here she is at the point of her great unburdening, and she can't even look at him. *Got* cancer, *had* it – it's a swirl of uncertain tense. The falsity of past and present and whatever shadow of whatever future lies ahead. I had a breast, I lost it. *Lost it!* As if, were she to look carefully enough, she might find it again. As for the rest of her, who yet knows what the hormone therapy will do? Sometimes it feels like an alien being has already entered her. How much of what is left, is me? she wonders. And whose voice will it be when she finds what it is she needs to say?

In the tangle of mangrove trees she begins to make out a map of sorts, her last few months located in the interwoven mass in front of her, the first shocking scan branching out to the next, doctor reaching out to doctor, date spreading to date, node to node. She reads the foliage as it reveals itself: a narrative of diagnosis and prognosis and treatment.

He listens to her, uncomprehending.

On and on she goes, locating opinions, then parsing them for him, each nuance. This world of bodily frailty she knows so well, for years lived vicariously, now inhabited afresh. She knows too much. She throws it at him, everything she can find. She has a need to overwhelm him, wants him to gasp for breath.

But when she approaches the end, when the surgery is done, and she has been discharged from hospital with a lopsided walk, her elbow tucked in and her forearm across her chest, shielding herself, and when her oncologist has given his latest prognosis, and she has commenced what she is told may be ten years of drug therapy, she doesn't care how long it'll take, she's just glad she's alive.

Even then, she is still not ready. She cannot yet bear his judgement, so she swings back into her story. She finds her own research, all the studies, all the peer-reviewed articles she's collected, all the blogs and on-line forums, a million women sharing their experiences. She tells him breast cancer has a long tail, echoing her oncologist, watching her husband to see that he understands.

James is dead-still beside her. She talks and she shivers in the deepening shadow. All the while she is aware of him staring at her, open-mouthed. If she continues, might she talk him into eternal silence?

A crow cries from somewhere behind them, *ark, ark*, and Penny stops, suddenly exhausted. *Ark, ark*, the crow says. The day is shifting. She closes her eyes and waits for either crow or James.

When he responds, it is exactly as she feared it would be every day since she decided to deal with it herself, not to burden him further. His words are exactly as she imagined hearing, the precise intonation even: 'Why didn't you tell me?'

But it's not really a question. It's not even a lament. *Why didn't you tell me?*

Penny had promised herself that if this is what he says, she won't fight it. She'll know and accept her fate. It would be a simple test to guide her way through the complexity of her longings. If, after all she's given over so many years, he still could only think of himself, if *he* could not recognise the stoicism in *her*, well okay. She'd turn her back on him and leave without a word, leaving him to mumble his *why didn't you tell me's* into the dusk. Her vow to herself.

But now that she hears it, it doesn't flatten her as she'd thought it would. It's a seal but not the one she'd imagined. Because she can't help but look at him and see his buggered old face on his oversized head, a tiring body, a lifetime in the breaking. She has been spectator and actor and if perhaps she could have left more of her own marks on him or gouged more out of him than she has, well, so be it: he'd still be buggered. Among the eddies and counter-eddies of emotion and hope and self-doubt and woundedness and falling cold, she shivers once and thinks: this is him. This is us.

Instead of walking away she slaps him. Hard.

PULLING AIR

When Phelan finds himself again, they are in the house and he is seated on the back steps. Penny is in the garden, turning a late-afternoon hose on. It seems he's been watching her for hours: observing her disappear behind a hedge as she kneels, then seeing her rise again, a weed he can't name pinched between her thumb and forefinger; knocking a loosely clenched fist against the rainwater tank to gauge the water level; scooping leaves from the frog pond.

Phelan tries to remember what she'd told him. It comes back in snatches. His memory's been patchy since Beckett, but this is time itself he's lost. Routine mammogram, he recalls. Stage two. Something about oestrogen receptors and lymph nodes. Then, mastectomy.

'Mastectomy?' he'd repeated.

'Mastectomy,' she'd said.

'That's when they—'

'Yes. They took off my left breast.'

He hadn't looked at her, not there, back on the path, in the forest, a crow scrutinising them.

He watches her moving out among the plants until she is done, and joins him on the steps. The silhouette of the great Norfolk pine at the back fence pulses, the falling sun behind it.

'What about chemo?' he asks, trawling through the little he knows about treatment. 'And radiation?'

'Like I said before,' she replies, 'I don't need it.'

'I thought—'

'No, not always. I'm lucky …' She pauses, as if the line to come is one she's delivered before, '… I get to keep my hair.'

He nods. 'And work?'

'I went back part-time after a few weeks' leave for the surgery and the recovery. Though not this week – they gave me this week off so I could … be with you.'

He nods again.

'The hospital has been very supportive,' she adds.

In a way he hasn't yet been. Though he knows she doesn't mean it that way.

'Great,' he says, as the logistics of her life these last six months begin to dawn on him: just how much she kept from him, the spaces she'd carved out of their relationship, how false the alternative existence she'd continued to describe to him while he was in Afghanistan.

An entire cycle has run its course while he was away. A water pipe shudders down the side of the house as the pump starts to pull air. And he has been entirely unnecessary.

SMALL BRUSHSTROKES

PENNY CLOSES THE bathroom door behind her, her nightdress in her hands, traces of soil beneath her fingernails.

Phelan picks up his *Meditations* from the bedside table where he'd unpacked it and opens it at random. The ancient words his eyes fall on contain no wisdom, nothing of comfort, nothing even to distract him. Their familiarity is, for perhaps the first time in his life, an irritant. He lays the book down and listens instead to Penny changing in the little room next door, hearing each shift of her limbs, tracking her movements in his mind. He hears water splashing in the basin, a handtowel pressed against her face, a drawer opening and closing. It strikes him that the woman in the next room preparing for bed is his wife. Not woman, but wife. The most ordinary of revelations. When did that metamorphosis happen?

Phelan hears her discarding the day's clothes, knows the precise moment she is naked, counts the beats of her weightlessness, hears her change into her nightwear then turn off the bathroom lamp. The band of light at the foot of the door disappears, and Phelan waits. But still she lingers.

'Let me see, Pen,' he says when she emerges from the ensuite.

She crosses the room as if she hasn't heard him, and places her old clothes into the wicker basket in the corner, her back to him. Such shoulders as hers, he thinks. It's the surest way to read a person – not the eyes, but the shoulders – and he sees now, only now, the slightest of pitches to the left, this change in her bearing.

'Penny,' he says again and she hesitates. 'Please, Penny. Please.'

She doesn't reply, crossing instead to the window where she pulls the curtains tight. When she turns to face him there is an entire room between them. She motions to the reading lamps on either side of the bed. He turns them off, first his, then, leaning across the bed, the frame creaking under his weight, hers. The darkened room. Penny gathers the hem of her nightdress and draws it to her thighs where she pauses momentarily, before lifting it up and over her hips and arms, shoulders and head, then dropping it carefully to the floor beside her.

She stands facing him, a silhouette in the stray moonlight. The symmetry of her old shape is changed. Her legs and her hipbones are all her, but her arms fall awkwardly beside her now, and one of her collarbones seems to have dropped, pulled down by the weight of absence. She said she'd lost her breast, but how can a man believe such a thing without seeing? The uneven fall of moonlight across her chest hollows it, as if her body holds darkness differently now, the shock not in the maimed flesh, or the scar, or any collapse of beauty. It's that this is not quite the wife he expected coming home to.

Behind her the curtains billow on the night breeze. She straightens under his gaze and in her bony shoulders there is defiance.

HE BRUSHES HER right nipple with his fingertips, gently, carefully, feeling it rise. Phelan kisses her then, his hand cupping her. He smoothes her skin with his tongue, recovering the shape of her breast. Then, slowly, he moves across her chest. He's unsure where he is going, this journey the pads of his fingers make across her altered body, her new skin. Her breathing shallows.

The side of his thumb works over her skin in small brushstrokes as he searches out the scar, as if he's working his way through a grid of uncertain territory, sector by sector till he's covered the lot and can declare it's clear. In time he finds it, low, across where her breast once was.

'I LOVE YOU,' he says, and Penny sobs in the darkness. Sobs and laughs and lies at peace. Is bliss just a form of acceptance? Its pinnacle?

She lies awake, overcome. He loves her, she him. Did she ever really doubt it? This certainty the reward for her heroic restraint, for her own sacrifice, for the lonely months of anxiety, of planning her healing without him. She feels for her scar, and it is almost a gift. A kiss, a consummation. Sleep.

WHATEVER IT MIGHT have been that woke him. Did Penny say something? But her breath is even and she is somehow still there, somehow sleeping. A dream then, though nothing of it remains.

Phelan's head throbs. He looks up at the plaster ceiling above the bed and in the ambient light makes out the rosettes in relief, thin-leafed vines twisting around each other in each corner of the room. The bay windows are open and palm fronds rustle in the night breeze. Penny's breathing catches, then quickly settles into a rhythm once more. This bed, this wife, this room, this house, this city, this night. How long it takes to come home. He drifts back into sleep.

But then there comes a great heat, his head and arms and feet pulsing with it. His throat becomes dry and swollen. There's dust on his tongue, kicked up by the men in front of him, now out of sight. Beads of perspiration are pouring off him, and his shirt is damp and sticky. He can smell hours of acrid sweat and grime on his body and almost chokes. The thumping and spitting of shells and rounds above his head, and the pulsing thud-thud-thud-thud of Apaches is almost deafening. He is alone and surrounded by noise, and he's trudging down a footpad by the side of an ancient stone wall stretching as far as he can see, to eternity and beyond. His gear is heavy. His limbs are like rock. He struggles to put one dead foot in front of the other.

In the wall ahead he sees a wire protruding from the mud, bright red. He is mesmerised by it, yet knows he mustn't touch it, knows what it is. But how interesting it is, so alluring in such a dun-coloured world. He should leave it for the sappers, but his hand is reaching for it anyway. He tries to pull his arm back, but he can't. It's an IED, it can't be an IED. It's an IED. It can't be. It's a beautiful little red wire, that's all. But he knows perfectly well it's an IED in the wall and he tries to twist his shoulder away, his whole body, but he can't, and his arm is still reaching, and his hand is going to pull the wire and he can't stop himself, and he's sweating and he's screaming and turning his head for the explosion and Penny is shouting now too, *It's just a dream, James, it's just a dream.* And he's sitting up gasping for breath and his heart is banging against his chest so it hurts, and when finally the terror retreats he fears what has followed him home.

'What is it, James? Talk to me. Tell me.'

In time his gulping breath subsides under Penny's calming fingers. The ragged world slows.

'I think I pissed myself, Pen,' he whispers into the death-silent night. 'I might have pissed myself.'

The indignities that accompany guilt. Knowing that men have lost control of themselves in combat since the first Stone Age axe hovered above the first Stone Age neck doesn't help. That at least he hadn't shat himself doesn't matter either. He doesn't know if he pissed himself before or after Beckett died, but he remembers he's trapped and there's fire all round and some of the fear is momentarily giving way to resignation, and Beckett is lying there still, and Phelan's waiting for something to come, for providence or fate, bullet-small or

Apache-large, and he's starting to smell himself, and to feel the acrid wetness on his thighs. And he doesn't want to get rescued like this. It's a thought he has, one he can never disown, and the only water that's left is Beckett's and he takes it and he leans back and he pours it over his trousers, over his groin, sluicing himself in this thicket of sound.

WHAT WAR CAN DO

THE NIGHT OUTSIDE their window fills with landing flying foxes, branches breaking under their weight, fleshy fruit thudding to the ground, hard-spat seeds, a demented carnival of whistling and screeching. On nights like this they are a chorus of demons on the wing.

Penny hugs him close.

There's not a bodily function she hasn't seen go bad, so it doesn't shock her. She's tended to years of broken men, wiped up oceans of piss and shit and semen, their pus and their blood. But still: James, her James.

She couldn't imagine a man less afraid than he. This man now shaking in shame in her arms. How he chased action in his early years, only for it to elude him, because there were too few wars in the eighties when he was young and ready. The administrative postings when they came were not his fault, he didn't seek easy paths, he did what was asked of him. So when he said to her, before Afghanistan, this time he might see action, she understood it wasn't just his career he was thinking about and the promotions that might come. It was deeper than that, truer than that, and she loved him for it.

'You can never ask anyone to do anything you wouldn't do yourself,' he'd said to her again and again. It had been his family's motto, he told her, and implicitly, theirs too. He had to test himself.

On the wall of his study was the framed handwritten letter his great-grandmother received when his great-grandfather – the first of the Phelan warriors – had died after a long life. She could almost quote it back to him, having stopped to read it each time she dusted the room.

9 August 1973
Dear Mrs Phelan & Family,

With regret I read of the death of your husband. As an old soldier who served and fought under him I thought it was my duty to write and convey my deepest and most sincere Sympathy to you and your family in your sad loss.

He was a brave officer and was loved by all his men who fought under him. He never asked his men to do anything that he would not do himself. He survived the Massacre at Bullecourt where a large proportion of the Battalion was lost. I myself was wounded twice in that battle. I pray that God will comfort you and your family in your time of sad Bereavement.

Yours sincerely,
Herbert Sullivan

She comforts James. Nurses don't need war to complete themselves, she thinks. Not like soldiers do.

Yet isn't it also true that all the great nurses were wartime nurses? Florence Nightingale in Crimea. The hundreds of heroes who returned from the Western Front with wounded soldier-husbands. Vivian Bullwinkel in Singapore. Ondaatje's Hana, a favourite of her book club.

She's lucky. He is a good man. She comforts him and wonders whether she might yet, in her own home, become a wartime nurse.

Whether her own wounding helps or hinders. Softens her or hardens. She stands before the bathroom mirror. Already this glass has revealed too much, has a power she fears cannot be harnessed, at least by her. I am no Amazon, she thinks – breast removed to better draw an arrow – and never will be. I am merely Penelope Phelan nee Richardson, standing erect as I can before my reflection. I am now one-nippled Penelope, mutilated Penny. Now have an unwanted pocket of fat beneath my arm, lose my balance, shrink. Some days I can laugh at the irony of my surgical souvenir, that it is *me* who is wounded, *me* who experiences phantom breast pains. Some days. I have been maimed by forces beyond my control. James may still want me, but do I want myself?

Look at what the war has done to us, she imagines whispering to him. She doesn't, though she might yet.

All her girlfriends have said it to her, her mother, her sister too, the whole phalanx of women who've pulled her along. Even though her surgeon resisted the idea as she'd expected he would, she still thought she detected in him a moment's hesitation that allowed for its possibility. *Stress.* The conclusion they urged on her. *It's caused by stress.* Penny understands well the inevitable human need to find a cause for cancer. To seek answers to unanswerable questions. She has never believed it herself, has never given her patients more than a sympathetic 'maybe'. Because her nurse's oath – her Nightingale Pledge – didn't include giving false hope or misleading advice. But it's hard not to wonder about the 'maybes' when they're yours.

Maybe it's the war that's responsible, she might say to James, as much to test him as anything else.

Do you really think so? she imagines her good husband gently responding, though he'd probably be entitled to a different reply, one she'd voiced to herself: *If you thought staying home was stressful …*

But she knows he would never say such a thing, because James doesn't believe in stress. Pressure, he's said a hundred times over the years, is real, but stress is a controllable response. Oh, those beliefs of his. How many years of polishing, how far they've carried him, and thus her too, his polisher-in-chief. He's a stoic in a post-modern world. What better place than the army for a man like him, who gets to quote his beloved Marcus Aurelius to kids starting out just as he had thirty-plus years ago, young officers, hard and ambitious. As if part of their initiation is to receive the Roman General's meditations, a lost wisdom, which, if they're ready for it, will guide them through a world most people find chaotic. The greatness of reason; the fragility of emotion. The triviality of the body. The majesty of the mind. All the aphorisms she's read, but which her husband has tried to live. *Let any external thing happen to those parts of me which can be affected by its happening – and they, if they wish, can complain. I myself am not yet harmed, unless I judge this occurrence something bad: and I can refuse to do so.*

For Phelan and Aurelius, stress is a moral failing. And yet here he is, sobbing in her arms, his mind having failed him on the battlefield.

What does your General think of you now, James?

'Look at what the war has done to us,' she whispers.

BLACK ON AQUAMARINE

PHELAN LIES ON the floorboards beside his bed, his knees pulled halfway to his chest, the hard, bright light of day all around him. Penny left the bed with a kiss to his forehead soon after the first magpies, but it has taken him an hour to get even this far. There's a heaviness in his body, and in his head, and the gym downstairs is too far. He lies on the floor, his fifty push-ups and fifty sit-ups ahead of him, one for each year, the annual increase a source of pride to him. He may not be getting younger, but he's not bloody-well letting age get on top of him. He sits on the floor, but not with his usual vigour,

96

primed for the day. Instead, he feels his bony arse, a flabbiness in his gut, his foggy head. He reclines, his hands behind his head. But the timber is cold against his shoulderblades, and after just one sit-up his head is throbbing and he lies back in the hardening daylight.

He could use this leave to catch up on everything he loves, but all he wants is sleep. And for the headache and mad ear-ringing to go away.

THE DAY CONTINUES in slow motion. Phelan moves through the morning. The house and the street and the neighbourhood and all the city below them to the east are almost stationary.

His wife by the fishpond, his wife on the phone with her mother. His wife taking her daily medication. His wife gathering celery sticks and apples, slicing them and feeding them into a blender. His sick, pale-skinned, worried wife.

He watches her in silence, moving in silence. He has been away. That he is back seems irrelevant. He is untethered, he is dispensable. Might she die? Is it possible? Is it that serious? He follows her into the laundry and stands at the door and asks her again about her treatment.

'How much more do you have left?'

'It's just the hormone drugs now.'

She seems genuinely optimistic. Is it just for show, for him? For herself too?

'What do the doctors think?' Phelan continues.

'The oncologist couldn't be happier.'

He nods.

'Here James,' she says, looking up, 'this is yours.'

She presses a business card into his hands. *Written on the Body* it reads, black lettering on an aquamarine background. The card pulls him out of his torpor. He turns it over but it is spare, just the name of the studio and the address.

Already Kira and what followed feels like it happened to someone else. It is as if all that has occurred in the short time since returning to Brisbane has wiped a little wartime folly from his slate. As if real life is of vastly more consequence than a night's escapade on a soldier's leave. But now his wife innocently prods him with it.

He says the name aloud, standing there in the laundry, Penny shoving his clothing into the machine, 'Written on the Body', as if reading the words for the first time.

Penny looks over at him. 'Are you talking to me?'

He shakes his head. But is she inviting him to tell her something? 'Thank you,' he says, waving the card, an attempt at nonchalance, watching Penny as she closes the washing machine door.

PHELAN LIES ON the padded gym bench and feels nauseous. There's no natural light down here, and one of the bank of fluoro ceiling tubes is fluttering. Fate's judgement is brutally efficient, he thinks: he cheats on her, she dies.

He lifts the bar from its stand, taking the weight, his elbows locked. What has he done? He lowers the bar to his chest. This is precisely what infidelity can do. He begins a set of ten, desperate for pain. If the beat of a butterfly's wings in the Amazon can unleash a hurricane on the other side of the world, why can't an affair in Sydney kill a wife in Brisbane?

HE CAN'T HELP himself. He looks up Written on the Body on the net. He adds 'tattoo' to the search engine, homing in on her, and the studio comes up. But there are no photos of her on the site, no bio either, just an online gallery and a short manifesto.

He reads:

Kira doesn't tattoo skin. She tattoos bodies. Her work celebrates the human spirit, and is inspired by nature, ritual and divine forms of sacred mythology.

He clicks rapidly through her portfolio and finds mandalas and Celtic knot-work and stylised leaves and kingfishers and angels on pristine skin. A monarch's wings. Rippling fish scales. Blacks and greys and blues and greens. He flicks through a blur of body parts, backs and shoulders and arms and wrists. Thighs and calves and ankles. The same hand – hers – marking them all.

But when he comes to a breast he stops abruptly, pulling his fingers from the keyboard as if he's suffered an electric shock. On the screen a thin silver necklace with a thread of small diamonds falls high against a woman's skin. Her right hand calmly covers her right nipple and much of the right side of her chest, her fingernails polished clear. But her left breast ... The woman's left arm is raised and out of photo, lifting her breast with its shower of tattooed petals into the centre of the image. But the petals are of no flower he recognises, no colour either. It is as if he's caught some fresh blossoming, a spray of petals emerging from the dark fold beneath her breast, moulding themselves to the contours of her body, miraculously transforming it, the place where her nipple might be protected by the gentle shadow cast by the petals. Her skin is tantalisingly revealed in the tips of the artist's translucent petals, before hiding again in the soft-brushed reds and grey-greens of the delicately inked floriade. As he watches, the breast disappears and something entirely new and beautiful emerges.

Does he misread omens? Despite cheating on her, perhaps she will not die.

NOWHERE AND EVERYWHERE

STILL NO SLEEP. Three weeks have passed since Beckett, his leave extended on medical advice, and Phelan's nightmares have only grown more vivid, repose more elusive, his judgements more damning. That as courageous as he might have been in going to Beckett, he should never have been on the patrol in the first place. An unanswerable what-if? And as brave as he might have been, when he got to Beckett he had nothing that mattered to give him.

He looks for sleep triggers in the dark, trying to distract himself, hoping to create a window for his exhaustion to enter and steal him away, if only for an hour or two. He runs through the list of men who've commanded the Australian Army, starting with the current Chief, lucky bastard that he is, and then, stepping back in time, each of the Chiefs of Army before him, then the long run of Chiefs of the General Staff, until eventually he reaches the two English generals who were in charge after Federation. There are milestones along the way: the wartime commanders, those who were knighted, the Catholics, those who went on to command the whole of the Defence Force. He knows them like a sheep knows its shepherds. He tracks them back through time, seeking a tunnel somewhere in the pre-history of this tribe of his, beyond names, that he might crawl into and disappear.

But he can't escape. He tries the other sleep-lists he's used over the years – national cricket captains, prime ministers, the names of boyhood pets – but nothing works. So he resorts to Hail Marys, a sleep mantra when he was a boy, masquerading even then as prayer. What fear does. He starts silently, decade of the rosary after decade, counting them on his fingers, and then more boldly, more desperately, his lips moving, murmuring the words.

It is with the first butcher bird's call that he catches himself, plummets into shame, moans from the shallowness of his undeserving fear. Warriors on patrol's eve are entitled to pray, sappers in a minefield, blood-soaked medics, Beckett in an irrigation ditch in falling light. But not him in his safe Brisbane bed. Oh the mockery! How his prayers mock his men.

TINNITUS COULD DRIVE a man mad, the remorselessness of it. Even when the ringing in his ears withdraws, the relief is precarious, a few days' respite at best. Because it always returns, and when it does it seems louder than ever. Constant cannon-shot. Whiskey helps as much as anything else, at least temporarily. He can't tell the doctor that, but it's true. And temporary relief is still relief.

He gets into his uniform and drives out to the Gallipoli Barracks at Enoggera one morning for his scheduled check-up, followed by lunch with the brigade commander. His goal for the doctor's consultation is just to get through it without giving anything new away, to kick the can of his return to Afghanistan down the road a little further, but not too far. The effort even that takes. By the time he reaches the Officers' Mess he is drained.

Phelan stands before the sliding plate-glass doors of the wall-length trophy cabinet, waiting for the base commander, his hands grasped behind his back. No matter how close he leans in, the collection of baubles behind the glass won't take shape. It's the fucking glare, he thinks, blinking. The ceilings in this newly built mess complex are too high, the floors shine too brightly, there's too much light blasting away, no secrets allowed, everything just too damned open and unwelcoming, not a single cigar ever smoked within these walls.

When he turns away from the cabinet two captains are standing in the archway looking at him. Before he can greet them they pivot and leave, the heels of their shoes squeaking on the floor. He is suddenly aware that what had been an empty room when he arrived, is now filling. How long has he been standing here staring into the trophy cabinet? Is it possible the nearby tableful of junior officers have dropped their voices to talk about him? The way they glance over at him, a look in the eyes of one or two, almost hostile. What is it? Scorn? They'll know he's on leave, of course, but do they read his mind too? Sense his weakness, his doubt? Is that possible?

AFTER PENNY'S DAILY morning meditation she goes online, so many messages of support, so many opportunities to practise living with gratitude for what she's got. One of her girlfriends forwards a thread to her, with an explanatory note:

> *Hi there Penny Love,*
> *This is all a bit strange. Probably shouldn't forward it to you, with everything you've had to deal with, but I thought you'd want to know. James too. It's just human nature, of course, to look for someone to blame, and no doubt it'll all blow over in a couple of days. But let me know if there's anything I can say to help manage it.*
> *Love you heaps, Bec xo*

Penny scrolls through the conversation, a discussion among a tight group of wives and girlfriends whose men are still over there. She doesn't recognise any of the names. At first it looks like they're just going over Beckett and what happened, but then she realises the conversation is not really about Beckett at all, but about James. And that it's more than just garden-variety bitching – that they're blaming him. Not with hints and innuendo, but openly!

She takes the phone out into the garden and sits on the bench with the laptop.

'Bec,' she says. 'What's this all about?'

'Sorry, Love. I didn't mean to upset you. But ... I know, I know ... it's outrageous, isn't it?'

'Who are they?'

'A couple have husbands who were on the patrol and are still out at the forward operating base ... Fiona Gruen is married to the commanding officer and Louise Starc – the really filthy one – she's married to a corporal at the base ... the rest, well other than the girl who forwarded it on to me – she's been a friend for ages – I don't know any of them ...'

'They're saying the patrol was only ambushed because the Taliban learned James was on it. They're saying there was no need for him to be there—'

'Army gossip, Penny Love—'

'That there is footage ...'

'No surprise. They all have helmet cameras these days.'

'That when the army's review is completed, James's career will be over?'

'Yeah, I know ... *that's* a truly feral thing to say. That's the thing it might be worth being a bit worried about.'

'But is there anything in it, Bec?'

'How do I know, Penny Love? But I doubt it. He's a hero. I mean, you know better than anyone what sort of man he is.'

PHELAN TURNS HIS ear towards the sound of the postman's motorbike as it buzzes and bunts its way down the street. He rises from the weights bench, drenched in sweat, and makes his way upstairs, wondering about the postman's route but unable to remember it. At the front window he furrows his brow, shakes his head, tries again to remember the route until he realises the engine noise has now disappeared at the end of a hilltop breeze. He feels an odd sadness come over him momentarily, so many losses. Beckett and now, possibly, Penny. Where do all the things one loses, great or trivial, go?

Phelan waits until the sound of the engine fades entirely before stepping out of the house. The bay and the sand island to the east are too far away to see at this hour, even if he'd looked. He scans the garden and the streetscape beyond. The street is empty. Phelan checks the letterbox for redbacks before reaching in and producing the bundle of mail, gathered with a thick red rubber band.

At the kitchen bench he sorts the letters into two piles, bills in one, the rest in another. He drops the rubber band into a glass jar squirming with them.

'Don't worry about any of that, James,' Penny says, preparing lunch. 'I'll sort it out when you leave.'

He doesn't notice she's hung a bright red cooking apron over her neck. That she's wearing matching lipstick and a change of perfume. He doesn't see her resilience. Because his thoughts are flitting, because he's opening bills, and thinking about their finances, about the mortgage, and how the quarterly electricity bill seems bigger than it should be, and whether or not Penny has cancelled the paper credit card statements because of the two-dollar fee, and he's thinking he's not going to ask her because that wouldn't be fair, but that means he's going to have to log on to check the account balance. That he needs to do it now, *right now*, and whatever Penny might think is more urgent it's not, because if their finances have got out of shape, then it's up to him to get them back into order, particularly given her health, and though Penny's kept the house brilliantly while he's been away, she misses things, which would be understandable given what's happened.

Penny reaches across the counter and rests her hand on James's forearm. He looks up, startled, wrenched from his thoughts by her touch. 'Talk to me, James,' she says. 'Tell me about Sapper Beckett. Tell me everything. It'll help get it off your chest, Darling.'

But it's not on his chest. It's inside him, in every sinew and every twitching fibre. It's entered his bones, which are heavy with it now, death-heavy. It's burrowing deeper, this very moment, even her request feeding it. His rushing heart, his fuzzy head.

'Tell me, James,' she says again.

He tenses.

'I can't,' he replies. It's an achievement to control his voice so he can get even those two words out.

'Why can't you, James?' she asks gently.

But in his growing exhaustion he suspects her kindliness is a front. She's too ready with her tenderness. What can it be but an attack? He's cranking up, the prickliness in his skin, he can feel it, tightening and tightening. *Leave me out of it!* he wants to shout at her, though he has enough restraint not to yell. Just.

Instead he covers his face with his big right hand as his jaw clenches and his whole head begins to shudder, clasping his temples with his thumb and middle finger to still himself, to stop from screaming, and when eventually the moment passes he takes a deep breath and leaves the kitchen, leaves the house, leaves the street.

BECKETT IS NOWHERE and everywhere. In the park Phelan overhears a male voice of a certain resonance, and knows it's not Beckett. Every kid playing every game of handball on the street is not Beckett. Beckett's name isn't mentioned in the cricket scores on the radio, though he has half an ear for it. Nor is Beckett beside him while he's doing push-ups in the morning, matching him, head turned, smiling, this soldier he barely knew challenging him.

Come on, Sir, is that all you've got?

That voice isn't Beckett either.

• • •

EVERYONE HAS THEIR psych debrief in-country before they return, even him. He'd insisted, even though it was just leave, not a permanent return. Never ask someone to do something you wouldn't do yourself.

'It must have been heavy, Sir,' the young psych says in his Tarin Kot room, the door closed for privacy.

The furrow in his brow is well practised, Phelan thinks, and no mask for what is probably just curiosity. Because of course this kid knows what happened – the bare outline is already common knowledge – or thinks he does. This psychologist with the job of ensuring no one's going to run amok when they get home, that no one's plotting mad revenge on some poor Arab family in some quiet suburban shopping centre in Bankstown. This kid and his ossifying diagnostic tools – someone's idea of best practice risk management. As if homeward-bound soldiers don't know what to answer already, as if they haven't shared the questions around, taken the piss out of it all, conducted their own mock interviews among themselves. This kid who's interviewing him about killing and being killed, who'll plot his results on a graph and work out whether Phelan is a risk to be managed.

But now that it's his turn, Phelan feels his heart race. What does the lieutenant with the soft hands and the pen hovering over a form really want to know?

Everyone knows what happened. Everyone will have an opinion. Phelan doles him perfunctory answers so he can tick his boxes. After every answer the kid looks up and asks the next question, clearly, slowly, articulating each word. It feels like a provocation, as if this lieutenant doesn't believe him. Phelan looks at his watch, doesn't hide it. Still the questions come, remorselessly. Drip, drip, drip.

Whatever it is this army psych really wants to know, Phelan will not tell. What it's like to go out into the field when you're not ready. What it's like to know they put on a patrol just for you. A vanity patrol.

Instead, Phelan tries to throw him. 'How long have you been doing this, Andrew?' Though Phelan already knows – there aren't so many of them serving in-country that you can't discover something about most.

'"This", Sir?'

'These interviews.'

'I arrived in January.'

'Four hundred and thirteen soldiers have returned since then. So that's four hundred and thirteen interviews?'

'Sir?'

'That's a lot of war you've seen.'

The kid is nervous.

'I haven't seen any of it myself, of course, Sir.'

'You interview enough warriors about their bad stuff, and their bad stuff becomes your bad stuff.'

'Vicarious trauma, Sir. Yes.'

'Are you okay, Andrew?'

'It's not all bad stuff, Sir.'

WHEN HE RETURNS to the house Penny greets him as if nothing has happened, as if she knew all along he'd return about now, having got whatever he needed to out of his system. She tells him that both the Chief of the Army and his friend Ben Donaldson have called, her voice straining for lightness but her eyes studying James's face for his reaction. He is aware of an intensity in her, something more than mere curiosity. Though his expression gives nothing away, the weight of returning the Chief's call is initially too heavy for him. He tries Donno instead, but the call goes to voicemail and he doesn't leave a message.

Beer? Phelan texts instead.

Where u been? Donaldson replies.

The Fox in an hr?

Have to be tomorrow, Bro.

Ok.

1400?

Ack.

Acknowledged. The thought of seeing Donno fortifies him enough to ring the Chief.

'WHAT DID HE want, James?' Penny asks when Phelan returns from his study to the kitchen, the call a lengthy one. He looks across the room. It is too small a space to hold a thousand-yard stare.

'An operational matter,' he replies flatly.

'What type of operational matter, James?' When he doesn't answer, she presses. 'James?'

'He wants to organise a time for an interview about Sapper Beckett's death.'

'Are you the interviewer or the interviewee?'

'It's all part of the process.'

'I've heard that the men from Beckett's base are blaming you …'

He looks at her. 'Who?'

'Gossip. Some of the wives and girlfriends.'

He takes in the information.

'Well,' he says eventually, grimacing, 'that's what I just heard too.'

COMMUNIONS

PHELAN STEPS FROM a cold shower after another night of fearful thrashing. He is dizzy and short of breath. He forces himself to shave. The night's anxiety is still on him. When he hears a raised voice in the street he starts, and his heart begins to clatter again. He grasps the edge of the basin with both hands to steady himself. When he looks up he sees Beckett's name in the mirror's damp.

'Why don't you see someone?'

He freezes. Penny's voice from the doorway.

'No one else needs to know,' he blurts.

'Know what?'

He shakes his head.

'What don't you want people to know about, James?'

'I'm so tired ...'

She looks at him and nods. 'Well that's what I meant. You need to see someone to help you sleep.'

He is still shaking his head. Slowly Beckett fades from the glass.

'You can't go on like this, James. You need to sleep.'

The lunch crowd at The Sly Fox is thinning, though slowly. Even for a Friday there are still too many suits for this side of the river, too many vapid conversations to try and ignore. He's arrived an hour early, but even after a third whiskey he can't settle enough to concentrate on the Sudoku in *The Australian*. He'd flipped through the paper from first to last when he arrived. There were no headlines, nothing about the war on all the pages dedicated to 'The Nation', nothing at all until 'World' where he reads a single column about the difficulties the Brits are having in Helmand Province. Beckett has been forgotten by the papers, of course, a relief, and thank god there's been no one else in the weeks since. But by Christ, even a swooping magpie gets coverage before the extraordinary work of our patrols. He pushes the ice cubes round his glass with his finger, not feeling the cold. It'd say something about him if a mere Sudoku clue could distract him from the toll of war.

'Who's responsible for putting that crap on?' Donaldson calls out as the chorus of Dexys Midnight Runners' only hit begins to throb from the wall-mounted speakers.

All the suits and the skirts turn their heads towards the tall man making for Phelan, his shaved skull and his green eyes and his black polished shoes glistening. He too is dressed in collar and tie and impeccably creased trousers, but without a jacket. He's been out ten years, and Phelan knows the years have been good to him.

'Crap name for a band, crap song,' Donaldson adds, breaking into a wide smile.

'Talk to the barman,' Phelan says, taking Donaldson's large hand, before suddenly clasping him close, chest to chest, holding him tight, surprising him. When Phelan releases him, Donaldson looks at him carefully.

'Sorry mate,' Phelan murmurs quietly. 'I'm just so fucking tired.'

Donaldson doesn't respond immediately to the unexpected concession to weakness. 'They used to have a jukebox here,' he says instead, looking around. 'You remember?'

Phelan nods dully, deflated. He fears he is on the verge of tears.

'It must give you the shits, JP. You go away to fight for your country, and what happens?' He makes Phelan meet his eye. 'They take your bloody jukebox away.'

Phelan smiles, but it is tired, resigned.

'Right-o. A drink then.' Donaldson glances at Phelan's glass, then clears a space between the suits at the bar. As Phelan watches his back he feels a pang of anxiety, an irrational fear that his friend is leaving already. He reaches for his glass to steady himself, drains the melted ice.

The two twenty-something couples who've been playing doubles end their game. The girls in their tight black skirts toss their cues onto the felt, not bothering to rack them, maybe not knowing, and wander away from the table. Their male companions know no better, and follow, the hand of one comically chasing his girlfriend's arse, just out of reach. Phelan shakes his head to himself and rises from his stool. He puts two gold coins into the coin slot, and rams the coin arm in. The balls release, drop, rumble and roll.

'How are you doing, JP?' Donaldson finally asks as Phelan sets the balls into position in the triangle, Donaldson's question coming in from an angle so Phelan can dodge it if he wants.

Phelan doesn't yet look up, intent on nestling the black into place. 'You heard what happened?' Phelan asks eventually, his hands resting on the triangle, the balls still corralled.

'I heard, I read, I saw,' Donaldson says.

Phelan nods.

'Mate,' Donaldson continues, 'from what I've seen, you've done bloody well.'

When he speaks, Phelan's voice is soft, barely audible above the music. 'What did you see, mate?'

'Bringing him home like you did. Greeting his parents. Addressing your men. Explaining what happened to the country. That must have been fucking hard, but you did what had to be done. You've got broad shoulders mate.'

Phelan is silent for a long, long time. He and Donaldson are school friends who went through Duntroon together. While Phelan climbed, taking every offered opportunity, promotion after promotion, Donaldson stayed closer to the ground, serving in East Timor and Iraq before getting out in his late-thirties and parleying battlefield experience into Dean of an all-male residential college at the university.

'Nothing's changed,' he quips whenever he gets the chance, 'I'm still trying to keep young men alive.' Without competition between them, they've grown closer these last ten years. 'You did what had to be done,' he repeats. 'Didn't you?'

Phelan lifts the triangle, slides it into its home in the table, and tosses. Donaldson calls true and breaks. They don't talk while they play.

We line up our shots differently from other men, Phelan thinks, his head over the cue. It's an article of faith that makes him feel strong. They follow their balls around the table, all sweet cracks and backspin, all the years of practice. Their control of speed, their ability to read a table's felt, know an unreliable cushion, judge the angles. How their balls fall perfectly into their pockets, all these small, temporary oblivions. As long as he plays, his life is in control.

'Can you remember voices, Donno?' Phelan asks between games.

'What do you mean, JP?'

'Some people say they can hear the sound of someone inside their brain, can actually hear the sound of their voice.'

'The missus you mean?'

'Hah, fucking, hah.'

'What happened, JP?' Donaldson finally asks. 'What happened over there?'

Before Phelan can answer two men in construction boots, who've been sitting on stools against the wall watching them, stand. Donaldson is beginning to reset.

'Doubles?' The wirier of the two asks Phelan. He has a thick beard and long hair pulled tight into a ponytail. His forehead glistens.

'Sure,' Phelan replies, his head turned away from the man to knock back his whiskey. 'Two shots on a foul.'

The man steps closer, steps into Phelan's face before he can react, the man's tiny burning pupils just inches from Phelan, sweat dripping from his forehead, stale Guinness on his breath. Whatever building site he's come in from, whatever else he's taken, whatever is amping him, however long he's been itching to orchestrate something, there's no doubt what he's after.

'Mate,' the man says, arrowing in, 'only pussies and soft-cocks play two-shot rule. Which one are you?'

Phelan can't answer. He is no longer in the pub, is no longer holding a pool cue, no longer caught in a room full of smoke on a lazy Friday afternoon, the fall of a gooseneck lamp on the wall. No longer capable of drawing on all the times he's had to defuse situations just like this, some bar-room warrior after a pub trophy. Instead, he's back in the Chora

Valley and there's a burst of fire overhead and his finger is on his trigger, and either he pulls it or he doesn't, and his nostrils are flaring, and blood is pumping inside him, rivers of it coursing through his veins, and there aren't even seconds in it, time both smaller and more immense.

Before he can act, Donaldson slides between him and the man he's about to destroy. 'Let it go, JP. Let it go.'

AH, THINKS PHELAN out in the street, sinking to his haunches on the footpath, a train rumbling overhead, is this what the army has been protecting him from? Is this what the scaffolding of hierarchy and regulations and orders and obedience has given him?

'You glad you got out, Donno?' he asks, looking up, knowing the answer but wanting to hear it again, now.

'Unreservedly. You could too, JP. There's a whole wide world out there.'

But he's moved a warrior's dead body. He's taken the last of Beckett's water. Is he any less culpable than the hordes that combed the battlefields of Flanders souveniring wristwatches or levering gold-fillings from jaws? What more is he that even he cannot know?

'Just say if you want me to ask around.'

'WHAT HAPPENED TO that lapis lazuli carving you said you'd bought in Kabul?' Penny asks.

It hardly matters to her, there are plenty of things more pressing. Still, if he'd brought it back, if he'd remembered to despite Beckett, and it was still tucked into a corner of a bag, then she'd add it to the collection of souvenirs he's gathered for her over the years, a little gesture of normalisation.

But he goes cold, waves the question away.

• • •

113

HE WANTS TO know, he doesn't want to know. He wants to know, he doesn't. It's like a game of 'he loves me, he loves me not', pulling petals off a flower. Whether to turn on the television news for reports of the war, whether to log on, whether to pick up the phone. Yes, thank God no one else has died since Beckett. But it doesn't take much for his brain to flip that around – no one has died because *I'm* not there, no more casualties because *I'm* not in command.

So it's me, is it?

When Phelan does trip into a sleep hole, blinded by alcohol, he wakes screaming. Or with his nightshirt drenched after lying in an irrigation ditch for hours. And some nights, at the edge of doom, he wakes with his hands around Penny's throat. He flees to the bathroom. He trembles, even as water streams from the shower rose all around him, his hands over his ears to block out Penny's sobbing in the bedroom.

WHILE THE WATER runs in the shower she is safe. Whether true or not, it's what she tells herself. Something to sequester a little space, time.

She's plenty of things. Loyal, good-natured, diligent. But not naïve. Not after A&E, the years in the general wards, what she's read, socialising with James's soldier mates, especially in the younger years. She's seen suffering, bodies ravaged by disease, beaten, burned, left to rot. She's seen what horror can do, felt its breath, its touch. There's little she can't imagine. She can conceive of villages wiped out by plague, cities destroyed by cataclysm, prisoners tortured for secrets, genocides, holocausts. But she could never have conceived of her husband's hands around her throat, strangling her.

His hands? Did something get into them, poison them, take them over, some malevolent spell at work? The hands that could, just days ago, cautiously, lightly, shyly even, seek her out. What could possibly have happened to them since then? Or was it in Afghanistan they became possessed, some dormant evil waiting to be triggered when he arrived back home, perhaps even by something she'd said? If so, might those ugly hands be severed from him, leaving her with the rest of him?

The water stops. She tightens. The ensuite door opens. Who is it coming out of the bathroom now? The sudden thought that it may be worse, that he may have armed himself, some knife or razor, aiming now to finish her. She lurches towards the bedside lamp and fumbles for the switch, finds it, flicks it on.

It is only James. Slump-shouldered, old singlet and boxer shorts, broken, pathetic, contorted by doubt. Seeing her sitting on the side of the bed, he starts to sob. He comes to her, kneels on the floor before her, lays his head in her lap. Gasping his apologies, his fear. Penny swallows. She slowly lifts her hand from her side, undecided. He is heaving with weakness and shame. She lays her hand tentatively on his back. Touches his contrition, his fragility, his terror.

But after tonight, how is it possible for her ever to sleep again?

HE LIES AWAKE, still. He knows the body beside him is Penny's, but as he begins to drift, as the devils in his head rearrange his thoughts and memories, whatever soft and malleable stuff fills one's skull, it morphs into Beckett. The hours they shared their irrigation canal bed, the intermingling of their bodily fluids, a communion that cannot be unbroken.

'SLEEP,' PENNY SAYS, rejoining him in the bedroom, an act of courage after the previous night. However she might find him. She'd left the room at first light for her morning routine, her meditation on the back deck, but it couldn't free her from his hands at her neck, at having to kick out against him for breath.

'Sleep,' she says to him again as he lies contorted on his side, red-eyed, hollowed. 'You *must* get something better to help you sleep.'

With James beside her in the kitchen she rings her GP, almost a friend now, so well has she got to know her. Penny describes his condition with perfect brevity, nurse to doctor. She explains what she wants for her husband, sleeping pills, maybe something more. The doctor will understand what she means. While Penny could get them herself from the hospital, slipping drugs quietly from the dispensary, she wants someone to see him too, someone other than the army medicos.

'Thank you,' Penny says into the phone, meeting her husband's eyes, nodding with relief, handing him the receiver.

'Come on down,' the doctor says to him. 'I can fit you in now.'

But Penny can see James is already retreating, manoeuvring himself to flee. Or formulating another plan, in his mind more pressing.

'Thanks, Doc,' he replies, 'but today is no good. How about tomorrow?'

Penny groans, turns away in exasperation.

'Well ...' the doctor says slowly, deliberately. 'That's fine too. However, in my experience it is important to respond promptly to these things. You don't want them to get away from you—'

'I'm good, Doc,' Penny hears her husband say, cutting the doctor off. 'I'm good.'

IF THERE'S ONE thing he needs, one thing his desperate exhaustion has fixed onto, it's to find a way of crawling out of the shallow canal he is stuck in with Beckett. To somehow prise himself from Beckett's embrace.

Forced together, Phelan realises how little he knows about Beckett. Phelan wears his name, but understands nothing about the kid – the man – not really. And what he thought he knew is draining away. He reaches for them – the few biographical facts anyone could discover, the stories he'd overheard Beckett's mates telling in the days afterwards, what Phelan thinks are his own memories – but they shrivel.

What Phelan has gathered about his life aren't even points on a children's join-the-dots puzzle, let alone stars in a constellation, *Orion* or *Aries* or *The Shield of Achilles*. Not even a handful of binary coding markers from *Call of Duty*, not nearly enough to bring him to life.

His parents received him at Holsworthy, then took him straight home to the north coast, to Yamba, for a private burial. With what rites, Phelan wonders, was he laid to rest? He guesses there'll be a grave, though it's Beckett's parents he really wants to see, Beckett's family. To accept from them whatever they might be prepared to give him. He can but ask. If there's a curse, then release. Otherwise, absolution.

CHARLIE

PHELAN LEANS FORWARD and looks through the car window, across the road to the lowset pale brick house, one of thirty in an ocean-front street of what appears to be an uncomplicated coastal holiday town. Beckett's parents can't see the ocean from here, even though it is just the other side of the dunes, and constant. The wind and the salt have, he observes, got at the front door of the house, which peels in the long morning sun, and what was once a front lawn is now sand, the beach reclaiming its own.

When he turns the engine off, the ocean is loud and insistent. What are you doing here? it berates him; you know better. Or, what took you so long?

Heat gathers quickly in the car, and when he opens the door the sticky air rushes in and around him like liquid. He pushes through it, swings his legs out of the car and stands. His knees creak; fifty years and a four-hour car trip. He is tired and he is old. He can smell Melaleuca in the air, sweeter than perfume. Phelan walks across the bitumen and up the pebblecrete driveway, past the white letterbox on its single white post, standing like an egret. He'd decided against his uniform – he didn't want to meet them on those terms, not this time.

At the top of the steps Phelan turns briefly. They deserve a sea view, he thinks, something for their grief. He turns back and rings the bell and hears its electronic chime echo inside the house. Sweat gathers under his arms, on his back.

The door opens. He recognises Beckett's father, strong, muscular, fit. Probably still playing local football. He is younger than Phelan remembered from the Holsworthy tarmac almost a month ago, this dead boy's father who, in his early forties, is himself still young. Beckett's mother stands behind him, looking over his shoulder, but not hiding. A halo of fluorescent light glows above her dark hair. She is as old as mourning itself.

'Who are you?' the father demands.

So they don't recognise him. He is as insignificant as he fears.

'We met before. In Sydney. I was in uniform. My name is Brigadier James Phelan. I accompanied your son home.'

As Phelan fumbles through what to say and what not to, more people emerge from rooms inside the house, filling the hallway behind Beckett's parents, curious about the alien voice. What is this, Phelan wonders, a month-long wake?

'Come in, hey. Come in, James Phelan,' the father says eventually. 'There are things we want to ask you.'

Phelan follows them into the silent house, passing framed photos in the corridor, one of a blond mop-haired Beckett, sixteen or seventeen, salt-encrusted, grinning, the nose of a surfboard in view, a clean swell in the background. Phelan glances through the open door of a bedroom where posters of cricketers are tacked to the walls. No one speaks until they are seated in the lounge room, water jug and glasses placed on the sitting room table, four of them seated here: Phelan,

Beckett's mother and his father, and an older man, a grandfather, Phelan guesses. An outer ring of family members lean against the walls, or fill out the lounge seats, kids perched on the arms of chairs, or crawling in and out of laps.

Beckett's father clears his throat. 'Colonel?'

'Brigadier,' Phelan replies, before adding hurriedly, apologetically, 'but it doesn't matter.'

'Would it have mattered to our boy?'

'I'm sorry,' he says, 'I don't understand.'

From the ring of aunties and cousins, one interrupts. 'He deserved a fuckin' general. You hear? A five-fucking-star general!'

Beckett's father waves his hand at her.

'Eeeeee,' she whistles and stops.

Beckett's mother hasn't raised her face from her lap. The grandfather's eyes are dark and still, waiting.

'Brigadier, tell us this. What happened to our boy after he died? After the battlefield. Where did he go? What did you do with him? Where did he lie? For how long? Where was he when your chaplain knocked on our door? When that notification team of yours parked their car exactly where you have yours out there now, and woke us and told us he was gone? Where was our boy then, where was he at that moment?'

Phelan is hopelessly exhausted once again. He can't possibly give them what they need. Doesn't even know what they're asking. When he answers, he speaks more slowly than he's ever spoken before. Answering multiple questions. Maybe there'll be an answer somewhere in what he says.

'He was never alone. We ensure there is always someone with him. The army has protocols. We have ... ways of looking after our ... warriors' ... bodies ...'

There is murmuring behind him, not the wild woman this time, but a chorus of low voices.

Phelan tells them what he can about their protocols, the minutest detail. It is a map of sorts he tries to lay out. He wants them to see there was more than just respect in it, that there is sacredness as well, that the army is capable of that. That he is too.

'And then, when it was time to bring him back home, I ...' all their eyes are on him '... I accompanied him in the plane. And then, after the flight home, when we landed ...' What does he say now? That he handed Beckett back to his parents? That they'd entrusted their son to him and all he'd returned to them was his body? He nearly does. Nearly slumps and says it, mea culpa, mea culpa, mea culpa, nearly beats his chest and nearly asks forgiveness.

Beckett's father grunts. 'And before that?' he asks. 'When he died. What then? What did you see? What did he say?'

The last words test. So much hangs on it, too much. The need those of us who are left have for wisdom, for reassurance of uniqueness, hope. But who among us could bear our entire life being distilled into one final utterance? This is not an examination Phelan needs to pass for himself. It's for Beckett he mustn't fail. He searches the room for clues on how to respond, a crucifix or a laughing Buddha or a totemic painting, but there is nothing to help him and he regrets breaking the man's stare.

'How did he die?' Mr Beckett asks.

Phelan wavers before the enormity of the question. Beckett's parents already know what happened. The army has briefed them. He looks up at the ceiling to think. Because there is falsity and there is duty, and before him is a young soldier's family, and Phelan's weakness is not their burden. 'I saw ...' he says, looking into the father's face again, '... I saw your son quietly close his eyes. The pain had passed. He was calm. I don't know where he went then ... you'll know that better than me. But in that moment I saw a warrior who was loved by his fellow soldiers. I saw a warrior who was a better man than me ... me who should have been his leader.'

There, he's said it. And it's true.

'Is that all?'

Phelan wants to groan, can't think of anything more, but understands what he's given so far isn't enough. What else? He gropes around for some harmless detail, no matter how small.

'He called me Charlie.'

Beckett's mother lifts her head.

'That's not my name, but that's what he said, "Goodbye Charlie". I had a sense ... I had a sense it wasn't me he was farewelling, but maybe all of us. Maybe in that moment, we were "Charlie".'

'Eeeee,' the aunt in the back keens, as the room begins to murmur and click and whistle, a collective acknowledgement of some truth beyond Phelan.

The mother starts to softly weep. The father places his gentle hand on her arm, and the room quietens again for Mrs Beckett and her weeping. Phelan averts his eyes. After a long time, the father turns back to Phelan.

'My wife's name is Charlotte. Our son called her Charlie.'

ON THE WAY back to Brisbane Phelan pulls over on the highway, the traffic streaming past, and staggers into the bush. A burst of startled galahs takes to the air and Phelan drops to his knees, retching.

MADE, NOT BORN

THE NEXT DAY Phelan turns on the cricket, a different sedative. He watches it, vaguely, for Beckett, looking for the players whose images he'd glimpsed adorning Beckett's bedroom walls. Some possibility of fellowship. On the screen batsmen bat, bowlers bowl, cricketers' cricket. Little human figures shrouded in white positioning and repositioning themselves against a green background, running in, then running out again.

If there's a narrative unfolding out there on the field, it's lost to him. This game he'd once understood so well has now moved beyond his grasp. It's hard to keep hold of anything – Beckett, what happened at Chora, the shape of his wife. He's got the interview to do, when? Next week in Sydney? He can't put it off again. But what has he got to say? What can he remember?

Between overs the same television advertisement repeats, an armed forces recruitment drive. Again and again and again the army asks him whether leaders are born or made. Phelan squirms. He could lie down. He could sleep. But the advertisement is insistent, drilling into him. Born or made?

'Made,' he answers finally. *'Made!'* Yelling it at the television. Lurching back to his old faith, his army family's creed. How good he suddenly feels. The recommitment is invigorating. Empowering. We make ourselves, he says to himself, regaining strength. It's how we respond to circumstance that counts, an eternal truth. The surge of power he feels just by acknowledging this truth, resubmitting to it, renewing his commitment. So simple a thing!

He looks at himself in the hallway mirror. He clenches his jaw and grits his teeth until the muscles in his neck tighten and the veins in his temples pulsate. His red face. All his vitality. He lets out his breath, drops to the floor, and commences his push-ups, driving away from the floorboards again and again. I have made this fifty-push-ups-a-day body, he thinks. I must ready myself to return. A medical examination to pass, an interview about Beckett's death to get through, then a flight back to Kabul and a command to resume. The confidence in him is feverish. Today I will shrug off the shallow breathing and the racing heart. I will ignore Beckett's insistent voice. I make myself. I lead. I am stronger than I have ever been.

The doorbell rings but Phelan refuses to be interrupted. Forty-six, forty-seven, forty-eight. He pushes his body, fierce as a zealot. I have not yet finished making myself, he thinks, whoever it is can wait. Phelan is rising to his feet when it rings again. He sucks in six breaths, each deeper than the last, steadying himself. At the third ring he calls out down the corridor, 'Coming!'

When he opens the door it is to a tall man he does not know. Though dressed in polo shirt and trousers, Phelan recognises him for what he is behind the dark sunglasses and the thick beard: an ex-soldier. He has grown his hair long, but his shoes gleam and his body is tight. He smells of fresh battle, the hunger for it. Recently discharged, probably now a private security contractor.

The man salutes, slackly, contemptuously – that old gesture from the vast wordless language of insubordination.

Phelan's resolve of just moments earlier, his mad certainty, flounders. Instinctively, unthinkingly, he braces up – the conventional response of the officer in civvies to a soldier's salute – his arms straightening by his side. Phelan looks past the man as he does so, trying to assess whether the man is alone. Behind him, stretching to the horizons north and east and south, the city goes about its business.

'Who are you?' Phelan demands.

'A messenger.' The man almost adds, 'Sir', but swallows it.

Phelan sees the struggle the man wages with the word, the little battle with himself, then the victory. Sees the stranger in front of him grow more powerful.

'Lieutenant Gruen wants you to have this,' the man says, and only now does Phelan see the envelope in his hand.

Phelan's gut tightens.

'But Lieutenant Gruen is in Tarin Kot.' He can't hide his surprise, feels himself slipping.

The messenger smiles. Or sneers. 'Yes. Where he should be. Keeping his men out of harm's way as best he can. Protecting them from hypocritical jokes like you.'

Phelan's heart pounds. He stands mute for long moments, at a loss.

'Lieutenant Gruen asked you to give me this?' he croaks eventually, his voice broken.

'Let's just say he wants you to have it. So you know what sort of train is coming down the track at you.' The man holds the envelope out but Phelan does not yet take it.

'What is it?'

The man laughs scornfully. 'What are you afraid of, Brigadier?'

'Who are you?' Phelan asks again. 'How do you know Gruen?'

The man just shakes his head. 'I'll let you in on a little secret,' he says, leaning closer, conspiratorially, as if about to raise his sunglasses to reveal his eyes, as if whatever he says next will be delivered in a whisper. But when it comes, it's a snarl. 'You're fucked,' he says. 'Accept it.'

'Get off my property!' Phelan finally shouts, his voice shaking. 'Get off. Now!'

When the man laughs again, Phelan knows it is at his desperation, his helplessness, knows he has nothing, is nothing. Knows there is nothing he can do to try and keep this out, his destiny.

The man tosses the envelope at Phelan's feet. 'Fucking pervert,' he spits.

FREEDOM

WHEN PENNY ARRIVES, her husband's yell echoing in her head, she sees the envelope on the floorboards, the open doorway and Phelan shaking on the threshold. She pushes past him, and when she finds no one on the landing, she leaps the stairs and runs down the path to the gate. But there is nothing. She goes out onto the street, and darts to the top of the local Jacob's Ladder, the long public staircase that falls down the western side of the hill to Newmarket train station. If there is someone at the end of the stairs, far away, they are a shadow now. She returns to the house, panting as she catches her breath. Phelan hasn't moved, frozen like Lot's Wife before some terrible prophecy.

She picks up the envelope, slips a finger under the flap and tears it open. The three images inside are freshly printed, carrying the smell of ink, and the paper is photographic quality, not merely A4. But what they're of she can't at first make out. She rotates the images in her hands, trying to orientate herself, leafing from one to the next and back again. They're from the same series, she can tell that, and it's dark wherever they are, though not yet night, not black. There are no faces, just bodies, shot close, as if in error. She selects one image and looks hard, trying to decipher it. She sees a belt, fatigues, a forearm with its hand disappearing into the dark folds of battle dress, nothing clear. Yes, she thinks, a camera has gone off prematurely and this is its digital detritus. But then, what does it have to do with James?

Penny looks at the second image. Her eyes are becoming accustomed to the darkness on the paper, the shifts in the positioning of the limbs. The creases in the fatigues show her it's a thigh she sees, submerged in dark water, a soldier's hips, the belt unbuckled, splayed, a muddy arm and hand suspended, masking tape around the wedding finger so the band won't catch, but the angle an oddity, as if belonging to a different body from the waist and groin and legs in the shallow irrigation canal.

Suddenly she understands where she is, whose arm, whose hand, whose taped ring, what part of it is her husband and what part Beckett, suspecting his shame runs deeper than merely pissing himself in battle. Trembling, she turns to the third image: her husband with a water bottle to his lips, looking directly at the camera, directly at her, the furtiveness in his eye wholly unfamiliar to her.

• • •

IT'S TAKEN WHISKEY to loosen him, but what shape he's collapsing into Penny doesn't know. She gently tries to pry facts out of him, but he is mute, smiling blindly back at her where she's moved him out on the back deck.

'How long were you there with him? What did Sapper Beckett say to you? What did you talk about? What's happening here, in this image. When did he die? How do you know? Is that your water or his? Why can't you remember?' But she knows the last question is unfair.

The bottle of scotch between them catches the afternoon's rays. He pours another glass, and holds the bottle up to Penny, offering to pour her one.

'Jesus, James,' she says, shaking her head in exasperation.

'It's true, Pen. I'm fucked.'

His first words.

At least *she* is trying to work it out, even if he can't. The three photos are frames from Beckett's helmet cam, she guesses that much. So everything has been captured, everything Beckett saw, even after he died: the river crossing, the hit, James joining him, all their time together in the trench, the camera continuing to film her husband as he lies with Beckett's body.

It won't be as it appears. It can't be. Whatever James is doing, there'll be an explanation. 'Talk to me, James,' she says again, but he is dumb.

He'll be assessing Beckett's wounds. Or making him more comfortable. Or tending him. There'll be a reason.

What is the protocol around patrol footage? she asks him. Who would have seen it? How many people? Where is it stored? For how long? But Phelan shakes his head, giggling foolishly, unable to remember, if ever he knew.

'Charlie,' Phelan murmurs softly, 'my cock, my nuts. Are they still there?'

Penny looks up from her phone, about to dial Bec. 'What was that, James?' she asks.

'It's all right, mate, you'll be okay,' he whispers to himself.

'Yes,' Penny says. 'It'll be all right, James. It'll be all right.'

'I want you to check, Charlie,' Phelan says.

'It's me, Love. It's Penny.'

Events are running away from her, whatever the hell is actually happening. Phelan collapsing, a campaign of some sort being mounted against him. Against *them*. They've got to get ahead of it, whoever's agenda, whatever campaign. She's got to understand it, find a way to push back, to somehow quench it before it becomes an inferno no one can stop.

'Bec,' she says into the phone, 'it's serious. I don't know what to do.'

'Come,' her friend says.

Before Penny leaves she looks at him sitting on the back steps, his head fallen, resting awkwardly on a timber post, a stiffening breeze lifting the collar of his shirt and pressing it against his neck.

'James,' she says, coming to him, her hand on his shoulder, 'I'm going to Bec's for an hour.'

He doesn't move, doesn't respond. She could stay with him, she could. But there's no time to lose. From the linen cupboard she brings out a silk sheet, wraps it around his shoulders, kisses him.

'An hour,' she says. 'Do you hear me?'

THE WIND PICKS up. A thin branch from the Cadagi snaps and falls to the ground, and Phelan stirs. For a long time he looks out at the gathering western dark, listening to the voices in the wind. When he finally rises he is purposeful. He finds the envelope where Penny left it in the kitchen and returns to the back steps with it, and another bottle of Dewar's. He slugs at the whiskey. The house is dark. Phelan fortifies himself in the moonlight.

The silhouette of the giant Norfolk pine glows strangely in the back of the property, dwarfing him, the house, everything. How the tree sways in the wind. How it strains and whispers. How it bends and does not break. He thinks about the family who had the place before them and how they used to string Christmas lights up the tree every year, the sixty-year-old woman climbing its branches to the very top where she'd fix a great white star, visible for miles.

He takes another slug, but when he goes to put the bottle down he misjudges and it hits the wooden step hard, bounces from his grasp and clatters onto the brick paving. As the liquor bleeds out, filling the channel between two bricks, Phelan lunges towards the bottle but trips and falls drunkenly down the stairs himself. His heart pounds as he sits on his arse on the hard ground. He finds the bottle and grips it fiercely in his hand, grips it till his knuckles begin to ache. He hears magpies quarrelling out in the night, or believes he does, and thinks he sees movement in the pine as it bends and glows in the beautiful moonlight, the stars appearing and disappearing between its wind-whipped branches.

He suddenly remembers the envelope and the photos and Beckett tells him it doesn't need to be like this. His knees creak as he rises from where he fell, or is that the Norfolk pine shifting in the wind?

He searches for matches in the pantry, feels for them in the dark, before returning to the deck. He squats before the barbecue and turns the wheel of the gas bottle, then the knobs on the burners, one two three. The gas hisses. But what does it say? He doesn't light it immediately. The gas is cold and smooth against his cheek, surprisingly pleasant. He strains to hear the message in its rushing. Only when he coughs and then gags, does he remember what he needs to do, and he strikes the match and there is a great whoosh of flame. Some part of him burns – the hair on his hands or his eyebrows or the back of his neck. *Pah!*

He turns the gas up until there are three rushing flames, each pushed sideways by the wind, three tongues leaning in unison, reaching forward, then flicking back, before leaning again, his little dancing fires. He reaches for the envelope and, listening hard, takes out the photos and tosses them onto the flames, one by one, watches them catch and burn. He nods his head, good, then adds the envelope and it too goes up.

But the flames are hungry and so is he. Phelan hurries inside, Beckett no longer directing him now, and into his office. When he returns it is with two boxes in his arms. He lays them beside the barbecue and goes back inside for another load, backwards and forwards, load after load, photos and certificates and letters and manuals. Uniforms and framed degrees. Histories and commentaries.

Phelan feeds them to the flames, piling them, creating a stack, tipping the boxes upside down, nearly smothering the flames. But this is not a night for suffocating, and his teetering pyre takes, and then burns, a great flame rising to the rafters above the covered deck, licking at them. He steps away, driven back by the heat, driven off the deck and down the steps and onto the back lawn where he stands and watches. The embers begin to swirl, flying from the deck into the house itself. Fireworks in the pond. Pages from his military memoirs shriek and catch and blow. The wind is howling now, the fire is howling, his blood is surging, yelping and singing.

He feels water at his ankles and looks down, startled. The water is too dark to see, too cold, but he knows he is in an endless irrigation ditch and feels it sloshing around his feet, rising. It would pull him under. He carries a garden chair to the base of the Norfolk pine, and steps up, reaching for the low branch and swinging his legs up till he stands there, part of the tree, and he climbs, branch by branch, away from the dank water, the drowning ditch.

He is birdman, he is possum, he is ancient cat. Higher he climbs, higher and higher, and when he can climb no further he sits and hugs the trunk, safe from the rising tides, the city and this burning house singing up to him, a lullaby to freedom.

PART THREE

BLINDFOLDED

Great Dividing Range, February 2016

THE BLINDOFLD HURTS. He shifts in his seat and stretches his stiffening neck, twisting one way, then the other. Neither of them has spoken for a long time, but it is not quiet and he is not worried – he's had the car's engine as company, the constant rumbling of tyres on road, the steady breathing of the Border Collie at his feet, and he is getting better at controlling the anxiety when it comes. If the blindfold hadn't begun to hurt he'd be almost content.

She stops at a fork in the road. Phelan's dog raises its head then clambers onto his lap to see where they are, and Phelan reaches involuntarily for the knot at the back of his head. He's been blindfolded since Brisbane, two hours.

'Not yet!' Penny says. 'It's not far now. It'll be worth it when we get there, James. Trust me.'

Phelan inhales quickly, his nostrils flaring like those of his snorting boyhood ponies, before releasing the spent air through his teeth, hissing it. Yes, he thinks, it's not far to go at all.

'Left,' he says to her. 'Take the left fork, Pen.'

'All right,' she says, humouring him. 'It's fifty-fifty, and you could be right.'

But he's not guessing.

Penny pulls the car to the left and takes the graded road as it follows the northern side of the ridge. The dog yelps excitedly and Phelan keeps the window down, his head cocked. The sound of the tyres on the corrugations is regular, soothing. He knows Penny will be concentrating, scrutinising the country on either side for markers, trying to make sense of the directions she's been given, desperate not to miss the final turn-off.

Phelan is awash in memory. There will be barbed-wire fences accompanying them on either side of the road, the long fence line broken intermittently by timber gates. They will pass a dam in a hollow to the north, its shrinking eye of water dark brown in the midday sun. Further along, on the southern side of the road, he remembers where a farmer used to park his tractor beneath a giant Moreton Bay Fig. He imagines the farmer – older now – sitting beside his tractor, his back leaning against the fig's trunk, his thermos beside him, inspecting them as they pass by. The road rises gradually as it skirts the northern side of a hill. They pass through the mottled shade of a corridor of gums before the road descends, a little more steeply, to the foot of the next hill.

'Twin children were murdered by their mother on one of these properties,' Phelan says, turning his blindfolded face to her, before leaning back out the window.

'So you think you've worked it out?'

He doesn't reply, says instead, 'On the right-hand side, somewhere around here, there used to be a potter's workshop.'

Phelan feels the car slow. Waits. Penny reads aloud the name of the studio from the slab of ironbark hanging near the gate. 'Members of the Public Welcome. No Appointments Necessary', she finishes. 'Well then, congratulations. You may as well take off the blindfold.'

'Not yet,' he replies. 'It's not too far now. On the left, we should come to stockyards.' He pauses. 'It's amazing,' he says, shaking his head to himself. 'Nothing has changed.'

• • •

But everything has changed.

She used to count her losses. A breast, a house, a husband – the husband she once had anyway – his career, their life. Everything.

There has been so much time for counting losses, so much waiting, thinking. For doctors, for medication to take effect, in hospital wards waiting for him to wake. Or sleep. He'd sit in front of the television at one of their rented houses, and she'd wait for his leg to stop shaking before placing a tray of food in his lap. Or she'd wait until some rage that had come over him blew itself out. Slow her own walking pace to his after forcing him out of the house for fresh air and exercise. Waiting for the clock to run down on a shift at work, sometimes because she was anxious to get home to him, others because she couldn't bear the shift to end.

For a long time, in conversation with friends or even people she'd just met, she'd talk about 'before the fire' and 'after the fire', a way of making sense of what was happening to her. Then, after a year or two, more brutally, more honestly, nothing left to protect, she changed it to, 'Before James's breakdown' and 'Since his breakdown'. Even on her good days, upbeat as she could be, the formula of words was freighted with resignation. On bad days, despair.

It was Bec who suggested rebuilding her library. 'It's something the girls want to do for you Penny Love. You just write out the list and then leave it to us!'

Bec bought her a notebook for the task. Partly, of course, it was a project to distract her. Dear Bec, darling Bec.

And it did for a while. She conjured an image of the library in her mind. So much of it was startlingly clear. She could walk along its length in her memory, picturing the spines of the books – the text of the titles, those with designs that wrapped from the front cover around the spine to the back, the undulations in size, the way some books rested snugly against their neighbours while others seemed to lean away. Instinctively she knew the task of cataloguing her collection was not one to rush, and that she'd need to linger over the exercise. She divided the notebook into sections, headings under which she'd record the titles. Years, with sub-headings beneath marking out the events of her life.

The simple act of writing out the name of a title in her notebook was enjoyable, a little moment of careful creation – or recreation – when her swirl of recollection became even more tangible and fell into order. The year her book club read nothing but titles with women's names, *Madame Bovary* and *Anna Karenina* and *Carrie*, their various tastes, the pleasure of listing them now. She smiles when she recalls their argument over whether the titularly anonymous *The French Lieutenant's Woman* counted. But greater than that enjoyment was what remembering gave and how it allowed you to disappear into other times, transport you to other places. Doubly transported, she thinks – first to the time of reading, then to wherever her memory of the book delivered her. Provincial France, St Petersburg. As far from life after the fire, after James's breakdown, as she could get.

Yet there were books she'd forgotten, or seemed to have. In her mind's library she could see the gap on the shelf. It was almost as if someone had taken the unremembered book from its home and not yet returned it. She'd wrack her memory, searching for triggers – dates, events – retrieving her experience of reading the books either side of the forgotten title, trying to step back into a feeling she might have had while starting the next book, attempting to detect an echo of the missing volume. The time she alternated between George Johnston and Charmian Clift, *My Brother Jack* followed by Clift's *Mermaid Singing* then *Clean Straw for Nothing* and *Peel Me a Lotus*. But the third of Johnston's trilogy won't come to her. She writes down the Clift she read next, *Honour's Mimic*, but for the life of her Johnston has disappeared.

'How's that list going?' Bec would ask.

'Getting there,' Penny would reply. 'Getting there.'

Occasionally she could prompt her way back to a lost book. But often, no matter what she tried, she couldn't retrieve it. At least not immediately. Because that's not how time and memory work. Sometimes a missing title would return to her as she lay in bed, sometimes in the shower, sometimes triggered by a word she read in a magazine or a patient's history – nursing a blind man bringing *Oedipus Rex* back to mind, that sort of thing – and she'd reach for the notebook, and jot it down lest it disappear again.

As upsetting as it was when she was unable to fill a gap in the shelves of her memory, more distressing was realising there were books whose existence she'd forgotten entirely. Books that didn't even occupy an empty space in her mind's library, books that had no relationship with the ones before or after, books that had completely disappeared. Of course, she was only aware of this forgetting when one of them suddenly returned to her, unbidden. It was like she'd been struck. Oh, no! Oh, no! Even then – the book revealed, the unreliability of her memory exposed – she often still couldn't put it into its proper place, couldn't remember whether it was a birthday gift or read for the book club. It unsettled her that an order she thought existed, didn't.

How many more such books are there? she thought, how many more she'd never remember? Surely, in the months after her diagnosis, she'd read more than just the three cancer memoirs she's written into her notebook. Had her own experience of the disease wiped all the others out? So the list stalled, and, ultimately, remained unfinished. Why recall a past if it's doomed to be incomplete, false? Why continue a futile quest? Start again, she thinks, better just to start again, start from here.

'That's crazy, Penny Love,' Bec said.

'I'm sorry, Bec. The library was such a lovely idea. Please, don't be disappointed.'

'Well come on then,' Bec said, rising from the café table they were sitting at, taking both their bags.

'Where?'

'If you want to start afresh, then let's start.'

In the bookshop, Bec says, 'Just one, Penny. Start with one. Just start. Now.'

'You choose, Bec.'

'No, Love. You can do it.'

Penny looks around her, the shelves overfull with books jostling against one another, competing for her attention. But it is silence she seeks. Just as she is about to back away it comes to her that a gardening guide is what she needs, and Oakman's *Tropical and Subtropical Gardening* is the nearest to her reach.

He is growing impatient now. The sun-bleached railings of the cattle yards must be just ahead, partially camouflaged in the shadows cast by the canopies of two stately gums. Pale grass will be growing high around the outside of the yards.

Sure enough, Penny says, 'Stockyards ahoy.'

'The turn-off is to the left,' Phelan confidently replies, 'immediately after the yards. It's a hard left.'

As he feels the car slow and swing north around the stockyards he remembers discovering a wallaby trapped inside the race, and how it had thrashed against the rails, staggering and leaping and crashing its shoulders in great resounding thuds against the timber. He'd tried to comfort the poor creature, but it had misunderstood, and as he neared threw itself against the yards even more violently. How close they'd been, a mere railing between them. Its frothing mouth, its bleeding ear, the way it had looked at him, the terror in its eyes before eventually finding the gate they'd opened for it.

'We're on a spur now,' he says, as if she is the blind one. 'We're almost there.'

The track deteriorates. Deep corrugations slash diagonally across the roadway where rains or heavy vehicles have worried away the earth. Fallen branches and dry leaf litter fill the crude earthen gutters on either side. They follow the spur north as it rises to a crest up ahead.

'When we get to the top of the ridge,' Phelan says, 'can we stop?'

Penny pulls over as the ridge levels off. Before them the spur falls away and widens into a plateau.

'Wow,' she says, 'wow.'

Phelan lets himself go now. His fingers struggle furiously to untie the knot behind his head, and when finally he manages it, he tears the cloth off and throws it to the floor. The light, after his blind hours, is staggeringly bright, needle-sharp against his eyes. He groans and shades them with his hands and blinks wildly, but still it hurts. Penny takes his sunglasses from the glovebox and hands them to him. He opens the door for the dog, and after composing himself, climbs out and stands looking ahead to the view at the end of the road. It catches in his gut.

To the north and east the plateau falls away over a steep escarpment which is nothing less than the rim of the Great Dividing Range itself, beyond which sky and air and the floors of wide valleys sweep towards the sea 150 kilometres away. On the western edge of the plateau a series of gullies cut into the earth, dropping in ragged terraces before falling out of view into a deeply shaded ravine. On the other side of the ravine is another spur, running parallel to theirs, and beyond that is another, bony fingers of stony earth clawing at the surface of the planet.

Closer, right in front of them, at the end of the road's final downhill stretch, Phelan sees the roofline of the 'Big House' of his childhood, the high pitch and the long sheets of corrugated iron and the three chimneys, the house itself obscured by the row of pencil pines on the garden boundary, shielding it from the southerlies.

Then, nearer still, he sees the cottage, a satellite of the house, high on its stilts. Though smaller than he remembered, it's exactly where it should be, set off to the right of where they're now standing, its water tank nearly as big as the house, and still green, still peeling. The simple pitch of its roof, its single chimney, the same chain-mail fence marking out the same arbitrary yard. Beyond it the cliffs of the escarpment are as close to the cottage as they ever were, a boy's crude homemade arrow's flight away.

'I'll walk the rest,' Phelan says to her, and without waiting for an answer sets off down the hill, his dog at his side.

PENNY WATCHES HIM hurrying down the track, as if he is drawn by a new gravity. She follows in the car, idling slowly down the slope, afraid that even the sound of the motor might destroy the moment. Anxious that if she did something to spoil it – and sometimes the smallest things have unimaginable impacts – then everything they've been working to rebuild might unravel again. A foolish thought, she knows, a debilitatingly high standard, but sometimes, even after all this time, she can't help it.

What she wouldn't give to wind things back to the moment James had slumped on the back deck the afternoon of the fire. *An hour*, she'd said to him, thinking that's all the time she'd need away, that he'd sleep the drink off, that what was more important at that moment was war-gaming with Bec a way to save her husband's reputation, his career, the life they knew. But what if, instead of leaving him, she'd stayed? How overwhelming the thought. If, if, if. And the question overshadowing all those what-ifs: how much was it *her* reputation as Brigadier Phelan's wife she was also protecting? Her life?

Regret is now something she and James share. Though not with each other. Because our regrets are, after all, wholly our own.

AS PHELAN APPROACHES the house his gait slows, and he stops, disconcerted, looking around, his bearings snatched suddenly away from him.

'What is it, Darling?' Penny asks, pulling up beside him.

He comes to her, unsteady, holding on to the top of the car door. Something's wrong.

It's not that the Big House has been let go, nor that its garden, once immaculate, is now a ramble of trees and bushes and surrendered flowerbeds. As a kid he was drawn to the wilder corners of the garden anyway. No, it's something else. He turns, taking in the slack fence line, and the crumbling piggery between the Big House and the cottage, and the nearby machinery shed, half-concealed by an insurgent passionfruit vine. The buildings and all the beautiful ruins are, in the geometry of his memory, precisely where they should be.

He looks up. The clouds are high, the sky beyond them almost purple. Two wedge-tailed eagles rise on a thermal, the birds opposite each other in the column of updraft, the solitude of each counterbalancing the other's perfectly as they spiral slowly upwards.

It's only then, his head tilted, that he notices the row of bunya pines set back on the western side of the road, and realises what is troubling him. His father had planted six, one for each of them, his parents and their four kids. But now, fifty years on, only three remain. They are wide-girthed and towering, each topped with great conical crowns. Of the disappeared, one has gone without trace, another is a stump cut too low to the ground to fashion even a seat, while the third is black and charred and broken, lightning-struck, Phelan guesses, two or three storm seasons ago. That's the problem with grand gestures, he thinks, with projecting emblematic meaning onto things. His parents are gone, yes, so that accounts for two of the trees, but only two.

Phelan lowers himself to the ground. He begins what he has been taught to do when he feels his skin begin to prickle, when his heart starts racing. When his irrational anxiety comes on. He breathes. He counts and breathes, counts and breathes, talks to himself, uses the words he's been given to turn himself around, mantras. After having come so far, he says to himself as it passes, I refuse to see myself as lightning-struck.

THE BIG HOUSE

IN LESS THAN two months, an early Easter behind them, they move in. They arrive mid-morning in their new Hilux, a practical vehicle they can use for farm chores as well as for Penny to drive to her work at the hospital. They have their most precious things with them in the cab – the jewellery she was wearing on the night of the fire and the few pieces they salvaged from the ashes of the bedroom, her uniforms, his weights, their laptops, his medication, the electric hot water jug and some mugs, the portrait of the Queen he's carried with him since recovery, some potted plants, the dog, his notebooks, Penny's gardening manuals. Everything else will come later, with the removalists – the furniture and the clothes, the kitchenware, the whitegoods, everything replaced by insurance and lugged from rental to rental till they rested for a few years in a suburban low-set and its garden.

Penny puts on the jug, and before she's had a chance to properly open the house up – the doors and windows stiff from being locked up for so long – the water has boiled and she returns to the kitchen to make a pot of tea for both of them. It is autumn. They walk down the long central corridor that runs from the kitchen at the back of the house all the way to the front verandah and the great bull-nosed roof above, Phelan leading the way.

'Imagine a runner along here,' Penny says, a few paces behind him.

But Phelan isn't there. He's remembering instead how for a week in mid-summer the corridor is perfectly aligned with the sun's path, and how its dawn rays stream right through the house as far as the kitchen, and then, if the back door is open, through it too and out into the fernery.

They step onto the sun-bleached verandah boards. The sun has already risen above the roofline and the verandah is in shade. Phelan and Penny sit together on the still-warm floorboards, their legs hanging off the edge of the verandah, not quite touching the ground. Phelan pulls the knuckles of his left hand, one after the other, settling himself. They look out to the east and the unimpeded view to the edge of the escarpment, and beyond that, sky and space. The dog is already out there exploring, nosing the earth. Phelan and Penny sit and rock their bodies gently and sip their tea, neither of them needing to talk, their shoulders touching.

FOR A WHILE, when she brought him home after his first stay in the Keith Payne Unit at the Greenslopes war veterans hospital, she took him to Mass with her, a practice she'd returned to in the first weeks after her diagnosis. It had to be the evening vigil because he was seldom up and moving for the Sunday morning service. Looking back of course, what she was hoping for was nothing short of a miracle. Not the laying of hands variety – she's too Catholic for that – more that the ritual itself might be transformative. That if he was open to the ancient rhythms of the Mass and allowed their verities to wash over and in and through him, that it would change him. Yes, heal him. That *she'd* never experienced the Mass in that way didn't matter. Because it's at our most vulnerable we're most open to change. She believes that. And, perhaps, it's also when we're most hopeful. At worst, the service would be one more stable thing he could build on.

He accompanied her for a couple of months, but as the days lengthened towards summer and it stayed lighter longer, he grew increasingly agitated inside the church building. On the final occasion he rose abruptly midway through the service and left her in the pews, walking deliberately down the centre aisle, his tired back to the altar, to sit on the church steps and look out at the setting sun. It seemed to her then, twisting her neck to check on him, that if there was a pattern in things he might hold on to, it was out there, in the dusk.

But she kept going. For a while anyway. Give me strength, she prayed, give me strength.

'WHEN IT'S ALL over I want to come back here,' he'd said years ago, before the fire, before the breakdown. By which she understood he'd meant his army career. 'Run a few head of cattle. Write the obligatory memoir. Keep a place the grandchildren can visit.'

'Maybe,' the young wife had replied back then, because it was far too early to commit and once she committed to something she tended to stick to it, 'maybe'. Though even then the idea of living on a farm thrilled her. She was the daughter of teachers, hers a childhood of evening board games, weekends of church and sport, camping holidays by the beach and pets – dogs, a bowl of goldfish, the budgerigars her father bred, the baby possum she nursed after its mother was struck by a car in front of their house. Later, with James, her gardens were tidy, but not overly manicured. She was both more practical and more romantic. She grew herbs and vegetables. She was delighted to find a small chook run in one of their first army houses, and loved the routine of gathering eggs in the morning and giving them to friends as gifts. But she'd also leave corners of her backyards untended so they could take their own shape, to thicken with vines or overhanging branches.

There were no grandkids of course, and his army career vanished soon enough, disappearing between one psychiatrist and the next. But even after the army granted him the pension they still had to wait: delayed by the stints in recovery – each supposed to be the last – the changes in medication, the loss of colleagues, the advent of new friends, damaged or dangerous. The remorseless descent through all the circles of hell.

She tried to find time to garden, to step away from her responsibilities as carer and hospital nurse so she could kneel in the earth and plant, wherever that giddying descent from trial to trial might end. She planted herbs and vegetables with properties to calm the mind: Swiss chard and cherry tomatoes and sunflower seeds. Oregano and St James's Wort. Herbs for the spirit, for herself as much as her husband. She read somewhere that a day in the garden was worth its weight in Valium. She tried to get James to join her, but he couldn't stick, the odd mown lawn or load of bark chips spread at her direction, that's all. A disappointment but there you go. So, soil for her fingers, earth for her hands. Gardening therapy. Prayer gave her strength, yes, but gardening was her salvation.

He might have wanted to retire here. She hopes it'll be the place he finally heals.

Though she has dreams for herself too, after so many hard years. Dreams of a great unbounded garden, sky-watered. She wants to wade through late afternoon grass until she reaches the horizon. She wants to see a cloud of butterflies. Watch meteor showers from her bedroom window. She wants to smell a paddock-birth and make marmalade from home-grown oranges and follow native bees to their hive. She dreams of seasons, up here on this plateau on the range, that the subtropical city on the river could never offer, could never understand. Where winter, as well as summer, was capable of killing. She has never swung an axe. She wants to split wood and feed it into a fire. She wants to come home from an antiseptically cleaned ward to a house that will keep them company, she and James, grow with them, teach them.

It's got to be a good sign it's happened so quickly. That after seven years of unrelenting labour, a route through the universe has opened up, the two of them now just strolling through. A mere two months from her first call to a local real estate agent – 'No, it's not on the market, but I'll make enquiries' – to settlement. The nodding approval of James's psychiatrist, Brisbane not too far to come back to for consultations. Her husband also accepting her one condition – though he will be the farmer, though it will be him who puts down crippled beasts and culls dingos – *she* will be the one with the keys to the gun cabinet. Finally, the ease with which she'd been able to transfer from the Royal Brisbane Hospital to Toowoomba Base.

Surely fate wouldn't be so cruel, so capricious, that it'd lead them here if this wasn't where they should be?

IN THE AFTERNOON he tells her about his history in the house, looking for evidence like an archaeologist might, excavating on his hands and knees. He finds layers of paint from his childhood, messages his sisters inked on the walls beside their beds, the puttied hole where a hook on the back of a door held a cow's skull. He finds, too, the cuts in the VJs where he'd lain in bed tossing his Bowie knife across the room, night after night till he learned how to get the point to shudder and stick every time.

PHELAN HANGS THE Queen on the back of the old kitchen door. So she'll look upon them while they eat, so she's visible from all the way down the corridor.

She also hangs in the common room of the Keith Payne Unit, where she's been since her silver jubilee year when a group of inpatients painstakingly assembled her – all one-thousand pieces – and, once completed, set her jig-sawed portrait behind its glass and walnut frame and ceremoniously hung her above the billiards table. And there she has endured, down generations of veterans from Vietnam to East Timor and Iraq and Afghanistan.

Each day of his stay she smiled kindly down at him in her pure white dress, and her diamond crown and neck piece, Her brooches, the wide azure sash draped across her breast. 'Not royal blue,' he'd explain to any nurse who cared to listen, a meaningless term, 'but azure'. There's no judgement in her kind eyes, no counting his failures. And if he was responsible for Beckett, she seemed to accept that too, as she accepts all things always, and in her heavenly way comforts him that there's really nothing to fear.

She soothed him daily when he was in the unit. When some stupid old bastard from Vietnam had the volume on *Apocalypse Now* up too high, she intervened with her benevolent smile. Let it go, she counselled. After seven days without alcohol and then eight and then nine and when the nurses on pill parade were lousy with their Seroquel, she was there. When Penny didn't answer her phone, *her* presence at least was calming. When Phelan surveyed the spines of the books in the Unit library – his head askew, the Seroquel demanding it – and spied one with the name *Haroun* in its title and he began to sweat, irrationally, she was there. When he stopped at the whiteboard and read the week's activities, and saw crosswords again and despaired at what he'd sunk to, fucking crosswords. The cafeteria that had to be endured, Phelan trapped between bodies in the queue, the scraping chairs, the clattering cutlery, the trays dropped to the ground, the dishwasher's two-and-a-half-minute cycle, the hundred competing bullshit conversations, the whole fucking entirety of that angry chaos. She was dependable in a crisis. Then, when it was his turn to introduce himself at the group sessions and he was going over the words in his brain before he said them – *Jim. Army. Thirty years. Discharged* – he knew she'd give him courage. She was there while he learned that whole damn language of group therapy – self-talk and crystal balling and catastrophising and fight-or-flighting and mindfulness – smiling, agreeing that it's a load of horseshit, but persuading him it can't hurt.

She was there, too, over his shoulder, when he sat in the common room to compose his first poem in the notebook they gave him to record his feelings. When all he could hear was the sound of his pen scratching on paper. *My heart is a broken pencil*, he'd written, the first time he'd given those words – *my heart* – shape. Neither she nor his psych seemed to mind that they belonged to someone else. That he'd stolen them. You can be forgiven for all sorts of things, she said to him.

As PHELAN MOVES about the house he glimpses the cottage through the row of pines, its windows boarded, its gutters rusting.

'Did anyone ever live there?' Penny asks, following his gaze.

'There were always people up there,' he replies. 'Mum and Dad rented it out. I don't think they got much for it – it was too far out of town – but it was a bit extra for the kitty all the same. No real estate commission, no tax either, I guess.'

Phelan recounts how his parents preferred having families there, but that they were hard to find. He remembers a golden six months with a couple of boys their own age, all of them sitting tall on rusting tractor seats like they were thrones, or exploring the gullies after rain, or pegging stones into a wasps' nest in the high fork of the gum that cast its shadow over the small dam.

He remembers an old woman who had a heart attack in the cottage one year, and how it was his job to stand on the track and direct the ambulance to the cottage in case it overshot and pulled up at the Big House instead.

But mainly it was men who lived there. Men trying to 'make a new start of it', his father's phrase. *You've got to help a bloke who's been knocked down and is trying to get back up again*, his father would say and his mother never disagreed. These were men who worked in the abattoir, or in the market gardens around Allora, or on the roads with the council. Men who'd leave the cottage in their Fords or their Holdens at precisely the same time every morning, but who returned at all hours, ragged and sometimes unruly. As if you could control how things began, but never how they ended.

He remembers being woken one night by the sounds of a brawl gusting through his bedroom window. And other occasions when police cars would crest the ridge and stop at the cottage, and they'd watch, agape, as constables fixed their hats to their heads and knocked at the door before disappearing inside.

'I remember one man in particular,' Phelan says. 'He'd been in the cottage for a month before we even saw him, maybe longer. Each day, each week that passed, empty beer bottles – tallies – would gather on the steps of the cottage. There was no one to take them away. The collection of empties grew and grew until the stairs were so crowded there was no way of getting down without knocking them over. It was as if he was entombing himself in there. Then, one afternoon when we got back from school – it was a windy day – we saw him. He was younger than we imagined. And there he was, standing alone in the middle of the paddock wearing an old army jacket and holding a homemade kite to the air. He looked like the loneliest man in all the world.' Phelan pauses, seeing the memory differently to his childhood self, infused now with melancholy. 'We went up to him after a while – because you can't be frightened of a man with a kite – and sure enough he offered us his string, as we'd hoped he might. But he never said anything. He just wiped the sleeve of his jacket across his eyes from where he'd been weeping, and stood there until we were done.

'You knew these men were trying to get back on their feet again, but as a kid you couldn't begin to guess what had knocked them down in the first place. And you didn't want to.'

• • •

149

IT FEELS, AFTER six years, that she and James are finally on their feet again. Being led by hope, fragile but real. In the first year, James hadn't remembered his own birthday, let alone their wedding anniversary. Penny brought him cakes in the hospital for both events, candles and sparklers, balloons and streamers. A naïve attempt to spark him back to life, pity on the face of at least one nurse. *You'll be okay*, the sparklers said, *I'm here, I won't let you go.*

Well she didn't let him go, hasn't. But six years is a long time, and there were days she lost enthusiasm. In truth lost heart. Years when it was easier to let an anniversary slide rather than torture it into place. Risk it overwhelming her, taunting her. When they eventually resumed marking their wedding, it was her husband, rebuilding himself, who did it, bringing her breakfast. *Thank you*, he said, his voice quavering with both gratitude and terror, *thank you.*

Penny knows the terror has not retreated, but still she hopes, this first day, as they begin to feel their way into this space, that they might at least return to the same bed. She dare not hope for desire – the medication and whatever it was designed to cure having killed that off for good, that much she's resigned to – but perhaps the intimacy of a common bedroom isn't beyond them.

She takes his hand and leads him to the master bedroom, with its built-in wardrobes and the bay window, and the shadows on the wallpaper where paintings had once hung.

'So, is this where you were conceived?' she asks brightly, as they stand together in the centre of the empty room.

'Not on the floor, that's for sure.' But she can see him thinking about it, now, for the first time. He was the eldest, and his parents had bought the farm before he was born, soon after they were married. 'It's possible,' he says. 'Yes, it is possible.'

'We need to choose our room,' she hears herself say.

The therapists had insisted on teaching him not just a new language – a vocabulary of emotions, some of which he's sceptical actually exist, shades of feeling cut so fine as to disappear into meaninglessness – but also a new way of thinking: how to express need. How to listen to others express theirs.

And as he studiously practised, week after week, so she also was forced to learn, and in turn, to teach.

But some moments are too big. Theoretically she could say to him that now, after being where they've been, after six years of rebuilding, six cycles, each a new eternity, after deciding on a new start here at the farm, that now was the time for them to start sharing a bed once again. She could tell him that she's adjusted so many expectations, shed so many hopes, but she's clung on to this one. That she can endure his nightmares and his dream-cursing. That she's prepared to be woken by his tossing. That she wants once again to wake to the sound of his breathing. That's all.

Instead, she simply says they need to select their bedroom.

He senses it. Not all, but enough.

'This should do, don't you think?' he says, and her heart soars.

MAPPING COUNTRY

HE MAPS THE boundary of the property, setting out with the dog. They can't yet afford a motorbike, so he walks along the fence line, marking out the posts that need replacing on a mud map he's drawn in his notebook. He records the broken strands of barbed wire, where sections have grown slack and need tightening. He estimates how much new wire he'll need. He lifts branches off the fence where they've fallen during storms, inspects the gates, notes where the termites have got in and how all the gateposts could do with a coat of sump oil. He limps around his property on dry knees, three days in all.

It's a miracle of sorts, being able to set aside his ruminations like this, his obsessions, his lonely projects. Not to feel compelled to switch on his computer at daylight and disappear into an online world of news websites, of army media releases and obituaries, of internet communities knitted together by grief and anger. Not just Beckett but beyond. All the Afghanistan killed, all its wounded, his quest to find a place for himself in a greater world. A miracle! That he can walk his way past his obsessions, that this land and its imperatives offer him this.

And how the country comes back to him as he walks, an entire childhood of it, adventure upon adventure. The thing that surprises him most, the thing he'd forgotten – or sees differently now – is how battle-drenched even this land is. How war-flavoured his childhood had been.

As a kid the firefights were always guerrilla contacts. It was something about the topography. The country was perfect for ambushes – the long grasses of the western paddock, the deep, viciously eroded gullies, and after rain, the creek and its three pools. Phelan hobbles across the country now on stiff knees. He steps over the same places where, as a child, he'd lie on his stomach in the grass. Lying for hours, propped on his elbows, the red-painted stock of his replica rifle keen against his right shoulder, his left eye closed, his right peering down the curtain-rod barrel, the grasses waving in an afternoon breeze.

Even as a child he could wait. He could listen too. The whistling grass, a cackle of cockatoos overhead. Rolling onto his back and counting the birds like they're a squadron of jets before rolling back over and commando-crawling forward, breaking the head of a stalk of grass and tossing it into the air to see which way the seeds float, circling his older cousin perched on a boulder. Learning what downwind means. And that in every tactical advantage lies a weakness, that while his cousin has a three-sixty view around him, he's also exposed. Phelan the kid tosses a small rock so it lands with a thud in a different quarter. He watches his cousin's head snap around, the thrill of manipulating the moment. He watches the back of his cousin's head, and lines him up, eye and barrel and trigger.

PENNY FOLLOWS THE sun. She leaves the bunya pines behind, heading down the slope towards the creek, an old calico bag over her shoulder, in it, gloves and hand shears. When she hears a light plane in the distance she stops and scans the sky but can't find it, waits instead till there is nothing left of it before resuming.

She smells the water first, then hears it, sees it. A spring, no more than a soak at the base of a granite outcrop, a single lily among shaded reeds. She presses the moist ground with her fingers, feels it give. The insects grow accustomed to her. She moves slowly down the fragile watercourse, plant by plant, clipping sprigs of herbs and handfuls of grass, breaking off branchlets and their leaves, placing everything carefully into her bag so when she returns to the house she can lay it all out neatly on the kitchen table for identification.

Though today she barely knows what she is looking for, in time she will know how to use these plants. She will come to learn when the rains fall due, what a good season looks like, which grasses are native and which introduced, how the land responds to drought, what it must do to survive. All is before her. Today she begins.

The damp ground becomes a creek, which leads to a small rock pool. Penny takes off her boots and tucks her socks inside, before stepping into the shallow water. She chases her own ripples to the other side of the pool, crawls over a natural dam and continues down the creek, rock-hopping. A dragonfly hovers above the water up ahead, as if signalling the way.

As the banks steepen, lantana grows down to the water's edge, funnelling the water into deepening shade, crowding out the creek until finally there is a wall of it before her. Light filters through from the other side. Penny bends her head low to continue but an overhead branch rips off her hat and tears at the back of her neck. She winces, before collecting herself. She recovers her hat where it is caught, then drops to her knees to crawl beneath the lantana tangle to the other side. She wrestles her way through, jeans soaked and eyes blinking in the bright light. Penny hears the sound of cascading water nearby. She moves slowly forward, stepping tentatively onto a large flat rock at the top of the waterfall to survey the country as it opens out before her. From here the creek drops its way into a valley below before joining a larger creek that disappears out of view to the north. On the other side, gullies and sharp spines of rock rise again. And not a house in sight, not a road, not a single overhead electrical wire.

She places her boots and her hat and her bag beside the pulpit rock. The sun is warm on her face. She peels off her jeans and lays them beside her to dry. Feels the sun now against her pale thighs. How long since they've been exposed to the sun like this? She looks at her soft thighs. There's not a colour anywhere out there among the scrub and the rocks and sky anything like her pale pink flesh. She is nearly fifty. Has her flesh ever glowed like this before?

The scratch on her neck starts stinging, and Penny reaches for it, the blood still moist. She slips out of her long-sleeved shirt and inspects the bloody collar, then kneels beside the hurrying creek, first to cup water onto the back of her neck, then to work the blood out of her shirt.

Penny sits. She pulls her legs to her chest and rests her chin on her knees. A yellow butterfly flits down to drink from a puddle she created when she splashed water over herself. So delicate, so beautiful. Penny smiles as it flies away. 'Come back tomorrow,' she says aloud, 'and bring your friends.'

She stretches out her legs and examines herself. These fine legs of hers, these thin ankles, the dark skin around her knees, her puckered thighs, the folds at her belly. You've hung in there, she says to her body. Then, a sudden impulse, and she looks around again, a rush of daring. Should she? But she doesn't even answer her question, not consciously, and strips away what's left of her clothes. You've done better than hang in, you're a bloody marvel! She laughs again and crawls into the creek and sits in the cold water, her buttocks on the stony bed, feeling it rush around her. Then she lies back, allowing it to course over her shoulders, over her collarbones, finding its way around her right breast, pouring into the space where her left breast once was, torrenting over her scar, sweeping down her belly and her waist and her legs, all of her.

THE GRASS IS high and the turkey's nest is half full of water. Phelan can't wait until he's repaired all the fences before starting to stock the farm. He figures two paddocks in good order are enough to rotate twenty head of Hereford, and while they're fattening he'll make his way around the rest of the property. So he sorts and cleans out the shed, making space for all the tools and materials he envisages collecting in this exciting new life of his. He gets tips from a neighbour about where to buy supplies, and makes the twenty kilometre run into town every other day to stock up on wire and timber, a strainer, tools he's never used before but which will become as familiar as a rifle. He buys an axe and a chainsaw second-hand, and the old labourer who sells him the gear offers him jars of nails and screws and rusting hand tools just to get rid of them. He debates with himself whether to get a motorbike or a quad, and settles on the four-wheeler, telling Penny he'll be careful on the slopes.

Penny is with him when the first beasts clatter down the ramp of the truck, the driver poking their rumps with a length of poly piping, ten steers and ten heifers. Phelan leans into the cab to write out a cheque on the hot vinyl seat.

'There you go, Charlie,' he says, handing it to the truck driver, this habit he's developed since one of his hospital stints – no longer calling men whose name he's forgotten 'mate' but 'Charlie'. Another splinter of Beckett, one he's unaware is lodged in him.

And then, when the truck has pulled away, he turns to Penny, a fearful ecstasy upon him. 'Look at them,' he says, his hands on her shoulders, shaking her and beaming. 'This is going to be great.'

'It already is,' she replies.

TWO DAYS LATER, at dusk, Penny hears a distressed bellowing from the direction of the turkey's nest and gathers her husband from where he's soaping the day's labour from his hands under the laundry tap. They cut the ute's engine near the base of the dam's earthen walls where their little herd of cattle mills around, agitated. Her count comes up one short. Penny climbs the wall, following a muffled moan. From the top she sees the animal in the muddy water, stuck fast, the water line above its belly. James joins her on the dam wall.

'We'll have to get to it quickly,' he says, 'before exhaustion sets in.'

'How?'

But her husband is already leaping down the slope to the ute where he searches behind the bench seat for rope. There's just a single length, not long enough.

'Stay here,' he calls up to her, 'I'll have to go back to the shed for more.'

Penny shuffles down to the water's edge. 'There, there, old girl,' she soothes. The cow's twisting neck. Its big eye. Its fear. The fading light. 'There, there.'

When James returns it is with a large torch and three long pieces of rope, each a different size, twenty metres in all.

'How is she?'

'Quietened a bit,' Penny replies, 'though whether that's good or bad …'

James hands her the torch. He squats before her beam of light and ties lengths of rope together, fashioning a lasso of sorts before standing on the bank and throwing the lasso towards the cow's head.

But it falls short, striking the animal's russet hide in the torchlight. He pulls it in and throws again, this time hitting the cow's nose. Time and again he throws and misses, begins to curse, feels his inadequacy.

'Darling,' Penny says gently, 'one of us is going to have to wade out.'

'But *we* don't want to get stuck,' he mutters.

She persuades him she should do it. Because she's lighter and less likely to sink, and because he's stronger and if they tie a length around her waist, he can pull her out if she gets in trouble.

Penny takes off her boots and her jeans, and places them neatly on the rim of the dam wall. When she steps in she finds the water surprisingly warm, so much of the day's retained heat lapping at her calves, swallowing her thighs. It is the mud and the silt that is cool between her toes, cool as it envelops her feet and sucks at her ankles. In her hand is the second length of rope. Though she sinks into the mud, she is still able to pull her feet out, first one then the other, and wade slowly towards the heifer, the line around her waist tight, calling to James to let it out, to give her space.

When she reaches the animal her shoulder bumps its girth and it takes fright and begins to thrash, but its legs are trapped and it soon gives up its struggle. She talks to the animal, a lullaby's melody, telling it what she is going to do. She reaches beneath the water to feed the rope under its belly, but can't get far enough, so she presses forward further, her cheek against the beast's flank, its blood pulsing by her ear.

'I'm just going to slide this under you ...' She stretches her arm out beneath the water again but still can't get the rope far enough under its belly to pull the end up from the other side. On her third attempt she takes a deep breath and sinks her head into the dark water.

This time Penny is able to reach through the water and the mud and push the end of the rope under the heifer's body. That much done, she releases the rope and lifts her head out of the water.

'Well done, girl, well done,' she pants.

She manoeuvres her way around the front of the cow to its other flank, beyond the throw of James's torchlight, whispering to it, stroking its neck as she goes. She finds the end of the rope and pulls it through, enough of it so she can throw it up and over the cow's back. She returns to the other side, and ties the rope into a loop, guessing at the knot, testing it.

'All right girl,' she says, 'let's get you out of here.'

Penny calls to her husband on the bank, and turns. She begins wading towards him, dragging her mud-heavy legs.

He leans out to her with his hand, unties the line from her waist and then ties it to the end of the length she has positioned around the heifer's girth. He gives her the torch while he climbs back over the earthen bank to the ute where he will fix the rope to the vehicle and will climb into the driver's seat and will call out to her before starting the engine, checking with her that it's okay to reverse and take up the slack and begin to pull the beast from the dam to safety.

But for now she sits on the dam wall, dripping, strong, elated.

DUET

THEY DRIVE TO Brisbane after a month, for her to visit her parents and catch up with friends, for him to see his psychiatrist.

'In the States they run writing courses solely for vets,' his psych says to him in her rooms at the clinic, trying to gauge his interest before gazing away beyond his shoulder into a pastoral scene on the wall. She sighs. 'The Americans lead us into these wars, hey? And now they're trying to lead us out.'

Whatever the hell point she is trying to make.

'Well,' she continues, turning back to him, 'there's nothing like that here, but most universities have a creative writing course. It's a way of meeting people. You might get something out of it.'

'Writing therapy?' he says.

'Something like that,' she replies. 'Why don't you give it some thought?'

If he responds, it would be to call it out as bullshit. He reaches for his cigarettes instead.

'Not inside,' she says, dropping her voice to a sterner register, 'you know that Jim.' But her eyes continue sparkling.

'See you in a month, Doc,' he replies brightly, thinking how much he'd miss these consultations.

THEY WORK TOGETHER in the stockyards, separating the heifers from the steers in preparation for the arrival of a bull. Penny is at the gate, Phelan in the pen behind the cattle, the dog – which would only get in the way – is chained on the back of the ute.

'Get orn,' Phelan yells, slapping the animals' rumps, isolating the heifers, one-by-one, and directing them towards the gate. 'Get orn.'

Penny controls the gate as each heifer approaches, widening it to allow the animal into the next pen, quickly shutting it on a steer trying to follow the heifer through.

'Get orn,' Penny yells too, picking up the cry, a dusty chant she joins in with James, almost a duet.

They'll have the bull for two months, two of their heifers' cycles. Increasingly, Penny feels the animals are as much hers as James's. She wants to be there when the bull arrives, and insists he arrange its delivery for a day she's off-roster. She wants to see what beast they'll be setting among their heifers. Proud and strong, she tells him.

She's not disappointed. He is a beautiful creature with a clean white head, polled, with tightly curled hair on his crown. Behind his still head are a powerful neck and muscular shoulders. He eyes them in the yards, first him then her. He paws at the soil and his bright pink nostrils flare before he sharply turns his great head away to sniff their cows on the breeze.

'JAMES,' SHE SAYS, 'I'm thinking about a new breast.'

The verandah is as good as anywhere to raise it, the two of them looking out at the eastern horizon. The birdsong, the buzzing grass, the tin creaking as it expands above their heads. Already she's discovered that some words vanish out here on the verandah, while others sink roots, that it's a mystery what survives.

'You don't have to, you know.'

'But would you like me to?'

'It's not about me, Pen,' he says, with surprise.

She could be wrong, but thinks she hears a note of indignation. She can ignore manufactured hurt, she thinks, but not the implied judgement in these old beliefs of his: that if she wants an implant it's because of some weakness of hers, some moral or psychological frailty. That the body is only ever something to be overcome.

But beauty? Joy? Does he still not understand why people dance? Sing? That there are things worth celebrating? Such as battles won. Even generals do that.

Of all people, she thinks. Haven't you learned? Where was your stoic philosopher general with his CBT when you needed him?

Of all people.

WRITING CLASS

PHELAN STUDIES THE lecturer from the outer semicircle of seats. The man's neat beard, his slicked back shoulder-length hair, his tan dress boots that others might mistake for RMs. He's supposed to be a serious writer. They say he's worked cattle out west, won literary awards, grown his hair long, set novels in brothels and on barques and by the banks of creeks.

Having relented to his psych, here Phelan is, one of two dozen first-year writing students introducing themselves to the group. It's as strange a situation as any he's found himself in before – though unlike the others here the course isn't part of a degree, except that if he likes it the uni will offer him credit down the track. Phelan can't ever see himself wasting money on enrolment fees. He also can't believe, as he watches the lecturer sitting cockily on the desk at the front of the class, manipulating biographies out of his students, that he's subjecting himself to yet another trial by introduction. At least in the Keith Payne Unit they were his people. As his turn approaches he swings between saying nothing and saying everything. *Jim. Army. Thirty years. Discharged. Been knocked down. Trying to get back up again.*

'And what about you, James?' the novelist asks him carefully. 'What brings you here?'

Phelan is suddenly aware that the lecturer, having been contacted by his psychiatrist, already knows exactly who he is. And either feels sorry for him or is intimidated by him. That this whole introduction thing is a farce, and that he has no manifesto he's memorised like all the students before him have, that there's no one here he wants to impress. And that he'll be fucked if he's going to tell them his psych thought the course would be better than continuing with cognitive behavioural therapy.

'I really don't know, to be quite honest,' Phelan answers. 'Trying something new.' He doesn't mean to, but he sounds petulant rather than genuinely uncertain. Those students who had not already been politely giving him their attention, now turn to look at him with interest.

'And what would that new thing be?' the lecturer presses, offering him a chance to redeem himself. Phelan is obviously the oldest in the class, has probably lived more and ought – surely – know why he's here.

'Looking for my inner Hemingway,' Phelan says, attempting a joke.

'Even Hemingway didn't find that,' the lecturer remarks, smiling generously before turning to the eighteen-year-old girl next to him.

PHELAN CAN'T WRITE in the house. He doesn't want to spoil it and whatever delicate thing he and Penny are creating there. Instead, he sits on the edge of the escarpment at dusk, after hours of trying to repair the bore pump but getting nowhere. It takes the westerly wind to prise some lines out of him.

'Dinner's ready!' Penny calls from the verandah, cupping her hands to throw her voice. But when he doesn't hear, or pretends not to, she has to stomp out to the front gate and across the paddock, and rest her hand on his shoulder and tell him it's time to come in.

I HAVE LIVED flat for six years, she thinks, laying her right palm on her chest where her left breast once was. She looks at herself in the long mirror and breaks into a sudden smile, this parody of a patriot's gesture: hand on heart, all truth to tell, a life readied for sacrifice to a greater cause. She drops her hand and stands tall. I am more than my body, yes I know that, but my body has held true for six long years now. My old flesh has rearranged itself, become more fluid, more elastic, has learned better not to resist the gravitational pulls of all the suns and moons passing overhead. Knows better how to survive. It has proven itself. *I* have proved myself. And I no longer wish to live flat.

With or without him. It's good he doesn't mind. Does it matter that he may not care? *It's not about me*, he says. Of course it's not, James. But is it true anyway, that it's got nothing to do with you? The scars we bring into our bedrooms. The tattoos. The maimings we share with our husbands and our wives and our lovers.

• • •

162

AN HOUR OR two at sunset isn't enough. He's not ready to come in for dinner, feels himself resenting it, finds ever more secluded writing sites, lingers into the night. Soon enough he takes to sleeping out.

'It's not you,' he says to her. 'Please understand, Pen. It's not you,' he tries to explain but falters. Phelan hefts a swag to his shoulder that first time and strikes out with his dog. The two of them leave in the late afternoon, a clear winter sky, moonless, the falling cold. They sleep in the dead-centre of a paddock, Phelan measuring the distance between fences before rolling out his bedding. The smell of canvas on buffel grass, the warmth of a dog's belly. There are meteorites in the east. He loses count. He writes in the dark, the darker the better, not caring to see what words he's reducing to paper. It's the moment he seeks, prolonging it in the darkness, line after unseen line. He sleeps. A stone appears beneath him in the night, and he shifts his body to accommodate it, curving round it. The ground is not so hard.

When he wakes it is still dark, and no bird has yet stirred, but the stars have withdrawn and a fog is creeping in. He lies motionless as the mist thickens, some great benevolent spirit rising out of the earth. The light, when it comes, is slow and diffuse, as if there is no east, as if the laws of the universe have shifted. There is dampness on his cheek and the magpies on their branches are a long way away.

Only in the light does he read what he's written the night before. Among them are lines for Penny. Just a few, just scraps, some striving. However beautiful or ungainly, whatever they might be they're a love song. Thank you, they say. Forgive me. Once more.

In the spreading dawn he hears the Hilux engine starting. His dog rises, and leans close, licking his face. Phelan follows the sound of the vehicle as Penny pulls out from under the shed and heads slowly up the road and over the ridge and beyond to the hospital for an early shift.

When he returns to the house he tears her poem from his notebook and sets it on her dresser.

• • •

SHE RETURNS TO an empty house and a poem. She takes it from her bedroom, pours a glass of wine and sits out on the verandah to read it. Is he out there somewhere watching? She reads:

The seasons, though, had ceased to turn,
there was nothing left to love or learn.

Let him see her cry then, let him.

'It's not you,' he says to her again, later.

It doesn't help that she knows it's true. Or that there's no point asking him what it is. Because he won't know. That he's hoping his poems might give him an answer.

Night after night he leaves. Penny prepares meals for him, and leaves them out. She imagines him re-entering the house in the morning after she has gone to work and eating quietly, standing at the kitchen bench, scooping casserole or pasta into his body. She sees him washing the dishes and drying them and putting them away before carefully hanging the tea towel back on its rack.

She thinks, as she returns from a shift to an empty house, that it's like she's feeding a wounded animal, coaxing it closer, building trust. Then she thinks, no, not an animal – not a dog or a horse, not even a patient – but a ghost. She's living with a shade.

EACH NIGHT FOR a month he does this, taking the dog and finding somewhere different on the farm. He sleeps on the banks of the dam and wakes to the bowed heads of creatures drinking, one eye on him. He lies down between the buttress roots of the Moreton Bay Fig, beneath its heaven-concealing canopy. He sleeps on the escarpment, moving further along it each night, positioning rocks between himself and the fall. Writes his nocturnal poems.

He remembers pitching tents when he was a kid, and tries to

remember that kid self. Tries to think back to the boy hammering a peg into the ground with an oversized mallet and striking rock. He remembers trying to straighten that bent peg, using the flat of a nearby stone like an anvil to bang the kink out of it. Trying, getting close, but realising that once bent, you can never get a peg perfectly straight.

MORE THAN A BODY

FROM THE HOUSE at night, alone, there are so many lights. The stars and the moon, and the orbits of the satellites she sometimes follows with James's telescope. The universe those satellites have created, the worlds they've realised.

There are also the lights of the valley, the headlights on the snaking highway to Brisbane moving in waves like scales. Nearby on the spur there is the cottage, dark inside, but the iron roof glinting with moonlight. And beyond it, over the ridge, invisible from the house, back past the cattle yards, and across Boundary Road where the wall of the escarpment swings east, there are the lights of the large houses erected by the town's professionals, leaning into the valley.

They could do it together, she'd thought. They'd sit quietly at the table, side by side, and she'd tip the pieces out, and together they'd turn them over, their hands reaching and deftly flipping. She'd set the lid of the box up, facing them, so they could examine the image of the jig-saw. His hands would move as keenly as hers, till all the pieces were face-up. Then they'd sort the pieces by edge and colour and shade. They'd mark out the border, like a picture frame, and when that was done they'd pause and stand and stretch and look at what they'd achieved already. She'd open a window, and behind her his breathing would be steady at the table. Then they'd start to fill the puzzle in. They'd divide it up. The sky for her and the buildings for him. Or vice versa, it hardly mattered. The hours would pass, and the angle of the sun too, and there would be cups of tea, and the jig-saw filling out, and maybe they would talk and maybe they wouldn't and either way it wouldn't matter, and his hand wouldn't tremble as it hovered over a piece of dark green foliage, and she wouldn't kneel on the floor to pick up the thousand pieces he'd swept off the table in a fit of fury. No. Together they would start to rebuild a little jig-sawed world, and they would lose themselves in it, and when it was done it would be complete.

What's wrong with her that she hasn't left him? It's the question her girlfriends ask. What sort of weakness is it, that she's still here? That she has continued to stumble in his shadows. Is a poem or two all it takes to keep her? His neediness. His gratitude. A marriage. Is hope even necessary? Love and faith may be enough. She has grown stronger herself, but is it only so she might dig a hole into which she will fall? Yet he's not a bad man. Just wounded, just weak. Not what's wrong with her, but what's right with her that she's stayed.

Quietly, sadly, Penny makes up another bedroom for her husband to return to when he is finished with his sleeping under the stars.

But she too, has the sky. And the farm and all its joys and consolations are hers as much as his.

IT IS SHE, when the birthing season nears, who researches how heifers calve, what signs to look for, what to do if things go wrong. She reads. She watches videos. She speaks with vets and with neighbours on Sunday after Mass at the tiny wooden church in the nearest village. She jokes with the midwives at the hospital and prepares a box of equipment that she sets aside in case she needs it: shoulder gloves, lubricant, rope, clean rags. She checks on the heifers twice daily, feeling their girths, examining them for signs of readiness.

And it is she who rises first to walk across the paddocks to discover if any of them have dropped overnight. It is she who kneels and watches their first heifer lick its baby as it lies on the earth, moments-born, splashes of red and yellow birthing on its rust-brown and white body. She watches as it dries the calf's wet coat, warming it with its rough tongue, the calf with one foreleg folded under its new body, the other splayed forward, its filmy eyes. The calf rises to its legs, it falls, it rises again. So much uncertainty, so much wonder.

She goes to get her husband to share this with him, amazed.

'JAMES, I'VE BOOKED the procedure.'

'The reconstruction?'

'Yes.' She waits.

'Great,' he says, realising it is he who must speak next. 'When?'

'Next week, Tuesday.'

'Up here?'

'No, Brisbane.'

He doesn't ask why she hadn't told him she'd decided to do it before making these arrangements, doesn't ask about the consultations with the surgeon she must already have had, all the preparations.

'That's great, Pen. It'll be great. Tuesday. Okay then.' He smiles. 'This'll be my chance to visit *you* in hospital!'

'You don't have to … it's only a couple of days and … Bec has said she can be there.'

'Pah!' James says, waving her away. 'After all you've done for me, I'm glad I can look after you for a bit.'

WHEN THEY RETURN to the farm Penny locks the bathroom door. She lifts her nightshirt over her head and turns to the mirror and still doesn't quite recognise herself. She pulls the points of her shoulders back. It's a funny word, she thinks, *reconstruction*, what we do to vanquished countries after war. Yet so much promise too! She examines herself again, side to side, comparing. She has grown past any ideal of perfection, or even symmetry. As she looks at her new flesh now, so full, so rounded, so well sculpted, she wonders if it will fall, wonders how it will age. She presses her fingers against the skin beneath her right nipple, then cups her breast, feeling its weight. She looks at her new breast, perhaps a little high on her chest.

Of course she is more than her body. But this is her body, all of it, and it is good.

THE SURVIVAL OF POETRY

TOWARDS THE END of the semester he reads aloud to the class, a fragment of something longer.

'You've got something to say,' one of his fellow students says, an undergrad doing the course as relief from a politics major. 'About the war, I mean. Like, you can read media reports for a year and you won't really learn anything. Not really. But that poem … like, that's really what the war might have been like.'

'Might have been?' Phelan bristles.

'Yeah,' the student replies blithely.

'So you didn't believe it?' Phelan accuses.

'Sorry?' The student grows uncomfortable. He'd only meant to praise.

'Might have been, or was?' Phelan spits, combusting. He points his finger at the kid across the reading circle, this sudden ferocity.

The room plummets into silence.

'Because unless it's *was*, unless it's *was*, then …' Phelan falters. He doesn't even know himself what threat he's making, what's on the other side of it.

'*Was* then, all right?' The politics major raises his palms in the air in mock surrender. 'Your poem captures what a soldier under fire in Afghanistan *would have* felt, *did* feel. Okay? And yeah, I believe you.' And then, when he sees Phelan is shrinking, says, 'Satisfied?'

How he wishes the years of therapy and drugs were behind him. He'd love to shed it all, like a skin that's served its purpose. That kept him together when he needed it, kept him safe, as safe as you could expect. But then sent him off when he was ready, steadier. Art can't record the sequence of it, no poem can say this, then this, then this. No song either. Birds and cigarettes and portraits of a queen he'd grown to love in there.

AT THE END of her shift she goes to the gym, sometimes with a new friend from the hospital, sometimes by herself. She jokes with the instructors who rotate through the front desk, changes into her exercise gear – loose first and then, as the months pass, tighter, skins – and then hits the equipment. The room is filled with discovery. She looks at herself in the mirror, again and again, marvelling.

She takes her body out into the paddocks, or it takes her. There is a deeper pleasure now in lifting a bale of hay out of the back of the ute, grabbing it two-handed by the string and swinging it out and onto the ground for the cattle to feed. She stays out longer in the garden. She wears singlets in the heat, beads of sweat gathering under arms. At the fridge she drinks cold water straight from the bottle, slugging it, her raised arm firm, muscular, glistening.

PHELAN FINISHES THE semester, and the lecturer arranges for a sample of each of their work to be collected in the university's online writing journal, and it's his poem, 'Waiting for Beckett', that then gets picked up by the local paper.

The journalist who tracks him down to the farm is determined to describe him as a 'war poet' but Phelan laughs dismissively.

'This wasn't nineteen-fifteen, Charlie,' Phelan says offering him a cigarette on the verandah, 'when all those English poets enlisted to fight out of Idealism. In this country *we* join the army because we want to become soldiers, and once we are soldiers we want to fight. Because that's what soldiers do. Understand? None of us were poets or writers or painters first. We were professional soldiers. Infantrymen. Signallers. Commandos. Engineers. Professionals, not artists dabbling in war on the side.'

'Well if that's the case,' the reporter presses, 'would you say the war uncovered you as a poet?'

'Seriously? All I've done is have one poem published. And in a student journal!' Though, he's beginning to enjoy this. Maybe it's the attention. Maybe it's the absurdity of being called a poet. Or the vanity of it, so little to be proud of for so many years. Maybe it's just the chance to hold forth with someone new.

'Do you have other poems?'

Phelan waves the question away. 'Would I say the war uncovered me? Fuck no. And you can quote me on that. There was no *un*covering going on. If anything, what the war did was cover us over with an invisible shroud till we near suffocated. Though perhaps,' Phelan continues, musing, 'perhaps you could say the war turned me into a poet. If that's what you call it, Charlie. Didn't uncover a poet, but forced one into being.' He turns to Penny. 'What do you think, Love?'

However, before she can answer – half-fearing what she might say – he adds, 'Though you always knew I had a poet in me, didn't you?'

She rolls her eyes.

But the journalist misses the wink and looks relieved, pleased the interview seems to be back on track.

'Is there anything,' he asks eagerly, reading a prepared question from his notepad, 'apart from the subject matter, that makes war poems different from other poems? Is there something about the proximity of death that allows them to speak more honestly about life?'

Phelan's turn to roll his eyes. 'Charlie, for most soldiers, it's the proximity of months of boredom that's more distressing than the possibility of death.'

'But what about *you*? Was there one particular thing that happened to you? One event you can look back on now and say, "That's what did it. That's what made me into a poet."?'

Phelan goes suddenly cold, the fun killed off as quickly as a single well-directed question. Beckett having joined them now on the verandah, taking his rightful place. How foolish to think I might have been able to control an interview like this, how presumptuous.

The journalist stares at Phelan as he rises and tosses his cigarette over the edge and drops his hands beside his body and shakes them urgently, repeatedly, as if trying to exorcise something, before walking quickly to the other end of the verandah, turning immediately and coming back, sitting again. The journalist looks at Penny in alarm.

Phelan pulls the knuckles on one hand then the other, so hard the journalist winces. When he's done he lights up another cigarette, and draws deep. Uncomfortable as it is, the journalist knows enough not to excuse himself now, knows that whatever he's witnessing will be the most important part of his story.

When eventually Phelan speaks, he is surprisingly calm. 'The first thing to understand,' he says, recalling his psychiatrist's initial diagnosis well enough to misquote her, only the smallest of tremors in his voice, 'is that poetry is a normal reaction to extreme trauma.' He hopes he can keep the sarcasm out, that he sounds as coolly ironic as he intends. 'While not everyone exposed to trauma will respond with poetry, it is normal to do so. Accordingly, no stigma ought to be attached to writing, or indeed even reading, poetry. For those who *have* been turned into poets by war, it commonly occurs after exposure to enemy fire, participation in armed combat, the sight of wounded comrades and civilians, witnessing the death of fellow soldiers and civilians, and indirect threats to one's own physical security.'

The reporter nods his head cautiously as he tries to follow Phelan. 'Which of those happened to you?'

'It doesn't matter,' Penny says, quickly intervening. 'No soldier is untouched by war.'

'Of course,' the journalist says to Penny. 'I understand these things can be personal. I'm sorry.' He turns back to Phelan, leans forward again and says evenly, 'but if it's war that makes a war poet, then for war poetry to survive we need to keep finding wars to join. Like we fight to test our equipment, and – as you said – to make sure our soldiers are ready for battle, right? No point having an army if we don't use it, hey? What would you say about that?'

Phelan glares at the smug little shit.

'I'd say who the fuck wants war poetry to survive, that's what I'd say.' Then he reaches across to the digital recorder on the coffee table between them and turns it off. 'And what I'd also say is – fuck you. Fuck Afghanistan. Fuck war. Fuck poetry. Fuck us all.'

WAR POET

'POETRY NORMAL REACTION to War Trauma, Says Veteran', ran the headline. Though only a local paper, he should have guessed someone would contact him after the article was published. Because the army knows everything.

'Jim?'

He recognises the Chief of Army's voice immediately. Though Peter Willey wasn't yet Chief when they'd worked together in Kabul.

'Sir.' It's automatic, the acknowledgement of hierarchy. It also gives him a moment to try and control the anxiety biting at his stomach, enough time to remember – how had he forgotten, even momentarily? – that they'd once been friends.

'Good to hear your voice, Jim.'

It's been four years, Phelan reckons, maybe five. Friends, but rivals too, competition spawned by ambition. Of course, by the time he helped get Phelan's disability pension over the line, Phelan was no longer a threat to him.

'Good to be heard, Sir.'

'Cut that out, Jim. How are you doing old fellow?'

'It's taken a little while but I've retired to that hobby farm we used to talk about.'

'Herefords, wasn't it?'

'Your memory is as good as it always was, Peter. They're beautiful animals. Penny and I have started with a few, but if all goes well, we'll build the herd to a couple of hundred.'

'That will keep you busy.'

'Not as busy as I bet you are,' Phelan responds, the formulas for conversations like this coming back to him.

'Ah … I must admit that many is the day I wish I had a small piece of countryside to retreat to myself.'

There's a brief pause. Phelan no longer ruminates about how, had things worked out differently, it could have been him sitting where Willey is now. But the Chief nevertheless senses danger, and moves on smoothly, taking control again.

'And your health, Jim? You sound … better?'

'It's a day-by-day proposition, Sir,' Phelan says, retreating.

'I read the article, Jim. It was very brave of you.'

Phelan laughs. 'Brave? As in, brave and foolish?'

'Brave is brave, Jim.'

There's another pause.

'Did you read the poem too?' Phelan asks.

'I did. It's very powerful. I can't say how good it is – I'll leave that judgement to people better qualified than I am – but it hit me in the gut.' There is the pause in the conversation that the purpose of the call would always require. 'But, I think you need to be careful.'

Phelan doesn't give the Chief any help.

'The *Toowoomba Chronicle* won't be the only media interested in your story. There are a lot of people listening right now. You've got Australia's entire military listening in. The whole country wants to know about PTSD and what we're doing about it.'

'What exactly do I need to be careful about, Peter?'

'Trauma is one thing. And it's a hell of a thing, don't get me wrong, a hell of a thing …' the Chief pauses, not in hesitation, but for emphasis, '… but asking whether we should have ever gone to Afghanistan in the first place is a whole other ball game. That's a political decision, and we—'

'—are only soldiers.' Phelan finishes the sentence for him, and, before the Chief can respond, adds, 'But that's the thing, of course. I no longer am.'

'You were never *only* a soldier, Jim. You were a brigadier. Yes, I have a duty to the men and women who are over there, or are on their way. All of my officers have that duty. And my duty extends to their families, and to the families of each of our brothers who didn't come home. You used to have the same duty, Jim. I don't want our people and their families to think the army itself doesn't believe in the mission. Because if they hear *you* don't believe in it, they might wonder if *I* don't.'

But Phelan won't be disarmed by soothing words. 'Well, do you?'

'Jim—'

'Fifteen years we've been there, Peter! Fifteen years we've been waiting. For what? Victory? Would we even know what that looked like? We decide to leave, yet we stay. We withdraw our troops from combat operations so instead they can teach the Afghan soldiers to do the shooting. The American's bombing campaign intensifies and the result? The Taliban expand their territory. We've got a rope around our neck, Peter. We're loitering beside a leafless hangman's tree waiting to be rescued. But when? By whom?'

'Jim, we're there, and there's nothing I can do that is going to change that ...'

'But maybe *I* can,' Phelan replies quietly, the first time he's given it any thought.

'You'd be fooling yourself.'

'That's one privilege of retirement.'

'Then think of the families of those men who died, Jim. Think of them. They need to know their men died for something.'

'They died for mateship.'

'It's not enough.'

'And they died serving their country.'

'It's still not enough, Jim. They need to know their boys died doing the right thing. Jim, all I'm saying is be careful. That's what I'm saying. Because I'd hate to lose you entirely.'

'What do you mean? I've already left.'

'If you turn your back on the army, if you disrespect it, there's no coming back.'

HE'S NO WAR poet. He knows that. And he's no activist. He'd sent no missals from the front line, so why would he start now? Nothing submitted to any of the journals or newspapers while he was away, so long ago, no poet's pseudonyms. There weren't even any letters home he'd describe as being either vaguely poetic or doubting of the war. No anthems for doomed youth, no Sassoon-like declarations of wilful defiance published in *The Herald* or *The Australian*, no emails to Penny about poppies, despite the fields of them all around him.

Lose you entirely.

Phelan can't get the words out of his head. He can't work out what they are – threat or curse or fact. But surely the army has no hold over him any longer. Surely. Since being run out of it by Gruen – a short, sharp campaign he was too weak to resist – he's had as good as nothing to do with it. In five years there has been a line of text beside the fortnightly deposits in his bank statements, an annual record of benefits paid, the odd piece of bureaucratic correspondence.

But, and but. Every night he still lies down to dream with Beckett. The guilt. Being chased out by Beckett's platoon. The shame. No matter how hard he's tried, the army still has him. The complex grip of family. What he'd give to be lost to it entirely, what he'd do to be freed.

Perhaps, he thinks, perhaps I *can* do something. So, when other media outlets pick up the story, and when he is invited to do an interview on national breakfast television, Phelan figures there is, in fact, nothing at all to lose.

INVITATION

PENNY SITS WITH him in the Toowoomba studio while a make-up artist does something to his face, preparing the talent for yet another piece commemorating the Great War. When she first made contact the news producer had warned them that the station's audience was tiring of the interminable centenary anniversaries, but that war poetry is a fresh angle, one they were keen to try. Her husband is resolute, his dark chequered jacket a new one they bought together for the occasion. He's learned his poem by heart in case they ask him to recite it. She touches his wrist in good luck and he looks at her, before turning away and following a station-hand into a new room where he sits at a curved table to be interviewed by the hosts down in Martin Place.

She nervously watches him through a bank of screens as he places his folio of poems on the table. He's been clutching them so tightly his knuckles have gone white. They're so slight, she thinks, his cryptic grasps at freedom. Is it pride she feels? Yes of course. It may not be a Medal for Gallantry in front of him on the table, but there are many varieties of courage. What he's been through, she thinks, what we both have. And maybe, maybe what he's going to do *will* help others – she's proud of him for that too. So why the doubt? Because it's been years since he's done anything public and maybe he's not ready. Because who can predict what will come of this. And because maybe *she's* not ready.

HE SITS AT the interview table and imagines Beckett beside him. They put an earpiece in and tell him where to look. There's a crackle as the sound comes on. He can hear the hosts in Sydney laughing at each other's jokes, bantering like a married couple. Then they cut to an ad break before his interview, and the cameraman leans out from behind his lens to give Phelan a thumbs-up.

A gesture as innocuous as that. Phelan sees the thumb and flashes giddy, cuts away, is suddenly in the field, the roar of rushing meltwater in his ears, acknowledging Gruen as he sets out across a stone bridge. His heart pounds. He sees Gruen's thumb, he sees his own upraised in reply. The mockery of it. No, Phelan thinks, the situation is not all right. He starts to sweat, feels the coldness of the studio, the starkness of the lights, everyone watching him from a distance.

Then, unexpectedly, Beckett laughs. It's like an explosion beside him and whether Beckett is laughing at him, or the situation as a whole, he can't tell. It's the first time he's heard it, but it's unmistakeably Beckett, full-throated and cacking himself at some lunacy.

Can't you see it? Beckett seems to be saying between bursts of glee. *The absurdity of it all?*

177

Phelan shakes his head, but still Beckett roars his invitation. Fuck it, Phelan thinks. Fuck it.

PART FOUR

THE BEAUTY IN SORROW

Sydney, January 2017

KIRA FEELS BLAKE lifting the doona at the end of the bed and crawling in, nuzzling his face against her calves like he's a puppy, the rest of his little body curled tight into itself, looking for its own warmth.

'Come up here, Blakey,' she murmurs sleepily.

His body balls even more tightly at her feet. She searches him out with her toes – feels his curved back, his shoulders, the mop of thick hair at his neck. When she brushes his cheek with the sole of her foot he draws away, burrowing his head into a hollow in the old mattress. She follows him, catching his earlobe between her toes and gently tugging it. He squeals.

'Ssh!' she hisses.

Most mornings she wouldn't care – she's at least the equal of the neighbours through the wall, can scream just as loudly back – but it's Flores outside on the lounge room sofa she doesn't want to disturb. Her arms are still sore from where he grabbed her last night and shook her, a spray of spit in her face, his brother Prince due for parole and Kira desperate for something to change.

'Give it back to him,' she'd pleaded, the business Flores has been managing for him while he's been inside. 'Just hand it back. We don't need it. It'll kill us. It'll finish us off.'

And his response, half-crazed, 'It's too late for that. It's mine now.'

Throwing her against the wall, yelling at her to shut up, to shut the fuck up.

'Ssh,' she whispers again urgently to Blake in the lightening bedroom, her finger against her lips.

Her son recognises this voice of hers, fear, and lies still.

Some rare mornings she hears the thin cries of birds in the lull between trains. Sometimes train song. Sometimes the morning currawongs even seem to sing in answer to Blake's breathing. But not today. This morning is heavy, songless.

'Time to get up Little Man,' she whispers eventually, trying to make it playful. When there's no response she says more firmly, 'Come on, Blakey, we've got to get you ready for school.' Some exhausted, silent, royal 'we'. If she lets go of that creed there won't be anything left to hang on to.

Still nothing, so she climbs out of bed, his body remaining motionless beneath the covers, and unpegs the sarong she'd hitched across the northern window as a curtain when they moved in here a month ago. Weak sunlight fills the room. Where does Blake go? she wonders. What better world than she can offer is he tunnelling towards this morning?

Kira goes to turn on the television, hoping to lure Blake out of bed. She takes the batteries out of the back of the remote and swaps them around to make it work, before flicking through the breakfast television fare, keeping the volume low, settling on a station for no better reason that a roulette wheel lands on one number rather than another.

She has turned away from the screen, back towards the bed, when she hears his voice. It grips her by the shoulder and pulls her roughly back around, urgent in her ear, resounding. She stares at the screen, transfixed. She knows him immediately. That same pock-marked face, the jowls, the short thin hair parted on the right. But so much older, somehow darker, crosshatched, the sort of ageing years can neither cause nor measure.

'I'm not alone,' he is saying. 'But people are afraid to speak up. They think it will damage their careers.'

'They think the army won't understand?' the male host, a household name, asks.

'What I should have said,' Phelan says, correcting himself, 'is that it *will* damage their careers. It's a certainty. And yes, the army does not understand.'

'If you had a message to the army,' the female co-host says, 'what would it be?'

'One day we'll evolve beyond this,' the soldier she once tattooed says, not with wisdom she thinks, but resignation. But there's a beauty in his sorrow, as if he might know its depths.

There follows a silence longer than breakfast television usually allows. Kira reads the caption at the foot of the screen: *James Phelan, Former Brigadier, Poet*. And beneath that, *Toowoomba*. Each word is disorienting. She'd never cared to know his rank, and as for his name, Phelan – she must have heard it that night, but she hadn't remembered, hadn't ever needed to. Not really.

'You write about one of the men under you who died in Afghanistan …' the male host says eventually, before falling away, even a conversation-shaper as accomplished as he is not knowing how to finish.

Kira watches former Brigadier James Phelan, poet, slowly unbutton his sleeve, then start to roll it up. The care he takes. This, too, she recalls, his purposefulness. She watches the faces of the enthralled studio hosts at this unscripted act. And for one perfect moment, Kira knows exactly what's coming. It's as if he's rolling back his sleeve for her alone, signalling to her through the screen. This revelation intended for her. The camera pans to a close-up of Phelan's arm, his old skin, her tattoo, *Samuel Robert Beckett*.

One day we'll evolve beyond this, she hears. *One day.*

• • •

183

KIRA HAS SEEN her clients on Facebook and Instagram and on television before. She's seen her work in the *Daily Telegraph* as an identifying feature of a 'person of interest' to the police. On corpses pulled from the harbour or out of Darlinghurst alleys. But not this. Blake is calling her now, Mum, but she ignores her son. James Phelan is talking and revealing himself, and the camera is closing in, but she's incapable of hearing any longer what he's saying.

He rolled up his sleeve for her before, years ago, when his skin was bare, before time, before, it seems to her now, the record of her own history had begun.

She swirls back out of Hurstville and this bleak flat, away from Blake, away from Flores. Away from their collapsed relationship, so many promises laid to waste. Everything that's been crushed out of it, every smothered dream. She pulls away from the woman she's become, trapped, uncertain. She pulls away from the thousand spites, all the ugliness she's brought into the world, or convinced herself she has. All the bitter dealing, every daily revenge. How much squalor can fit into a day. She's reversing the last six years of her life's evolution, every changeling spirit she's laid to rest. All those stillborn escapes.

She hears a long-ago soldier's voice and leaps into the sky, soaring above the years. She remembers. She returns. And once again she's diving beneath a moon-swept ocean, and the water is clean and her body is strong and desire is good and she is powerful.

'WHAT THE FUCK are you crying for?' Flores demands, shirtless in the doorway, hung-over. He is sour now, the previous night's anger gone.

'Nothing.'

'Tell me.'

'Lost love,' she says, throwing it at him, looking him in the eyes, forgetting Blake is in the room.

'Bitch,' he spits back, but without conviction.

She laughs, bitterly. It's possible he's even more wretched than she is. He sheds his trousers, tossing them onto the bed, not caring where they land, not seeing the lump under the covers.

'Hey!' she says, remembering, 'Watch out! Blake's under there!'

Flores looks, sees.

'Sorry mate,' he says contritely, patting Blake's back twice through the doona.

'What's become of us, Flores?' she whispers to herself when he disappears into the bathroom and the shower starts to run and Blake emerges from their broken bed, wide-eyed. What's become of me?

So, he was a brigadier.

Kira retreats to the back room between clients. Flores is working on an all-afternoon sleeve, a pumped-up bicep. She can hear his voice above the Velvet Underground, holding forth about the glory days of tattooing, bemoaning the celebrity tattooists and the backyarders. In his glory days Flores could tattoo all day without pause, lost in his work. Now the tattooing is a sideline, a front. And when he does tattoo he's slower, distracted, irritated even. She reckons she has ten minutes before he'll start wondering where she's gone.

She looks up Brigadier James Phelan on the web, the sound muted. There are hundreds of entries about him, most of them from the two-thousands, dated. She reads articles with quotes by him in Afghanistan, flicks through a montage of images of him, watches army media interviews on YouTube with his name sewn neatly in black into his uniform. I've marked Blake's clothes like that at the start of the school year, she thinks, only on the inside. She sees the brigadier in the passenger seat of a four-wheel drive, turned towards the camera, smiling with what she guesses is Kabul blurring past through the window behind him. She sees Phelan in webbing on patrol, the shape of him with his body armour and ammunition belt and goggles and helmet make him less human than the village urchins in the foreground. There is another photo of him at attention, arm angled in precise salute, with a flag-draped coffin moving towards the open tail of a giant cargo plane. You could almost believe you're accompanying someone to war like this, she thinks.

And then there are a handful of recent references, a local newspaper story, the morning's television piece. She re-watches it. The characters' mouths move silently, until once again she sees her tribute. She finds an email address on a page linked to a university writing journal, *Contact the Writers*, and clicks on it. His name populates the *To* panel of a new message screen, *jamesphelan60@gmail.com*. She sits back in her chair, looking at the screen and the name from a distance. Her heart races. She deletes the new message box, and only then feels her blood slow.

She tries thinking back to that night when this brigadier saved her from Flores's brother's friend. But there has been no saving herself from Flores's brother, or from Flores himself.

What's become of her? What curse was laid by whom that night?

THE LOVE OF BROTHERS

THAT NIGHT. ALL those years ago. The next day.

It's mid-morning and she's a black cat slinking home. She can almost feel herself changing form, padding softly up from Central Station, moving quietly in the shadows. She barely understands it, the way different creatures inhabit her, moving in and out. She arches her neck and looks up from the dirty Saturday street at the first-floor windows of the studio, and on the floor above, the windows of the apartment she and Flores share.

There is nothing to be ashamed of. If Flores is back, he is back. Wherever he was last night, it was the universe's choosing. The curtain of their bedroom window has blown out and flaps against the building's brick wall, licking at the daylight. So he's back, she thinks, and then, practising – because she'll need to explain herself – she conjures him in her mind and says firmly to him, *About time.*

She quietly climbs the stairs. She stands in the centre of the empty studio and feels the after-tremors of last night's violence. The turbulence buffets her still. The floorboards in their sleeping quarters above her head creak and she makes her way up the second, open flight of stairs.

Flores sits on a Bentwood chair at a small desk against a far wall, facing her, his back to the desk, waiting. Leaning against the wall beside him is his brother, Prince. It is he who speaks, pushing off the wall with the heel of his boot.

'You shouldn'tve called the cops.'

They look so alike they could almost be twins – the same height, their broad shoulders both pitch forward as if crossing a finish line, their two wiry frames, both of their hair clipped short, the angular faces of both brothers darkly stubbled. But Flores has a stillness his brother doesn't, a steadiness of eye. Or he used to.

She can't think quickly enough to work out how Prince knows about the police, so she just asks.

'They came back with more questions this morning,' he answers. 'Just left, didn't they.'

'Oh,' she nods.

'I've been trying to call you all morning,' Flores says. Kira feels the interrogation begin. Even just a few months earlier, this wouldn't have been possible. But neither was what she did last night, nor Flores's doubt now.

'My battery died,' she replies, dropping her handbag on the floor. She may have to apologise for something, but not for that.

'So where have you been?' It is Prince, the brothers doing some sort of tag-team she hasn't seen before.

When she answers, it's to Flores. 'You weren't here when it happened. I was scared. I took a taxi to my mother's place.' She looks him in the eye. She has not lied. Whatever Prince is muttering, she ignores it and doesn't take her eyes from Flores. When he nods, she knows he believes her. 'Did the police tell you what happened?' she asks.

'A robbery,' Flores replies.

'An *attempted* robbery,' she corrects.

'You still shouldn'tve called the cops,' Prince repeats.

'You weren't there Prince,' she snaps, and aggressively kicks off her shoes, watching them slide along the polished floorboards, clattering against the wall.

'Is that some sort of accusation?' Prince retorts.

She laughs derisively.

'And another thing,' he continues, drumming his fingers against the wall, 'who was the dude the police said you were with?'

'Get out of here, Prince,' she says, more exhausted than exasperated.

'Well who was he?'

'No one ... a walk-in ... a soldier.'

Prince grunts dismissively. 'A hero fucking soldier.'

'He saved my life,' Kira flares, not that Prince warrants it.

'That's a bit melodramatic isn't it?'

'He had a knife. Your mate was off his head.'

'Hey!' Prince bites. 'I never met him before in my life.'

She looks piercingly at him. 'I haven't even told you who it was. I haven't even described him to you.'

She looks at Flores. See, she wants him to understand. See how dangerous your brother is.

'Don't go blaming me,' Prince says. 'Got it? Don't, right.'

'Get him out of here,' she says to Flores.

Kira leaves them for the bathroom and closes the door. She hears the brothers talking, their voices low at first, Flores, and then a burst of Prince, but not loud enough to make out the words. Kira splashes water from the washbasin into her eyes, then presses a hand-towel against her face.

There was a time, being an only child, when the ferocity of Flores's loyalty to his petty criminal younger brother was attractive to her. Principled Flores. But that was before she'd met him. The second born of the Rodriguez boys, they called him 'Prince'. More likely after Machiavelli, she began to think. Neither of whom were smart enough to stay out of prison. Certainly not this Prince, with his street dealing and his low-level gangster contacts. He'd draw Flores in if he could. If he hasn't already.

When she returns to the room Prince is gone. She lowers herself onto the futon, where Flores joins her and starts rubbing her back through her singlet. She resists, her body still cold, still tight.

'He's a prick,' she says.

'Yeah.'

'So, what are you going to do about it?'

'Nothing today. Today I'm looking after you.'

'Yes, today,' she says. 'Now. I need to know. He's poison and I need to know what you're going to do about it. Last night happened because of him. He'll bring all his crappy karma with him and we'll get swamped by it. I almost did. Look at me, Babe. I could have been killed last night. You know that, don't you?'

'I know.'

'You believe me, don't you?'

'I believe you, of course I do.' He pauses. 'But he's my brother. You don't abandon your brother.'

Why not? That's just clichéd, lazy thinking. She thought him above that.

'He needs my support right now, Babe.'

189

'What's that supposed to mean?'

'It means love. It means faith. It means hope. They're the things you've got to give.'

She's only ever read the words on him before, never heard him say them. They both look at the inside of his left forearm at the same time, *1 Corinthians 13:13*, and then at each other, awkwardly now. There's a long silence between them, as long as it might take a relationship to end.

'I could have been killed last night.'

'I know.' He reaches for her singlet, but she brushes his hand away.

'I don't want him around anymore, Flores. Okay? I'm not telling you to choose, Flores. Okay? I'm not. Give him whatever support he needs. All I'm saying is, I don't want him around here anymore. That's fair isn't it?'

'All right,' he says, and only then does she allow him to kiss her.

On his back, disappearing into the bathroom, is his great *Ancient of Days*, Blake's masterpiece, the great bearded god measuring the order of his universe from his sunstruck cloudbank. But we are full of *dis*order, she thinks, and though sometimes it is sweet, not today. Not today.

'Flores,' she says later, 'are you awake?'

He groans.

'Flores?'

'Yeah Babe?'

'Where were you last night?'

He props himself on his elbow, looks at her, but does not answer.

'The tattoo gods looked after you last night, Babe,' he whispers, touching her hipbone with his forefinger. 'They give and they take away with the same hand. If they give, it's because you earned it. They looked after you last night.'

THE TATTOO GODS

WHAT HAD SHE done to lose the favour of the gods? A question she's asked herself time and again these last years. Was it really such a grave offence she'd committed, or was she merely their plaything, moved into position as part of a cosmic rivalry she'll never fathom? All she'd done was sleep with a lonely old soldier, fresh home from a war. A single night with a sad old bugger she'd never see again. Desire? Sure, but so what? As much a gesture of thanks, an act of kindness even. Nothing Flores needed to know.

She could point to worse by Flores, a hundred grievous betrayals, both before and after Phelan – of her, others, his own tattooing deities. A cascade of small unkindnesses that in time begot savagery, more than a person should be asked to bear. Where are their judgements of *him*? Why do the gods remain silent? Damn them! Their tithe has been crippling, and still they demand more. Not just of her, but Blake too.

It was Flores who named him. She had to allow him that. 'An angel,' he'd said, nuzzling the baby in the dark, still wired from a late session, a pair of wings he'd tattooed using ink they'd made themselves from scratch, still pursuing their grand tattooing dream, reaching higher than ever for tattooing virtue. 'And no one does angels' wings like Blake.'

If she was proprietorial about raising him, it was partly because Flores was becoming so distracted. Because the tattoo gods refused to commune with the gods of economics. Crafting their own ink – collecting the material, grinding, making the pigment, then mixing it – took time. They priced their tattoos as art, as entire cycles of creative being – birth to death and beyond to eternity, but they were prophets to a paying too few.

And it was not just their own dues, but the money they needed to make to pay off Prince's suppliers, the uncertainty of whether his brother would turn up despite being warned off, and if not him then worse. Then the police and the law, and if Prince being jailed gave her some relief it was only ever temporary and didn't extend to a moratorium on his debts.

She nursed Blake in the studio, weaned him there. She took small jobs, roses as often as possible, a hibernation of her ambition, yes, but for a time her flowers became better, somehow purer. Kira fitted her clients in around Blake's feeds, a bassinet on the floor. Sometimes she worked the pedal with her left foot and the bassinet with her right, her body a conduit for the vibrations from the machine to her baby. An immersion, she thought, a baptism for the boy.

She tied a piece of material around her chest, so the child could rest against her in this pouch, so she could walk, and sit, and eat and he could feel her heart and she – if she closed her eyes – his. Sometimes she drew while she fed, pulsing with creative currents that other days faltered. Once, exhausted, she rested her head in her palm, closed her eyes, and woke to find her pencil in the child's fist. She brought her pad into her lap so the child could mark paper instead of air. Sheets of notepad she'd fold away for whatever future might await him.

They moved to a cheaper studio, and then cheaper again, working hard to take their regulars with them, trying to maintain the name, Written on the Body, which continued to mean everything to her, even as she spent fewer and fewer hours at the studio when Blake started yanking himself to his feet and pulling at power cords and knocking over ink caps.

It was disorienting to be away from the studio. Impossible, some days, to navigate, and brutally lonely. Inevitably, Flores took on another apprentice, paying him nothing till he started paying his own way, which meant he was tattooing months before he was ready. Which meant their dream was done, and they were surviving on turnover and add-ons. Piercings and the necks of drunks.

Shrinking behind ink

She can't remember exactly when she realised Flores was dealing, though she'd probably known it subconsciously for a long time. More and more he'd leave mid-afternoon if the booking list was empty, and not return, staying at his brother's. At first, their finances improved, a miracle of sorts – that while there were fewer clients, there was more cash coming in.

'It's not how many clients,' Flores told her, 'it's whether they're the right type of client.' It had been one of his sayings since she met him, so she didn't suspect anything, not from the words alone. And she was relieved the pressure was off.

But then she started coming in and examining the booking diary and it'd be empty for whole weeks, not even any regulars. Then his brother was sent inside again and still Flores stayed away at night. And when she asked, he spat at her feet, as if the question was an impertinence.

The first time he hit her she heard, above his fury, between the pushes and the slaps and the closed fists, between his bone and hers, the sound of something tapping against the window behind her.

The places the mind can take you when you need it to. The door to the apartment was locked so there was nowhere to run; she'd tried to fight back but he'd quickly overwhelmed her. So her mind left her body to its fate, led her to turn her head away from Flores, to follow the odd little tapping sound at the window. And there, attracted by the light in the apartment, was a Christmas beetle bunting against the glass. *Tap*, it went, *tap*, then wheeled around and flew at the glass again, thumping into the windowpane, its shimmering metallic colour. It'd been years since she'd seen one, since she was a kid, and now this poor little beetle with its glossy rainbow-coloured back was tapping at her from outside, prepared to die to get in.

At some point she became aware that Flores had stopped, and was beside her on the floor, uttering pleas of contrition and shame, lifting her, cradling her in his lap, petting her hair, sobbing, 'What have I done? What have I done?'

In the morning, she conspired with him to be ill for a week. In the morning, he played Lego with Blake before leaving to buy creams and icepacks and wheat bags from the chemist. In the morning, she found the Christmas beetle's body resting on the ledge outside the window.

'Never again,' Flores promised. But he'd dragged her across a border to a land she'd never conceived crossing, and part of her could never return to safety. She knew that. 'Never again,' he vowed, but it wasn't Flores the tattoo-poet making the promise, it was a functionary in an opaque distribution network doing runs to the western suburbs when directed to, every now and then icing up.

'It's all good, Babe,' he tells her, 'it's all good.'

IT DOESN'T TAKE long for a body to disappear entirely. Kira is proof. She covers herself. Not her neck, not her face, but she hurries to fill the rest of her body. So many protective tattoos to stand beside her Celtic warrioress. A great Christmas beetle for her right shoulder, for the angel who'd come to her rescue. She asked Flores to tattoo that one, explained to him its significance, believing his vows, hoping that if Flores did it, the ink would be a seal of sorts, a blood oath. But after the second time and then the third, she turned to other tattooists. Dragons and tigers and eagles.

'Who the fuck's work is that?' he'd ask.

She knew better than to tell him.

'You shouldn't be letting anyone else touch you, Babe. You fucking shouldn't. Just look at yourself. You're ruining yourself, Babe.'

But she wants to become impenetrable. Messages of courage and strength on the backs of her fingers. Skulls. Roses growing from bony eye sockets. She shrinks behind her ink. She builds a wall around herself, aiming to disappear behind it, untouchable.

Until the return one morning of Brigadier James Phelan. Until the moment she hears his voice, sees her own tattoo, imagines his strength. Without even being aware she's doing it, she weeps.

Have the tattoo gods sent him again? she wonders. Is he their emissary? But what message is the soldier carrying: hope or damnation?

Between his thumb and forefinger

'Kick?' Flores proposes.

Blake nods enthusiastically.

But nothing can be taken at face value.

'I'll come too,' Kira says, standing, not wanting to let Blake out of her sight.

'Whatever,' Flores grunts.

She looks out the passenger side window of the red Audi A5 Flores has been looking after for Prince these last twelve months, stored in a secure garage around the corner, a low thump of bass from the speakers.

At the park, Blake runs ahead. Kira sits on a grassy mound watching the soccer field. Nearby, older boys shoot hoops on the cracked bitumen basketball court and two young mothers bend over each other's second-hand pram and console one another. Flores is still strong, still muscular, an athleticism that used to be benign, beautiful. He kicks the first ball to Blake, but misdirects it, and Blake has to run to retrieve it.

Even Flores seems anxious about Prince's release this time. Prison has never broken his brother, nor ever rehabilitated him, only strengthened him. The networks he expands inside, the fresh loyalties he attracts. But what has Flores been up to while his brother has been away? Has he been caretaking Prince's share of the business, or cutting in, squeezing him out? Who owns what? she wonders. Who owns who? And who, ultimately, owns me?

After ten minutes, Flores leads Blake away from her on the knoll, towards some empty goalposts and the tattered netting draped over the crossbar. They're out of earshot now, and she feels a flutter of anxiety. Flores stands in goal and crouches while Blake shoots, Flores casually stopping each shot. Each time he rolls the ball back to the boy, who tries again. And each time Flores reaches out and stops it, rolls it back. It seems cruel.

She watches as Flores gestures for Blake to come to him, watches as the man bends to the boy to impart something, some fatherly lesson about soccer and life. A sudden wave of panic washes over her. What the hell is he saying? she wants to know. What poisonous advice? What faux verities about blood and loyalty? With what words might he destroy a still innocent child?

Flores pulls away from the game to take a phone call, then another, a flurry, and they have to leave.

BACK AT THE apartment the doorbell rings. Kira starts. Every knock on the door these days, every turning of a key, every buzzer, causes her stomach to tighten, her heart to quicken. Flores coming home at some odd agitated hour, or a visit from one of his 'business associates' as he calls them, or a friend who'll collect him for a drink or a long session of weights. If he's home, it is she who answers, Flores watching on. It is always for him. Kira can't remember the last time she had a visitor – does anyone even know she's here? She gets the door and the phone, collects the mail from the wall of boxes in the lobby. It's become a form of servitude.

How entirely she has become attuned to him and his moods, always aware of whatever room in the apartment he's temporarily occupying, whatever thing it is he's doing there, weighing how long it will take, whether it's simple or not, whether he's cursing it. How much time she has before he'll emerge, seeking her out.

We evolve like this, with survival mechanisms. She's part-dog, with her heightened hearing, and part-insect in the way she detects vibrations in the walls and the floor, the shifts in the currents of late-afternoon dust motes falling across a bank of louvres. Her thousand different antennae. It's got so she anticipates his activity. How she has grown to hate herself.

But today she resists. Some premonition.

'I'll get it then,' he mutters, another blade of resentment.

She hears Flores answer the door, then a pause as he steps out onto the landing, followed by back-slapped greetings and grunts of primal acknowledgement. Flores closes the apartment door on her, Blake in his bedroom. The murmur of voices continues outside, Flores and his visitor. She is, for this moment at least, safe.

The phone rings. She stands in the kitchen and picks it up. It's the real estate agent. Already the rent is late.

'No, it can't wait,' the agent says forcefully, 'I need to speak with him, now.'

Kira walks slowly down the hall. She leans forward towards the glass eye in the door and brings her own eye up to it. Flores's back is to her, his shoulders broader than usual under the distorting effect of the lens. Whoever he is speaking with is still on the landing, just out of view. But there is something about Flores's stance, as if it has hardened into contest.

Even as she bends and peers, Flores reaches abruptly for the handle, sensing her presence. She leaps back from the opening door.

Prince is harder, bigger than ever – his chest, his arms, his neck, his abdomen, the product of his twelve-month sentence to a prison gym. He attempts a smile, but it is twisted beyond recognition and quickly settles into a more comfortable sneer.

'You won't even allow your man to welcome his brother into his own home,' he says to her, but the greater accusation is aimed at Flores, belittling him. There was a time when Kira used to meet Prince's eyes, could wave him and his antics away. No longer.

Flores turns, wanting to take his humiliation out on her. 'Who was that on the phone?'

'The real estate,' she answers. 'They say it's urgent.'

Flores reaches towards her, Prince watching the slow trajectory of his brother's right hand as it nears her chest, and then, with calm deliberation, pinches her left nipple through her T-shirt.

'Tell him I'll call him back,' he says, twisting her nipple between his thumb and forefinger, before releasing her.

SECOND CONTACT

KIRA HAS CHOSEN this life, twice. First, she chose a life of tattooing with Flores. Then, after Blake was born, she chose life with Flores. She can only forgive herself the first decision. If not forgivable, perhaps the second can be reversed.

But she must be careful. Anyone might open her email, her end or his, and at his, maybe a wife, perhaps a secretary. Yet this may be her only chance. She composes and recomposes the message in her mind for days.

> *Dear James, I hope it is not presumptuous to think you might remember me from when I tattooed you!*

I will never forget that night. I have thought about it often – partly because no one has saved my life again since! Is that too dramatic? I don't think so. Perhaps I should have tattooed your name on me in gratitude! I still have the stencil of your friend Samuel Beckett's tattoo, and I wondered, after seeing your interview, whether you might want it.
Best wishes, Kira

It's a monument to restraint. She hopes she's been able to hide her desperation. Conceal also the falsities the note holds. She wants him to recognise her, but how much of her is there left to recognise?

PHELAN WALKS LAPS of his office, circling the glowing computer screen, unable to break away, unable also to stop for fear he will impale himself upon the shards of memory. Kira!

It's not so much memory as feeling that has him swirling out and around and back again. Maybe not even feeling, but remembrance of feeling, returned to him through a thousand distorting filters.

I am still here, the words that flash like lightning, *are you?*

He could delete it and trash it and walk away, and perhaps forget. But he knows he has not forgotten yet, so there's no true prospect of that. If it's not about forgetting then, perhaps it's the same as staying sober. The daily recommitments and the baby steps.

Ask yourself, James: Is this good for you or bad? Ask: Do you want to go back there, having come so far?

She's still in Sydney, he learns from the web, and still tattooing. Though her studio is at a different street address, it has retained the name, the same manifesto, the same website layout. As if gathering electronic dust.

Banging harder on the keyboard doesn't help, but he doesn't know that yet. Doesn't know either that you can't type at the speed of a racing heart. He writes:

Dear Kira, What a surprise. And thank you – for the offer of the stencil, but also just for making contact. The answer is yes. Perhaps I can visit next time I'm in Sydney? I still have to thank you properly. Yours, Jim

And before he can reconsider the message and all its lawless echoes, it's gone. He rests his head in his hands. What is there to thank her for? There is an erratic pendulum in his heart. What exactly? Material for a poem or two. His exile. A fist of lapis lazuli that went astray six years ago and which, when the memory of it comes upon him, refills the pool of his guilt.

LEAVING, COMING

THERE IS A single frenzied hour of packing the Subaru station wagon with clothes and bedding and toys and the half dozen things she says to herself she can never abandon, the lapis crane she's stored among her trinkets, her Nikon, her metal briefcase with her Micky Sharpz and as much tattooing gear as she can fit. She stops at the bank first and empties their account, before picking up Blake.

When she arrives at school his teacher looks into her eyes in the corridor outside his classroom and knows, gathering a term's worth of lessons into a satchel and kissing Blake on the top of his head and brushing his fringe from his eyes then taking Kira's own shaking hands and saying to them both, 'Go well.'

Phelan wants to thank her properly. She grasps it, believes it. She arcs around the city on the M4, Blake's face turned to the window. Remember to pay the tolls when you stop tonight, she tells herself, or the infringement notices they'll send to the flat will reveal your route to him. Don't speed either, and beware red-light cameras. This discipline she forces on herself, the effort it takes to quell her instinct to get as far away as she can, as quickly as she can. To flee, flee, flee.

SHE KNOWS HE'S north, Toowoomba, but has no other clues.

'Mum,' Blake says eventually, 'where are we going?'

She adjusts the rear-view mirror and looks at her son in the booster seat he's almost outgrown. She looks at him and all the years the two of them made believe he was a king and the seat was his throne and he would issue giggling edicts to his subjects, her. But now she sees his white singlet beneath his blue-chequered school shirt and the seat belt cutting diagonally across his little chest restraining him is no royal sash. All the old dispensations are gone, she thinks, going, going, gone.

He's looking at her, waiting.

'We're going on a holiday,' she says, sick in her stomach as she says it, but sensing too she's just the last in a fellowship of women who've used those precise words to tell that same fairytale. To help make him believe it, she says, 'We're going on an adventure.' Why not? 'We'll see things that'll make your classmates jealous.'

'Is Dad coming?'

'No Blakey,' Kira says. 'He's got to stay home and work.'

THERE ISN'T A house she's visited across their years together – either with him or alone – that he won't ransack to find her. She'd abandoned her mother years before, and though her mother had no part in this life of hers, no responsibility for it either, he'll visit her now, and Kira wonders if what her mother learns will horrify her. He'll locate her childhood friends and her art-school mates and have his business associates watch them till he's sure she's not there. He'll call in favours, he'll recruit anyone who owes him, no matter how small, no matter how reluctant. Sydney's not such a big town.

THE MOTEL WHERE they stop, exhausted, halfway up the highway, has free WiFi. She's not bold, she's desperate. She wants to scream *help* but doesn't want to lose him. She checks the time, just after eight, and Blake asleep. She writes:

Dear Jim, I'd love to see you again. As luck would have it, I'm going to be passing through Toowoomba the day after tomorrow on my way to Brisbane. Perhaps we can meet somewhere?
Warmly
Kira

They'll get there earlier than that, tomorrow she hopes, but it'll probably be late, and she can't afford to scare him. Hopes feverishly she already hasn't. Before Kira crawls into bed beside Blake she puts out their clothes for the next day and repacks the wagon so all they need to do in the morning is check her email, dress and leave.

PHELAN WAKES AT two, as he often does in the house. Sometimes he returns to sleep. Not tonight. Even if he hadn't dreamed of her, he is alive with her, the night is breathless and his heart will not still. When he turns on the computer in his study, Kira's name is there too, glowing in the dark. He closes and locks the door before sitting down to her message.

He understands just one thing from what he reads: he's going to see her again. The rest is flash and fire and he knows the sky above the tin roof is blazing with stars, and somewhere up there her silhouette is giving the night its shape, her body astride him, her hips, her tongue. This great uncompleted need, dormant for so long.

He's stirred in a way he thought he never would be again. He'd resigned himself to a new self – that the man he's been rebuilding for so long was without desire. The changes wrought by years of medication, creeping age, all the shifts in his relationship with Penny he doesn't entirely understand. That she has given so much to him that perhaps his body knows not to ask for more. Whatever it is, his desire shocks him, threatens to burst through.

Luck's got nothing to do with this, he thinks.

I can't wait, he types in the light of the pulsing screen, his fingers trembling. *There's a café at Picnic Point. Let's meet there, tomorrow, Saturday. Can you make midday?*

His blood pulses with her as she returns to him, once again swimming back to him from the vastness of the Pacific Ocean, her skin glistening, his body aching.

KIRA PULLS OUT of the motel at dawn the next day, elated in a way she couldn't explain. Behind her Blake has disappeared into *My Neighbour Totoro* playing on the DVD player she's hooked over the back of the passenger seat. She winds down the window to hear the morning roar. She reaches out. The cool air buffets her hand. She allows it to pass through her fingers. How smooth, how easy. And yet now, finally, she has something solid to reach for, a tomorrow from which she might pull herself to safety. She feels herself surge with something she's hasn't felt for a long time. A tremor of life, hope.

Almost a miracle that the world is offering her this once again. Phelan.

AZURE OR COBALT?

BY DAWN, LYING on his night-tossed mattress, Phelan is swinging wildly. Penny moves around her bedroom, preparing for work, unknowing. Phelan unlocks his room and steps out into the morning hallway, desperate to recognise something of himself. Through the square of frosted glass in the door at the end of the corridor a tribune of daylight is glowing. He blinks.

'Good morning,' Penny says from behind him, startling him.

'Morning,' he mumbles. He can't turn around to face her, the swell of guilt too great. He hears her standing there in the hall for a long, long time, waiting for him. When she gives up and returns to her bedroom and her make-up, closing the door on him, Phelan doubles over, sick in his gut.

He has to get out, opens the door and hurries from the verandah into the garden and through the gate, and across the paling summer grasses in the paddock out towards the escarpment, his dog trailing him, nudging him for a pat he can't give. He sits, lights a smoke and looks out. An unseasonal mist has pooled in the valley below. The dog whimpers and Phelan slips his hand under its collar, feeling the rhythmic rise and fall of its chest but unable to fall in with it. A second cigarette, a third, half a pack, just one more.

He waits until Penny is gone. There's a note on the kitchen table. She'll be back at four. Text her if he wants her to pick anything up on the way home, a kiss and a hug, *xo*. A drink, he thinks bitterly, I could do with a fucking bottle of whiskey.

Once upon a time, a lifetime ago, he'd been constant. Once upon a time he'd known what to do, knew what he wanted. He'd thought that steady man was returning. He'd thought that man was back, or nearly so. During all his ruminations about Beckett, through the years of his fixations and his painstaking regathering of fragments of himself, she'd been invisible. He'd somehow severed her, disappeared that night from his memory, erased it from what had remained of his life and what he and Penny had been rebuilding. But now! Now she comes rushing back, a torrent, throwing him off course again, sweeping him away, taunting him, and it is Beckett who remains, burning at his shoulder. Beckett, mocking him. My cock, my nuts.

'Fuck,' Phelan screams at the ceiling. *Fuuuuuck*. He scratches at his shoulder with his fingernails, great agitated gouges. Fuck. Fuck. Fuck. They cleared the beer out of the fridge years ago. Still he goes and stands and stares. There's an opened bottle of moselle that Penny's begun drinking occasionally after her years of saintly fucking abstinence in support of him. He pours it down his throat, dizzy, gone, the taste of it. Fuck her that she's got the Hilux with her in town, and that the quad bike is in getting serviced and that he's trapped, and there's no bottle shop, no pub, nothing in walking distance. The old anxiety overwhelms him as he stands in the small kitchen in the Big House, a fusillade of competing compulsions. He rushes out to the verandah, his wild eyes groping for the horizon.

He chains the dog to its kennel, and sets out in search of something to drink. The fleeing sound of his boots on the concrete path from the back door to the gate to the gravel road. He hurries past the three bunya pines on his right, oblivious to them. He is vaguely aware of the cottage on his left as he starts his determined march up the rise and then down the other side to the yards. After that he turns east and forces his body between two strands of barbed wire, catching and tearing his shirt. The barbs bite at his flesh as he pulls free and when he feels his burning skin it feels good. He continues his march on the other side, more slowly. He reaches the edge of the escarpment and skirts it south, pushing his ungainly way through the afternoon bush, scattering the birds and insects, the fallen bark bursting under the soles of his boots, all the bushcraft of which he'd once been so proud, gone.

He does not see the bandicoot hole for the long grass and steps into it, tripping, falling, twisting his ankle, cursing. He lies back, feeling the pain, feeling his ankle begin to swell. But he knows not to rest too long and rises, limps on.

At the boundary fence to the first of the mansions he stops. His ankle is throbbing, the cut on his back too. As he catches his breath, he looks for movement behind the windows of the house ahead, but the curtains are drawn, and there is no car in the carport either, no clothes on the line. He crawls awkwardly between the fence wires, taking more care this time, and hobbles across the exposed grass, increasing his pace now that he is in the open, alert to danger all around him.

Phelan reaches the cover of the house, presses his body against the wall and stops. He's controlling his breathing now, gauging his environment, measuring the distance to the end of the wall. He feels uncomfortably light, almost naked. His chest is exposed, his head, and he's already received a flesh wound on his back. There's an old rake propped against the side of the house ahead of him, and he takes it, holding it crossways. It's good to have something in his hands, some weight to balance him. He slowly circumnavigates the house, peering through the windows and the glass doors, stopping at intervals to put his ear to the wall, listening. Satisfying himself it's empty, he finds the spare key on a hook under the tank stand.

Phelan opens the living room cabinets, one by one, till he finds the spirits shelf. He pushes the bottles of rum and gin aside until he finds the whiskeys, rummaging among them, glass clinking against glass. He unscrews the cap on a bottle of Jameson's, snapping the seal, his fist tight around its thin neck. Then the sting in the back of his throat. His burning, blinking eyes. The smoke of burning abstinence. His nerves beginning to calm.

He finds a tumbler and drops into an armchair facing a pair of enormous sliding glass doors that frame the east. He can almost smell the light outside, the dryness of it in his throat. He slugs and gazes and there is the glass and what is beyond the glass, and he flicks between the two in search of some distracting optical effect, anything, but he is suddenly exhausted from the trek and closes his eyes.

THERE'S AN EXPLOSION in the room, a great bang and a shuddering and Phelan throws himself to the ground and he is rolling for cover, his heart rushing, his head beating, some fuck somewhere, some fight, some flight, the suck of death. Fuck, fuck, fuck. It's him that's going to explode. The reverberations of the detonation are roiling around the room and he can hear through the echoes a scratching, and sees the glass is still intact, and the scratching is on the other side of the pane and he is sure Beckett is clawing towards him, but there's no bloody hand yet reaching slowly up the glass. Still the scratching, louder, more insistent, and he uncurls himself, and is on his knees and it's good that the glass hasn't shattered and it's good that it's still just him in the room, and it's good that while the room is reverberating there aren't shells coming in too, one, two, three fucking hundred.

When eventually he stands, what he sees is a kingfisher stilled in the gloam beyond the glass, its body crumpled on the decking where it has fallen after flying into the door. Still Phelan's heart thuds. He finds the latch and slides the glass doors. He kneels and picks the thing up and lays it in his great shaking palm, still warm. There's a cross-breeze ruffling its feathers and he's unsure whether it's dead. Azure or cobalt? he wonders of its wings. There's a tremor, and a heart, and its beak parts, its hardness on his skin too, and as he holds the creature in the cup of his trembling hand it levers itself up with a wing and grasps his hard forefinger with its iron claws and steadies itself. The whiskey is inside, but he waits here for long minutes as the bird rests on his hand, gathering strength before remembering something out there in the bush or in the air, and pushing against his hand, taking flight. Gone.

The hand that held the bird that holds the whiskey. He pours another glass, and then another, a setting sun's worth, opens another bottle, and finally it is dark and his head is empty and his hands have stopped their trembling and he's forgotten the bird and maybe he's asleep.

Refugee

She drives through the long day, Armidale and Glen Innes and Tenterfield and Warwick, towns that looked more substantial on the map than they are passing through. Finally, Toowoomba, whatever that means, the first of the Aboriginal names this side of the border. Already she's further north than she's ever been before.

She has left almost everything, as refugees do. Her entire portfolio is back there, all the drawings and the paintings and the stencils she's kept. Her history told in leaves of paper and cardboard. Kira imagines him tossing them out. Not for him the melodrama of tearing them up, or burning them, or tipping them out the window into the street. He'll calmly carry them, load by load, down to the skip in the alley behind the apartment block till the bin's full, and he'll wait until the collectors lift it on their mechanical arms and the bin tilts and tips and her life of drawing is upended into the back of the council rubbish truck. She can almost hear the increased pitch in its engine as it accelerates away.

But she has the pictures in her head. She lies awake at night and tries to retrieve them. Stronger than her memories of the drawings are the bodies. She could track them down, she thinks, those arms and backs and thighs and hips. Those parts of herself on other people's bodies moving in the world, showing her off. It amazes her, when she stops to think about it, that this very moment her tattoos are cleaning kitchens and writing judgements and driving buses and dealing cards and making love and publishing poems. What that map would look like.

She could go to her website, she thinks, and – if he hasn't yet pulled it down – click through the images in her gallery. He could easily have shut the site down, eliminated that part of her too. It's irrational, but she fears even checking, easy as it would be. The fear? That somehow, if she clicked onto the website, it'd lead him to her. Even crazier is the fear that she'd be sitting at a computer in some council library somewhere, and the moment she clicked on the webpage link, he'd appear on the screen, looking at her, watching, and that he'd then know where she was – seated before what monitor in what library in what street in what town – and come looking, track her down. That if she clicked on her own site, she'd give herself away.

So, she's a refugee, seeking strength, protection, possibility. The one last man, that's who she's after. The one who might take them in, and who might have the power to protect them. The one upon whom she and Blake, surely, have as great a claim as anyone.

'Who are you?'

Phelan is blinking, and shaking his head, and staggering to his feet in the blinding whiteness of the new world. But it's just a man in a pale blue shirt and suit trousers, and Phelan groggily assesses it is no one to fear and drops back into the armchair, squinting against the fluorescent ceiling lights. The stranger still has his car keys in his outstretched right hand, frozen in the moment of placing them on the kitchen bench.

'What are you doing in my house?'

Phelan's head is spinning. He reaches for the tumbler, which is empty, and then the bottle and drains the last of the man's Jameson's. He stands and limps towards the man, his right hand outstretched.

'Do I know you?' the man asks.

'Brigadier James Phelan,' he says, drunk. 'Poet. Husband. Arsehole.'

Then Phelan unsteadily points back across the ridges and through the bush in the direction of the Big House where Penny will be beside herself. He points to the vague north, as if that is where Brigadier James Phelan might be found.

'Afghanistan?' the man asks, thinking lame leg, thinking IED.

'Yes,' Phelan slurs, his swollen ankle just another thing to shame him.

WHEN PENNY COLLECTS him, he is weeping. She apologises to their neighbour, who waves her away.

'It's nothing,' he says patiently.

She had thought these embarrassments were behind them.

Her husband sobs that he doesn't deserve her. She gets him into the passenger seat and lays it back so he can curl up and cry as she drives him home. 'I love you, Pen. I love you.' Her eyes are on the road. She asks nothing. Outside the gate of the Big House she opens the car door and kneels on the grass and strokes his head till the angle of the risen moon strikes them both.

By the time he gets into the house he is emptied out, except for his pounding head. She gives him Panadol, and then Valium and settles him into bed, the radio on in the kitchen, the bedroom shades drawn, frames of rectangled moonlight around them.

What, she thinks, has triggered this? It's not always obvious, not always anything significant, sometimes just three nightmares in a row. But there's usually something. Perhaps he's just deflated after the euphoria of the television interview and all the activity that followed, the messages of encouragement, the thanks for starting a 'national conversation' about what the war is doing to us. Tomorrow, she thinks, I'll ask him tomorrow.

THOUGH DARK HAS fallen, Kira finds the caravan park on the southern edge of town. In the office the manager is watching the Saturday night league on a small television perched on the reception desk. He doesn't look at her as she checks in, only breaking contact with the screen to count the cash she hands him as payment for a bed.

PHELAN WAKES IN the night, panting. The images are still stampeding through him and over him, and his ears are ringing and the gore on his hands is sticky and won't go away, and he's wiping and wiping and wiping them against his pants, and when that's no good he's trying to shake his own bloodied hands off the end of his arms to get away from every little piece of Beckett that's still clinging to him.

He spills a glass of water down his front as he tries to drink at the kitchen sink, and still the images of Beckett pulse before him. Phelan presses his fists into his eyes until his eyeballs hurt and he's temporarily blinded.

Don't come, he emails her.

ALL HER PROTECTIVE SPELLS

IT IS RAINING lightly when Kira wakes. She looks at her son making origami cranes on the bunk of the onsite caravan, his little hands deftly folding sheets of bright yellow paper. She can't afford to tire. Blake needs her to be vigilant, not just for the things she fears, but all the demons out there whose existence she can't conceive of, let alone comprehend. Does she look at the boy too often and too much? This itself turns into an anxiety; that under her gaze the boy might atrophy, or become pressed out of the shape he was destined for.

Kira locks the caravan and steps across the gravel to the common room to check her emails. She hopes Phelan will be there, but fears Flores will. That he will have got over the shock of her leaving, and will now be working on a plan.

She logs on to a barrage of messages from Flores. His name fills her inbox, line after line. It's as if she's already doing her penance, as if it has already been written out there on the screen, again and again, a hundred times.

Kira's hand shakes as the cursor hovers over his name. Should I, should I, should I? She gulps and then clicks hard on the last email from him before pulling her hand back quickly, as if the mouse and keyboard themselves might harm her.

Put the money back and I won't come looking for you.

Fuck. She can't breathe. Fuck, fuck, fuck. She bangs down on the keyboard, hits the delete key and holds it, wiping away his name, sweeping away all the other names in there as well, Phelan too, clearing her whole inbox, then clearing trash. Getting as far away from him as possible, eliminating him, cleansing herself. But as she sits in the chair gazing at the empty inbox, hugging herself, rocking on the chair's spindly legs, a new email comes in. It feels like retaliation.

There's nowhere to hide. Put the money back in first. Then bring Blake back.

She stares at the message. It seems to fill the whole screen, seems to pulse, until the blood behind her eyes starts throbbing in agreement with it. She stands, worried suddenly about Blake alone in the caravan. Bang. Delete. Shut down.

WHEN THE RAIN stops she asks for directions to Picnic Point.

'It's up on the range,' the manager tells her, looking at her now. 'At the end of Tourist Drive. You can't miss it. All roads lead to Picnic Point.'

'Rubbish,' the man's wife interjects, appearing through the doorway from their flatette. She wears large owl-wise dark-rimmed glasses, has bare shoulders, and startling fluorescent blue hair. She carries a paperback novel in both hands.

'Rubbish yourself,' he retorts before rising from his chair and abandoning the reception to his wife.

'Love,' the woman says to her, setting her book almost reverently on the counter, 'this isn't Rome. But the view you get from up there is second to none ... Second to none ... There's a bit of a café, though you'll get cheaper coffees elsewhere. And there's a good park for the young 'un to play in.'

The woman pulls out a tourist map of the town, and marks the route in red pen, before going on to circle the nearest corner shop and the town centre and the skating rink which is half-price for kids on Sundays. Kira is only half-listening, distracted by the woman's hair. Not the brightness of the dye – Kira's done similar herself – but the surprise of it, here, on a wet morning, at a caravan park like this, with a husband like that. It's comforting, reassuring even, as if all things are possible, even still.

'Thank you,' Kira says, grateful for every simple act of kindness.

'You're welcome, Love. Just passing through are we?'

'Visiting friends and relatives,' Kira answers, still smiling.

'You're not from here though? Sydney?'

Kira is startled. 'How did you know?'

'Your plates, Love.'

Ah. Yes.

'Visiting the boy's father, are we?' the woman asks, gesturing her head to Blake who's standing barefoot in a puddle outside. Her smile is intended to be matronly, but the intrusion stuns Kira and she looks at the woman, agape.

'Well,' the woman says, registering Kira's reaction, 'then you must have left him behind. Look, Love, there's nothing to be worried about here. We see it all. It's usually one or the other for the mothers that visit us from interstate. Just let us know if you think there's going to be trouble, that's all. Better for us to be able to help out, step in early. You know?'

• • •

KIRA ARRIVES HALF an hour early and parks down from the lookout, beneath the pines. She gives Blake a water bottle and biscuits and puts on another *Hayao Miyazaki* anime for him.

'I'll be just up the top there,' she says to the boy. 'You stay here, Blakey. Okay?' But he is already lost in the images on the screen, filling with wonder.

She stands on the viewing platform jutting out over the valley. She is oblivious to the vista, examining instead each vehicle as it nears, watching their drivers emerge, each a spark of trembling hope. Will he even recognise me? Kira thinks about how much of her has been covered, how many new tattoos she's collected since her Celtic warrioress, how many reinforcements her talismanic protector has called in over the years. A menagerie of guardian beasts. All those protective spells she's tattooed on her skin since. *Hope* and *strength* and *carpe diem*. Heavy words that somehow seem to mock her.

Midday passes. She wanders over to the café and scans the tables inside. She speaks to a waiter, but there's no booking for a Phelan. She returns to the platform where tourists and lovers come and go, pointing or resting their elbows on the railing or pushing coins into the mounted telescope and bending and pressing their eye against the glass. Twelve-thirty passes, and then one o'clock. She checks on Blake, who's fallen asleep in his seat, and restarts the disc in case he wakes.

One-thirty. Perhaps he got here before she arrived, she thinks. Perhaps he'd observed her from some discrete vantage point, seen her with Blake. Fled.

SHE STANDS IN the doorway of the caravan park's office.

'What's up, Love?'

'I ...' but Kira can't speak and bursts into tears.

The woman comes from behind the desk and puts an arm around her.

'There, there,' she says. 'What's happened?'

Kira composes herself, and tells the woman she's lost her phone with all of her addresses and phone numbers. That she's now got no way of contacting her father, who will be worried sick about her.

'You don't know where he lives, Love?'

'He's new to town,' Kira answers, producing a copy of the newspaper article she'd printed out at the studio, showing the woman a photo of Phelan. She wouldn't happen to know him, would she?

'He doesn't have a number in the phone book?'

'I don't know,' Kira stammers, not having thought to look him up there, not ready to speak with him by phone anyway.

The woman puts his name into the online directory, but nothing comes up. 'Being a brigadier and all, he'll probably have a silent number. Let me see what I can find out, Love,' the woman says, retreating into her office to make some calls to her grapevine of friends.

'He's out on the range at Preston,' the woman says when she returns ten minutes later, watching Kira carefully. 'Does that ring a bell?'

'That's it!' Kira exclaims, feigning recognition. 'Thank you, oh thank you!'

The woman clicks her tongue, then comes around from behind the counter and takes another map from the carousel of tourist pamphlets in the corner of the reception foyer, writes down the address and marks the route.

'While there was no entry in the directory for your father,' the woman says, handing Kira the map, 'the number was there under his wife's name and initials. And the address. He and ... your mother ... moved out there maybe a year ago.' The woman pauses. 'She *is* your mother, isn't she?'

'Families are complicated things,' Kira says, without meeting the woman's eye.

Two women and a boy

KIRA DRIVES DOWN the long dirt track to the house and pulls up near the shed with the white ute parked inside. It is late afternoon. She'd half-expected to be greeted suspiciously at the gate like in a scene from a rural-gothic movie, an apron and a shotgun, but the house seems still. She waits. She sits in the car until Blake begins to whinge.

'All right Little Man,' she says, pulling on his purple gum boots.

She's about to knock when the door opens. His wife, Kira understands immediately, even though she has no picture of Phelan's wife in her head. This woman is a similar age to Phelan, if younger then not by too much. Her face is weathered but open, a neatness about her – hair pulled back from her forehead, plucked eyebrows, cheekbones high in the western sun. Though her eyes are tired, as if she may not have slept, there is a solidity about her in the doorway, deciding who will pass.

'Yes?' the wife says, looking from the woman to the boy and back. 'Can I help?'

'Hello,' Kira replies. 'I ... we ...' she says, trying to meet the woman's eyes, before she herself chokes and bows her head.

The boy looks up at her, startled, as his mother's chest begins to heave.

'Mum?' he says, and when she does not answer, he says it again, scared now, 'Mum, what's wrong?'

PENNY GLANCES ACROSS to the car but there is no one else with them. Just a wagon packed high with boxes and bags, a jumble of domestic items hard against the inside of the windows, as if pressing to get out.

'Who are you?' she asks. The woman's heavily tattooed hand grasps the boy's. The anger in those tattoos, Penny thinks, the fierceness of that grip. She resists an urge to retreat silently back into the house. Breathe, she tells herself, and she straightens.

'I ... I ... I ...' the woman stutters through her sobbing. 'I'm a friend of Jim's. I mean ... I used to be ... I mean, the poem ...'

Then it hits Penny. 'Are you the tattoo artist?'

The woman nods.

'You're the one who gave him the tattoo?' Penny knows she's now at the edge of a precipice, feels it in her body, but can't yet imagine what's at the bottom. 'From Sydney?'

'Yes,' the woman says, then adds, 'we've just driven up.'

'Today?'

'Over the last few days.'

And then, after a pause, a quiet in which both women are only vaguely looking at each other, in which both of them are instead reaching back into their own universes for some principle that might stabilise this moment, some memory. After that long pause the woman summons up the courage.

'Is Jim here?'

'What's your name?' Penny asks.

'Kira.'

'Kira who?'

'Dyson.'

Penny nods slowly, not knowing how to fit the information into the fragile matrix of her life, what weight to give it. But the longer the two of them stand facing each other, the stronger Penny feels. Perhaps it's the tattooed woman's obvious vulnerability and neediness, or the look of bewilderment on the face of the child. Maybe it's also that this is her home, her threshold as much as James's. And that she'd been right about something setting him off, that her instincts are good. That she can trust herself.

'James is not here right now,' she replies. By which she means he's not standing there with the two of them and the boy. Whether he's asleep, or still hungover, or cowering in his room, Penny doesn't yet care. 'What do you want?'

THEY SIT ON the front verandah with cups of tea, Blake with a lemonade. He nestles against his mother on the day bed, leaning into her even as he sips, listening to the sound of her talking, the cool melamine cup in his little hands, the vibrations of his mother's voice. Penny holds a plate of chocolate chip biscuits out to him. Blake stretches forward and takes one.

'Have a couple,' she says, and then to Kira, 'I'm afraid we don't have much here for kids to play with.'

Penny watches the tattooist lift the small china teacup to her lips. Her awkwardness with it – she's not a regular tea drinker. Her dark lipstick, her dark fingernail polish. Penny reads the lettering on Kira's fingers, *L-O-V-E* and *H-O-P-E*, and sees other markings – inked rings, a lightning bolt, clef notes, a yin on the back of one hand, a yang on the other. She realises too that what she'd earlier thought was shadow at the neckline of the woman's T-shirt, is ink. She looks away and out across the paddocks.

'He could climb on top of the harvester,' Penny says to Kira suddenly, pointing at the old Sunshine rusting near the side fence, 'and have a good muck around on it.'

'Is it safe?'

'As safe as anything else around here.'

The tattooist nods. 'There you go Little Man,' she says to her son, 'go and have a play. It looks a bit like a spaceship doesn't it? See the seat? See if you can climb on top of that. I'll be right here watching.'

When he's gone she tells her story to Penny, the violence and the threats of it, how she had no choice but to leave. That she'd seen James on television. How he'd saved her once before and that perhaps, just perhaps, he could put her up for a bit now while she caught her breath and thought things through and made a plan and found her feet and …

Penny feels herself harden as Kira falters then hurries on, trying to repair her misstep. She tells Penny she's got cash, isn't a sponge, but that whatever happens she can't let Flores find her.

'We're desperate,' Kira pleads, looking at her, not yet sure if she's a foe. 'I hoped Jim might be able to help.'

Penny tries to weigh all of this, to pick the lies from the self-deception from the mere bullshit. The seconds build, long and ominous, until the silence looms over this visitor, increasingly insurmountable.

'There wasn't anyone else I could think of!' Kira blurts, and Penny accepts the desperation is real. Can see it in her eyes.

Even so, Penny waves the pleading away. 'Flores is your husband?'

'He thinks he owns me,' Kira answers miserably.

'And he doesn't know where you are?'

'No.'

'Where does he *think* you are?'

'I don't know.'

'Come on!' Penny snaps at her. 'Think. What's going through his head now? Where does he think you've gone? Friends, relatives? Where?'

'None of my old friends – and that's what they are, 'cause I haven't seen them for years – know anything about Jim. Never heard of him. Even if Flores tried to torture it out of them,' she smiles blackly, 'they wouldn't know to tell him.'

'Can he track you?'

'No.'

'You're sure?'

Kira looks away, thinking.

'The car? Whose name is it registered in?' Penny presses.

'Mine …'

'Mmm.'

'Don't you believe me?' Kira asks eventually.

Penny gazes at the boy, sitting proudly on the harvester's iron seat, his hands out in front of him as he grips an imaginary steering wheel, turning this way, then that.

'That doesn't matter right now.'

COTTAGE BY TORCHLIGHT

THERE IS SOMETHING monstrous about this creature on her verandah. Her body swarming with skulls, flexing faces and otherworldly spirits, the woman's once-tender flesh now strangled by devil skin. And the boy in her thrall – how long can his innocence survive? If still it does.

Studying her, Penny feels the touch of something on her own left ankle and looks down. There is no crawling insect or breeze-blown butterfly there. Instead, the mark she has not noticed for years, not even after Samuel Beckett, has begun to prickle, and she is forced to remember.

HOW MANY YEARS? Forty-odd, something like that. She is twelve, and beside her is a boy her age. They are crouched together on the concrete floor of the abandoned dairy, sheets of corrugated iron torn away from its roof and walls by years of summer tempests. More light than shade falls on the exposed slab. It is Easter break, and it is late afternoon, and the pack of Marlboros he has brought with him lies carelessly tossed, a rectangle of red and white on the grey concrete.

'You first,' she says, by which she means she will do him.

He nods. That is the extraordinary thing, more exhilarating than their bodies touching, or the headiness of cigarette smoke pulled into her lungs. That he trusts her to do this thing neither of them has experienced before. That he would simply nod and lift his right leg into her lap.

'All right,' he says. 'Do it.'

She looks him in the eyes. All their other glances before this have been furtive, their kissing a way of avoiding having to look at each other.

'Are you *absolutely* sure?'

'If you are.'

And so she picks up the nail they'd levered out of one of the fallen rafters. She wipes it on her shirtsleeve, rubbing the rust off. She doesn't look at him again. She presses the nail against him above his ankle, and draws it across his skin.

'Harder,' he says.

She tries again, but still can't break the skin.

'Here.'

He takes the nail and pulls out his pocketknife from his shorts. He swings his leg away from her and positions the nail so its point is against the concrete floor. He cuts at it with the knife, as if the nail is a twig and he is whittling its end into a little spearhead. His scraping blunts the blade of his knife rather than sharpening the nail. But he does manage to scrape off a couple of lumps of rust, and when he is done he bends his leg into his own lap and leans over it, digging the nail into his flesh and ripping it open, scraping, bit by bit, her initials into him, wiping away the blood with the palm of his left hand, wiping it onto his shorts.

'All right, now you.'

She gives him her foot in the end and closes her eyes, she feels him scraping at her and cries out, but his hands are hard around her ankle and she does not want to pull away, will not pull away. Eventually he is done, and there he is, his two initials, S and F, etched into the flesh beside her ankle. Throbbing now, forty years later, in the safety of her own house.

PHELAN'S HEAD THROBS. He'd been lying in bed, falling in and out of a queasy sleep all day, when he heard the car arrive. When Penny answered the front door he carefully opened his bedroom door. He didn't recognise the voice at first, but it was a woman's and it could only be her. Kira! Here! Now on his verandah, having somehow tracked him down. From his bedroom he hears little of the conversation. Instead, trapped in his room, he tracks what is happening through the shifting of weight on the floorboards. He'd assumed Penny would turn her away, or that Kira herself would leave if she thought he wasn't home. But now here they are, the two of them, talking. He returns to his bed and lies on his side. It is growing dark outside, dark as an irrigation ditch, and he is trapped. If he emerges unscathed, it will not be him who decides. He can't come out now, not after so long, not after choosing this way. He'll just have to stay in his room until one or other of the women has determined what they want to do with him.

There are things Kira could say that could raze everything. Could destroy Penny. Ruin a marriage. Is that why she's here?

PENNY WAS RIGHT about *something* having disturbed her husband and sent him careening backwards again. Now she knows – it is Beckett once more, Beckett in the form of the tattooist who'd sealed the name on his skin. Beckett who cannot be escaped, who must be faced. If the tattooist can help, Penny thinks, then what is there to lose?

'How old is your boy?' Penny asks.

'Eight,' the tattooist says, before adding, 'he's never been on a farm before.'

It doesn't matter whether or not she's lying. What she knows *is* true is that it's been a long time since a child has visited their home, Penny thinks. 'His name is Blake?'

The tattooist treats the question as part of the interrogation and rolls up her sleeve to show the name in ink, proof.

'All right,' Penny says, 'you can stay. Just until you get on your feet.'

KIRA FOLLOWS PENNY across the paddock to the cottage by torchlight. Penny helps Kira prise open the cottage windows while Blake nuzzles the dog on the steps. When they're done, Penny hands her the torch so she can explore the building by herself.

Kira goes from room to dusty room, her shoes crunching on the lino floor as she steps on desiccated rat droppings and collapsed insect carcasses and the fallen nests of wasps and starlings. The sound echoes as she passes from living room to kitchen to two bedrooms, exploring the enclosed narrow verandah and the bathroom. From a back window, Kira sees an outhouse with a tin ventilation chute protruding from its corrugated-iron roof.

Underneath the cottage, in the torchlight, there's a cement basin on a small slab of concrete, fibro sheeting on three sides, the fourth open to the elements. Kira turns the tap and the house shudders and she wonders how many years are being released. The water, when it comes, gushes rusty brown. Penny joins her under the house and, taking the torch, locates the electrical box. Penny flicks all the switches there are, and the cottage begins to hum.

'I'll bring some linen over,' Penny says.

'We're okay for linen. A towel would be a big help, though.'

Kira tries the lights when she returns upstairs, and in the main bedroom climbs onto a wooden chair to swap a working bulb for a blown one. She checks the mattress of the old brass four-poster for mice and, finding none, wraps sheets tightly round it, before, with Blake's help, dragging the bed into the centre of the room, away from the walls. They crawl into bed, exhausted, the mother's body curving around the boy's.

Blake wakes her in the night, shaking her shoulder. The bedside clock pulses red, and though it is not yet midnight there are giant jaws gnawing at the walls around. They hear a wicked screeching in the dark outside and in the ceiling an army of feet run one way then the other and Blake is scared, and Kira, hushing him with guesses, is too.

OUT OF THE MIST

A STRANGE AND magical mist billows over the edge of the escarpment, damp on their skin. Already, out here, the night and its terrors have receded. The early light is muted, almost playful. It's as if the rising sun has stalled and hovers in the enveloping shroud of fog, waiting for them to set it once again on its course.

A bird calls – Kira can't tell what – its song clear, the only sound in all the umbral world. She holds Blake's hand as he leans out over the edge to listen, perhaps to even spy it.

'Careful, Little Man.'

'Muu-uum,' he complains.

'We don't know how far it is down there,' Kira says, her words struggling to find shape in the mist. 'It might be steep. We wouldn't want you to fall.'

Away through the fog behind them an engine kicks into life, followed by headlights. A quad bike, she guesses, Phelan. She grips Blake's hand more tightly and watches the lights as they leave the house and approach the cottage a hundred metres away. The fog swirls. It lifts and descends, thins and grows dense once again. The bike appears briefly through a hollow in the mist, an old man hunched over, dog between his legs. He sees her too and momentarily releases the throttle – whether in surprise or doubt she can't tell – before changing direction, and making for her. The headlights, the fog, her son, bird answering bird at her back.

By the time he pulls up, and the dog has leaped off, they're staring at each other. He with his hands still on the handlebars, as if he might yet wheel around and return to his sanctuary, she with her fingers gripping her son's hand. He cuts the engine, swings his leg over the seat, and stands.

In the flesh he is more broken than he'd appeared on television. Or perhaps he's collapsed even further since then. He'd spoken with such clarity on screen, but now his shoulders are bent. She looks at his neatly combed hair, and the scars from minor surgeries on his forehead. His skin is a delta of capillaries and his cheeks are swollen, as if time and again the words he's needed to speak have got stuck there. Whatever else he has done, she thinks, he has achieved vulnerability.

HE RECOGNISES HER immediately, despite the changes. She is thicker, stronger. Tattoos now cover her like a suit of armour: both arms, her wrists, the backs of her hands, her fingers with rings of ink. Her warrioress is still there, though she seems crowded, stooped, as if she is just another weight for Kira to carry. The hair that had once been long has now been cropped. It is still dark, but looks freshly dyed and he thinks he detects the remnants of purple near her left temple. He's so tired.

'Kira,' he says. His tongue is thick with effort. He wants to say, what have you been doing all these years, what have you been up to? He wants to ask her about her life. He wants to say sorry. He wants to say thank you. He wants to swim and to dance.

Instead, he says, 'Where have you been?' As if she's late. As if he hadn't told her to stay away.

'I liked your poem,' she says.

'Why?'

'I don't know,' she shrugs. 'There was something in it I recognised.'

'Beckett?'

'Something else.'

A black cockatoo bursts from out of the mist, screeching. Blake flinches, then, seeing it above them, points excitedly, wide-eyed. A second appears, following the first, all wing-beat and eddying fog, so close to them in the distorting light, so close you can see a flash of red tail feather. So close you could touch them.

'Wow!' Blake exclaims when the birds have vanished, and the dog has disappeared after them, chasing air.

'We don't see many black cockatoos here,' Phelan says to the boy. 'You're lucky.'

The sun glows through the mist, strengthening.

'Your wife …' Kira starts, then falls away, not knowing what she had intended to say. The fog quickly fills the gap. She starts again. 'Your wife is very kind.'

'Yes,' Phelan says, 'I love her.'

CREATURES IN THE LANDSCAPE

PENNY BRINGS OVER a broom, a mop and a bucket filled with cleaning products – creams for the fridge and the bathroom, powders for the oven, sugar soap for the walls. Rags for the two of them. They move from room to room, knocking mud nests off architraves, sweeping away spider frames, dusting picture rails and sills, wiping stains off the walls themselves.

She prompts conversation, tries to get to know a little more about the tattooist, but the woman is walled off. Penny gives the boy a hammer, and asks him to bang in the nails in the skirting boards where they've pulled away from the walls.

'He's a good kid,' she says.

'Thanks,' the tattooist replies.

THE SECOND DAY Kira works alone in the front room, once an open verandah but now enclosed by louvres. She painstakingly cleans the glass with the vinegar and newspaper left for her on the stairs, while Blake draws faces on the back of a used envelope he found behind the old couch. The room lightens. The lino on the floor is faded and cut, wounded by the years. She mops it but it remains cut and wounded. She beats the dust from the armchair and Blake helps her carry it back inside and into the front room.

'Well done, Little Man.'

'Mum?'

'Yes, Manny?'

'I miss Dad.'

KIRA WATCHES PHELAN limp from the house with a crowbar over his shoulder. He is like an ancient warrior-monk with a staff, setting out to protect a footbridge from bandits. She loses sight of him on the other side of the house.

There is work she wants to do, so she leads Blake down the track that runs along the spur to the house Phelan has just left. There is no sign of him in the yard, but how much does she have to say to him anyway? She has taken risks enough just to get here. She takes a rake from the garden shed and gathers the leaves and twigs on the lawn into piles. Blake sits on the verandah folding paper. She can't think what to do with the piles, so moves to the verandah and the front entrance, sweeping them down. It's not such a bad thing about the piles of leaves, because the wife will see what she's done. Then she feels the pang of conscience. *You donate in secret,* her father used to say, *you don't shout about your good deeds from the rooftop.*

But this is a transaction she's proposing, or at least an acknowledgement of a debt she wants to show she'll find a way to repay. Because the cottage is perfect – it's private, it's a refuge for a while, and it's as isolated as she could hope. And it's protected. Yes, by a broken warrior, but still protected.

THE FIRST DAY at school Kira walks Blake to his classroom. She's fully covered, gloves and upturned collar, hiding her ink. The teacher is a recent graduate – narrow-hipped, tight-skirted, stockinged. She points to a desk with Blake's laminated name card already taped to it. Kira scans the room but when she bends to kiss him, he is already moving away from her, his attention caught by some activity in the corner.

'Look how quickly he's making himself at home!' the young teacher chirps, sensing Kira's unease.

Kira nods vaguely before dragging her gaze away from Blake and the little group of kids he's joined, and directing it at the teacher, trying to take her in, her wide eyes and lipstick.

'He'll be safe here, won't he?' Kira asks, unable to keep the need out of her voice, that vein of desperation.

She goes to Blake in the corner and kisses him on the head before she leaves.

All day she waits in the car across the road from the school gate. Even when she grows hungry, she stays rather than abandon her post to get something from the corner store at the end of the street. She watches people come and go, filtering them for danger. The second day she does it again and then the third, until the principal comes out and leans into her window and tells her there's no need for her to stay, that it's better if she doesn't, says that she must have other things she needs to do.

But there is nothing I have to do more important than this, she thinks.

To DISAPPEAR — THE great trick, the great feat. To brush the scent from your tracks with a branch snapped from a nearby tree, like in the boys' adventure books Kira read as a child, the books originally her father's. You sweep your footsteps clear so all that remains is the swirl of leaves drawn across the dirt. Because only the rarest of eyes is capable of reading the way the tips of leaves have been dragged across the earth. These *Boy's Own* truths. In time the rain and the stampeding footfalls of the day will obliterate even the evidence of the ruse and there will be nothing of you left. Except, perhaps, the little mound of ash left over from where you burned your sweeping branch at the side of the river. White ash trodden into the ground by the feet of nocturnal creatures, or blown across the landscape in the first rising wind, a scattering no eye could possibly interpret. I left no trace, she tells herself, and while Flores's eye was rare when they first met, he's destroyed it since.

But Kira starts to doubt herself. The loneliness of it. She and Blake, and the pleasantries at the school gate. Or the conversations she's started at supermarket checkouts, taking her cue from the covers of the women's magazines. One day she returns to the caravan park on the pretext she might have left something behind, and listens to the blue-haired woman's chatter. The woman is as good as a stranger, but her talk is, at least, one familiar thing.

Sometimes after school she takes Blake to the library where he'll lift origami manuals from the shelves and fold paper at the low children's desk. She finds a picture book for kids who have to flee 'angry houses', and snuggles beside him into a beanbag.

She buys paint from a hardware store in town and, after checking with Penny, paints the door of the cottage red, bringing colour to it, good luck.

At night, after Blake goes to bed, she opens her silver case. She takes out her tattoo machine and feels the weight of it in her hand, playing with the screws, turning it on, creating music. She counts the needles on her needle bars, rolls rubber bands between her fingers, shakes her ink bottles. She sighs.

Where is this going? she wonders.

She cleans their house each Monday morning, thoroughly, trying to pay her way. If Phelan is still there when she arrives he either quietly leaves the house through the other door, or locks himself in his study. He can be so still. Does he think she doesn't know he's in there?

WHEN PENNY BUYS half a dozen leghorns from one of the farms on Boundary Road she thinks the boy might enjoy collecting the eggs, and pulls in at the cottage on her way back to the Big House. The tattooist comes down to the ute with Blake when Penny asks if they want to have a look. They watch as Penny lifts one of the cardboard boxes from the tray to the ground, then kneels and folds back the top flap.

'What do you reckon?' she asks Blake as he peers in.

There is a burst of wing-flap, and the boy pulls back, alarmed. Penny laughs.

'Here, look,' she says lifting the white hen from the box, pressing its wings against its body. She cradles it against her breast so it can't get loose, then reaches for the boy's hand. 'Let me show you.' She guides the boy's fingers towards the bird. 'Feel the feathers. They're soft, aren't they?' Look at him, she thinks, the purity of his amazement.

'They're going to live in that coop over there. See? By the pines. And you know what? I'm going to need someone to look out for their eggs ...' Penny looks up at the tattooist, who doesn't object. 'Do you want to come down and help?'

Blake visits twice a day, with food scraps in the morning then to collect the eggs in the afternoon after school. The first few times his mother goes with him to inspect the coop and accompany him as he walks the eggs to Penny's back door, Penny always giving the boy some to take back to the cottage. Soon enough, these become Blake's responsibilities alone.

KIRA THINKS ABOUT Flores daily, though the edge has come off. No longer does she wake at birdsong as she did those first mornings, startle-eyed, heart pounding, fear-filled, having forgotten to take some nameless precaution. The strangeness of dawn here has its own power, its own pull, equal to the pull of her fears. At first she hears a wall of undifferentiated bird noise, so loud it drowns the sound of Blake's breathing in his bed across the room, Kira lifting her head to check he's still there. When she lies back again she forces herself to remain still while her heart subsides. She closes her eyes again and tries to isolate what she hears. She attaches words to what she experiences – squawk and tweet and whistle and trill and coo. She counts eleven distinct sounds, though cannot yet picture the bird making the call. There is a scratching on the roof overhead, and she thinks crow, and listens till the bird alights in a burst of claw-on-tin. Then, whatever bird it was now airborne, she asks herself: Why crow? Why not pigeon or kookaburra or magpie? What memory has she drawn from, she wonders, or what process of deduction has she used that she is unaware of?

She rises. She doesn't touch Blake's cheek as she leaves the room. It might wake him. In the kitchen, making coffee, that routine she's brought with her, Flores returns. She can't shake him. He is there as she prepares breakfast for Blake and as she readies him for school. Some days Flores joins them momentarily at the kitchen table, and sits silently, arms folded, pinning her with accusations, weakening her. What she's destroyed, what she's taken from him. She slumps. Perhaps he's right. But here is Blake, and here she is, and beyond her doubt and

231

her turmoil there is calm, and here, on the other side of the wrenching, she feels safe, and if her coffee scalds the back of her hand it is because she has clumsily knocked it over, not because it's been thrown at her, the entire universe boiling.

PHELAN IS AWARE of her as a new presence in the landscape. A counterweight to the house he shares with Penny. She is there through the curtain of pines and across the paddock to the cottage, her arrival giving the days a new patterning, a palimpsest yet to cohere.

'Why don't we invite them down for a meal?' Penny asks.

'No,' he says.

'She's lonely, James.'

He ignores her. 'Can you give me a hand with the feeder this afternoon?' he asks.

But Penny won't be distracted that easily. '*You* need it too, James.'

'No.'

'You need to face it.'

He looks at her, startled. 'Face what?'

'I don't know, James. Whatever it is.'

HE LAYS HIS book down but misses the bedside table, and the volume thuds against the carpet. He can barely bring himself to care whether it's woken Penny in the room next door. He's been forced to face things for years. It's fucking exhausting. He lies with the torchlight resting against his cheek, directed to the ceiling. He begins counting the drifts of spiderweb, but comes back to Beckett. And when he fades into sleep, Beckett accompanies him.

• • •

HE CAN HEAR them down the dry creek bed, following his boot prints in the sand, the surest of trails. But what if he can't outrun them? Ahead there's a log fallen across the bed. He veers off to the right, laying tracks towards the right-hand bank as he goes. At the log he leaps up and onto it, but rather than follow it further up the bank – the quickest route out of the creek bed – he turns acutely left, running back along the log across the full width of the creek to the left side where the tree's root-system lies exposed where it toppled, taking some of the earth with it.

He scrambles and pulls himself up and over the roots and the lip of the bank before rolling away on the flat land, staying low till he judges he's out of sight of his pursuers below. He's up and running through eucalypt forest now, weaving between trunks and shafts of sunlight, the ground a carpet of leaves. His trail is still not hard to follow, but he knows it'll take longer than if he was still in the soft sand of the creek bed. Eventually, when he's got nothing left, or thinks he doesn't, he drops to the ground beneath an old gum, panting, sheltering behind its trunk. He wills himself to silence.

There's nothing yet from behind him and he hopes they're in the country beyond the other bank, fossicking for his trail. As he places the palm of his hand on the ground to rise, he turns his head, nothing deliberate in the movement, and freezes. At eye level, eighteen inches away on a fallen branch, are three frogmouths, grey and weathered as the sun-bleached branch on which they're perching, still as dead timber, their eyes closed into tight slits.

He watches their hard beaks as he levers himself carefully off the ground, but when he begins to rise, one of them lurches towards him, snapping its beak and hissing, *Beckett, Beckett, Beckett.*

BIRDSONG

SHE HAS NOT heard birdsong since she was a child, not properly. Her tattooing life in the Sydney streets was filled with birds, but on the skin. The sounds of the city drowned out the squawks and chirrups of the few living there, the pigeons and mynas and crows. But all the birds she's tattooed from flash designs passed down from generations of tattooists: how many hundreds of swallows and doves and eagles she's sketched and traced and inked, squeezing so much meaning into so few species.

Out here, the flash seems emblematic and flat. Here the variety of wings and birdsong is dizzying. She begins to categorise what she sees, what she thinks she hears, separating them into rough groupings. All the black and white birds, the parrots, the small bush birds that refuse to stay still long enough to get a proper sense of them, the hawks that hold aloof over the valley. From the library she borrows a field book with colour plates and sits on the landing at the top of the stairs in the afternoons. When she picks Blake up from the school bus she practises the names of what she has seen: butcher bird, pardalote, wattlebird.

SHE HAILS PHELAN one morning on his way to his cattle, and he stops, reluctantly. They've not spoken since that first day, avoiding each other for a month. Kira produces the field guide and turns to the plate with a pair of whipbirds sketched, male and female.

'You can hear them,' she says, 'but you can't see them.'

'Wait here,' Phelan says to her.

When he returns from inside the Big House, it is with a pair of binoculars. He hands them to her, wordlessly.

She expands her vocabulary from the back door of the cottage. Pale-headed lorikeets flash past, apostlebirds drop to the ground from a stand of gums, squawking and turning over fallen leaves. She finds a long caramel feather on a mid-morning walk and it's weeks before the heavy rustling she hears in the undergrowth turns out not to be the wallaby she'd guessed, but a pheasant coucal. She hears the long shrill whistle of a kite and looks out. The bird glides westwards, the tips of its wings bowed downwards. If she were close enough she could hear the whisper of the air across its feathers. The third time she sees it she tracks it to its nest of sticks set in the big eucalyptus by the dam.

A WHIPBIRD ANSWERS its mate, their calling and the buzz of the early sun on the windowpane. She lies in bed listening, imagining what they're saying to each other. I'm here, says one. Me too, replies the second. Where? asks the first. Over here, the second answers, just over here. Can't you see me? I'm here. You're safe.

After a while she hears a man's footsteps outside, the shifting weight of each step as the soles of his boots roll over the gravel, the small pebbles crunching against each other, their uneven surfaces rubbing together. Strangely, she is not afraid. She rises, bringing his binoculars with her.

She meets Phelan at the foot of the steps and follows him quietly towards the cliff. She lies on the ground where he motions her to, and trains the binoculars on one tree then another, narrowing in until she spots them, plain and mysterious.

LATER THAT DAY, Phelan stands beside the forty-four-gallon drum they use as an incinerator to burn off their weekly rubbish. He drives the crowbar between the earth and the foot of the drum, using a stone as a fulcrum. He levers the bottom of the drum off the ground, then reaches forward and pushes it over and onto its side so he can shovel the build-up of ash and debris into the cardboard box he'll walk to the edge of the cliff and tip into the wind.

As he works he pulls out the rubbish that has not burned down. He'll decide later what to throw back for a future burn, and what to stack – mainly bits of metal that should have been separated. As he thrusts his shovel deep into the drum and scrapes the spoil towards him, he finds a burnt tennis ball. Had he thrown it there himself, he wonders, tossed it from the house verandah months ago, testing his aim? His shot memory. He holds it in his gloved hand and squeezes it. He hears a hiss of air, and lifts it closer to his ear, squeezing again. He smells the little puff of ash. He takes off his gloves. This ball. He rolls it in his palm, feels it on his skin, in his fingers, feels its weight in his cupped hand. This beautiful blackened ball.

Phelan tosses it lightly, and the ball leaves his hand by an inch and falls back. He tosses it again, rolling his fingers over it, ash coming off on his skin. Again it falls back into place, its weight leaving and returning. He tosses it again and again, higher and higher, until its arc reaches above his head and he must look up and see its shape against the sky. This little darkened sphere rising and falling against the blue. His hands catching and throwing. Ever higher he throws it, and he moves his body into place beneath it, his palms together creating a nest for it, his hands growing darker catch by catch. When he misses and the ball spills from his fingers onto the ground, he bends to pick it up.

'Hey Boss!' It's Beckett, but he is laughing. 'Yours!'

Sapper Beckett is clapping his hands, and pointing, and the tennis ball the Afghan boy has struck high into the air with his makeshift bat is black against the bright sun. Out of the corner of his eye Phelan sees the boy racing away for a run, but with his head turned and his startling green eyes trained on him, hoping he'll drop it.

A dozen other village kids are also watching him from their fielding positions in the hard-packed dirt street as he moves back from where he'd been wicket keeping, towards the spot where the ball might land. Boys with shaved scalps who've joined the game, others in embroidered skullcaps. Girls in pale blue dresses, their loose scarves falling from their heads.

Phelan is laden with combat gear and backpedals awkwardly, his eye on the ball, almost tripping, this big old cumbersome soldier.

Will he catch it or won't he?

Sapper Beckett is hooting and hollering, trying to put him off, the kids joining in, a wall of boisterous noise.

Catch it or don't.

Be here or don't.

He watches the spinning ball as it drops towards him, his gloved hands cupped, ready.

'Got it!' he yells out, before he's even caught the ball, ahead of the moment, excited, elated. This moment.

PHELAN STARTS AGAIN, resumes his tossing. This ash-blackened ball. These inconsequential dropped catches. The perfection of the ball's weight and its colour and its parabolas and the sky and his hands and the memories of his hands. Beckett's laughter. All the ash on him, a benediction. And when he begins to weep it is like rain and if there is life to be born here he is ready to open.

NOT ALONE

HE SHAVES AND irons a shirt. He faces himself in the bathroom mirror before dressing, twisting shoulder-ways.

'Hello there, son,' he says to Beckett.

He leaves the house, passes through the back gate, turns towards the cottage and marches towards her. The clouds are high and bright and moving swiftly north where they will, he knows, dissolve beyond the horizon. He counts his broken steps in groups of a hundred, breaking the journey, tallying the bundles in his mind. So much counting over so many years: inventories and fighting strength and unspent rounds. He passes the collapsed piggery and the rusting harvester. A blue-tongue turns and disappears into lantana shadow. He is ready.

The cottage stands before him, perched high on its stilts. He pauses at the foot of the steps, his hand on the railing for long seconds, feeling for her movement inside. He hoists himself upwards, but the door opens before he reaches the top step and Kira fills the space.

WHEN PHELAN LIES down he grimaces. His old body.

'Does it hurt?' she asks.

'Of course,' he replies, but lightly, thinking, *it should*.

Shafts of light fall on him through the window and for the briefest of moments his head is still and one side of his face is glowing and all the blemishes on his skin are illuminated, the scars and blotches and nicks, the bark of him glowing sagely in the afternoon.

'Wait,' she says, before beginning, and closes her eyes, her left palm resting on his bare right shoulder. He watches her, wondering where she is going. Her head is motionless. Her nostrils twitch, once, before her breathing slows and the creases in her forehead begin to disappear.

Is she praying? he wonders. Penny yes, but surely not her. Through the window behind her Phelan sees a hawk dive towards an invisible prey. Eventually he also closes his eyes and feels the warmth of her hand on his shoulder, and then the sun on his face.

When she speaks again it startles him.

'So,' she says, examining her work, 'Samuel Robert Beckett.'

'I want something else, something new.'

'Sure. What'll it be?' as if mimicking a bartender.

'Anything,' he says. 'You choose. Anything.' Because what he really wants is to be opened up, to hurt, to feel alive.

'Let me think,' she says, and then, when she returns, asks him whether he wants to know what she's decided.

'I trust you,' he says. But everything is stiff. His old man's back, the side of his face planted on the bed, his turned neck, his shoulders, the hardness of his cheekbone. He is stiff and dry. When he blinks it feels as if his eyelids are scraping against his eyeballs. Better to keep them closed. Better just to give his other shoulder to her needle, hand himself over to her pain. When he stirs it is because of the cry of a cockatoo, heralding a shift in the weather.

He opens his eyes and sees her gloved hand pass beside his face to the ink table. There are bright red marks on the tips of her fingers.

'Is that ink or blood?' he asks, coming out of his stupor.

'You don't know the difference?'

She means, he thinks, you of all people. But her surprise doesn't tip into incredulity, doesn't try to shame him, even in jest. The little laugh that follows is, he thinks, aimed at herself. She hurries on.

'There are so many reds.' She runs through them, like reading from an industry catalogue. Some have mercury in them, others cadmium or iron. Or metal oxides. The naptha chemicals. To say nothing of blood, and the way it changes colour.

When she is done she leads him to the bathroom mirror.

Kira has cut a lone red poppy into him, delicate, double-skirted, dark-eyed, sitting high on its stem, utterly singular.

'What do you think?' she asks.

HE EXAMINES HIMSELF again back in the Big House, elated, the breeze building too, moving into the leaves and branches outside.

There is poppy and there is skin. There is a glistening shoulder and a ruffle-red flower come into being by a tattooist's hand, the blossom's dark outline etched into flesh. The poppy may rest, but the flesh, the body, the blood?

You are not alone, the flower whispers to him, a lullaby across a thousand fields, a thousand lands. You are not the first, it sings, its red-cupped face, its voice coming to him on an ancient wind blowing over the eastern escarpment, and sweeping over the Hindu Kush, and skitting across the English Channel. It is the breeze that has breathed spirit into a thousand poems. A thousand vows of remembrance.

AT WORK IN THE FIELDS

HE TAPES THE stencil of the poppy to the wall above the computer in his office. He gathers the information about the war dead that he's haphazardly collected over the years. All the articles, all the obituaries and memorial pages, all the snippets of information that have nearly drowned him since his breakdown. He navigates the internet now with a clarity of purpose, gathering updates, flashes of feeling he collects from Facebook. He creates folders on his computer for each soldier.

He reaches out beyond the killed in action. He sends off emails, reconnecting with people he hasn't spoken to since he left the army. He hooks into support networks, roiling grief-posts. He rings old colleagues. 'What do you know? What have you heard?' The names of those who died in-country are easy, their lives of valour and sacrifice. It is those who have died back home who are harder to find, their stories darker and more complex. He is offered private numbers. He rings mothers and spouses and brothers, histories of grief and denial and reconciliation. Wells of pain too deep for a dropped stone to ever measure. Still, he gathers them, treading as carefully as he can – their names and their stories, as true as he can find.

HE RETURNS TO her after a week and hands her his list of names.

'I need more poppies,' he says, fire in his clear eyes.

'So many?' she asks, part surprise, part sorrow.

'A field.'

Each day, after Penny leaves for work, he comes.

A poppy a day, Kira suggests, and he agrees.

'So, tell me about him,' she says with the first press of needle to skin. It becomes part of their daily ritual, working down the list. 'Tell me about this man.'

And he does. He recounts what he's learned about the soldier, his eyes closed, the hum of her machine drawing what he knows out of him, the buzz becoming a melody and his ragged words, lyrics.

He tells her about each of the men, details of their lives, of their deaths, of their families, where they were born, under what sign. Who they loved. Who loved them. Sometimes he has a lot to tell. Some days there is little beyond the soldier's bare biographical dates. Even then he lays them out for her like stars on an astronomer's map.

But always, always, he tells her where they died, and he tells her how. He doesn't spare her. Or himself. He tells her who died alone, and who in the arms of comrades. What their final words were, if he knows, whispered or typed or scrawled in blood. There are clean wounds and there are bodies blown.

Sometimes she shudders at the detail, and pulls away. To look at a different horizon through the window, to breathe a fresher air, to gather herself.

'Are you familiar with *The Iliad*?' he asks.

She shakes her head.

'It's the story of the Trojan War. A long war, like this one, ten

241

years of it ... well, not quite as long as this. Anyway, what Homer does is capture every single soldier's death. He describes every detail – that Diomedes' spear struck Astynous above his nipple and his sword hacked off General Hyperion's shoulder; that Patroclus was struck not once but twice, the first time between the shoulders and the second in the lower belly, the spear going right through him; that Achilles stabbed Deucalion, not just in his arm, but in the place where the tendons join the elbow; that blood soaked one warrior's hair but not another's.'

She waits for him.

'How our deaths are as unique as our lives.'

'You remember the girl I was working on before you that day?' She watches him looking at her, fixing on her, as if trying to draw the memory from her.

'The large girl?' he asks. 'The one with the skulls on the inside of her wrists?'

'And under those skulls?'

He shakes his head.

'Scars,' Kira says. 'From where she'd cut herself.'

The girl couldn't have been much younger than his soldiers, than Beckett.

'And those skulls,' he asks, 'were they her idea or yours?'

'Sometimes,' Kira says, taking courage, hoping it won't sound absurd, 'it feels as if we're in the business of accommodating death.'

But then she falters. Phelan waits. However long it might take.

'Sometimes,' she continues, 'sometimes I can smell it on a person. You break the skin, and the scent of death hits you. When that happens, you wish you were doing something else.'

He wants to ask her about himself. Instead, he says, 'So you're not a tattooist at all. You're an exorcist?'

• • •

KIRA FEELS HER own blood flowing. She explores the top of his back – the ridged and hollowed canvas of it – feeling its contours, navigating it with her fingers, working out where to plant each poppy. She wants, when she is finished, for them to move with the shifts in his musculature, like they might sway for a zephyr passing across a field, the red blooms bowing and lifting their heads as he moves.

She had almost forgotten what tattooing can do, how you can lose yourself entirely. Blake's playground scuffles fade to nothing when she presses her foot on the pedal and the electricity starts to flow. She stretches skin between thumb and forefinger and her dwindling savings are of no consequence. She wipes away blood and ink and it is the most urgent thing ever required of her. Flores is nothing, nowhere.

She finishes a poppy and she is immeasurably stronger than when she'd begun it. Taller somehow, more confident, formidable. Perhaps Flores can feel my strength, she thinks. And knowing how strong I am, he dares not come after her. She thinks, buzzing in the beauty of the skin she has just transformed, Flores knows and he has given up. He accepts this, she thinks, we are safe.

THE LIST HE'D shown her just days ago is already incomplete. It grows with the war. Phelan's task is to keep it current, to ensure he misses no one. He hands her an updated tally.

They tattoo in the morning for an hour or two on the single bed they've dragged from the second bedroom into the front room. She tattoos, opens him up and allows him to talk. When they are done Phelan covers his back with his long-sleeved work shirt, and goes out into the paddocks and the sheds and the yards.

Sometimes she watches him throw hay from the back of his four-wheeler, or disappear into the toolshed. Other days she goes down to the Big House where, as she's arranged with Penny, she cleans, helping pay her way. Then, each weekday without fail, she leaves the plateau mid-afternoon to collect her son from the school bus.

They circle around on the plateau making room, each for the other. Sometimes he looks up from his work in the afternoons to see her car returning, other times he can only hear it, counting the minutes until it reaches the cottage. Phelan is coming to know things about the kid too, the way he slams the car door and bounds up the cottage stairs before Kira's door has even opened. He's seen the kid trip mid-stair and recover, as if nothing happened. He's watched them disappear into the cottage, boy and school bag, mother and boy.

PENNY SENSES THE shifts in the life of the farm, the new pre-occupations in her husband. There are the hours at night in his study and the jobs he's not getting to during the day. And there's the way he circles back before bed to ask her again what she remembers of the war-taken, scribbling down whatever titbits she might have to give. At first she thought he was collecting material for a poem. But there's also a fresh vitality in him, a crispness to his footfall on the floorboards in the mornings, a purposefulness to his breakfast routine. There's more laughter too. And more of the old playful teasing.

But she's no fool. Whatever James's quest, whatever she's encouraged him to face, she knows it's stronger than her. She may not see everything, but she knows enough to know that. The daily trips he makes while she is at work, through the pines and across the paddock to the cottage, a track forming in the grass. What potions does the painted woman mix inside? What spells does she cast? Has she stirred something that Penny had thought the years of James's medication had anaesthetised forever?

KIRA OPENS BLAKE'S room. A turned handle, a tongue receding, a cone of torchlight reaching out across the floorboards. Blake lies on the single bed like a sleeping lordling, three or four mattresses layered on top of each other, his face to the wall, beautiful. A pale mosquito net stretches out from a brass frame above his head, tucked firmly under the uppermost mattress. Beneath the net, her son's chest rises and falls. Beside the bed, set on a silky oak lowboy, is a line of folded cranes of different sizes, looking out at the room.

She lifts the mosquito net and whispers his name softly, her hand on his warm shoulder. But as she touches him, she feels something leave her too, an echo of the old soldier, and wonders how many spirits of how many tattoos have fled her fingers to nest in her son? Wonders what the cost of a tattooing life has been. This boy, this exquisite boy exposed to so much. Having chosen tattooing, having then chosen Flores, this third life she has now chosen, this one here on this farm with former brigadier James Phelan and his wife, at least for now, this is for her son.

CAVES AND WATERFALLS

'Can I ask you something?' she says at the end of a session. 'A favour?'

Phelan swings his legs off the bed.

'It's about Blake ...'

He waits for her to go on.

'It'd be good to get him outside more. He's great with the chickens, but ... could he, after school ... maybe he could ... accompany you one afternoon?'

Through the rear-view mirror Phelan can see the boy standing in the tray of the ute, holding on fiercely. Phelan wonders if he is small for his age. Beside the boy are the chainsaw, his gloves, the sharpened axe and a pile of hessian bags. He slows as they approach a creek and Phelan leans his head out of the window and yells to the boy.

'Hold on, big fella. It's going to get rough.'

Phelan drops the Hilux into the shallow creek bed and then up the other side where he makes for a stand of trees on the northern aspect of the bluff. When he pulls up he leans forward for a better view, his face close to the glass of the windscreen. He nods to himself, switches off the ignition and climbs out.

'Let's have a proper look at these, hey?'

The boy trails him through the trees, Phelan inspecting them for the diameter of their girth, how straight, how tall. He wants to get three posts out of each trunk and stops before a likely gum before looking up at its height. The boy looks up at the man. Eventually Phelan grunts before returning to the truck where he hands the axe to Blake, wide-eyed. He tucks the gloves into his belt, and swings the chainsaw off the tray. The weight of it, the substance of it, its perfect fit.

'You stay here. Beside the truck. Okay?'

At the base of the tree Phelan pulls the cord and the chainsaw's engine comes to life. It's as if some vital, animating force deep inside it has woken. He measures the tree again, its weight, its fall, and sets the chainsaw's teeth against its trunk. Smell the smoke, hear the two-stroke engine, feel the teeth sink into the tree's bark. How light the saw becomes, the machine hungrier now than even he is, seeming to have a need apart from his own.

There is the moment he is feeling for, when the tree begins to go. On one side of the moment it is still tree, on the other, timber. Feel for that moment. Reach for it. Know it. That's the thing, that's where the rush is. How many triggers he's pulled over the years. But there's distance in time and space between pulling the trigger on a weapon, and the puff of dust or the dark mark on a firing range target. Here he's still connected, still one through body and shoulder and arm and engine and biting teeth. Bayoneting a man in a trench may have been like this, he thinks. Or killing a beast with a knife or a hen with an axe. The life-force transferred, the strength gained. But only that which is necessary is sacred. Whose words were they? Aurelius's? His father's?

The tree succumbs, and he turns the engine off so he can hear the sinews snap, and the rush of air as the canopy crumples, the crash to the ground, the vibrations that reach him through the earth.

'Here, come,' he calls out to the boy.

Blake approaches, though tentatively.

Phelan walks the length of the trunk, stepping out the three posts he's after, before cutting them from the fallen tree. When he looks up, the boy has his hands to his ears. After the three sections are cut and rolled away, Phelan takes the chainsaw once more and draws a long line down the length of each section, bark deep.

'Pass me the axe,' he says to Blake, turning off the saw and resting it on the ground beside him. 'Now we need to take the bark off.'

Phelan raises the axe high above his head before bringing it down, not blade-ways but in reverse, striking the wood instead with the rear of the axe-head. A dull thump. Again and again he hits the wood, moving up and then down, softening the bark with each stroke, loosening it from the timber beneath.

'Watch now.' He kneels and grips the bark with his fingers where he'd cut it length-ways with the saw, and pulls it towards him. It peels away easily. Blake leans over the section of trunk and does the same, grasping the bark and pulling it and, small as he is, away it comes.

Blake looks at Phelan, his eyes sparkling, and grins.

PENNY WATCHES HER husband collect Blake from the cottage, watches the boy clamber up and into the tray of the ute where the dog is waiting excitedly, hears the engine noise fade away over the ridge. She changes out of her uniform. She takes a bottle from the fridge, pulls on her boots and makes her way across the paddock.

When the door opens she holds up the bottle. 'Can I tempt you?'

She can't work out if she's interrupted the tattooist. The woman's face is inscrutable, at least to her.

'Sure,' Kira says. 'I'd like that very much.'

Too bad if she doesn't really, thinks Penny.

There are no wine glasses in the kitchen cupboard, so Kira finds two tumblers, holding them out while Penny pours. Penny places the bottle between them on the kitchen table, bare but for a camera.

'How's the cottage?'

'Good ... Great ... Perfect,' Kira says finally. 'Thanks.'

Penny nods. The kitchen is neat, she notes, it is clean. They both drink quickly. 'Blake's a great kid, isn't he?'

'He loves it here, absolutely loves it,' the answer just enough to cancel out the question.

Again the conversation flounders.

'You're a photographer?' Penny prompts, nodding to the camera.

'I used to do a lot. I enrolled in art college after school. Yeah, I enjoyed taking photos. I thought ...' But the tattooist trails away.

Penny perseveres. 'Have you found anything around here to photograph?'

'Actually, yeah.' A spark of life, a little less caution. 'The birdlife ... some of the birds are pretty amazing. The colouring on some of the parrots is incredible.' Kira picks up the camera and scrolls through some shots she'd taken that morning, a dozen wild budgerigars feeding on grain she'd tossed onto the grass. She hands Penny the camera.

'Beautiful,' the older woman says, looking at the first image. 'Are there others?'

'Just scroll through yourself.'

'You don't mind?'

Kira waves the question away. 'No, no, no. There are no secrets in there.'

• • •

IN THE MORNING Phelan goes to Kira. In the late afternoon he takes Blake with him as he catches up on chores. They finish felling the trees they need, wrap chains around the slippery, debarked logs, and haul them to the yards where they set up makeshift drying racks. While they wait for them to dry Phelan leads Blake around the property, circumnavigating it over the course of a month, painting sump oil on the good posts, straining the barbed wire in stretches and running new lengths of wire in others. When the new fence posts are ready, they drop them, one by one beside the rotten posts they'll replace, then return to the first of the old posts and start digging it out. Once a post seems loose Phelan ties a chain to it and, with both of them in the cab of the ute, Blake peering through the back window, Phelan nudges the truck forward, pulling the stump out in a cloud of dirt. It's painstaking work – if they extract one in an afternoon it's a good day.

Even when he tires, Blake doesn't abandon the work. Phelan looks for things he can do, little tasks. He tells him stories as they work, recalling his own childhood, the farm becoming an adventure-land of waterfalls and caves and hidden treasures.

'DO YOU REGRET any of them?'

It's the third time Kira has accepted a drink from Phelan's wife, but she is determined to hold her past close. Phelan's wife lifts the glass of moselle to her lips as if the question is as inconsequential as the weather, but how the woman burns to know.

Kira looks down at her arms, the knit of ink. The beautiful and the desperate. Then looks up at the other woman, still her landlord. 'I'm not sure we know each other well enough yet.'

Do I regret any? she asks herself. Every part of my body wants to scream yes. The pair of feathers Flores tattooed on her in the beginning. The cheap wallflowers she'd inked to shorten her worst days, or the useless skulls she had done after her intuition started going awry. Flores's name, that proof of loyalty he'd demanded from her. Some days she wished she could rip off her epidermis, tear up her thirty-year-old skin and start again.

But you can't. She knows that. You can't pick and choose. A tattoo captures a moment. And then it is gone. Whatever particular yearning or fear that births a tattoo and propels it into the world cannot last. Every ensuing need, every fresh desire, differs from the tattooed moments that have already passed into history. All a tattoo can do is speak of one time, one place. Who we were, not who we are.

She hears that wise voice sometimes, but in the task of surviving each day there is no time for meditation, no time for philosophising.

Phelan comes to her in need, and she can disappear. He offers her that opportunity. Those moments of sweet relief, maybe strength, maybe rediscovery. Maybe something to endure.

ONE SATURDAY MORNING when Penny is rostered off, James brings her a glass of squeezed juice, oranges from one of their trees. He holds the refrigerator-cold glass out to her. She sits up in her bed, propped by pillows, and drinks it as he stands there.

She smiles and wipes her lips with the back of her hand. 'Delicious!'

James beams. Then, after the briefest of pauses, he begins to speak, telling her everything, shedding his shirt, showing her his back. But this is no reprise of the revelation of his Beckett tattoo. This time he is excited, and his enthusiasm is free of doubt.

Penny kneels on the bed and examines him. Ah, she thinks, so, the tattooist. Penny counts the poppies, counts the days he's been at his project. He and the tattooist. But is that all? Tattoos? Then, looking at him, open, dismisses the notion. James is too like a child, is beyond deceit. At least for now.

On her bedside table is the pen she uses for her nightly crossword. 'Don't move,' she says, reaching for it.

She turns her husband around so he is facing her. 'Kneel,' she says, and he does. Then she presses the nib of her pen onto the skin at the left of his chest, drawing a little blue heart there and piercing it with an arrow. Her initials, then his. Whatever you and the tattooist are doing, don't forget you are mine.

NEEDLESONG

PHELAN BRINGS KIRA yet another new name.

'Corporal Milan Djokovic, thirty-four years of age. Two children, two girls. And an ex-wife. Standard, that. An infantryman. On his first tour he'd been part of a unit providing cover on small hearts-and-minds projects in Tarin Kot. They'd slept the night on a classroom floor after erecting monkey bars in the playground. The next morning they were escorting some engineers down an alley on the way to a nearby mosque to install new speakers, a simple metro patrol. They walked out of the alley onto the street moments before a car bomb went off. The blast threw Djokovic back into the alley. He herniated a disc in his back, but that's not what did him in. It was attending to the civilians killed and wounded in the explosion. That's what did it. That's what he couldn't forget. Schoolgirls among them. And that he himself had two girls.'

'And then?' she asks.

'He started unravelling after he got home from his second tour. He did a third to try and get ahead of it, but it was no good. His marriage began to deteriorate. He went into treatment, but it didn't pull him back. He'd been accepted onto a crew of veterans sailing the Sydney to Hobart yacht race – it gives them a sense of teamwork again, mateship and competition – but he didn't get to the starting line. Corporal Djokovic jumped off South Head. He wrote in his suicide note that he didn't want to take the place of someone who was more likely to benefit from the trip.'

Kira tattoos *MD* in black on the flower's stem, planting it for him.

ONE SUNDAY, PENNY watches Kira and Blake leave the cottage and cross the paddock to the Big House, the boy carefully carrying a box in his arms.

'This is for you,' Blake says at the back door, holding the box out.

'What is it, Love?' Penny asks.

'Something I've made,' Blake replies, 'a present.'

In the kitchen, over tea, Penny unwraps the brown paper covering the shoebox. She folds the paper and lays it aside to re-use, then carefully lifts the lid from the box.

'Oooh,' she murmurs, 'it's exquisite!' She lifts the first of two origami cranes from the box, their yellow wings bright in the kitchen light.

Blake smiles, proudly.

'Did you make these all by yourself?'

'I can show you!' Blake blurts, and produces a sheet of paper he'd tucked into the belt at his back.

Penny watches as the boy folds the paper on the table, turning it over and pressing it with adept hands.

'If you make a thousand cranes you get a wish,' Blake says as he folds.

She thinks about the novenas of her childhood, and her own father leaving the house early on the first Friday of the month to go to Mass before starting his day's work. *If you can commit yourself to it,* he'd explain, *if you can accomplish nine first Fridays, then Jesus promises he will forgive your sins immediately before you die.*

She wasn't a child to pick fights with her parents, but all the same she'd asked, *So all you have to do to get to heaven is go to Mass nine times?*

It's harder than it sounds, her father told her, *life gets in the way, all sorts of things — you get sick, your children get sick, holidays, work.*

'Is that so?' Penny says. 'Where did you hear that Blake?'

The boy pauses, and looks down at the folded paper in his hands. 'I don't know. Somewhere,' he says quietly, his confidence faltering. 'I think it's because no one could ever do it. You'd get bored. It'd take too long and you'd get bored and stop. A thousand is a lot of cranes.'

THAT EVENING PHELAN takes a call.

'What do you think you are doing?' the voice asks, an old voice, unforgotten.

'Gruen?' Phelan responds. They've not spoken since he left Tarin Kot with Beckett's body, but Gruen has shadowed him ever since.

Penny looks up from her book, startled, colour draining from her face.

'It's been a long time, hasn't it Brigadier Phelan?' The mockery of what Phelan had once possessed, of who he once was. 'We never thought we'd have to see you again.'

The Gruen who greeted Phelan at his forward operating base, had doubted him even then. Gruen the seer. Phelan has nothing to hold on to now, no air to breathe, nothing to stop his mouth from drying or blood pounding in his ears.

'What do you want?' Guessing the answer, fearing it.

'We all saw you on television, Old Man,' Gruen continues evenly. 'It was like you'd come back from the dead.'

Phelan has nothing to say.

'You've been making contact with people again, haven't you? You wouldn't be thinking of doing anything like that interview again, would you?' Gruen continues, Phelan understanding now that Gruen is calling to finish him off.

'It was because of *you* Beckett died.' Gruen puts it to him like a prosecutor to a trapped and broken accused, all its remorseless logic, the accumulated weight of years. 'You don't get to be his advocate, Old Man. Not then. Not now. Not ever.'

Phelan tries to respond, but can't form the words. There is sound, plaintive, a whimpering before a raised axe.

'What did you say?' Gruen asks through the phone, wanting to hear Phelan attempt a defence, ready to pounce, to kill.

'I know,' Phelan blurts it out. 'I know!'

Gruen is taken aback, though only temporarily. 'What do you know, Old Man? Say it!'

'I know that it was my fault.'

'But do you?' Gruen presses. 'Do you really? Or is it just that you know *his mates* hold you responsible, that *I* hold you responsible, that in time history will too.'

'Of course I know. Of course I do. As if I'd need *you* to tell me.'

'As if you *didn't* need me to tell you!' Gruen snarls, losing his equanimity. 'There's no one better than me to say it. Because he was *my* soldier to protect. It was *my* base and *my* patrol. *My* watch. And he was *my* boy. And if you hadn't come, he wouldn't have been killed.'

'I know that,' Phelan says again. 'And I know that's what you think. You made all that abundantly clear a long time ago, Tony. And I've had a long time to think about it. You are right. I was wrong. If I hadn't been there, Sapper Samuel Beckett would not have died. And I will never forgive myself.'

Seven long years of silence.

'It fucked you up, didn't it?' Gruen says, even now pushing further forward.

'Being responsible for a young man's death can fuck you up,' Phelan replies. 'Yes, it can.'

The two men fall back.

'Has it fucked you up too, Tony?' Phelan asks after a while.

'*I* can live with my responsibilities without them fucking me up.'

'Well good for you. Good for you.'

254

'We saw that you got a tattoo of his name.'

'We?'

'The boys. Those of us on patrol that day. Those of us who shared that base together.'

'You saw my tattoo?'

'You showed the world when you did the interview, Old Man.'

'I'm not afraid to talk about Beckett.'

'And to talk honestly about your role in it?'

Phelan pauses. Clocks tick. Tattoos sting. A wife watches. 'I'm not afraid of that either.'

They both weigh Phelan's answer, what truth there might be in it.

'The boys get together every year,' Gruen finally says. 'Those of us who are in Brisbane. Every ANZAC Day we hire out the first floor of The Victory.'

'It's a trap,' Penny says.

But Kira's needles disagree. *You can do it*, they hum, *you are strong.*

VICTORY

Phelan stands in King George Square, close to the parade's route, lost in the gathering crowd. He hears the hiss of a coffee machine in a cart at his shoulder. A mother brushes dandruff from the shoulders of her son's dark jacket. The wheels of a baby's stroller squeak and car horns squabble. People are talking everywhere, though even if he were to pause and lean close he still couldn't hear what they were saying, as if no matter how much he may wish it, there are conversations to which he can never be admitted. It's his first parade since he was a kid where he's not in uniform. All the civilian boots hurrying across the square to join the bulging crowd are out of step. A voice comes over the loudspeaker, momentarily parting the static, a man's voice, but too high Phelan thinks, too hurried, swallowing his words, as if something as mundane as delivering a message to an ANZAC Day crowd can make a person anxious.

Overhead are clouds and fighter jets, on the ground fifty thousand upturned heads. Stirred or benumbed? Phelan feels the whiskey flask against his left breast, filling the inside pocket of the jacket Penny bought him for his breakfast television interview. On the outside are his medals, two sides of the same jacket.

He finds a toilet cubicle and slugs down his Jameson's, feels it hit. He straightens, sighs and straightens further, slaps his cheeks.

The bells of the City Hall clock tower chime ten o'clock, demanding to know what he is doing here, why he is spectator not marcher.

He feels her tattoos on him, his whole body is alive with them, not just his skin. She's humming for him, whispering to him. *You can do this*, her tattoos murmur. *You can.*

It propels him forward, through the thick streets, vibrating with people. It is afternoon now and the day is glowing. The close crowd carries him for a city block or two. Then, as he nears The Victory, he slows. The couple behind him have to swerve suddenly to get round him. Would they be cursing him if he was in uniform?

Phelan stops completely when The Victory comes into view. He leans against the wall of the building on the corner of Edward and Charlotte, and looks across the intersection at the pub. A giant Maori in a black-and-white security uniform stands guard on the footpath outside, patrolling the side door leading upstairs to the private room where the boys have been drinking since late morning.

He yet could go, he yet could stay.

As he watches, tossing up what to do, Gruen emerges from the pub, alone. Phelan's gut tightens. He feels the building hard against his shoulder. Gruen steps onto the footpath and puts his phone to his ear, his thin lips moving. He gestures as he talks, cutting shapes out of the air with his right hand, giving orders to someone. As Phelan has not done for a long time.

You can do this, Kira's tattoos whisper to him.

But do what exactly? Watch Gruen on his phone as he'd watched him on his army radio in the Chora Valley? The angle of Gruen's head and the rope of muscle running down the side of his neck are entirely unchanged. Brisbane and its babbling streets disappear. Phelan watches Gruen receive intelligence. Watches him process it, move his men around. Watches him bring in air support all over again. Where is Kira here, where Penny? Phelan closes his eyes. He breathes. He tries to count the battle away, one two three, but a shell explodes nearby and his eyes snap open and Gruen is looking directly across the street towards him.

Phelan jerks his head back sharply. His heart, his skin, heat at the back of his skull. He slides into a doorway, panting. What shadow there is, what shade. He tries to make himself small. These people passing by on the footpath in front of him, these old men, these parents with their children in their hands. This same throb of battle. The smell of piss from somewhere far away, so close. This crowd of boys, this Beckett-filled street. Beneath this molten sun, sheltering in this shallow doorway, this no-space. Phelan's legs weaken.

'Old Man.'

Does he feel his legs at all?

'Phelan,' the voice tries again.

Ah fuck.

'I'm glad you've come,' Phelan hears Gruen say.

He opens his eyes. Gruen's hand is on his shoulder now, patting him.

'Come on up, Old Man,' Gruen says. 'Join us.'

It is an ambush, he thinks, Penny is right. But I have no choice.

ALL THEIR HEADS turn when he enters the room. They look at him, amazed. It is as if they themselves have called him forth, as if the intensity of their denunciations over the years has made him real. As if from somewhere in their cauldron of accusations they have found the spell to summon him for sentencing. And now here he is, among them! They look at him goggle-eyed, astonished at their power.

Gruen signals the barkeeper to cut the music.

'Boys,' Gruen says, pausing for effect before yelling. 'Here he is!'

The men roar. An ambush *and* a sacrifice, Phelan thinks.

Gruen raises his arm to quieten the room, his boys before him once again. At moments like this it's as if he's still their commanding officer in Afghanistan, as if they're all still hunkered down in their forward operating base in the Chora Valley, the last remaining representatives of humanity, no one to rely on but each other. He might be about to deliver a briefing, preparing them to step out beyond the wire, urging them to keep their heads down. Sweating to keep them safe. When he speaks again it is clearly, evenly.

'Let us give James Phelan credit where it is due. We invited him here, and he has come. He didn't need to, but he has. That takes courage.'

A number of men snort derisively. Phelan thinks he hears the click of a closing door, sealing him in. Gruen raises his hand again. Silence follows.

'Phelan has something he wants to say. Let's hear him out.'

Phelan looks around the hostile room. They come at him, pressing forward, wedged still in the Chora Valley, working to cut themselves free. They'll kill him to get out, he knows that. They have to. He desperately needs a drink, but he'll have to do this without one.

'If ...' he starts. 'If I hadn't ... been ... on that patrol ...'

They listen to him stumbling and gulping, trembling before them, and realise what they have in front of them is not what they imagined they'd get, nor what they wanted. They barely recognise him he's so broken, so pathetic, incapable of issuing orders, let alone expecting anyone would follow them. Where there had once been a soldier, even a career-arsed brigadier you wouldn't cross a proverbial dirt track to piss on, now someone else entirely has taken his place, someone it's hard to be angry at.

'Spit it out,' someone hisses, but he's shouted down by others.

'If I hadn't been on the patrol,' Phelan continues, 'then there probably wouldn't have been an attack, and ... and Sapper Samuel Beckett would probably still be alive. And ...' There is no way out for him now. 'And I didn't need to be on that patrol. There was no sound operational reason for me to be there. So I must carry the responsibility for his death.' Phelan looks around the room. He tries to meet their eyes, even if just one or two men, but he can't and looks down. 'He was a mate of yours, and I'm sorry.'

They look at him and his pitiable apology, some embarrassed for him and wanting it over now, for someone to put Phelan out of his misery; others furious. They turn to each other and battle over him, as if he is no longer there, whether he be hanged or not.

He watches from the centre of their competing, safe for as long as the fight continues. He has lost all authority. He understands that. Once he could have made or broken men's careers, fancied he could have even broken the men themselves, that he had that power. Now he is a scrap some of the men want to save, and others long to see burn. The judgements themselves are no harsher than those he's reached himself. They ring with a purity in the spoken air, crisper, cleaner – he's weak, unreliable, vain. He closes his eyes. It's more than a relief. There's gratification in it. Though it's not the damnation that hurts – it's the counter-arguments. The voices who refuse to judge, the compassion. The so-whats, and who-gives-a-shits, and the first stones, and glass houses. It sounds weak, even to Phelan's ear. These men who are not trained in mercy seem to him, at that moment, reduced by it.

The longer the debate over him goes on, the more they are all tainted by it. Indecision is always fatal, a once-upon-a-time mantra of his. The trick is knowing what has died. He is Barabbas. Get it right this time, he thinks. There is no one else, no choice.

But Gruen says, 'Let him atone. Let him try. Watch him try and make amends.' Gruen is almost whispering. The room is leaning in to him, tongues lapping, as if his words are the last remaining droplets of sense. Just watch.

'You're not buying his fucking PTS fucking D line are you, Boss?'

'Look at him,' Gruen says quietly, 'look at him.'

All their turning heads. All their withering gazes. These marksmen, Phelan thinks. Finish this, finish it.

Too much silence.

'We get that you feel guilty, Sir,' one of the men says, breaking it. 'But that's only half of it. We saw the interview you done, Sir. About how war can fuck you up. About how the army can do more to help. About "destigmatisation" and all that. And good on you. But then you bring Becks into it. What the fuck? I mean why the fuck would you do that? And that's the problem see? You say you feel responsible for Beckett's death, but then you take responsibility for his memory, see? They're separate things. The war fucks people over, spits them out, no one there to catch them. All right. Fix that up. Good on you. But leave Becks out of it. You can't do that, see? You can't give a man's life away, and then take his memory.'

Echo and silence. Long and deliberate and reaching back with precision. Phelan is there. Gruen is there. Beckett is. Each man in the room.

'Fair enough,' Phelan says, 'but he shouldn't be forgotten either. No matter how the war takes them, they shouldn't be forgotten.'

Phelan takes a step backwards from the bar table. The tight fist of men around him opens slightly, clearing him a space. They watch as he unbuttons his shirt. Those not yet at the table gather from the far ends of the room. They see Phelan's chest hair, his pale skin, his softened gut as he pulls his shirt out from his trousers. All talk, all drink, all music, all shifting weight from foot to foot ceases. Phelan peels off his right sleeve, and they see Beckett. They know it already from Phelan's interview. Even so, seeing Beckett's name there on Phelan's pink skin, reading his name there among them, is a shock.

Then Phelan peels off the second sleeve. His shirt drops to the floor and the men see his back, his field of poppies, each bearing its initials.

They understand, they know. They don't need to count, they know. They lean forward and find their mates and see themselves and the price of war and they know.

Then one of them, Joseph Ng, wounded after Beckett, rolls forward in his wheelchair, rapping the men in front of him with the back of his hand to make them shift.

'Let me see,' he says to Phelan. 'Kneel down, will you,' and Phelan does.

Ng reaches out. He jerks his head suddenly, an involuntary tic, and his reaching hand shudders before resuming its course. They watch his trembling finger, see it land on the back of Phelan's left shoulder. Tap Phelan's flesh, gently brush the tips of his fingers against a poppy's petals. Watch him lean in closer still to examine him, making as if to pluck the poppy, to lift it off his skin and smell it.

'Excellent fucking work,' Ng says.

A GOOD LEG

HE BRINGS NG to her, carrying him across the paddock in the afternoon light. She goes out to meet them at the foot of the stairs.

A word of greeting, perhaps *Come*, *Welcome*, not yet understanding who he is and why he's here, but she is touched. Phelan lifts the soldier up the stairs, the young man's face raised in uncertainty, his right arm around Phelan's shoulders. Upstairs, Kira sits Ng on the bed set out on the enclosed verandah, while Phelan returns to his ute for the wheelchair.

When he gets back Phelan pulls her aside in the kitchen and asks, his voice low, 'Can you do this?'

'What, exactly?'

'A tattoo. Whatever he needs.'

'He'll pay for it?'

'Or I will.'

Kira looks at him. Phelan is animated by something she hasn't seen in him before. She doesn't immediately answer.

'He's scared,' Phelan presses. 'He's lost one leg, and half the other. He's just arrived home after two months in the military hospital in Germany. He's got it all ahead of him still – more surgery, new legs, therapy. But he wants to keep what he's got left. He wants ... well, he'll tell you what he wants better than I can.'

Kira shakes her head. 'Well, I'm scared, too, Jim. I mean, who is this bloke? He could be anyone.'

Only then does Phelan see Kira's anxiety, she who came seeking refuge. Whatever fear bringing an unknown soldier to her sanctuary might seed in her. Whatever risks she imagines it might bring, however it might expose Blake.

He nods. 'You don't have to do it.'

She sighs, shrugs her shoulders. 'He's here now.'

'Hey,' she says as she approaches him from across the room.

'Hey,' he returns, swivelling his chair towards her. His cap is resting in his lap. His short dark hair, his wide-darting eyes. He's mid-twenties

262

at most, she thinks, but his trousers are pinned up, the left above the knee, the right below it.

'Where are you from, mate?'

'Sydney, Darra, Vietnam,' he replies. 'Take your pick.'

It's only now, standing beside him, close, that his neck and head jag suddenly away from her, before slowly settling back into place.

'What's your name?' she asks.

'Sapper Joseph Ng. The brigadier said you're the tattooist.'

She gestures to the bottles of ink in neat rows on the top of the table.

'You were the one who did his back?'

She nods, then takes a chair in the corner of the room, facing him at his level, so she might see him better. As she lowers herself, he watches her, his head whipping violently to the left again, before returning smoothly to neutral, as if a hydraulic timer is at work within him.

'You're an artist,' he says looking across at her, hauling the words out of himself. The immense effort it takes.

'At your service, Sapper Ng,' she says, bowing her head as she speaks. The gesture risks parody, but it is sincere. Then the whiplash of his tic. She waits for him to settle, then smiles.

'You and Phelan,' she says, pointing her head towards the Big House as she mentions him, 'obviously know each other.'

'Not really.'

He jerks again, and Kira measures the time between tics. The soldier's unique rhythm.

'Have you been tattooed before?'

He nods, showing her the work on his biceps.

She names the tattooist, and he nods, impressed. She waits for his tic, and then, when the spasm has passed, asks if he knows what he's after.

He reaches into his breast pocket for a page from a glossy magazine, unfolds it and holds it out to her. A great dragon, nostrils flared, scales glistening, its eyes looking out at the world and all its threats.

'Where do you want it?'

He wheels across to the single bed. 'Can you help me up?'

She gets underneath his armpits and lifts as he twists and slides from his chair to the bed. She steps back as he shuffles out of his pinned trousers. Usually she'd turn away, but she worries it might offend him if she did. The soldier sits tall, his T-shirt falling to his black Y-fronts, 'Bonds' stitched around the elastic. His two withered thighs shine in the half-morning.

'Here,' he says, rubbing his right thigh. This thigh is complete, the stump of his leg below his knee. Kira watches his hand caress his skin. 'This is my good leg,' he says. 'I don't want the doctors to take any more of it. I want a dragon to ward them off.'

She moves around him, resting her hand on his thigh, feeling the ridges of his quadriceps, the contours of him, the texture of his skin, comparing what she is discovering about his leg with what she knows of all the other thighs she's worked. She touches his hips, both. She moves around him, changing sides. She almost speaks. Where, how, why, but restrains herself. She leaves him and his thigh and returns with another lamp which she sets on a chair dragged close. A yellow light.

AN HOUR LATER she sets to work, inking to the vibrations of his body, pausing every forty-five seconds, lifting the tattoo machine just in time, coming to know his body in waves.

His skin glows, his thigh giving off its own light where she cuts it. Self-fulfilling. The hours pass. She rotates him, repositioning herself too. As she turns her head to refill her line of caps he reaches into his trouser pocket and pulls out a hip flask. She looks up at the sound of the cap being unscrewed. She imagines a genie escaping. He does not meet her eyes as he lifts the flask to his lips. She says nothing until he offers it to her.

'No thanks,' she says, too curtly.

'It's a family heirloom.'

She looks at the worn brown leather casing. 'Alcohol makes blood run,' she says.

He responds with another slug. 'Then run, baby, run,' he mutters to himself as he screws the cap back on before tossing the flask across the room. It hits the wall, and thuds to the ground. Kira sighs.

'All right then,' she says, collecting it, and taking a shallow mouthful herself before setting it down on her work table, behind her rows of inks, a tall dark peak shadowing them. Later, she gets them both water. Then dry biscuits from the kitchen.

She tires before he does. The machine grows heavy. The pads on her fingers whiten where the blood has drained from holding it so tight for so long. She straightens her back. It's as if he's not even here, and instead has left her a chrysalis to pattern. The low whistle in the west where the falling sun brushes the eucalypt leaves on the ridge, singeing them, wisps of smoke curling into stars.

She lays down her machine and stretches, and thinks, abruptly, where is her son?

'Let's stop for now. Let's finish this later.'

'Later? What the hell is that? There is no "later".'

She knows he's right, that she might lose her place, but she doesn't care. Hopefully Phelan will have him. She goes to the window and pushes it open as far as it will go, listening in the direction of the Big House, looking. And there he is, through the pines, Penny beside him, shifting a hose from the base of one orange tree to another. Kira bends over the soldier once again. He knows how his dragon is progressing at the front of his thigh, but hasn't asked to see what she's done on the back, hasn't tried to twist his head or seek a mirror. He's listening to his skin, she thinks.

It is past midnight when she finishes, sore. She asks him what he sees.

'Hope,' he answers.

She leaves him on the bed and returns with her Nikon. 'May I?'

'What for?'

'I don't know. Habit. Pride. To remember. To make it last.'

She takes a photo and shows him. He sees his leg, his skin breathing fire. He sees his courageous leg beneath the skin, all its hunger, all its leaning into life. He tells her it's beauty he sees.

'I've never used that word before. Beauty.'

She nods.

'Thanks.'

She sees his pride and suspects it's been a long time since he felt that.

'Take some more photos,' he says to her.

Kira claims a shutter full of images.

Ng hugs her under the stars. 'Thank you,' he says.

THE SOUND MOTORBIKES MAKE

IN THE BIG House, three days after Ng, Phelan hears the sound of approaching motorbikes, Harleys.

'The keys to the gun cabinet, Pen. The keys, quick!' he yells.

Penny hears, sees, hurries into her bedroom, before emerging, throwing the keys to him where he stands in the corridor.

Phelan unlocks the cabinet. The magazine is full. He slides it into the .303, his heart thumping. Click, snap. That precision contains his swelling emotions, their sharpness, their certainty. There is not yet any order to his thoughts, only peril and instinct. The old grooves. He slings the gun over his shoulder, feeling the rifle strap at his collarbone, the stock against the small of his back, feeling even the safety catch in position against him.

Out the back door, through the gate and onto the dirt road, and his first view. Already the bikes have arrived, their stands kicked into place, two riders swinging their legs over and off. Their synchronicity. The two men move slowly, as if bossing Phelan with their nonchalance, one throwing his jacket over his seat, the other stretching his arms, reaching for the sky. Their heads face each other momentarily, a word or two, no more, before turning towards the cottage.

Phelan's quick stride turns into a trot as the first of the men takes the bottom step. He tries to control his breathing, tries to think. Kira hasn't appeared at the top of the stairs. Surely she won't. Surely she's latched the door and retreated. But there is no back door from which to escape, and the windows are too high for jumping. At least Blake is at school, safe. The calculations begun.

At the top of the cottage stairs, one of the men raps. The knocks reverberate through the air like small detonations. The other man turns to look out, away from the house. Something about his pose, the set of his neck, his sweeping eyes, seeking movement before object. The man sees Phelan at a jog, hears Phelan calling out now, his weapon in his hands – 'Get away!' – the two men at the top of the stairs, exposed, these heartbeats. One throws a leg over the handrail and slides, the other drops to his haunches, shrinking on the step.

'No!' they yell out. 'Don't!'

Still Phelan runs, faster now, raising his rifle as he approaches. The target is splitting, one of the men is at the bottom of the handrail, nearly on the ground, and if Phelan allows that to happen he'll lose his advantage. His blood is beginning to surge in him, the language of blood, now! now! now! But the man who's remained on the stairs is yelling and holding out his hands, his two palms out, and is calling *Brigadier! Brigadier!* and it's confusing. Phelan blinks the uncertainty away from all that is familiar to him – the cottage, the drill, the gun in his hands, the blue sky, his childhood home. Yet still there is something, a word tossed into the air, and Phelan's walk slows and the man rises from his position at the top of the stairs, his head and shoulders framed by the door now, Kira's red door, and the man calls out *Brigadier Phelan!* and the voice is like one he's heard before, and behind the man with the outstretched white palms the door opens and it is Kira herself.

'YOU SHOULD HAVE let me know.'

'Yeah, we shoulda.'

'This is my property,' Phelan continues.

The land maybe, not Kira.

'Yeah,' Surawski says. 'Sorry.'

Under the shade of the fig Phelan knows them, corporals Surawski and Gislason. He knows them from the patrol briefing, these two somewhere in the line with him, having their gear checked like him, stepping out through the gate like him, each man patting the head of the base goat. These are the brothers he'd meant when he'd spoken at the ramp ceremony, the men he was addressing, Surawski and Ng and Gruen and Swift and Hillman and Gislason and the others from the platoon. Knows them from what he's learned afterwards. He remembers them from The Victory, these two drinking quietly together in a corner, like lovers, Surawski's fingers coming forward to touch his back after he lifted his shirt, following Ng. Another one needing to touch to believe.

'She may not have been in,' Phelan hurries on, the adrenalin still in him, jagging him this way and that. 'It could have been a waste of time.'

The three men watch as Kira moves towards them, a jug of lemon cordial in one hand, a tower of four glasses in the other.

'Text me next time, call me,' Phelan murmurs before Kira reaches them in the depths of the shade. 'I'll organise it. Let everyone know.'

'Sure,' they grunt, 'sure.'

GREATER THAN THEY THINK

IN TIME THEY come. Some word of mouth. Some soldiers' grapevine. They wind their way up the mountain, in carloads or alone, each of them coming for her. It is as if they know her already, are aware of everything she has done, believe in what she can do.

Phelan greets them first at the Big House, as arranged. Sometimes they will drink tea or coffee, all their loaded teaspoons of sugar on his verandah. They will smoke or talk shit or share their plans with him, Phelan nodding like a sage.

He only leads them across the paddock to her if Blake is safe at school, the one condition Kira has set, that Blake remains invisible. Their boots and their thongs and their sandshoes crunch in the dry grass, the air around them glowing and humming, the blue sky deepening with each step, the high-floating clouds. Phelan delivers them to her as if he is Charon and they are immortal warriors and this paddock is the Styx, and these men will return. He'd taken their coins from them in the Chora, before he'd become a ferryman, when all was aflame anyway and the only direction was out. Now he pays them back.

DAY AFTER DAY they come to her, and she receives them, one by one, refusing none. She has this duty. To tattooing as much as to these men who need her.

She gets to know each of them before she inks them. To learn what they want, why they're here. She then needs time to draw their designs. Sometimes they bring her photos, or pages from *Skin & Ink* or *Tattoos Downunder*, or images they've printed off the net. Sportsmen's tattoos. Other soldiers' ink, often marines. She looks at their images, nods and asks them to talk. She might lay the image aside, out of their line of sight, and ask them to describe it.

'Why that?' she might say to prompt a conversation.

A couple hand her pieces of folded paper on which they've sketched their own ideas. One of the drawings includes notes at the bottom of the page with the symbolism of each element of the design explained.

'You can strangle a tattoo with too much meaning,' she says to him.

'I don't understand,' the soldier replies.

'It's like a relationship,' she says.

'I'm single', he answers.

'You've got to allow each other space to change, grow,' she says.

He grins. 'So are you married?'

The wisdom doesn't feel like hers, if wisdom it even is. Something a preacher read out at a wedding she went to once, oaks and cypresses and not growing in each other's shadows. What does she know of relationships? Don't fuck around, don't take gear that'll kill you, don't fucking lay a hand on me ever again.

But she knows this – that her best work requires her to understand her clients, whether their bodies are soft or hardened, why they are there, what they want. Kira knows too that she needs the money. These men travel great distances for her tattoos and they pay her what she asks for, more than street rates, without blinking. They pay in cash. She keeps a tally in her notebook and hides the growing wad of notes in the ceiling. So she saves. It's an opportunity to make money that she cannot let pass. Because she must look beyond this time, beyond this refuge. Because she cannot afford to sell herself short.

She will not tattoo images of real people. She will not tattoo weapons, or slogans of war. She will not tattoo angels' wings.

'Why not?' one of the men challenges her. 'That's what I want. Like Johnathan Thurston.'

'You need to discover what it is you really want,' she replies. 'Come back then.'

'I know,' he insists. 'For years I've wanted wings, big ones, on my back.'

'But you are not Johnathan Thurston. You are better than that – you are yourself.' She says things like this to them, and they like it.

But she says to herself, shaking her head sometimes when they leave – Who the hell do I think I am? I am not William Blake. I was never Flores, back when he was a tattooist. No wings he ever tattooed have helped me fly. Or allowed me to flee. If anyone has settled for less than they should have it is me! But not anymore. My son needed me to leave a long time ago. My son didn't need me to stay with Flores. I'll make my own wings, dollar by dollar, feather by feather. For Blake. For both of us.

SHE TELLS THE men they are greater than they think. She tells them they know everything they need to know. She speaks to them in a foreign language, even to her. She uses the words 'love' and 'skin' and 'healing' and 'faith'. The men look at her as if they are spells falling from her lips. At the end of a session, their bodies afire, her every word is wisdom. She says, '*You may bleed.*' She says, '*There may be pain.*' She tells them not to scratch or pick scabs. She tells them to stay out of pools and to change bandages and to apply lotion. She tells the future and they listen, needy, rapt, and submit to her.

She tattoos roses growing from Surawski's skull as he squirms in the chair, anxious about what he'll say to his mother. Lantana berries for Starc, whatever childhood memories he's trying to recover. Earnest young Thyme asks her to tattoo the Shield of Achilles on his left breast and tells her he wants to be a father one day. She tattoos *Best They Could Do* neatly beneath the horizontal scar scored across the side of Howe's neck where a round took the edge of him and no more. And Swift, the secret orchid keeper with his secret tattoo, whatever she is now complicit in, that too-tender part of him.

And still they come. I need to be careful with them, she thinks.

One of them wants a large back piece done in one sitting.

'Let's do it over three days.'

'Why?'

'It adds up. I'll be breaking a lot of skin for you. I don't want to hurt you.'

'You don't understand then,' he replies.

She nods. 'All right.' She wounds to heal.

PHELAN COURIERS THEM across the paddock to the cottage before retreating to the house where he watches, or becomes agitated not watching. But the surveillance is of a quiet timber cottage, a soldier's car stilled outside his house for hours. There is nothing to see. Men enter and disappear, the house itself gliding lazily through cloud-shadow. When they emerge, hours later, they are like men exiting a confessional, or a lover's apartment.

Is it envy Phelan feels? That he is reduced to this? That he goes from necessary to superfluous in an afternoon?

PENNY WATCHES ALL these soldiers returning to their lives. Before the fire, before the breakdown, she and James had often entertained. In the later years of his career they hosted gatherings of officers with their wives and girlfriends or, increasingly, their husbands. And in the very early days there'd be barbecues and poker nights, all the amusing rubbish the soldiers would speak, pumping themselves up, bringing each other down. This is different – their house has become a waiting room for the patients the tattooist is seeing across the paddock – but all the same it's good to have people in the house again.

Usually they'll have gone by the time she returns from the hospital, though even then the traces they leave behind add something to the house – boot prints in the dirt, cigarette butts flicked off the verandah, the echo of their excitement on her husband. Better still when she gets home after a shift and they're still here, putting off the drive down the range. She changes out of her uniform and joins them on the verandah, admiring their tattoos, enjoying their banter. And if James is away with Blake she'll laugh and tease the boys, sometimes even flirting lightly, confident in her body.

His journeys of exploration with Blake push further afield. In the winter hours after school they set off for the ends of the property, some task to be attended to. To check on the cattle. To ensure the troughs are full. To check the turkey's nest, or a fence. To paint the sump oil he's collected onto the gateposts to ward off termites. To smoke out a rabbit hole before filling it in. Stones have begun to emerge from the back paddock, rising out of the earth. They collect them, one by one, and walk them to the base of an old eucalypt, clearing the field, building a cairn in the shade of the tree.

Blake discovers tadpoles in the top pool. He scoops his hands futilely into the water and almost topples in. While the boy is at school the next day Phelan bends an old metal coathanger into a circle and stretches mosquito netting over it, stitching the cotton gauze into place with needle and thread as he did fifty years earlier. He smiles when he is done – the joy of boyhood, of creating, of gift-making.

'Come with me, Big Fella, I've got something to show you.' Phelan presents the net to Blake who sees and understands, and sprints out of the shed. Phelan finds a bucket and follows the boy to the pool, where he is squatting on the bank, net lowered. The boy lifts it out and half a dozen tadpoles squirm and bounce and flick droplets of water at him.

'Look at this one. Wicked!' And Blake reaches in to catch the largest in his fingers.

• • •

'So, YOU LIVE here?'

There is something about the way the soldier examines her tattooing room, as if trying to see through the walls to what's beyond. Something in the fact he's come alone. And in his agitation, a small-eyed meanness. Half the men are on things, but this one, this former sergeant, is close to the edge.

'What's the brigadier got you up here for then?' the sergeant sneers as he drops into the armchair.

Kira was about to ask him about himself, but freezes. She realises suddenly how the farm has been a shelter from this, too. Arseholes.

'That's enough,' she says quietly.

'*Just* tattooing, hey? Is that all?'

She stands. 'Mate,' she says, her voice firm and clear, 'that sort of talk is not going to happen. You carry on like that, you're going to have to leave.'

In her gut is the memory of the night with the junkie, Phelan to her rescue, and Phelan across the paddock now too, just a yell away. The last thing she's going to do.

'His tattoo bitch, hey?'

She shakes her head slowly, as if disappointed for him that he hadn't listened, but in truth it's an enormous exercise of self-control. 'I told you not to carry on like that,' she says evenly, taking one deliberate step towards him, before suddenly striking him with her open right hand, slapping him fiercely on the cheek.

'What the! What?' He covers his head with his arms.

'Get the hell out of here, you pig!'

The sergeant wilts, unnerved. 'Whoa, whoa,' he says.

'Out!'

'Just a joke, Sister. It was just a joke. Calm down.'

'What would your brothers think of you? What would Sapper Beckett think? The memory of your dead comrade.'

They're just words, not hers, trying anything.

'I'm sorry,' pleads the sergeant, 'I'll behave.'

'Not today,' she replies. 'Come back when you've got some manners.'

To THE EAST Kira watches a great cloud illuminated by spasms of lightning. The cloud is distant, too far for thunder, or the breeze working against it. The cloud is self-contained, like an atom that will not be split, bolts of lightning flying from one end to the other. Another streak of horizontal lightning – greater than the rest – threatens to burst the cloud open, all its depths, the entire world of it. But for the war within itself, Kira thinks, the giant cloud might have moved unobtrusively across the sky, its very existence a secret. She sits on the steps and watches the show.

Is this how Flores's tattoo gods settled their arguments? she wonders. But here I am, and they cannot touch me. Not tonight. I am leaving them behind.

GALLERY OF LIMBS AND TORSOS

AFTER TATTOOING THEM, she takes photos of her work. Early in her career she would photograph every tattooed body and post the image online. Or, if it wasn't a piece to share, she'd simply store it away, compiling a catalogue of her work. Back in the days when she designed and drew and created, and what she created was unique. When she tattooed daily, when she dreamed daily. That was a long time ago, back when the studio was more than a front for Flores's dealing. When tattooing mattered to them. Now she looks at her work on these men and once more thinks, this is good.

She downloads the images from her camera and admires them at night when Blake is asleep. Her roses are as beautiful as any she's done before. She's proud she had them in her to give to Surawski. Look at Ng's dragon and its one missing scale, its vulnerability more compelling than its fierceness. A glistening shield, wet with the sweat of battle. She compares her work with what other artists are doing and it's not bad, she thinks, not bad at all.

The soldiers rise from the chair or the bed, their tattoos done, their skin aflame. They pose for her, these men she has marked but will probably never see again, and in this moment they are at the centre of the universe, and she is there with them.

She prints the images off and surrounds herself with them.

PENNY ESCORTS BLAKE across the paddock. She's carrying his school bag for him, the carton of eggs they filled together too. He's been anxious to get home after opening up the palm of his hand on a star picket. Usually such an easy child, he seems to have resented that he's had to wait at the Big House this afternoon while Kira finishes work. Little displays of petulance. She wouldn't normally walk him home like this, but he couldn't wait for his mother to get him and Penny wants to explain what happened, what she's put on the gash, give Kira some antibiotics just in case.

Blake runs ahead. When Penny reaches the top of the stairs the door is wide open. From one of the bedrooms she can hear the sound of the mother comforting her son. She doesn't want to intrude. To her left, the door to the enclosed verandah where Kira tattoos is ajar. The makeshift studio glows in the afternoon light, the bed, the armchair, Kira's stool, a table with an array of tattooing paraphernalia. But the walls. Penny steps inside. The walls are covered with sheets of A4 paper, images of the bodies Kira has been tattooing.

Ink on skin on ink on paper on wall. Positioned with care, the black and white images clustered together on one wall bleeding into a group of colour photos on another. So many limbs, so many torsos. The marked hands and wrists. A glistening thigh, a dimpled arse cheek. The muscle-taut skin. Scars. Not the men's, but the war's. Or perhaps, Penny thinks again, they're just domestic cuts and scratches and blisterings, wounds of civilian life. She sees neat lines of stitching. Fist-sized hollows where dark beasts of war once fed. The stumps of an amputee.

Penny moves around the room, taking in the walls of tattooed skin, unaware that as she moves she's tucked her hands behind her back like she's a gallery patron, peering close. She murmurs to herself, nods reluctantly, begrudgingly.

So, they really are quite beautiful, these images of tender skin and their exquisitely fresh wounds. She can tattoo, this woman, she can take photos too. Then suddenly, she thinks, where is James?

Penny scans the images, seeking out not Beckett or poppies, but her husband's bared body. When she finds it – the oldest among so many young men – she thinks, yes, that is him, this artist has captured him.

FROM THE GARDEN of the Big House Phelan sees a camera flash, not knowing what it is, catching only the unexpected flare of light as he pauses against the trunk of a cypress, and looks across at the cottage. Nearby, Blake is swinging his legs over the side of the verandah, banging the heels of the new pair of RMs Phelan has bought him.

'Mum's nearly finished,' Blake says, seeing the flash too, seeing Phelan come off the tree and squat to get a better view of the cottage.

'Can she have dinner with us?'

'Of course,' says Phelan. 'Of course she can.'

PHELAN, WHEN HE stands alone in her studio, feels his own skin tingle, begin to hum. Some song of common wounding, of universal suffering. He stands in her makeshift gallery, overwhelmed by what

Beckett has put in motion. Surrounded by these men he is coming to know, he quietly weeps. If Kira touched his shoulder now. If his mother did. If Penny could see this. If only they all could.

TRIBUTE

ONCE AGAIN HE is alight, madly. Once again Beckett enters him, speaks to him, urges him to act, though this Beckett is different. Not so much a remembrance as an artistic vision. The single tattooed name on his shoulder has now been joined by a platoon of tattoos. This new Kira-born vision. To take Beckett to the country, to take him and his brothers to the world! Who would not want to join him, who could not see its truth?

It doesn't take much to interest a journalist contact, and then – a morning of calls and a coffee down in Brisbane later – a publisher. He shows her the images he's taken on his phone of Kira's photo wall, magnifying them on her laptop so she can see for herself.

'Yes,' she says, short blonde hair, deliberate, experienced, encouraging.

'It's art,' he says.

'And it's an idea we can sell,' she replies.

PENNY WATCHES HIM at his project.

'You're mad,' she says. And in truth she is not sure whether the mania propelling him from the farm and back into the wider world will blow out after a few days, and he'll collapse onto a pile of empty whiskey bottles.

But the days turn into weeks and the fever of activity does not break – the phone calls, the emails and the trips down the range to the city. The refining of the original idea. The spreadsheets and the timelines. All the consents. The conversation with the Chief, the flights to Canberra and the lengthy negotiations with the army.

'It's a tribute to Sapper Beckett,' he says, 'and a celebration. Not just of Beckett, but all of them.'

'Who is *she*?' they want to know.

'It doesn't matter, Charlie,' he says, waving it away. 'It's not about her, but them.'

'But without her, there is no them.'

'She's "The Tattooist". That's enough. Otherwise, she is anonymous.'

'Won't people want to know?'

'People want to know about heroes. There'll be one on every page. *That*'s who people will want to learn about.'

He coordinates the photo shoots with the men, organising them into the photographer's studio in Brisbane at the nominated times, watching them turn into models, flexing their bodies. Flashes of ego and delight. The power of solidarity.

The life flowing through him as he crafts words to accompany the photos, lines of poetry, lyrical complements. Laughter not curses. This new cycle of, what? Happiness?

It is too much. 'Not just mad, but cruel,' Penny says to him.

'Cruel?'

She'd encouraged it, she knows that. But she'd thought that whatever it was he couldn't face when the tattooist first turned up here, that wound – resistant to therapy and medication and love – whatever it was, the tattooist might help him shift it. Bloody fool she's been. Because there's been no release. Worse – Beckett's hooks are even deeper into him. The tattooist's as well. The tattooist! How Penny has humiliated herself. She has given her life to this man, but it's not her he's celebrating.

279

'Here I am,' she says. 'Here I have always been. You can't even see me.'

'Pen! Don't say that!'

'But it's true, James!' she says. 'Beckett … Beckett will destroy you. He'll destroy whatever is left of us. You'll let him. You will, won't you?'

His distress is like a child's, uncomprehending.

'Oh Penny! But the book is a *good* thing. It'll help people understand the war.'

'It will destroy us. Is that what you want?'

'Of course not. No. No. No. I'm sorry. You're everything, Pen. Everything. I … I—' He reaches for her, but she pulls away. She will be no partner in his unsparing zealotry, will give him no encouragement, no succour.

'You're on your own with this, James.'

WHEN IT IS finally done, and the first copies arrive, three weeks before release, Phelan carefully wraps one for Kira. He lays the sticky tape beside the scissors on the table in his office and rises.

At the back door of the Big House he pauses, gazing out. Penny looks up from the kitchen table.

'The stars are brilliant tonight,' he says.

'Where are you going?'

He shrugs. 'The tattoo book.'

'Aah.'

PENNY LETS HIM go, walks down the hallway and enters his office. She pulls a copy out of the box, sits in his chair and begins to flick through. Thinks, can't help it, when *was* the last time you gave me anything?

• • •

'WHAT'S IT FOR?' Kira asks.

She knows it's a book, big and heavy in her hands. But neither her nor Blake's birthday is near, and the anniversary of their arrival – an event Penny had politely marked with a cake – had passed three months ago.

'You'll see,' Phelan says, feigning calm, control.

Partly it's the weight of it that makes her pause. She's shed so much, and has no instinct to accumulate.

'Come on!' Phelan urges. 'Open it.'

There is a mighty expectation in him. She feels the weight of that too.

'Mum!' Blake goes to wrestle it from her, but she keeps hold.

'Let's open it together, Little Man.'

'This will endure,' Phelan says, his eyes beginning to flame. 'Longer than me and my skin. Longer than Ng's and Surawski's. Longer than a platoon full of tattoos. A whole army-full.'

She's not sure what she's looking at, this album of her tattooed soldiers. A temporary blindness falls upon her, an opaque film clouding her sight. She turns the pages slowly, with ungainly fingers.

She sets the book on the table, open, face-down. It is heavy. She feels giddy. It is too late. Everything is changed. Motes of dust float around the glowing bulb. Kira lifts a cupped hand into the throw of light and holds steady. Whatever might fall into place.

'Are you all right?' Phelan asks after a while. His eyes burning still, yearning to ignite her.

She shakes her head and drops her arm. Looks at him. His thin hair. His puffy cheeks. A fire beyond her dousing.

'What the hell have you done?'

SHE SITS ON the top step of the cottage just before daybreak and looks out. Directly in front of her is the row of cypress pines and behind it, the Big House. You have to turn your head to avoid it. She does.

Gazes at the lightening of the east, all the sky beyond the escarpment, softening. The creatures of this place are stirring – the chooks and the cattle, Phelan's dog, the carolling magpies. They've been good to her. And to Blake who, soon enough, will climb from his bed, looking for her.

Kira is not sure what, exactly, she is surveying; what alchemy of time and circumstance. The trail of soldiers to her door has fallen to a trickle, though now Phelan has bound them to her she can't easily turn them away, coffee-table book or not. She has saved enough cash, but enough for what? A new identity? A new home? That would no doubt please Phelan's wife who seems to oscillate between suspicion and tolerance.

She hears her son's feet hit the floor. When he doesn't find her in bed, he calls out for her, 'Mum! Mum!' and she thinks, there are chooks to be fed and breakfast to be had and a school bus to be caught, and whatever the hell I'm going to do, it'll be for him.

WHAT TO FORGIVE

SO THIS IS where Phelan has escaped to, Gruen thinks, turning onto the gravel road and following it along the plateau. He stops his LandCruiser at the top of the rise but doesn't get out, surveying the country, knowing it already from the satellite images, but there's still the thrill of entering the map, owning the coordinates and feeling the images come to life around you.

He sees the old homestead, the cottage, the escarpment to the east and the north, sees the land gullying away to the west. A nice view, Gruen thinks, but there's only one way in and one way out. These trade-offs. That lesson from his first season in Chora when they'd set up their outposts on high ridges overlooking insurgent valleys.

Thinking they'd control the valleys, but really it was the valleys that controlled them.

Gruen sees two figures, man and boy, climb over a ridge to the west. He checks his watch. Phelan will have seen him. Gruen moves his vehicle forward to reach the house before Phelan does.

'Hello, Old Man,' he calls when they are in earshot, the boy carrying an empty yabby trap in his arms.

Phelan points the boy towards the Big House and the kid leaves them, looking over his shoulder.

'If you've come for a tattoo it's too late.'

'For your book, it's too late.' Gruen smiles at the retreating boy. 'Whose is he?' he asks. But Phelan does not reply.

'You're the only one not in there, you know,' Phelan says. 'Every other member of the platoon. All your boys. Every one got a tattoo, every one is there in the book.'

'Beware groupthink.'

'Hah! But of the two of us, *I'm* the one who has left the army.'

Gruen holds his gaze. 'And even then you haven't been able to let go,' he says quietly.

Phelan can't meet Gruen's eyes. He sighs, and as he does his shoulders drop. His eyes fall to the ground, and then, embarrassed, he lifts his face to the sky, as if distracted by something up there.

'Look Old Man. The book is fine. It's beautiful. The men love their tattoos, and they love the souvenir. All the media coverage. They're proud to be part of it. You've given them that. It's a fine thing you've done. A fine thing. But that's not why I'm here.'

'Well then?'

Gruen pulls out a ziplock plastic bag with a USB stick inside, and holds it out to Phelan.

'What is it?'

'You know.'

Phelan's mind is writhing. He can't find anywhere for it to settle.

His eyes shift from the bag and whatever riddle Gruen is laying out, whatever danger lurks inside, and stares hard at him. 'I've got absolutely no idea what this is about.'

'But you will,' Gruen says. 'It's about Becks.'

Phelan takes the plastic bag.

'And it's about you, Old Man,' Gruen adds.

'What the hell?'

'I owe you an apology.'

Phelan shakes his head. 'And this?'

'It's the footage from the helmet cam.'

'The what?'

'The helmet cam Becks was wearing when he died.'

'But why?'

'Because this way you'll have everything. This way you'll know what to forgive yourself for,' Gruen says.

THE HELMET CAM. His room and a laptop, and on his desk a transparent ziplock bag with a red memory stick inside. The clean plastic and the neat lines and the fresh metal and its smallness, cool and anaesthetised in its little plastic bag. *You and Beckett* Gruen had said. *You and Beckett and a helmet cam.* Phelan could destroy this little red splinter of history. He could toss it over the escarpment for it to crack open on the rocks below or wedge in the roots of a strangler fig for the weather to do its work. Or he could slide it into a drawer and try and forget about it, hoping it will somehow disappear in the dark.

He stares at it inside its plastic bag, blood red, his temples beginning to throb. Phelan sees the tiny green light, hears the camera whir and then click. There's a violent pull at his gut. He hears neither Penny arrive nor Blake leave. She's just there, standing beside him, resting her hand on his shoulder. She doesn't ask what he's doing, staring at the little plastic bag on his desk. Says nothing about the bottle of

Jameson's and the tumbler resting on his thigh.

'That was Tony Gruen, wasn't it?' she says. 'The vehicle that just left? The one I passed coming in?'

Phelan nods.

'This is from him?' She doesn't really need an answer to that either. She picks up the bag, opens it and squeezes the stick out, as if pressing ointment from a tube. It slides onto the palm of her hand and she inserts it into the laptop, fetching a second chair while it loads. Phelan's hands shake as he pours another whiskey.

PENNY DOESN'T ASK him if he's ready, nor ask herself either. She recognises the name beneath the icon on the screen, Chora Valley, and the date and opens the drive. A video. Outside the window the row of pines glows amber in the setting sun.

The footage expands to fill the screen, and suddenly it is 1645 hours on 4 November 2010 and they are in Afghanistan and they are on a narrow path, and they are Sapper Samuel Beckett and they are approaching the hour of their death.

Phelan gasps and his body recoils and in its reeling away from the screen his chair topples and crashes to the floor and he stumbles from the desk till his back thuds against the wall behind him, and he is jammed into the corner of the room, and there is nowhere else to go, and his hands are over his face, and he is trying to breathe, and he begins to slide down the wall till he is crumpled on his knees in the farthest corner of the darkening room, his head and hands pressed against the floor. He begins to bang his forehead and to groan, and Penny is beside him. Reaching for him, rocking him, nursing him.

She lifts him up and leads him out of the house. The entire western sky is aglow. She holds his hand. He is stiff. She walks him along the road, past the cottage and up to the top of the hill and then back again.

There is the sound of their shoes on the gravel, the sighing sun, the first stars bursting into being. At the gate to the house she turns him around again and they head back up the hill. She is exercising him, back and forth, up and down the hill and back up again. The cottage lights turn on as they pass. Kira's and Blake's silhouettes would be visible if they looked. The sun disappears.

Phelan shudders. Penny feels him tremble and then slowly begin to sob. He moves to pull his hand from hers, but she clings tight. She leads him back to the house, back to the computer. She rights the fallen chair. The room is dark but for the glowing monitor. They step onto Beckett's path once more. Penny grips Phelan's hand as they go, checks he's ready, their shoulders touching.

There is a mud wall to their left, waist-high, and beyond the wall an almond grove. The camera swings from the trees in the grove to the ground at their feet, to the buildings up ahead to their right, and back to the trees. Rays of sunlight pierce the trees – a short, brilliant kaleidoscope – then disappear. The path stretches ahead in a silent rhythm of bootstep. They march to the beat of an inevitable countdown, their hearts constricting.

They swing around to see what is behind them, too fast to fix on anything in the arc of stripling shadow and febrile light. They see a patrol of men behind, soldiers on the path, others among the trees. Way back in the distance a river and a bridge they've just crossed. One of their colleagues signals to them, a raised hand. They turn their head again – only a few more degrees – and there is Brigadier Phelan. Their gaze pauses on him, a juddering moment of dislocation, before sweeping on, halting, and turning back again, past Phelan, past the others, back to the path ahead, and back, eventually, to their steady footsteps on the ground.

But he has recognised himself.

Penny too. Her husband is beside her, and simultaneously trapped inside the footage on the screen. She has experienced so many versions of this narrative already. She has imagined it. She has read accounts of it. Has sat in storytelling circles in the hospital while Phelan tweezered parts of it from his brain. Has felt her husband convulse to it, nightmare after nightmare, beads of sweat pouring off him, little spheres of toxic memory seeping into their bedsheets, poisoning her too. And she has seen three still images ripped from life and all its bloody context, dark with portent, brutally effective.

The blast, when it comes, is almost a relief. There is a flash, but it is too bright to illuminate anything. There is jagged flash, and then there is storm, and in the spit and chaos of that cosmic tempest only swirling particles of dust exist. Phelan and Penny are buffeted by the ferocity of the static on the screen. It is all around them. Their ears are pummelled by every violent sound their imaginations are capable of conjuring. A nihilistic roar.

Then darkness. Dust and dirt and devil breath. As the world slowly lightens, it is because the storm is blowing itself out, and things begin to reconstitute themselves. The dust begins to settle, the earth to fall back into place.

They watch and wait and moment by moment things take shape, but what? It's as if their sight is damaged, as if specks of dust have blown onto their eyeballs. Only gradually do their eyes adjust to their new world.

The first thing they understand is that there are two planes, one of dark and one of light. Then they realise they are no longer upright, but lying on the ground, their heads at an angle to it, the dark earth close by, eyelash-touching distance away. Through the grit and dust, past a nearby dark mass, the trees of the grove slowly emerge, backlit, trunk after trunk. The angle of their heads resting on the ground causes the trees to run horizontal to the world rather than upwards. It is disorienting, but the trees are the first certain things, and their eyes fix upon them. They are learning to see in this new world. Other things – a snapped twig, pebbles, rocks, a mule tethered to a distant boulder. What looks like a bird's nest in the branches of the nearest almond tree may be a hive or a burl.

They realise the elongated dark mass close to them is their right arm, stretched out as if in sleep, their hand pulled into a fist. Their head is not moving. Their eyesight is fixed. Penny wonders if they are dead already.

PHELAN KNOWS THEY are not. Not yet.

He knows what is happening around them, though they cannot see. He knows a firefight has begun. He knows the practice of warfare is unfolding about them – locating the source of enemy fire, returning it, signalling to each other, estimating how many enemy there are, giving cover, screaming, *Man down! Man down!* He knows too, that he is closer than anyone to the fallen soldier, knows that by whatever impulse, by whatever alchemy of training and instinct and fate, it will be he who runs-scrambles-dives-falls and then lands beside Sapper Beckett.

Phelan's arrival, when it comes, is violent, breaking the peace. One moment they are gazing languidly out through the trees, the afternoon light as golden as any fairytale's, the silent earth a steady pillow for their resting heads. Then a soldier's body explodes from nowhere and lands in front of them. The earth shudders. They cannot see all of him – his camouflaged torso is too huge and takes up most of their field of vision. His weapon lands awkwardly between them, his gloved hands gripping it tightly. They recognise Phelan's forearms, the neatly rolled cuffs. Even then his skin was old.

There can be no looking away now. There is no sound, but they see Phelan speaking.

Phelan remembers. His first low, urgent word, *Sapper!* His body coursing with adrenalin, filling with an unfolding moment he doesn't yet understand. *Sapper!* And his hand reaching for Beckett's shoulder, shaking him, fearing already it is a corpse he's trying to force a response from.

Then Beckett groans. Or cries. Some animal noise, some ancient trench-wail. Phelan recognises it, knows he's finally here. At Tet. Or Milne Bay. Or Fromelles. Gettysburg. Jericho. The very plains of Ilium. How many humans have expired like this? Ten million, a hundred million? What brotherhood of the slaughtered is Beckett about to join?

But then, after the cry, a word. *Charlie*, the wounded man says, *Charlie.*

You're all right soldier, Phelan says instinctively, *you're going to be all right.*

Phelan takes off his gloves, and lays them aside. He removes Beckett's dark ballistic glasses, and Beckett blinks and groans again. His eyes wide, blinking madly, as if he's entering the world afresh. *You're going to be all right*, Phelan says again as Beckett turns his head to him, looking at him now. Is it terror or is it wonder, Phelan thinks, something newborn in the sapper's shutter-flashing eyes? *Charlie*, the soldier says again. Phelan doesn't know what to say, whether to acknowledge the name, or even how to. Whether even to say anything at all. He puts Beckett's glasses back on to help with the light, to ease the blinking – *There you go mate* – and pulls down Beckett's vest from where it has risen up around his throat.

Phelan's radio sparks. He chooses his words with care. *He's alive, Lieutenant. But wounded.* They're for Beckett as much as the patrol commander. Fuck! he remembers suddenly. He hasn't even examined him yet. All these seconds passing, and he hasn't even done that. But what an examination it is. He'd thought at first glance, diving beside him, that Beckett's right leg was folded under him, that the blast had only landed him awkwardly. In truth he wasn't capable of conceiving, in those first few moments, that Beckett's leg was gone. Obvious now he's looking, but he hadn't seen it, couldn't see it. Now he's aware of the blood gushing out, darkening ripped trousers, darkening ground. His hands fumble and grope from pouch to pouch. Where did he pack the field dressing? If he was combat-ready he'd know instinctively. He ignores the radio. Fuck. He rips the bandage out, but what sort of fucking job is he asking it to do? Where to try and get a handle on Beckett's thigh and how to staunch the blood. He rummages through Beckett's webbing and finds a tourniquet nestled against the chest of his plate carrier, larger, and ties it to Beckett's stump. His hands are dark red and wet now. There's a thigh without a leg, and all Phelan is doing is trying to hide this truth.

And then a plea. *Charlie, my cock, my nuts. Are they still there?*

Phelan's not sure he's heard right. *It's all right, mate, you'll be okay.*

I want you to check, Charlie.

This calm. This seriousness, and Beckett lifting himself up on his elbow and trying to roll his hips so Phelan can get at him.

Okay, mate, okay. Just—

The rounds are still flying overhead. Phelan touches Beckett's cheek.

My nuts. Tell me, Charlie. Tell me.

Phelan is looking into his eyes now, and the sound of the firefight around them and the blood-mud ditch is somehow fading away, replaced by this urgency.

Have a look Charlie.

Phelan's heart is pounding. He unbuckles Beckett at the waist, and reaches into his trousers. Phelan feels Beckett through his jocks. He's moist, but it's not blood, not yet. *You're all there, son*, Phelan says, their helmets touching, fire above, *you're all there*. But as Phelan holds him in his hand he feels the warmth begin to leave him. *There's nothing to worry about, got it? Nothing to worry about. You just hang on, son. The medevac will be here any minute. Any minute.*

Thanks Charlie, he says. Or Phelan thinks he says, thinks he remembers.

Beckett closes his eyes and his body relaxes.

But now what? Does Phelan keep him awake or help him sleep? No answer comes, nothing he remembers. Nothing announcing itself as wisdom. No grace, clear and sure. Just the fear of impotence, a gaping terror, wide-jawed. He takes his water, splashing it over Beckett's face, roughly at first, then more gently, cooling Beckett's forehead, cupping some into his hand and raising it to Beckett's lips. Once he starts tending him he can't stop till he's emptied his last water bottle, washing dirt from Beckett's cheeks, his fingers leaving muddy prints on the boy's skin.

Phelan's mouth is suddenly dry. Looking back, this is the moment that changed everything, this. If he'd chosen differently he might have survived. That's what he'll later think, a thousand times, ten thousand. That if he'd chosen a different course at that precise point in time, he might have been able to confront his judgements, might have got through this war, this life, more or less intact. But his mouth is parched. He swallows and his throat chafes against itself, and for a split second he cannot breathe for thirst.

He looks at Beckett again. Beckett at peace. He knows what he is about to do is wrong. But there is no stopping it, and he leans in to Beckett, and rolls him, searching his pouches till he finds water, and slugs it, the radio cackle-cackle-cackling. Phelan slaking his need.

When he is done he turns towards Beckett's face again. As he looks, Beckett's repose breaks. A fluttered eyelid, a groan as long as eternity, something expiring, something, what?

After Beckett dies, he radios it in, one KIA. The words pour from the radio, calm but urgent, louder than the rounds, more insistent, but Phelan can't put them into any order. He sloshes the last of Beckett's water over the crotch of his trousers, where, he realises, somewhere in all this he's pissed himself.

He lies back and waits. He sees a falling star or an insect trapped in a shred of light. The radio noise seems to disappear into the vestiges of the day, and the fast air arrives. There is roar and there is vibration and above him Apaches rend the sky. The fabric of the very universe is torn, every star undone, every bird winged and tumbling. If the world were to explode, would the sound be any louder? Where would deaf Icarus land? Beside him here in this ditch?

He sees the rockets leave the helicopter, one-two, and then the compound disappears into a cloud of dust that in its own good time will fall and settle. The molten wax of Icarus's feathers. The picture books would have the beautiful boy tumbling to earth, feathers detaching as the wax melts, his body falling faster than the feathers floating high above him now. That look of terror on the young prince's face. That knowing.

But where are the paintings of ruined Icarus after he'd hit the ground? Where the depiction of the limbs so busted they are unrecognisable, the burst organs, the blood seeping from mouth and nose and eyes?

Yet it is not Icarus beside him. Beckett's body is not proof of pride, lest it be a nation's. Not the cost of folly, unless it be his country's. Lest it be his. Phelan cannot look.

Three soldiers join them after the Apaches have cleared the insurgents from their compounds. The hands of one – the medic – are moving frantically.

'He's gone,' Phelan says. The medic ignores him. The other soldiers are yelling at him now.

'Are you wounded, Sir? Are you hit?'

Suddenly all the sound is in his head, the steady pulse of his blood building until it stabs at his temples, his eyes. The roar of the falling sun. Phelan grabs at himself, trying to knead the pain away with his knuckles. Then the medevac passes slowly overhead.

The soldiers stretcher Beckett's body back down along the road to a clearing as if following the path of the chopper, the medic close behind. Phelan jogging now too, other soldiers surrounding him, shielding him, ready, despite everything, to take a round for him.

PLATEAU OF LOVE

HE WEEPS BUT Penny does not go to him. His head is in his hands at his desk and he is shaking in the dark, but she is calm. She is detached from all this. He shakes Beckett free, sob after sob. This release. Releasing him, releasing her.

What had been her war, too, no longer is. No longer is Beckett a black hole sucking her inexorably towards his centre, no more is he a malevolent creature reaching his clawed hand towards her. There is only this weeping man and this night. Everything changed. Beckett has died again, for the last time.

She leaves her husband. In the kitchen there are teapots and water tumblers and cheap crockery. There are shelves stocked with food and medicines. At the other end of the phone, if she needed them, or when it is time to bear good news, are her mother and her sister and Bec. She is calm and she is sure. The glow from the fridge light is miraculous as she opens the door to get the water jug, a burst of illuminating wonder. Even though she's not yet sure what she is celebrating. On the verandah she can still hear him sobbing behind her as she bends to put on her boots. He will not die from this. He will be okay, and now, finally, there is a chance they will too.

She does not need a torch. She knows the way. There are the shadows to guide her. The arch of the timber trellis. The edges of the path. The line of cypress pines. A beast lows in the valley. It is a beautiful sound. The cottage ahead is lit up. She sees Kira's silhouette moving, first in one room, then another. There is, after all, nothing to fear, nothing to forgive. This is the thing she wants to tell her, but how? She doesn't know, but she will find a way. And the growing boy, his birthday approaching, his beautiful life ahead of him. This plateau of love and forgiveness. There is, after all, a place for all things.

Too Much Light

BLAKE LEAPS DOWN the steps with the birthday kite in his hands. From the cottage, Kira and Phelan and Penny watch him go.

'Shouldn't you show him what to do?' Penny says to Phelan.

'He'll work it out,' Phelan replies.

'Thanks,' Kira says to both of them. 'For everything.'

Phelan bends to pick up the torn wrapping paper with its sailing-boat patterning. He carefully peels off the sticky tape, then lays the paper flat on the table, smoothing it out with his hardened fingers before folding it once, twice, and leaving it neatly in the centre of the table for Kira should she ever wish to use it again. 'Come on,' he says to his wife, reaching for her hand.

Penny hesitates. She wants to stay. She wants her husband to leave so she can make tea and the two women can talk for a while, nothing else in the day ahead to get to. She meets Kira's eyes and smiles.

'You go, James,' she says to him, 'I'll stay here and help for a bit.'

Phelan looks at one, then the other. We'll all be okay, he thinks, standing there in the kitchen of this refuge. Each one of us, in our own way, always.

The little room is glowing. The old lino on the floor and the cracked benchtops and all Blake's cranes on the windowsill and every cup and every saucer in the drying rack dance in the sunlight and Phelan is overwhelmed.

'You go,' she says to him again, and blows him a kiss.

'Let me …' Phelan says. His chest is swelling. His wife is beautiful. His wife is good. And Kira is here, extraordinary. He has an overwhelming need to share, to give, to thank.

He takes a cane hand-basket from the top of the fridge without explanation. 'I'll be back,' he says. 'I won't be long.'

The two women look at each other. He sets out, fixing his old

Akubra – stained and creased and collapsed at the brim – firmly on his head.

As Phelan leaves the cottage he watches Blake throw the kite into the air above him and then run, his string hand behind him, the opposite of fishing in the creek, trying to get something to fly away instead of bringing it in. Even when the string sags, and the kite falls to the ground, Phelan smiles. Blake looks up and waves wildly towards him.

Phelan watches as Blake heads towards the escarpment where there's always a breeze, and smiles. How much the boy has learned here on the farm. How confidently he stands by the edge, holding the kite's thin vertical dowel between his fingers, waiting for the breeze to strengthen before launching it up and out, throwing it like a spear. The yellow diamond lifts and then lifts again, working its way towards some unseen current above the boy's head, the kite straining against him, flapping against the wind. Blake feeds out more line, turning his wrist again and again as he shucks off loops of string.

Blake turns, beaming, and gives Phelan a thumbs-up. Phelan returns it. The kid'll be okay too, he thinks, the kid'll be okay.

Phelan follows the fence line where stray buttercups grow in the shade of posts. He cuts them with the blade of his Leatherman, and lays them in his basket. Onward he moves, eyes to the ground, scanning for colour. When he finds a wildflower he kneels and snips it near the base of the stem. He gathers dogwood and boronia and, among an outcrop of boulders to the west, a flannel flower. He recalls once coming across a spotted sun orchid on the other side of the hill behind the cottage, and veers towards the stand of eucalypts rising above the crest.

As he climbs the hill he snaps a head of silver wattle from a stunted bush, and lays it in the bed of flowers. He drops to his hands and knees when he reaches the top and enters the eucalypts, lifting long shreds of bark from the ground, choosing three curlicued strips for the basket, fossicking.

'I GOT A tattoo once,' Penny says.

'Really? You?'

'I know!' Penny says, 'I know!' She tells Kira the story, the two women at the table shaking their heads and laughing, Penny taking off her sandshoe when she is done, showing off her ancient welt.

'I might have something for that,' Kira says.

'What do you mean?'

'Come with me.'

Penny follows Kira out of the kitchen and into the front room where she worked, where her gallery of printed soldiers remains. Penny takes in Kira's tattooing gear, neatly organised on shelves, the bed still set up like a masseuse's table just in case, Phelan's book on the coffee table.

But there is another object that catches Penny's eye, a small azure statuette standing among the ink bottles that she hadn't seen when she was here before. She reaches for it. She raises the fragile bird to her eyes, turning it. Its legs are impossibly slender, but its breast is bursting as if in song, and its wings are spread as if they would encompass – or smother – the world.

'Where did you get this?'

PHELAN SENSES THE van before he sees it, a splinter of white through the trees. He looks up. The van stands on the eastern side of the turkey's nest, driven, he assumes, through the stock gate, across the paddock and parked here so it's invisible from the road. Phelan remains stationary for a full three minutes, counting, watching. All is still.

Then he rises and leaves the basket at the base of the nearest gum. He scans the side of the hill, the field, the horizon, but sees no human form.

As he approaches the van his gait slows, staying out of the line of its side mirrors. A new model Mercedes with tinted windows and New South Wales plates. He slows further, inching forward now, till he raises his head and peers through the darkened glass. The van is empty. He tries the doors, but they are locked, the rear door too. He returns to the driver's side window and presses his forehead against the glass. There is a baseball cap hooked on the rear-view mirror, a cigarette packet on the dashboard, chewing gum wrappers jammed into the ashtray. On the floor at the passenger's side he sees a collection of loose tools – wire-cutters and pliers, cable ties.

Then, laid out in the middle of the bench seat, he sees the tattoo book, opened to his own image on the flyleaf.

'IS ANYONE HERE?' Phelan pants as he stands in the empty kitchen. No answer. He begins moving slowly through the cottage, searching.

'Hello?' he says, quietly, tentatively. 'Hello?'

He finds the two of them in the enclosed verandah off the kitchen. Whatever he has disturbed, it doesn't now matter.

'Where is Blake?' he asks urgently. 'Where is he?'

Kira looks at Phelan and knows. She knocks over a chair, and runs across the room, through the kitchen, leaping barefoot down the stairs, wild, somewhere ahead of her an abyss.

Penny watches her go, and turns to Phelan.

'What is it now, James?'

Danger.

THE YELLOW KITE lies discarded on the ground. Kira turns a circle beside it, scanning the length of the escarpment, the ridge to the south, back to the cottage and the road, then to the row of pines in the north and behind them the Big House. The squawking galahs in the distance are nothing. Think, she tells herself, think.

'FUCK!' PHELAN CURSES, only now thinking he should have disabled the van. 'Fuck! Fuck! Fuck!'

He returns to the kitchen and grabs the keys to Kira's wagon from their hook. On the road he changes gear, spitting gravel. As the wagon accelerates he glimpses Kira standing in the paddock, Blake's kite in her hands, jerking her head briefly towards the sound of the car before turning back to the eastern horizon. The wagon rushes up the hill, Phelan keeping his head, flying up and over and down, the crunching suspension, the gum trees rushing past. He veers towards the paddock gate on the left as he approaches it, but doesn't stop, taking it out, the lengths of cross-timbers splitting, fence wire snapping and whipping against the sides of the car.

In the distance he sees the van across the paddock where he'd left it beside the turkey's nest, empty, a jab of relief. It may not be too late after all. The car ploughs through the long grass as it speeds towards the van, its wheels shuddering against the corrugations in the earth until it hits a submerged log and Phelan is thrown forward, his chest slamming against the steering wheel. The car comes to a halt, its engine revving madly. Phelan groans, turns off the ignition, and stumbles out.

BLAKE'S HEAD RISES above the edge of the cliff a hundred metres away and Kira gasps. She screams his name in wild relief, and he looks up at her, and even as she starts running towards her son she senses confusion in him, a turn of the head, a looking back.

Her bare feet tear across the ground, but she cannot run fast enough to stop the fear. She cannot run fast enough to quieten the squawking galahs or catch the fleeing clouds or escape the pitiless sun or return to Sydney. She cannot run fast enough to turn back time. And she cannot run fast enough to stop Flores appearing behind her son.

Flores seems larger than before, the product, perhaps, of her frightened imaginings. His glistening shaved head, his sunglasses, the black collared shirt, the straps of a backpack around his shoulders. He steps from the shade of the great fig into the sun beside Blake, huge, confident, and smiles at her.

Somewhere a half-thought reaches for her – why isn't Blake coming to her? She slows pace, falters, the weight of dread gathering in her. Flores places a hand on Blake's head, and Kira feels it like a punch to her stomach, gasps. *We are one*, he'd said to her again and again. *We cannot be parted. The tattoo gods – they decree it.* Was that before or after Blake? Is he any less manic now? She forces herself on, staggering under the doubt.

What words are there, Kira thinks? There are so many from which to choose. Are there words of hope she has not clung to, tattooed so she can't forget? A grief she has not confronted in skin, a fear? She has urged wisdom into a thousand needy bodies, a thousand ancient verities to guide a thousand aching souls. Words of love and honour and pity and pride and compassion and sacrifice. Her own skin is aflame with meaning. What words?

Flores waits for her. Blake's eyes are wide beneath Flores's steady hand. Man and boy are like a statue, the clay of them setting before her.

Kira is close enough now, whatever doom may be. Her heavy steps cease, she looks at Flores and she says, panting, 'He is not your son.'

But he doesn't hear. He strokes the boy's hair in reply, as tenderly as he ever has. Perhaps it's that he doesn't believe. He smooths Blake's brow. His expression could even be one of pity for her.

'Ah,' he says calmly, 'I see.' Just standing there, smiling smugly, patting her son.

'He is not yours!' Kira's voice rises. 'You can't take him!'

'A boy needs his father,' Flores says, laying it out as if what he's offering is clemency. 'Come back home, Kira.'

'But you're not his father!' she screams. '*You* are not, it is not you.'

She can't bear to look at Blake as she continues to scream. If Flores won't hear it the universe will.

'YOU. ARE. NOT. BLAKE'S. FATHER.'

She means it as an accusation. But the rest of what she has to say is confession. The words themselves tell her, force her to lower her voice.

'The brigadier is, Jim is.'

Now the words are out, every other sound is sucked away, every bush insect and every bird and every breath of wind. A silence the like of which the world can never have known descends on this plateau above this valley beneath this sun, and it is her duty to fill it.

'You're not Blake's father, Flores. I'm sorry,' she says, sensing the shift. 'I'm sorry, Flores.' But no words are big enough to fill this space. They can open it, but they can't fill it.

She sees a twitch of muscle. Something in his neck or perhaps it's a tightening of his forearm, maybe just a catching of breath. His body trying to hold back a truth it's known for a long time. The change in him, when it comes, is swift. Suddenly, he is a man without a son and he collapses, dropping to one knee, his hand falling from Blake's shoulder to the ground, holding him.

'I'm so sorry,' Kira says, stepping forward. 'I'm so sorry.' Only now does she turn her gaze to her son. 'I'm sorry,' she says again, this time for Blake.

Mouthing it to him now, 'I'm sorry Little Man, I'm sorry.' Her reaching, trembling, hands.

Released, Blake moves away from Flores to join Kira, confused, but never again to be his son.

• • •

PHELAN WATCHES FLORES shrug off his backpack, watches him unzip it. Knows what is happening before he sees, runs, keeping his head still, the brief moment breaking into ever smaller parts, shorter frames.

He watches the gunman's shoulder movements, Flores's splaying right elbow as he ratchets the backpack open, tooth by tooth. Kira embracing Blake, the one immersed in the other, both oblivious. Phelan closes in on Flores, but knows he will not make it. Flores's hand enters his pack. Phelan gathers himself. He will not make it. He doesn't need to wait until he sees the gun; the change in Flores's face is enough. It is barely perceptible, but he knows it well – the surge people feel at the moment of arming themselves. Sometimes invincibility, always strength.

He knows what he must do. He is decoy, distraction, and, inevitably, target.

'Hey!' Phelan yells, 'Hey!'

Phelan stops running. There are still thirty metres between them, and there is no cover. Every little upwind sound is magnified, the shifting of three bodies to face him, each gasp, each sob, Flores's safety catch flicking off. Phelan recognises the raised weapon, a standard-issue Browning. He dives and hears the rounds, one-two, but the thud he feels is his shoulder against the ground, and as he comes out of the roll and looks up Flores is walking steadily towards him, arms raised, the handgun pointed at him.

This firefight, here. The two rounds echo and rumble still and he might be lying in long Preston grass or a ditch in the Chora Valley, the same storm breaking overhead, the same sky. How the world contracts. How the world draws into itself. He feels the third round hit his left arm. Burn and burst and useless flesh and bone. Above the pain he hears his name. There is no emptiness out here in the windswept field. Only that which is essential. Sky and pain and Kira calling his name.

That Flores is bearing steadily down on him hardly seems to matter. Because there is not just the one voice now, but two. He hears not just Kira, but Penny too, and they are both calling for him, those two voices, one following the other, over and over, intertwined. It is almost song.

A second bullet enters him, ripping out his breath. The sound of his blood gets louder. Still he hears Penny crying his name, closer, Kira also, these two women. The shadow above him now is Flores, he knows that, but it is woman that fills the air.

The next shot he hears is memory. Some vague recollection of a different weapon, his own. But it has no bite, not this round. It is sound without moment. Even so, Phelan's eyes want to close now. He thinks he sees a Penny-like shape in a receding field, a beautiful composition of the woman he loves, her feet set, his rifle against her shoulder, her eye at its sight. He hears another shot, and Flores collapses out of the sun's way.

There is suddenly too much light and Phelan must shut his eyes. Still there is his name, still Kira and still Penny. And now Blake.

EPILOGUE

'CAN YOU DO this?' Penny whispers.

'Yes,' Kira answers. 'I think I can.'

Kira cups the older woman's breast in her hand. All their nervous talk ceases. There is only breathing now. And skin and breast. Kira is gentle. She is respectful. She'd thought she'd be uncertain, clumsy even, but it's not like that. She explores the other woman's skin with her fingers, her thumbs, learning where the flesh has been removed, where the skin has been tightened, where she's sensitive. She circles the horizontal scar, but on finally reaching it, runs her forefinger evenly along its length, its little ridgeline of experience.

'Can you feel it here?' Kira asks.

'Only a little.'

'And here? And here?'

Kira reaches for her gloves out of habit, but pauses. No, she thinks, discarding everything that is unnecessary. As she presses the design onto Penny's skin, she looks up at the older woman's face. Penny's eyes are closed and she is breathing evenly. When Kira peels the stencil paper away a minute later, the purple outline of a hibiscus flower envelopes Penny's breast.

She adapts to the changing skin and all its shifting textures. She stretches it where the fatty layer is intact near the armpit, but where it is thin and taut over the implant Kira turns the machine down and

305

finesses it, as a lover might brush an eyelash from a beloved's cheek, softly, softly. At the scar she pauses before crossing it, feels it again with her finger, the little knot. She takes care the needle doesn't catch, before moving up and along the outline of another petal, embracing the curve of the implant.

They break for water and to stretch.

'I don't want to look,' Penny says. 'Not till it's done.'

Kira hangs a sheet over the wall mirror, even though she finds it unsettling, as if this makeshift shroud has temporarily banished some part of her from the room. They talk about lorikeets and galahs and the colours of feathers.

'Well,' Kira says finally, 'I think we're there.' She removes the cloth.

Penny climbs off the bed and sets herself before the mirror, naked from her waist, her hair still falling down around her shoulders. She stands and looks and begins to weep.

Kira lets her go, leaves the tissues she normally uses to wipe off ink and blood where they are on the trolley. There's a dignity in the woman's tears she won't attempt to erase. She sits still on her stool, her back straight, concentrating on her breathing, not wanting to do anything, no matter how small, to disturb this moment. All the colour of weeping.

After what seems to Kira a very long time, Penny speaks, though her eyes remain on her reflection. 'It's, it's a shock. It's—'

Kira's stomach tightens. Please, she thinks, please let her like it.

'I don't know why I'm crying,' Penny says, turning now to look at Kira.

'No?'

'It's not like … I guess, you steel yourself. Well, you have to, don't you?'

The women look at each other.

'Well, I did anyway.'

Penny touches her skin as if it is new. As if some miracle has appeared from some hidden universe, the first hibiscus, and all the world is made new again. Her breast, her body, each glorious tear. The good in it all once more.

'It's beautiful,' she says, and Kira gets up now, the two women weeping, embracing each other, enfolding one another, the two of them. Now.

ACKNOWLEDGEMENTS

THIS IS A work of fiction. Any similarities between the characters and events in this book, and the lives of soldiers posted to Afghanistan since the war started in that country in 2001, is coincidental. A number of accounts of the experience of that war have, however, informed this work, including interviews with soldiers, both serving and retired. I am indebted to them for sharing their stories so freely, and often courageously. Among the written accounts I am indebted to are John Cantwell's *Exit Wounds*, Mark Donaldson's *The Crossroad*, Chris Masters' *Uncommon Soldier*, James Prascevic's *Returned Soldier* and Gary Ramage and Ian McPhedran's *Afghanistan: Australia's War*. More generally, Lieutenant Colonel Dave Grossman's *On Killing*, and Jonathan Shay's *Odysseus in America* were valuable resources.

The epigraph is from Robert Fagles' translation of *The Odyssey*, Book 8, lines 99–103. The line on page 60 is adapted from a line in the W. Marsden, T. Wright and Peter Harris translation of *The Travels of Marco Polo: The Venetian*. The extract from Marcus Aurelius' *Meditations* on page 96 is from Martin Hammond's translation. The first two lines on page 305 are adapted from Anna Akhmatova's *Requiem* translated by Stanley Kunitz.

This book is the product of the great generosity of many people who have shared expertise, read the book in manuscript form, and offered encouragement or direction. My very deep gratitude to: Hamish

Ashman, Laura Bridger, Desley Campbell-Stewart, Alisa Cleary, Rachel Cleary, Stuart Crozier, Mick Donaldson, Robert Ferris, Steve Foley, Rodney Hall, Patrick Hamilton, Tatiana Hamilton, Matthew Horan, Georgina Isbell, Peter Jensen, Krissy Kneen, Quentin Masson, Audie Moldre, Gwenn Murray, Jo Rennick, Scott Seefeld, Max Walters, Tony Woodyatt, Samay Zhouand and Zmarak Zhouand. I want to especially thank Nicole Brosing for being my tattooing guide and unreservedly welcoming me into her studio to watch and learn a little about the art of tattooing.

To the dedicated folk at the Gallipoli Medical Research Foundation and the Keith Payne Unit at Greenslopes Hospital who seek to understand and tend the wounds of war: my respect and gratitude, and in particular to Miriam Dwyer, Madeline Romaniuk and Trish Mossop.

At UQP Madonna Duffy is a publisher extraordinaire who I want to especially acknowledge and thank. Indeed the entire team at UQP has been magnificent. This book has benefited greatly from the wisdom, experience and fine editorial eyes of Julia Stiles, Christina Pagliaro and Jacqueline Blanchard: thank you.

Finally, thanks to Alisa, Dominic and Liam for the greatest of support.